DUNGEON LIFE

DUNGEON LIFE

BOOK 1

Khenal

Podium

To Aranya, who was more confident in the story than I was,
and who encouraged me to start posting it in the first place.

Cover design by Istvan Straban

ISBN: 978-1-0394-5394-4

Published in 2024 by Podium Publishing
www.podiumaudio.com

Podium

DUNGEON LIFE

Chapter 1

As I behold the dusty basement, I wonder if I made the right choice. The car crash was instant, at least. The angels don't exactly pay much attention to why people die, but a semi barreling down a hill is usually because of failed brakes. They told me I could go see about the pearly gates or get reassigned. Apparently, accidents like that are a bit of a loophole.

Also apparently, those isekai stories are a thing. There were a whole bunch of different worlds out there to send adventurers and such to, but I wasn't all that interested. That kind of thing is fun in a game, sure, but in reality, you only get one life. Or two, I guess? I was about to leave to talk to Saint Peter when the lady angel presenting the options tried one more. It was to become a dungeon.

I was incredulous, but also intrigued. How does one become a dungeon?

Well, one gets hit by a semi, I suppose. But how does one actually be a dungeon? Would it be like Dungeon Man in *EarthBound*? It was such a strange option, and she looked so desperate to fill that position, that I shrugged and accepted. I figured, worst case, I'd end up back there eventually, and I could just head to the gates instead.

After accepting, I started to just . . . dissolve, and the angel seemed so happy, telling me I wouldn't regret my decision. She was wrong, as watching my feet fade away filled me with regrets pretty quickly, but I had already agreed, and I can't stand backing out after agreeing to something. Even if it seems like it's going to immediately suck.

Which brings us to the basement. Do note that I said *behold* and not that I looked around. As far as I can tell, uh . . . I don't have eyes. It makes sense, if I'm a dungeon. I'm just curious what kind of definition of a dungeon equals to what feels like a run-down house. If most of those isekai stories are like playing an RPG, I feel like this one is more like a city-builder, like maybe *Dwarf Fortress*. I just hope it's not as difficult.

I feel like I'm a floating viewpoint, and it's pretty surreal. I can also kind of focus out and feel the whole house. I even have a few little indicators for things. For one: I have denizens, which feels grandiose to call some rats and a bunch of spiders. I also have invaders in the form of roaches and flies. What I don't have is any idea how to do anything.

After observing around a bit, I notice a tiny little orange gem that pops up with the word *Core* above it. I don't know what it is, but the cupboard I found it in is labeled as my *Sanctum*, so that's probably important, even if the gem is super tiny. More like a shard or a chip than a gem. Either way, I'd really like to put it somewhere more secure than just a cupboard.

The spiders seem to want to protect it, though. I've seen them weaving an impressive tangle around it. Well, impressive for spiders. Maybe they just like the little glow it gives off? The flies definitely do. I watch one of my spiders finally scuttle up and bite into the first of the captured flies, and I feel something weird.

Mana Gained!

Yeah, weird. More little notifications pop up as the spiders dig into their meals, each showing over the little flies before fading. So, I get mana from the spiders doing things.

What does mana do? It's gotta do something, right? If this is like a city builder, I probably use it to build my city of spiders and rats, though that still doesn't answer how.

I try mentally yelling at the rats to do a backflip or file my taxes, but they ignore me. They do occasionally eat a roach, which seems to have more mana than a fly, but I get the feeling that's not saying much. I focus back on the spiders, since they seem to be actively, if accidentally, protecting the core. I notice one just starting to build a new web, so I try to give it a command.

Hey. Spider. Weave a heart into your web, instead of it just being a circle.

Whoa. That took a bit of my mana. Not a ton, but more than a couple flies would give. And sure enough, I can already see the little spider weaving a heart for her web. While interesting, what does that actually do for me?

I mentally sit down to consider. Denizens seem to be on my side. Invaders seem to be against me. I get mana for killing invaders. The core is probably important.

I mentally nod to myself as my next task is decided: get the core somewhere safe. Where would be somewhere safe? The cupboard is safe-ish, but I feel like I can do better. Pretty sure I'll need more mana to do that, though.

Did I call this a city-builder? Because I think it's an idle game, and I can't even click things to make it faster.

I did find a few things of interest, at least. I found my . . . spawners, I guess? There's a rat's nest in the basement, and the little room under the stairs leading to the second floor has a spider egg sac. I mostly discovered them on my quest to find something to click. When I focused on those two, though, I was presented with the option to spawn rats or spiders, respectively, for a mana cost. Spiders are dirt cheap, while rats are a bit expensive, at least at this point.

I spawned one of each anyway, and after a little timer ticked down, a spider crawled out of the sac. Not a spiderling, but a grown spider. Similarly, an adult rat came out of the nest in the basement. I tried clicking them, too, and discovered they are much easier to command than the normal spiders and rats. Looking closer, they're listed as Spider Scion and Rat Scion. So I guess I have kinda creepy little avatars?

Well, with creepy little avatars, I can at least move the core. The rat can't exactly get up into the cupboard, and the spider would be too vulnerable out in the open, but teamwork makes the dream work! It's not too difficult to get the spider to web the core and carry it, though it does seem a little bigger now. Maybe it's from me having mana? Either way, I need to get this thing secured sooner rather than later.

With the spider holding the core, I have it dragline down to land on the rat, and we're off to the races! And by races, I mean basement. There's a little hole in the wall under the stairs that seems like a great place to put the core. The rat can just barely squeeze into it, and the little space is about the size of my fists put together . . . Well, my fists as they used to be. It's gonna be wild getting used to not having fists.

I even get the idea to have the rat gnaw a bit of wall from a different part of the basement to make a cover for the little hole. With the spider's webbing, the whole thing seals up, and you'd never know it was there. It even changed the title of the little space to *Secret Sanctum*, so I'm pretty proud of that. Seems like my mana generation has taken a hit for it, though. Probably because there's no little glowing source to attract flies.

I found more things to click.

Or rather, I have enough mana that clicking things actually gives me options now. Specifically: I can make traps. Or grow traps? I don't know what else to call it. When I click a door, I can make it have a squeaky hinge . . . which doesn't sound like much of a trap to me.

The description is interesting, though.

Squeaky Door
Detectability: Moderate
Chance to Trip: Guaranteed

When opened, the door emits a loud squeak from poor hinges, alerting all denizens up to one room away.

It's not like roaches and flies will be opening my doors, but for bigger stuff, that could be nice to have. I spend the mana to do it, mostly just because. I also set a rotten floorboard in the main room of the house.

Rotten Floorboard
Detectability: Impossible
Chance to Trip: Low
The rotten floorboard will snap under a careless foot, briefly immobilizing the intruder and alerting all denizens up to two rooms away.

Playing with traps gives me something to do besides just spawning more spiders and rats. Only the first ones are scions, which kinda sucks, but the new ones are cheaper, at least. They also seem kinda weak compared to even the normal critters. The normals seem to almost listen to them, though. I started having my spiders build webs around my various windows and other places flies could get in, and the normal spiders seemed drawn to them.

Similarly, I had my rats actively patrolling for roaches, and the normal ones started frequenting those areas more, and so ate more roaches and got me more mana, which I've been spending on upgrades for my rats and spiders. Well, upgrades on their spawners, at least. For the spiders, upgrading the egg sac seems to just make more egg sacs, which will passively spit out more spiders over time.

With the various entrances mostly covered, I set a few of my spiders to just webbing up the basement, which the normals seem to take to with gusto. Anyone arachnophobic is going to stay well away from my basement. They even register as a swarm now, instead of individual spiders, which is encouraging.

I've only been able to afford one upgrade for the rats so far, though. As far as I can tell, it just spawns slightly tougher rats now. Which is fine; it's not like roaches are dangerous to them.

Oh.

That could be, though. Someone just knocked.

Chapter 2

My front porch has felt fuzzy to me ever since I got here. Maybe it's technically outside my borders? I can feel someone standing there and what sounds like speech, but I can't make anything out; not like they're speaking a language I don't know, but more like they're underwater. Or I am. Either way, I'm pretty sure my front door isn't locked. I don't think I even can lock it. I can trap it, but I can't just keep people out. Probably for the same reason I can't just keep flies and roaches out.

I decide to spend a bit of mana to pull everyone back, my rats and spiders all scurrying to whatever hiding places are available. Whoever is out there is either in no hurry or has great timing, because the door only opens after everything is hiding.

My first thought is to wonder why an elf decided to come visit.

Yeah, I know what an elf is, and I'm not all that surprised. I've played DnD. The only people who lose their crap over an elf are people with the hots for Legolas.

This one doesn't look too far off from that. He has the similar bearing of grace and agility, though he doesn't have a bow. He wears fairly simple leather armor with a pair of quality daggers at his side. Straight brown hair tops his head, ending about at the shoulders. Slightly pale skin says he has a naturally pale complexion which fights with the sun regularly. His eyes are green and piercing, though he looks almost bored rather than attentive. He's also talking to himself . . . or into some kind of recording device.

"Can confirm house is a dungeon. I could feel its attention when I knoc—shit!"

Hah, suck on that rotten plank. I even got some mana for that, which is the first time I've gotten it for something besides killing things, which is nice.

"No, I'm fine. I managed to find a rotten floorboard. Nothing came to try to eat me, though."

Oh, right. If I'm supposed to be a dungeon, I should probably at least make a token effort. I wouldn't want to be rude.

I spend a bit of mana to send the wimpiest rat to go see what he's about. I spend the extra for a normal, not one of mine. I wouldn't want the normals to follow one of mine and swarm the guy.

I don't think I need to worry about that, though. His eyes lock on to it as soon as it enters the room, even with furniture and stuff in the way. This guy might be a bit high level for me.

"Level one rat, single, passive spawn." The elf pauses for a moment as the rat continues to approach, the little thing not even aware it's been spotted yet. "Roger. Engaging." He whips out a knife and tosses it at the rat, killing it instantly. He's definitely too high level to be slumming it in a newbie little dungeon like me. I got mana from him killing the rat though. That's weird.

Huh, that's also weird. He's not listed as an intruder but as a delver. I'm pretty sure I've seen the roaches get a spider or two, and I didn't get any mana for it, so why for him? As I think on it, he looks around and talks to his device . . . or team. It seemed like someone was talking back.

"No sign of the Sanctum, nor any other specialty rooms. The one under the stairs is close to becoming a spider lair, looks like. Level three spider swarm in the basement, and a level two rat's nest. No hostility aside from the single rat; looks specialized for pest control still. No resource nodes . . . one minor chest in the attic."

Whoa, wait, hang on there, Elf Guy. Resource nodes? Chests? I can do that?! And hands off my chest! I'm no lady, but you should still buy me dinner first!

I briefly consider siccing the swarm on him, but decide against it. He didn't sound too concerned about it being level three. I don't want to waste those kinds of resources for them to just be killed . . . though with what happened with the rat, it might be alright? Nah, we'll save that for later. For now, I should put up at least some kind of defense for the chest.

"Lots of movement; looks like it wants to protect the chest. The swarm is staying put, though I see a new one forming on the stairs up. Level one swarm confirmed."

Yeah, what's your stupid knife going to do against a swarm of spiders, huh? Oh.

Skills are a thing. He doesn't shout the name of his attack, but a few flourishes of his knife send winds to scatter my swarm and destroy the webbing they were putting up. I got a bunch of mana from that, though, and he didn't even kill many of my spiders. He just dispersed my swarm.

Okay, uh . . . need to stall him.

"Swarm dispersed. Minimal damage done." His bored look shifts to a smirk for a moment. "I told you I know what I'm doing. Besides, this one doesn't seem actively malevolent. If it was, it'd bring out the big guns and try to bury me in rats and spiders all at once. Or would have put a spike under that rotten floorboard."

While he takes his time climbing the stairs, I spend some mana on more than just moving rats around. I can upgrade my traps, see?

Squeaky Door
Detectability: Moderate
Chance to Trip: Guaranteed
When opened, the door emits a loud and annoying squeak from rusty hinges, alerting and attracting all denizens up to one room away.

It's subtle, but it's there. Now, stuff doesn't just know when a door is opened—they are incentivized to go look instead of just hiding. There's another upgrade still, but it's a bit expensive for me just yet.

Now, to see what Elf Guy does with my new trap.

"Ugh . . . upgraded squeaky door. I hate that trap. It's not just annoying to the denizens. Alerted . . . two level two spawned rats and four level one passives. Engaging."

He pulls out two knives, and I'm worried he's just going to do the same to my rats as with the spiders, or even with that first rat. Thankfully, it's either on cooldown or he just doesn't want to expend the effort. He still takes out each rat with a single attack, but my brave little rodent soldiers do their job of slowing him down a little. None of them even come close to biting him, but they make a good effort. With their sacrifice, my last defense is in position, at least. I seriously doubt I'll be able to take him down, but if I can even score a hit, I'm gonna count it as a win. And if I keep getting mana for what this delver kills, I should have enough to do something interesting.

"Successful encounter. I don't see any other movement, but I don't think it's just going to give me that chest. Proceeding with caution." He quietly continues toward the ladder to the attic, and I'm already a bit proud of making him cautious. I hope he's not too cautious, though. I want to take at least one of his HP to keep. At least, I think he has HP. My spiders and rats don't, which is probably why he can take them out in a single attack.

As he climbs into the attic, I can hear a bit of surprise in his voice and see a small smile on his face, which now looks attentive. "Confirm boss encounter, level two mixed rat swarm . . . with scion buff. Negative on scion position. Engaging."

He does his Windblade attack again, but the rats are heavy enough they can't just be scattered like the spiders were. They're definitely blades of wind, though, as I see many rats in the swarm sliced into. The rest surge forward, and he acrobats around my dusty attic, occasionally sending another blade of wind at them. They get close a few times, and I think the scion buff he mentioned might be making them a bit tougher, as I see a few rats actually wounded and still trying to attack instead of simply dead from any damage.

Still, the outcome was clear from the start, and soon, the swarm loses cohesion and scatters. "Boss complete. Checking chest now." He walks over to the chest, and as he lifts the lid, my Rat Scion pops out and bites his hand before darting away, leaving him startled as he watches it vanish into a hole in the wall.

"Stupid mistake; didn't get the XP from the boss fight, so it wasn't over." He shakes his head before continuing to talk. "XP gained. *Now* boss is complete. Chest contains . . . potion of minor healing," he relays as he plucks it from the chest. He pops the cork and drinks the potion, causing the little bleeding wound on his hand to quickly fade.

"Dungeon is cheeky but not overtly hostile, despite lack of resource nodes. Dungeon is suitable for low-level small parties up to the attic; basement is forbidden. Path to Secret Sanctum is probably down there somewhere. Note that dungeon already displays unorthodox methodology and ability to adapt to delvers. Intruders at minimum; dungeon seems to prefer a clean house, dust notwithstanding."

That seems to finish his report, and he heads for the ladder. I don't bother sending anything else to mess with him—partially because he's cleared me, I guess. That's just how you do when you're cleared. The other part is because he doesn't do more than simply peek into the basement, respecting that I want to keep something to myself. But I mostly don't want to spend the mana on it.

I have just enough to upgrade *me*, not just my spawners.

Chapter 3

Upgrading myself was definitely a good idea. My porch doesn't feel fuzzy anymore! I can even feel my roof and a little of the land around myself, too, though there's a little tower thingy on my roof that's still beyond my reach. I can feel movement outside, but I can't tell if I'm some creepy house in the woods and that's trees swaying in the breeze, or if I'm a run-down house in the middle of a huge city.

Even better, though: I have two new spawners! I have a nest of blackbirds on the roof over my porch, and I have an anthill in the yard. Of course, with new spawners come new invaders. Wasps have started showing up, and they love to harass my poor spiders. The spiders sometimes get them in the webs and eat them, giving me a nice bit of mana, but the wasps sometimes get the spider. I'm just glad I went a bit overboard with the spider spawner and they appear as fast as the wasps can get them.

I can also confirm that invaders don't give me mana for what they kill. Stupid wasps. There're also invader ants, which don't seem to be able to take over my hill, but I'm still a bit concerned about it. I'm going to be putting a lot of mana into that thing once I get more. The ants seem like they're designed to handle the roaches as well as the other ants, too, so they'll be able to pull double duty once I get them upgraded further.

And I'll want them to, too, because the last new invader is my new gold standard for getting mana: mice. The rats go after them, so the ants get to pick up the slack with the roaches.

The mice didn't come in from me upgrading my awareness, though. They came in after I made a resource node!

I checked all over everywhere I could find, and it looks like I'll be hosting herbalists for the foreseeable future. I managed to grow a little patch of herbs in the backyard, and even sprouted some mushrooms near the foot of the stairs in the basement. I'm going to make them work at least a little for the mushrooms, kinda reinforce the idea that the basement is for me, not them. And the mice love the shrooms, so I keep several rats nearby.

Oh, the room under the stairs on the first floor is now, officially, a spider lair. It even spat out a venomous swarm the other day. And speaking of spiders, my scion doesn't fit in my Secret Sanctum anymore. Little guy is a tarantula now, at least, so I have him in a little nest near the mushrooms to eat more mice.

While my spider is working on being a tank, my rat seemed to like the hit-and-run on the elf, and he's very sneaky now. If I didn't know everything about this house, I'd swear he's teleporting, but he's been making little tunnels throughout the walls that seem like only he can fit through. He's my little Scout. He's great.

And that's *Scout* with a capital *S*, by the way. My scions have titles now! The spider is a Guardian, and the rat is a Scout. It seems like they give different buffs, too. My Scout gives things extra awareness now, which I think means an extra room worth of distance for noticing things. The Guardian makes things tougher in his room. Since he's in the basement, that means the swarm in there is even more of a hindrance and more difficult for invaders or delvers to get through.

So, with a good Rat Scion, I decide to upgrade the nest several times. You know, give him more rats to buff and stuff. But after a certain point, I need to decide a path for it, which confuses me. Rats don't have paths. They're rats! Well, on Earth, maybe, but not here.

Let's start with the path I didn't take: plague rats. Yeah, no. If I'm in a city, I don't need to bring the black death, thanks. Besides, I think the one I took is more interesting: packrats.

I'm not exactly sure how, but they seem to spawn random stuff every so often and put them places. I still only have the one chest in the attic, but now, adventurers can look in my various drawers and cupboards and find interesting little things. Rough little gems, coins; sometimes, they'll even put some fungus caps somewhere. They love hiding stuff in the chest, though, which makes sense.

The blackbirds I quickly upgrade to crows, partially to help with the mice, and partially because crows are cool. They also like to collect shinies . . . Maybe that's where the packrats get the stuff. Either way, the crows also find the wasps delicious. I'm not sure that's how the food chain worked on Earth, but I'll take it. Good birbs. Protect my leggy-bois.

My real project, though, is with the ants. They spawn a bit differently than the others. For my other things, I just queue up what I want and *bam*, I get it. They also periodically spawn stuff on their own, too. With the ants, though, they only spawn workers passively, and I can't tell the hill to produce more workers. I can upgrade it, or I can trigger a nuptial flight.

I upgrade it several times, and then the option for nuptial flight starts blinking.

So I go ahead and spend the mana for it, just to see why. Well, that leads to interesting things. For one, despite having only the one hill, there are several different types of ants available in the mating flight. I steer clear of the carpenter ants, at least for now. I wouldn't be surprised if they can do actual carpentry eventually, but I'm just a house right now. I don't need ants chewing through my wood to find a place to live.

The option that sticks out to me, however, is the leafcutter. That's the ant that farms fungus to eat, and I think that'd be a cool one to use as my Guardian. Army ants and fire ants could be interesting for offense, but I like me some defense. I have her hitch a ride on my Scout down to the basement, and he stops by the mushroom patch for her to get a bit of the mycelia.

I had honestly expected her to just suddenly have a little bit of fungus to grow and nurture, but that works for me. I'll bet those mushrooms attract delvers almost as much as they attract mice, so I definitely want more of them. She's a pretty active queen, too. She puts her little bit of fungus next to my core—which is looking about like a marble now—lays her eggs, then heads out to forage. I mean, I guess she's safe enough in the house, especially after I told a few spiders to watch over her.

Only the flies seem interested in her, so the spiders were the obvious choice for protectors. She gathers a bit of paper to bring back for the fungus and sits down to just chew and process it. It's relaxing to watch her work.

Oh, my Crow Scion says we have delvers approaching. Multiple? This'll be interesting. I didn't get a chance to do much outside yet, aside from the herb patch. I also wanted to get a chest in the basement, but was more concerned with getting my new Guardian settled.

Ah well, they're here now.

Chapter 4

I approximate a squint at the "delvers" my crow alerted me to. Is he sure they're delvers? They look like kids, or maybe early teens? That awkward age that's old enough to get into trouble and young enough not to realize it. One looks a bit bigger and is green, so probably an orc or something. I can't tell if orcs here don't have tusks, or if his haven't properly grown in yet. Messy black hair sits atop his noggin, and curious brown eyes look around. The other is also green, but is shorter. Like, a lot shorter. Probably a goblin. This one has longer brown hair and green eyes. Once they step onto my property, I listen in on what they're saying.

The goblin looks nervous, but the orc is putting on a brave front. They look kinda dirty and poor, but seem mostly healthy. Are they from an orphanage or something?

The nervous one speaks up. "I dunno, Freddie . . . are you sure this is a good idea?"

"Sure it's a good idea! I saw the inspectors check this place out; it's definitely a dungeon!"

"Doesn't that mean we should stay away?" I'm with the scaredy-cat on this one. Dungeons don't seem like the kind of place for urchins to play.

"No! If it was a big established one, yeah, but this one's fresh! Old Staiven said he'd apprentice anyone with an ounce of magic if they could bring him some spellspores, and this is just the kind of place they'd grow! I think."

"But . . . you don't have any magic, Freddie."

The loudmouth just waves that off. "But you do! So come on! A party has to help each other!" Huh . . . that Freddie seems like a good sort, at least. I thought I was looking at a bully situation. But do these kids even have levels yet?

Well, I still can't lock the door, so I guess they're coming in. They each ready their weapons, which are just two different sticks, looks like. Freddie there has a hefty stick; not quite a club but it looks like it'd be up to dealing with rats and spiders. The other kid has a whippier stick with a little shard of glass tied to it, I guess to act as a wand?

I spend a bit of mana to send two wimpy rats to greet them; I don't want to overwhelm these kids just yet. It takes them a bit longer to notice than the elf did, but Wimpy's gasp alerts Freddie. The kid stands between his friend and the rats and yells at them, trying to scare them off, but these are my rats; they're not gonna run off. They have a job to do, and they are going to do it to the best of their abilities.

The two rodents scurry forward, and I'm just hoping the kids can run away before anything too bad happens to them.

I didn't need to worry, though. Freddie would have a good golf game back home; he sends a rat sailing into the next room. Wimpy, however, points his wand at the other rat.

"Frost!"

The little thing ices up and decides that running is preferable to dying. Which is fine by me; I still get mana for them being defeated, not just for them getting killed, which is great all around, really.

There is a pregnant pause before Freddie whoops in triumph. "Yeah, we did it! See, your magic is good enough! Now we just gotta find those mushrooms." He looks around, obviously without a clue as to where they could be. He heads for a cabinet, and Wimpy calls out to him.

"Be careful! You don't know if it's trapped!"

"It'll be fine, don't worry!" he says as he opens it up. His eyes shine as he sees the silver piece sitting in plain view. "Wow, a whole silver! We should come here more often!" The boost in mana I get as he takes the coin makes me agree with that idea, too. Packrats and crows were definitely the right choices for upgrades.

The two poke around the main room, gathering coins from various containers. Freddie is not as observant as Wimpy, though. That kid peers at the spiders in the windows and the rats hunting roaches, and keeps a distance as he watches. When Freddie makes to open the door to the spider lair, however, Wimpy actually grabs his hand.

"Not in there! Look," he says, pointing down at the slow stream of spiders coming from under the door. Freddie's eyes widen, and he backs up a bit.

"Yeah . . . I don't think we could handle a swarm just yet." Ah, good. He knows his limits too. I like these kids.

Wimpy looks around and points at the stairs going down. "Uh . . . I think the mushrooms will be down there. They like darkness." Freddie readies his stick, and Wimpy makes his little wand act like a flashlight, then the two slowly descend into my basement.

I actually spend a bit of mana to keep things calm down there. Everything knows the basement isn't for visiting, but I'm willing to give these kids a chance.

They seem to know they're getting in a bit over their heads, but the brave little buggers keep going, as careful as two kids can be.

The spider swarm hisses at the light and the presence of the kids, but don't attack. From Freddie's look, I think he might be arachnophobic. Still, he does his duty, standing between Wimpy and the swarm, even as his stick wobbles in his hand. "How long t-to get those mushrooms, Rhonda?"

Rhonda! A girl, then. Huh.

"Just a few seconds . . ." she says, sounding a bit sorry about the situation. She focuses on the mushrooms and plucking several of the bigger ones. Once I get the notification that she's gotten three units of mushrooms—I have no idea what a unit actually is, but it's more than just three caps—I decide that's enough for now.

I'm not a mean dungeon, but I feel like I'd lose my license if I just gave this stuff away. Not that I actually have a license, but still. I have my Spider Scion start to emerge from his little nest, in clear view of Rhonda. At the same time, I let the swarm start to slowly advance.

"Uh . . . Rhonda? They're coming!" Her *Eep!* of reply gets him to look and see the scion emerge. He's my biggest denizen by now, about the size of a dinner plate if you count his legs. To the kids, he probably looks the size of a horse.

"Run!" orders Freddie, and Rhonda is all too happy to oblige. The two book it, and I keep my spiders from giving chase. I get a bunch of mana for "defeating" the "delvers," and I can't help but smile to myself as the two slam my front door and lean against it, panting from the run and from the fear.

After about a minute, though, the two start laughing, relieved to have escaped. "That was crazy!" exclaims Freddie, riding the energy of his adrenaline tapering off. "Did you get enough?"

Rhonda nods and pulls a double-handful of mushrooms from her pocket. "Yeah! Old Staiven will have to apprentice me now!" Rhonda's happy smile slips, even though Freddie is still beaming. "But what about you? You still don't have any magic . . ."

Freddie shrugs. "I'll be fine. Maybe the Church of the Crystal Shield will accept me? We got in and out of a dungeon, after all!"

Rhonda smiles at that. "You'd make a good paladin, even if you're scared of spiders," she adds with a giggle.

Freddie gasps. "Hey, you saw the size of that Guardian spider!"

She laughs and nods. "Yeah, I also didn't argue when you said to run, hehe."

He laughs as well, and I get a new alert.

Quest Updated!
The Next Generation completed their quests in you! Mana rewarded.

Ooh, that's a lot of mana.

Chapter 5

So, what am I to do with this sudden windfall of mana thanks to those kids? I've got enough to upgrade myself again, and I do want to, but I want to make sure I'm prepared before I do that. My ant queen has been busy, her little workers finally hatched, and all've gotten to . . . well, work. I've been mostly spending my income to upgrade her, keeping my total above the points for me to upgrade myself, but not spending it just yet.

She can make majors now, which are just bigger and meaner ants. They're not all majors—she still needs workers—but invader ants are basically a solved problem now. Her workers have been digging into the dirt of the little Secret Sanctum, as I want my large marble of a core to be beyond the reach of anything strong. Fittingly enough, the ants are hard workers, and progress has been going pretty smoothly. A foot a day might not sound like much, but after a week, it'll take adventurers with picks and shovels to get at my core.

Which makes me more willing to let delvers into the basement. I've even grown a new chest down there, too, but nobody's shown up to try to get it yet. My swarm is now level five and venomous, but I know it's only a matter of time before some strong delver comes by to clear it out. There's even a magic dagger in the chest, so that's sure to draw someone.

Also sure to draw delvers are the new mushroom nodes. With my queen around, I can put new nodes in other little spots around the house for a discount. They're mostly in cabinets and cupboards and such, just a small patch for the ants to feed from and for mushrooms to grow. I'm kinda proud of my little ecosystem.

Oh, hey, Elf Guy's back. Maybe he wants that dagger? I focus in on him as he does a loop around my yard.

"Dungeon has expanded since last inspection. Crows refuse to shut up." Good crows. "Patch of herbs in the backyard, not high level. Birds upgraded to crows; anthill appears heavily upgraded, but no obvious signs of ants outside. Appears dungeon prefers to focus on interior at this time."

He gathers a bit of herbs from the patch before walking around to my porch and knocking. "Hmm . . . no movement inside after announcing my presence." Ah, so he could sense me shuffling my things around last time. He heads on inside and looks around the main room.

"Entrance busy with patrols of rats and small spiders. Dungeon not reacting to me this time; may be trying to lull me into a false sense of security. Spider spawner in the spandrel is now a minor lair. What? Spandrel?" He facepalms at whoever he's reporting to. "That's what the little room underneath stairs is called. Speaking of rooms, still no sign of Sanctum or other specialty rooms."

He seems to do a doubletake as he glances at the stairs to the basement. "Lesser chest in the basement, behind a level five venomous swarm with Guardian scion buff." He gives a low whistle. "Surprised it spawned a chest down there, though. Last time, basement was a clear no-go zone. May have moved path to Secret Sanctum." Hah, you wish, Elf Guy. I'm a smart dungeon.

He starts to poke through my various containers, pocketing the loot and getting me a nice bit of mana in the process. "Container loot above average for level, to be expected with both packrats and crows. I can sense several small mushroom nodes scattered throughout the house, so probably leafcutter ants as well. Dungeon seems to prefer to be cooperative, though not a simple toybox. Rat swarm upstairs still level two; most of house still recommended for new adventuring groups. Will examine basement to investigate report of orphans having been down there. From this growth, someone has definitely been in here."

I should have expected the kids would talk. They seemed really excited about those mushrooms, so someone would have asked where they got them. I hope those two were able to do their things. They seemed like good kids.

Elf Guy cautiously descends the stairs, and I make a note to put a rotten floorboard or five for next time. "Confirm spell spore mushrooms just past landing in the basement. Guardian spider nest nearby, and venomous swarm as well. Dungeon could have easily finished the kids off."

His eyes lock on to the chest in the back. "Chest contains a magical weapon. Permission to retrieve? Acknowledged. Engaging." Oh, he does want the toy! I spend the little mana it takes to alert the swarm and the Guardian spider. Tiny, as I like to call my spiderbro now, is definitely bigger than any spider back home could ever dream of getting, about the size of a cat. His aura not only makes the spiders nearby tougher but also makes them do more damage, too.

Nothing personal, Elf Guy, but you gotta pay the toll if you want the goodiebox.

"Deliberate pincer maneuver by the spiders. Dungeon definitely could have kept those kids if it wanted." He smiles and pulls his daggers. "This is gonna be fun!"

He decides to engage my scion instead of the swarm first, probably because with all the webbing around, he wouldn't be able to acrobat around like in the attic. He stabs poor Tiny, but the little guy seems to be able to take it. He webs one of the elf's feet as the swarm closes in, but that grin of his stays on his face. He kicks Tiny back and pivots on his stuck heel to unleash those Windblades of his at the swarm and the big mess of webbing. There are too many spiders for him to keep them all away, though, and he gets many little bites.

I can even see the little poison effect floating over his head now. It doesn't seem to have dampened his spirits, however, even as Tiny jumps onto his back and sinks his fangs. Is he going to leave soon? I kinda like the friendly rivalry we have; I don't want to accidentally kill him.

"Shadow Blade!"

Oh. I didn't need to worry about that. He seems to melt into shadow before flashes of steel permeate the room, and he even kills Tiny! No! My swarm is done, too. I wish I still had eyes to glare at the jerk who killed my Tiny!

"Whew, boss encounter finished. Confirm use of Shadow Blade; basement is for high-level solo or medium groups. Grabbing loot before scion respawns."

Wait, *respawns*!? I focus on my spider lair while the Elf Guy opens the chest to get the coins and dagger, and sure enough, I see a little portrait of Tiny with a timer counting down. I look over at my mana for that fight, and if I had a jaw, I'd need to pick it up off the ground. That's a *ton* of mana from that fight.

Elf Guy drinks one of his own potions as he ascends the stairs, and I let him go. I still feel a bit sore about him killing Tiny, but at least the little guy will be back before too long. As the elf reaches for the knob of the door, he pauses and glances back into the room. "Don't spend it all in one place. I'd hate to lose a dungeon like this."

Wait, *lose*?

Chapter 6

I'll admit—Elf Guy shook me up with his cryptic parting words. Well, at least it seems to confirm that my core and my Sanctum are important. Definitely keeping it secret for now. Some of his other words also make me curious. He mentioned other rooms. Other rooms like what? If they're anything like the Sanctum, I'll probably want to keep them secret, too. And if they're anything like the Sanctum, the room can be tiny.

I set my queen to digging out a few extra chambers for me and to keep expanding the Sanctum. The core is about the size of a golf ball now, so I can't get complacent with the chamber it's in; I wouldn't want it to get stuck. It actually doesn't take long for the first chamber to be finished, and when I focus on it, I see a couple interesting options: *Library* and *Lab*.

How's that supposed to work?

Well, no time like the present. I designate the first chamber as a library, and it pops up as a secret library. Cool. A small scrap of paper also appears. I focus in on it as I wonder what it does.

What's this?

Oh. It's like a little notepad. *Uh . . . erase?* Ah, good, that worked. I don't exactly have enough paper to just go putting useless questions like that on it.

The second chamber is about finished now, too, so I designate it as a lab, and sure enough, it's now my secret lab. No papers appear in it, however. How do I make it work, then?

I poke around a bit, though I don't get anything to pop up. Until an ant wanders through with a bit of mushroom in her mandibles. *Combine*, eh? Well, that has all sorts of interesting implications. I tell the queen to send a few workers to get some of the herbs from the patch and a bit of the spell spores, because I think it's experimenting time!

No, wait . . . it's visitor time. Oh hey, it's the kids. They're looking better now, too. Rhonda has a simple little robe on and a wand that doesn't still have bark on it. Freddie has some clothes on that look similar to denim, and a little wooden shield to go with his club. It still has bark on it, but it's a bit thicker and has a decent knot on the business end. Seems like a good upgrade in gear to me.

This time, interestingly enough, it's Freddie who seems uncertain about being here. "Really, Rhonda? *That's* what you want as a familiar?"

"Well . . . no, actually." Freddie seems to relax at her reply, at least until she continues. "That was a scion, so I can't make that my familiar. But there might be a different big spider like that to tame." Freddie visibly shudders at the idea of taming a spider, and I'm curious. A familiar? Interesting. I have been getting a decent number of odd larger spiders recently.

"So . . . how do we go about taming one, then? Beat it up and nurse it back to health?"

Rhonda looks aghast at the idea. "What? No! I have to befriend it!"

"How do you befriend a spider?" Freddie asks incredulously, and Rhonda looks a bit bashful.

"I'm, uh . . . not sure. Old Staiven has a bunch of books on familiars, but he says he believes in learning on the job." Freddie doesn't look very impressed about her mentor, and Rhonda can't help but quickly speak up to defend him. "He didn't send me out with nothing, though! He said I should find out what my familiar wants and provide it."

"Then what's a spider want, besides to crawl on people's faces while they're trying to sleep?" asks Freddie, shuddering once again.

Rhonda just giggles. "Well . . . food and safety, I guess? But these aren't just normal spiders here. They also want to guard their dungeon."

"But if they're your familiar, won't they not be able to stay here to guard the dungeon?"

"Um . . . kinda. But I had an idea for that!"

"The bucket?"

"The bucket!" she exclaims with joy, brandishing a wooden bucket with a small plank over the top.

"So how's that help the spider defend the dungeon?"

"We'll just catch some invaders then feed them to a spider!"

"Without feeding us to the spiders too," Freddie deadpans. Rhonda simply smiles and nods, and he rolls his eyes before continuing, "Okay, so what's an invader? Uh . . . us?"

She shakes her head. "No, we're delvers. We're kinda supposed to be here. Invaders want the core. Old Staiven said with a new dungeon, mice are probably the biggest invaders."

"We saw rats, though. Those're bigger."

"Those are denizens; they're also supposed to be there. Let's try to catch a mouse out here, then try to find a big spider to feed!" Huh, that's interesting. I set my crows to leave the kids alone and observe, giving them a chance to catch something.

"Hey, what about this big bug instead?" asks Freddie, holding up a large hissing roach in his hand.

Rhonda recoils a bit before steeling herself. "That'd . . . probably work?"

With that, she removes the plank, and Freddie plops it in the bucket.

I mentally shrug and leave them to their hunting because I can sense my two reagents are in the lab now. I even have a use for the scrap of paper in the library! Let me see . . . ochredill and spell spore.

Ochredill + Spell Spore = ?

Perfect. *Hey, ants. Come chew these two things up and mush them together.*

I'm amazing at science. A couple worker ants come to do my bidding, and they're soon chewing and mushing. It's taking a while, though, so I go see what the kids are up to.

I never expected a bucket of roaches and mice to be so easily identifiable by the sound, but it is. The kids look pretty proud of themselves, too.

"So, we have spider treats. What's the next step?" asks Freddie, seeming a bit more at ease. Kid seems the type to prefer doing rather than just talking, but at least he's smart enough to know to follow a plan.

"Well . . . now we go inside and look for big spiders, and see if any of them are tamable."

Freddie still doesn't like the quest, but he's not backing down, good lad.

"Well, let's go then." He leads the way back to my porch and heads inside, casting a wary look at my various denizens. I have them stand down, despite the big bucket of invaders they have, and the two start looking around.

"What kind of spider are we looking for, anyway?"

"I think I want some kind of hunting spider. Weavers are cool, but I don't want to have to deal with webs everywhere."

"So how do we find one of those?"

"Well . . . they'll be hunting, I guess?"

A hunter, eh? Well, the best laid plans of mice and men, as they say. Sure, I have a couple large jumping spiders wandering around, about the size of a hand. Those're probably exactly what she wants. But that bucket also gives me an idea to make their quest a bit harder.

Don't look at me like that. I'm still a dungeon, not a supermarket. Or a pet store.

I send one of my spiders to scurry through the room to get their attention. Then I send a couple more. They're kids, not the Elf Guy; I can't expect them to spot everything. Freddie is actually the one to spot the fifth spider I send through. "Like that one?"

"Yes! Don't lose it!" Rhonda says with excitement and dashes after the spider. They both try to be quiet, but have you ever heard a kid be fast? They can be fast or quiet, not both. Still, I get them to the kitchen, where my little trap is set for them. I do have a couple jumping spiders milling about, mostly because they hadn't wandered out after I sent them.

The real fun is up on the ceiling. Adorable little newbies haven't learned the importance of looking up yet.

Rhonda hands Freddie the bucket, who puts his club away to take it. Kid has a good mentor. If you have to choose between a weapon or your shield, take the shield. Rhonda removes the plank and levitates out a roach, trying to coax one of the jumping spiders to come eat it. Freddie is keeping a look out, but I don't think the kid has a great spot check, you know?

On the ceiling, my little traps prepare themselves. Ogre-faced spiders are cool. They have the usual eight eyes, but two of them are huge, probably because they don't make normal webs and don't hunt normally like wolfspiders. They make nets. And they need those eyes to aim those nets.

While Freddie is looking away from the bucket and Rhonda is distracted, one of the spiders descends, opens her net . . . and plucks a mouse from the bucket without being noticed. She returns to the ceiling and quickly enjoys her meal before preparing another net.

"Come on . . . tasty invader to eat!" tries Rhonda, having little luck feeding the spiders.

"Maybe they prefer the mice?" suggests Freddie, even as another mouse is plucked from the bucket without him noticing. Rhonda sighs and returns to the bucket, tossing the roach back in and levitating out a mouse. "I hope so," she says, sounding worried that her plan won't work.

I know the jumping spiders do prefer the mice, but the ogres don't really care either way. The two young delvers return their focus to the jumping spiders while another net plucks out a few roaches. The jumping spiders immediately notice the mouse, and the nearest one prepares to pounce. "There you g—eep!"

I guess she wasn't prepared for them to move quite that quickly. Probably fortunate for her that she was levitating the thing. The mouse is dispatched with a crunch and quickly eaten, and I can actually see a little bar over the spider's head starting to fill.

"It's working! Quick, give . . ." Her excited face turns to one of confusion then concern as she turns back toward Freddie. Sitting on the bucket for stability, her dragline keeping her weight off it, one of the ogre-faced spiders is staring at Rhonda as she chews on a mouse.

"Freddie . . ." starts Rhonda, not wanting to startle her friend. I, however, can see the little taming bar fill, and silently laugh as it looks like Freddie gets a notice.

"Taming complete? Wha—AAAHHH!" His outburst scatters the other spiders as he backs away from the bucket and his new tame. She simply holds the bucket now and reaches a leg in to pluck out a roach to eat as she watches her new master and his party member.

Chapter 7

Ah, those crazy kids. After Freddie found himself with a new *animal companion*, there was much consternation. He wanted to release it, of course, but that's only an option for rangers and tamers, silly boy. He definitely looked like he was considering cross-classing in the near future, though. Rhonda, however, still needed her own familiar, and the two got the bucket back with hopefully enough mice to spare.

They actually tracked down the one Rhonda had started taming, partially with the help of Freddie's spider . . . who I'm going to call Fiona. Fiona seems to take her new position seriously, as she netted the jumping spider as soon as she spotted it, which was significantly earlier than the two kids. I'm pretty sure the taming bar filled slower, what with the spider being restrained like that, but Rhonda got herself a familiar.

I let the two kids go on their way peacefully, and get another pile of mana for them finishing a quest as well. I smile to myself as they leave my perception, hoping they'll come back for some more shenanigans. For now, though, I have an experiment in the lab to check up on.

It's definitely done something, but I don't know what. The mush is faintly glowing yellow, which . . . might be a good sign? It didn't blow up or melt through the dirt, so I consider it a win so far.

Not knowing what else to do with it, I tell the queen to have a few workers eat some. If they explode or something, they're just a few little worker ants.

And hey, they don't explode. They don't die, either, which is even better. I watch the ants and notice a pretty immediate change. They're quick little buggers now, wow.

I tell the queen to keep tabs on them and turn to other things. I've been sitting on quite a pile of mana for a while now. My core is close to the size of a tennis ball, too, so I should do something with it.

Now, my new upgrades will let me expand up, out, or down, and they're all tempting. Up will let me get that little tower thing on my roof, which feels like a great place to put some stronger stuff, maybe something between the strength of the basement and the attic.

Out would give me more ground to look at, maybe let me see the fence or wall or whatever. The kids more or less confirmed to me that I'm in some kind of town. It's not like urchins can just go wander out into the woods and expect to come back safely.

Down is also really tempting, though. There could be caves there, or maybe ores or something. If I'm going to live up to the title of dungeon, I'll need to head deeper eventually, right? Although, deeper is probably also more dangerous, and I want to be ready for dangerous stuff.

Up it is, then. It feels weird to not have the run of the whole house when I *am* the house.

Ah, it's a belfry. Fittingly enough, I have a bat spawner in there, too. I don't know what my new invader is yet, though. Bats eat bugs or fruit, and I doubt I'm gonna get attacked by killer tomatoes. I feel like I have bugs more or less handled, so what will they throw at me? Feels like something sneaky, whatever it is.

Or maybe it'll actually be nothing? It wasn't all *that* much mana, and it didn't give me that much extra floor space. It more gave delvers roof access and the belfry than it gave me new rooms, so not all that much, really.

I decide to risk expanding out, since I still have a lot of mana to spend, and man, am I glad I do. I do, in fact, have a wall and a gate, but I also have a huge expanse of a yard. My new spawner is a personal favorite, too: snakes! Heck yeah, I'ma have noodles wandering around.

I upgrade my little snek den and the bat belfry until I need to choose a path, then leave it hanging for now. I want to see what happens with the new invaders before I make any choices.

Mana Gained!

Wait, what? A new mana thing? Where is . . . *aha!* One of my snakes got something! It's . . . a mole? Uh-oh. My Sanctum is still secret, but moles will eventually stumble over it and the core! Okay, I need more sneks, and I think I need them small, so we're going with vipers. I wanted constrictors, but no way is an anaconda going to be able to hunt moles.

Alrighty, sneks, go and . . . My snakes! Seagulls! I hate seagulls! The vipers fight back a bit, but these gulls are bad news, wow. My only real options to fight them in the air are my crows and my bats. I could make them vampire bats, but I don't think that'll do too much against seagulls.

I spend most of my mana to upgrade my crow's nest to a raven's nest, and the new birbs descend on the gulls like they're the new taste sensation. A group of crows may be a murder, but these ravens are definitely an unkindness to those stupid seagulls.

Aah . . . that's some nice mana income now, though.

Right, surface secured again, I need to secure the Sanctum. My Rat Scion has been working on my walls and various nooks and crannies, making all sorts of secret passages and such around, and I see a great spot for my new Sanctum. I'm glad he hasn't really been getting bigger, unlike Tiny. I thought he would be, especially after the nest spat out a dire rat the other day.

A Scout needs to stay lean, I suppose.

Anyhow, the location for my new Sanctum is going to be in the chimney of the second floor. Well, technically in the attic. There's never been a fire in there since I got here, and with the spiders and ants to build a little chamber in it, I can move my core!

Of course, I need to be careful about that.

First thing first: scion roll call! *Tiny! Keep doing your thing, buddy. You hang out in the main room for now. If you keep getting bigger, I'll need to give you an actual room for your lair, too. You're about the size of a small dog now. If anything says "Dungeon closed for renovations," it's a spider big enough to play fetch.*

Scout rat! Congrats, your name's Teemo now. Get the other rats on high alert, especially along the route to the chimney! You're going to have to be the one to carry the core, so I'm counting on you!

Queen ant! You're moving shop! We'll leave the lab and library for now, but get ready to hitch a ride on Teemo. Get as many majors as you can to eat the rest of the ball of go-juice. Oh, and how are those workers? They're still speedy? Awesome, we need to get more of that stuff made, but later.

Raven, Poe! You're my early warning and first line of defense on the surface! I don't expect the gulls will be able to do much, but keep an eye out. And if any delvers show up, do your best to discourage them. I don't want anyone inside until my new Secret Sanctum is secured!

Bat Scion! Uh . . . sleep tight? Not a whole lot for you to do right now, sorry. I'll get back to you.

Fluffles, my new Snake Scion! I see that MP bar, mister. You're running escort with Teemo. Don't go burning me down or something. Okay, we all know the plan? Then break!

Outside the new dungeon, the quiet port town can feel the shift in the activity of the old, abandoned manor. While before, the place had been almost welcoming, today it is not. People can see the ravens staring at them as they walk by and hear the occasional squawk of a seagull being intercepted as soon as it enters the grounds of the old estate.

The representative of the Dungeoneer's Guild stands at the gate, scribbling furiously as she takes down notes, her pointed ears occasionally twitching as she works. Suddenly, the mood seems to change, like someone flipped a switch. The ravens caw and relax, and the electricity seems to just vanish from the air. She notes that, too, for when the inspector next returns. It could be a sign of something having gone wrong.

Chapter 8

Ah, everything went right with the move! I even learned exactly what the go-juice actually does! Well, almost everything went right. Let me explain. My ants started moving my core through the tunnels and toward the crack in the wall when a mole finally found the core! I tell you, at that scale, moles are terrifying!

Queen, though, quickly rallied the troops to fend off the invader, and the little soldiers started zapping it! Lightning ants! Isn't that cool?! Anyway, I only had about a dozen lightning majors, but with them, the normal ones, and Queen directing them in the fight, the mole barely even got to touch my core.

It did take a tiny bit of my mana before they could push it back, but the affront of it touching my core seemed to send them into a frenzy. The lightning majors are all dead now, but that mole is also very, very dead. Queen got the ants moving the core the rest of the way, and Teemo soon got ahold of the orb and Queen, with Fluffles watching over them all.

With the mole incursion making me cautious, Teemo led everyone through a secret passage and into the crawl spaces in my walls. He wasn't taking any chances, which I definitely appreciated. It seemed like the various invaders could all sense the core was vulnerable, even if they didn't know where it was. I've never seen the invaders numbers that high! It felt like every hand, foot, talon, wing, claw, and tail was on the ground to repel them, and I can't help but be a bit proud of my denizens.

Thanks to the secret paths, my core was quickly placed in the new Secret Sanctum, safe behind layers and layers of thick spider silk and packed dirt, as well as the stone and mortar of the chimney itself. My Raven Scion even set his nest on top of the chimney, with various spiders actually protecting the opening from different insects. All in all, a very successful relocation, and I signal the all clear.

Everyone goes back to their normal doings, and I ping Tiny to head outside. I have an idea for what to do with all that free real estate, and I'll need his help.

I also set my bats to be fruitbats. I want to make me some agriculture, and is there any more cultured agri than a hedge maze?

See, I have all sorts of interesting things I can grow out here, and a thorn hedge is one of them. If I set them up right, I can make a maze. And if I'm gonna have a labyrinth, I'm gonna need something to live in it, and I don't have a minotaur. I do, however, have Tiny. I also have various larger critters to help populate the maze; a couple dire rats and even a small swarm of crows. That should be plenty to populate it, at least for now.

I also have the ability to make a ton of nodes out there. I've got several options for herb nodes, and a bunch of spots for various wood nodes, too. I go a bit crazy with spending my mana to get the thing up and running. I don't need to expand downward right now anyway, and the increased numbers of invaders means more mana production, too.

I haven't seen any delvers in the last few days, though. I had a few, aside from the Elf Guy and the kids, but none recently. I wouldn't mind a bit of extra mana from them doing stuff, but I'm not exactly hurting for it.

I'm definitely glad I made my bats into fruitbats, too. The hedge maze is a bit out of the range of Queen and her workers, and fruitbats are just the kind of things to help make my herbs and trees grow better. More herbs and trees should mean more delvers, right?

I even sprout a few chests out in the maze, along with the aforementioned various nodes, just to sweeten the pot. They're all listed as "Least Chests," which I'm pretty sure means they kinda suck. That might be from how I'm organizing everything out here, though.

See, in the house, it's basically dungeon business as usual. My critters defend me from invaders and challenge delvers, everything to the death or to retreat/ rout. Out in the maze, however, I'm setting things up differently. I've had Teemo out to teach the dire rats a few things, and I've also had Tiny practicing his webbing. He's approaching the size of a horse now, and I wonder if even the Elf Guy might have to actually try to be able to beat him.

Which would be difficult for me. See, if nobody comes to get my stuff, I don't get that bonus mana. So I have a new job for Tiny: hide-and-seek. I want to get delvers to explore the maze and to have to avoid Tiny. If he catches them, he'll web them up and dump them outside the maze. I think I can even have Fluffles levitate them from there to just outside the gate.

The dire rats will be playing annoyances, stealing stuff from the delvers as they spot them. I wonder if the delvers will consider the area even more dangerous than the house. HP is a lot easier to replace than stuff sometimes. I'm not too worried, though. I think challenge translates to reward levels—for the delvers and for me. It's a weird and different challenge, but one I hope will pan out.

And if it doesn't, well, I'll have more herbs and things to experiment with in my lab. I've tried a few other combinations, but so far, the Bottled Lightning—despite not being in a bottle—is my only success. I get the feeling that I don't want to mix everything one to one, but I don't think I have much other option at the moment. I'd need a bigger lab to upgrade it, but I want to keep it secret. I think that will have to wait until I expand downward a bit and can get into stone.

I have upgraded my library a bit and moved it into the wall not far from the chimney. It's not the most efficient as far as working with my lab, but it's secret and a bit bigger, giving me a full piece of paper to work with now! It might not sound like much, but I've been able to keep track of each combination I've tried in the lab.

Speaking of the lab, Queen has started to produce a specialized worker for in there. I've been calling them Alchemists because that's basically what they're doing. They've been slowly producing more Bottled Lightning for use in the rest of me. I actually want to get the basement swarm of spiders to be venomous *and* lightning powered! That'll be quite a boss fight! It'll also take a lot of Bottled Lightning to accomplish. I like that it seems permanent, but it's a pretty significant dose to achieve.

The lack of delvers still has me concerned, though. The maze is still growing, and while the fruitbats are occupied, other flavors of bat are just kinda milling around. Sure, some help look for moles, but the number of snakes is starting to increase now that I have enough ravens to handle the gulls. I focus in on one of the normal bats, wondering what I should do with it. There's not a whole lot of stuff to do at night, after all.

Oh, hey. That's a new option.

Chapter 9

I have an option for the bat, but I have no idea how it'd apply to a bat.

Mount Expedition

How does a bat mount an expedition? It's a bat, not an archeologist.

Well, only one way to find out. *Mount that expedition, my bat!*

Oh, number to send. Uh . . . three? It accepts three. Good. Where to? That's a good question. I already know basically everything in my reach. It's kinda cool, actually. Outside my walls, though . . . it's still a mystery.

Wait . . . can they actually go outside? *Bats! Your expedition target is across the street, past the main gate!*

And off they go, huh. Cost a bit of mana, but not too bad. The little guys do that bat flutter over the top of the gate and vanish from my awareness, and now I see I have some denizens on expedition. At least it looks like they should be back in a few minutes.

. . . Is it a few minutes yet?

How about now?

Still no?

Ah, there we go! *Welcome home, bats! What news do you bring of the world outside the walls?* A bakery? Seriously? I'm a dungeon with a bakery across the street? I'm not sure what I was expecting, but a bakery was not it. Well, that fully confirms I'm in a town. I just hope the whole "town around a dungeon" thing works better than it did in the first *Diablo* game. Yharnam? No, I think that was *Bloodborne*. Tristram! Or something like that, anyway. Well, as long as nobody goes and tries to jam my core into their face, it should go well, right?

Either way, I want more info, so I start sending out expeditions with my bats, keeping them in groups of three just because. I also give them larger areas to identify, which takes them longer but doesn't cost me extra mana. I guess it's because it technically leaves me vulnerable to have them out for too long. Or leaves *them* vulnerable.

While they explore, I look in on my library and see about sketching out a rough map.

And immediately run into a problem. I can only put words on stuff in my library. Or numbers. Or drawings. Wait, what? How can I draw a lightning major but not a wall?! *Queen, do you have any ideas?*

Nah, she's busy organizing her ants and following the list of combinations on my paper.

Do I need a map room? That seems kinda . . . specialized. A whole room just for a map? None of my room options were for a map room. I focus in on one of the little chambers that doesn't seem to be in active use by Queen, and see what my options are.

Armory is a bit beyond what I can actually use right now. Maybe if I get carpenter ants, I can give them little spears, heh. Garden? Yeah, don't need that anytime soon. Prison? That sounds like it could be interesting, but I don't need another complicated project; I'm still growing my maze. Workshop sounds cool, but I still don't have anything that would work in it.

War room? Why would I need a war room? What does a war room even do? I don't have wars to plan. I don't need to push figurines around a . . . map? Is that what the war room does? Because a cartography room would be too easy? It's also not exactly cheap, even as a little ant chamber. I mentally sigh and spend the mana.

A little bit of leather pops up in the new secret war room. There are two dots: Dungeon. Bakery. Well, at least it's some kind of map, though it doesn't even have a compass rose to say which way is north. As my bats start to come back, however, more dots appear. Looks like I'm smack-dab in the middle of a commercial district. Am I not the first dungeon here?

Elf Guy did say he didn't want to lose me as a dungeon. It could also just be luck in my spawn, though I don't know why someone would leave an abandoned manor with a big yard to just stay abandoned for . . . however long it takes a dungeon to happen. I doubt just any old random, ignored basement can suddenly become a dungeon over a weekend.

Most of the dots are pretty boring and probably not much use to me. Tailor. Cartwright. Haberdasher. Apparently, the town is big enough to have someone make a living making hats, so that's cool. Alchemist. Enchanter. Oh, hey, a church. I wonder if it's the Shield one that Freddie goes to. I wonder if Rhonda is apprenticed at one of the magical places, too.

I don't get any shop names, though, and I don't know if that's because bats can't read, or if I need to upgrade the war room to get more details. Either way,

I probably shouldn't spend any mana on it just yet. The maze is hungry, and nobody has come to visit in a while. I should double-check my scions.

Tiny is doing great. There's a small grove of trees growing near the center of the maze, and he's webbed it up good to make his nest. He hasn't gotten much bigger just yet, but I haven't been able to spare him much mana for it. He's still listed as a Guardian, which I've taken a closer look at. Basically, if he's in his guarding area, he buffs my stuff and gets some good buffs himself. I don't have any numbers to go by, aside from his level (level eight now, by the way), but I can see him moving quicker in the maze than not, so his transfer is complete.

Teemo is being the best sneaky rat and seems to be teaching my other rats things. He's still a Scout and making various paths all over the place, which seem to let my other rats get to where they're going to quicker. I considered making him electric, but I want to wait until I get venom for him instead. I named him Teemo; he should be able to do poison stuff. The packrats have been occasionally getting electrified, too. Queen must be doling out Bottled Lightning outside her ants occasionally. Fine by me. Faster packrats mean faster accumulation of goodies for delvers.

Speaking of Queen, she got a title I wasn't expecting. I had put her around the core to become a new Guardian, but I guess I should have expected she'd become my Alchemist with what I've been having her do. I definitely appreciate the discount on upgrading the lab. For her latest project, I actually had Teemo grab a potion out of one of the chests. That cost me about twice the mana I would have gained if a delver took it, but I want to test something. Now that I have an actual Alchemist, I wonder if Queen can analyze stuff. This trial-and-error crap is taking up way too much paper to keep track of. If I can get me some healing ants, or maybe healing spiders, that'd be cool. They could even weave their own bandages!

Poe is keeping a good lookout, and I might send him on an expedition come daylight. If Tiny is lord of the maze, and Teemo lord of the house, then Poe is lord of the yard. He's been coordinating with Coda and Fluffles to keep the moles and gulls at bay. I wouldn't be surprised if he gets some title of his own soon, too.

Fluffles has been growing well, but thankfully not as well as Tiny. I do want him to be able to get into all those nooks and crannies, after all. He also seems to be specialized in Kinetic magic, by which I mean picking up and moving things without hands, which is fitting, in retrospect. I've seen him snag a gull out of the air and bring it down for vipers to bite. If he keeps catching things like that, maybe I should get a jail soon.

Coda, the Bat Scion, has been mostly occupied with tending the maze and most of the nodes outside the house. He has also been making sure to keep the sonar bats on a good rotation to help Poe scan for moles. He's probably my least-effective combatant out of my scions, but he's doing a great job with the nodes and maze. I've been getting steady discounts on growing and upgrading everything out there, and I've even seen him getting seeds from the expeditionary bats.

So maybe I *should* get a garden or greenhouse or something, actually.

Finally! Someone's at the gate!

Chapter 10

Oh, I wonder who's there? It doesn't feel like Elf Guy. For one, there's too many feet.

I focus and see an actual party. Neat! First inside is some kind of half-bird person with a bow. Probably their version of Elf Guy. She has piercing blue eyes and a short, hooked beak like a hawk, with the brown-and-white feathers to match and a tail of reddish-brown feathers too. She has a modest but noticeable swell at her chest to make me call her a her under that leather armor.

Behind her is a dwarven fighter. Big red beard, big shiny axe, big shinier shield, smol legs: dwarf. His hair and beard are kept pretty short, but he does take the chance to braid his mustache as far down as his beard goes, about halfway down his neck. Him and the birb give a wary eye around the dawn-lit yard, looking more serious than the Elf Guy ever did.

Behind him comes an elf . . . or maybe half-elf? She doesn't look as graceful as Elf Guy, but definitely has the ears and the tanned pale skin he did. Maybe he's lighter on his feet because he's such a high level? Or because he's a . . . rogue or something. Either way, she's definitely a caster. She's got a blue robe with some embroidery, but not the conical brimmed hat. Her blonde hair is long and mostly tucked into the back of her robe. Her staff is painted white with a bunch of small gems bedazzled at the top. Is she a Light mage? Or maybe she's not specialized? That'd be interesting. I haven't seen anyone do multiple elements yet.

Wait, they brought the kids?

Poe peers down from his nest as he awakens and confirms it: that's Rhonda and Freddie. It's not like there's a second pair of kids with spiders following them around. Fiona, the net-casting, ogre-faced spider, has gotten a bit bigger and seems to have marked Freddie's shield with one of her webs. At least the kid doesn't seem scared of spiders anymore. Rhonda's jumping spider, Lucas, is riding on her hat, his big eyes keeping a lookout.

"Did we have to bring them?" asks bird lady, and I agree. I mean, adult supervision is probably a good idea, but that party looks like they want a more traditional dungeon-crawling experience. I don't think bring-your-kids-to-work day is a thing here.

"Hey," speaks up Freddie as he looks around. "The only person who's been in and out of here more than us is the guild Inspector!"

I mean . . . he's not wrong.

The dwarf chuckles and motions for Freddie to stand next to him. "Alright, laddie. You're our guide, so guide us. We're here t' take a look 'round and try n' see if aught has happened t'yer dungeon between inspections. So, what d'you see?"

Freddie and Rhonda both look around, and their spiders do as well. Aw, they're so cute. I'm glad they got spiders; the kids have terrible spot checks. Fiona and Lucas have great vision, I just don't know if they can alert the kids to anything besides simple threats. Rhonda speaks up first.

"Well . . . there's a lot more activity outside than there was before. Last time, we didn't get the feeling of a dungeon until we went inside, but now, we feel it passing the gate."

"Yeah," continues Freddie, pointing up. "There's also birds and stuff now, too. Look at the size of that raven up there." All eyes turn to Poe, who preens himself a bit. *No, I don't think you have a fanclub, Poe. Well, maybe the birb lady. She's squinting at you.*

"Raven Scion. Doesn't look hostile. You kids said they all were staring at people a week ago?" Huh, I don't remember that. The kids do, though, and nod their heads.

"Yeah, one afternoon, the whole energy of the place shifted. It went back to normal, but people have been nervous ever since." Rhonda fidgets and leans out like she can see around the house from the gate. "Should we look around a bit more outside before going in?"

Birb and dwarf both nod at that suggestion, and the caster lady speaks up. "Alright, Ragnar and Freddie up front. Yvonne, Rhonda, and myself in back." Freddie looks a bit nervous about that but doesn't make any moves to return to the back. Ragnar just smiles and nudges the boy with his shield.

"Ach, dinnae worry, lad. If aught happens, I'll protect ye. It's m'job, after all!" he says with a laugh, which helps Freddie loosen up a bit. Now, I'm all for a nice field trip and tour, but I need some mana! Where's my weakest viper . . . Ah, there you are! *You and a couple rats, let's give the party a nice encounter to gauge their skill.*

"Movement," warns Yvonne the birb as she nocks an arrow and the front line readies their shields. Around the corner come my little chosen fighters: a level one viper and two level two rats! Pretty sure Elf Guy could handle that fight without even batting an eye, but the party seems to be taking it seriously. Or at least taking the viper seriously.

"Leave the snake t'me, lad. I can handle a wee poison. Keep the rats off our squishies, aye?"

"Uh . . . aye?" Freddie replies. I can practically see his training running through his head as he slowly advances. Looks like good form to me, but I haven't exactly trained with a shield. "Fiona, net the left one." He hardly finishes the sentence before she does just that, immobilizing the one rat, though it doesn't look like it'll stick for long.

Ragnar swings at the snake and misses, taking the counter on his shield and keeping its attention nicely. Freddie is luckier and hits the rat with his hatchet before Rhonda sends a little icicle to finish the rodent off. Yvonne catches my snake with an arrow in the . . . neck? Do snakes have necks? Not far below the head, and that seems to end the little noodle. I'm a bit sad to see the little guy bite it like that, but I needs me some mana, and he's given me quite a bit for the cause. Besides, he'll respawn.

The other caster doesn't get to do anything before my rat escapes the web, and then escapes the encounter, giving me a nice bit of mana for the whole thing. Elf lady speaks up. "I sensed hardly any malice in that encounter. What do you think, Yvonne?"

"No. If the dungeon was murderous, it could have sent far more than a weak viper and a few rats. Just the Raven Scion up there may be able to handle all of us." *Oh, don't puff up at that compliment, Poe. You're probably not that tough . . . though you are level three. I think these guys are level one. I still can't quite tell.*

The encounter finished, the party soon rounds the corner, and I see them all stop and stare. I wonder what has their attention? There's the ochredill patch by the house, which isn't anything to be stunned by. They can see the anthill from there, though I don't think that's it, either. They can see the hedge maze, but it's hardly knee-high yet. There's the various herb and tree nodes in there, and the couple chests, too. Maybe they like the look of the chests?

Oh, nope. It's not that. It's Tiny. He's very plainly sunning himself not far from his webbed-up copse of trees. Rhonda manages to put to words what everyone is thinking.

". . . That's a big spider."

"I think that's the one that was guarding the spell spores the first time," adds Freddie.

"Well . . . I dinnae think yer dungeon has gone murderous on ye. That thing would'a been a much more deadly fight than the snake and rats." Everyone nods, and Yvonne squints at Tiny.

"That is strange, though. I've never heard of a dungeon growing such a large bramble field. Nor having such weak chests guarded by something like that."

Elf lady nods. "I think that's a question beyond our expertise. Perhaps we should check the house? If it really has been a while since anyone has delved, there should be some very nice rewards inside."

Oh yes! Poppa needs moar mana! You guys might level from some encounters, too. *Hey, Poe! Coda! Get me a few weaker fliers inside! I'ma rally the spiders and see if the party knows to look up, and see if the kids learned that lesson.*

Turns out, the kids *did* learn the lesson, while the party hadn't yet. Thanks to Rhonda and Freddie, they spot the ambush of ceiling spiders. Elf lady gets webbed, but everyone gets out of the fight with all their HP intact, and I get some more mana. Yvonne finds the rotten floorboard, and the looks on everyone's faces was worth far more than the mana I got for it.

There is loot a-plenty for them, too, and I think everyone is going to be able to get some kind of upgrade for their gear after this. Rhonda finds some stone-lily petals in a drawer and gasps at them, so I guess they're a good ingredient. I still haven't found a use for them yet, but I will eventually. Or rather, Queen will, eventually.

At the stairs up, I toss a spider swarm at them. I start to get concerned it might be too much for them until Rhonda and the elf lady cast their spells. Rhonda casts a Freezing Gale, while the elf calls hers Earth Pulse. Then the two raise their implements together and shout, "Avalanche!"

For a moment, I'm worried they might have overdone it. I don't think I'm rated for avalanches. Thankfully, it just seems to be the name for a combined earth/ice spell, and the swarm is frozen and/or squished. I wonder if I should tone things down, but I think that's about the difficulty I want for a decent encounter for them. The next few are fairly simple: a few bats, a few crows, a dire rat guarding a room with more containers than usual.

While they work on that, I decide to change the encounter in the attic. I like the rat swarm, but I don't think the party is quite equipped for a boss swarm encounter. If they don't smoke it like the spiders, everyone will be pretty quickly overwhelmed. Besides, I have a good idea for a different boss.

Ragnar is the first to climb the ladder to the attic, and he goes nice and slow. He's not exactly a stealth master, but I'm also not exactly going to let the encounter just rush him as soon as he's spotted. His eyes widen as he sees what I have in store, and he quietly climbs back down the ladder.

"What'd you see?" asks Yvonne, and Ragnar exhales.

"Two dire rats, lightning enhanced." Looks are exchanged as everyone weighs their options. On the one hand, there's a chest up there with quite a bit of loot by now. On the other, there's some pretty serious potential pain between them and it. Ragnar seems to get an idea.

"Aelara . . . you know Protection from Elements, aye? Can y' teach the lass?"

The elf lady, apparently Aelara, considers that for a few moments. "Perhaps. It's not a particularly difficult spell. Would your master disapprove, Rhonda?" she asks the girl, not wanting to step on the toes of the one she's apprenticed to.

"Well . . . he does believe in learning on the job," admits Rhonda, and Aelara smiles.

"Ah, he sounds wise, then. Now, I'll only be showing you how to protect from electricity for now. You can work against any element, but that will take a bit more time to teach than we have."

I pay attention, too, and write what I can in my library. Fluffles will be practicing this later, definitely. I'm pretty sure the rats' lightning will still do some damage to the group, but it should be much more manageable for them now. The casters look pretty tired by the time they're done, though. "I'm afraid we'll be down to simple cantrips for the fight itself," apologizes Aelara, and Rhonda nods. Personally, I'm impressed the kid had enough to cast it on two people.

As the party starts to ascend, Freddie offers a plan. "I think I can keep the attention of one of them with Lucas and Fiona's help. You guys can focus on the other with Ragnar, then get mine?" Ragnar chuckles. "They'll focus on yours first, lad. I'm nae gonna let ye try to tank one o' those for longer than needed."

Yvonne and Aelara nod, and Freddie nods as well. Ragnar is the first to climb onto the landing, and the time for planning is over. I keep the rats from leaping forward, letting the party climb up and organize themselves briefly, then allow the rats to attack.

Yeesh, "lightning enhanced" indeed. Definitely glad they had the foresight to protect from lightning. Everyone looks a bit crispier than they'd prefer, but nobody is grievously wounded, even if Ragnar's beard is smoking. Him and Freddie leap to their plan, and it seems my rats need to recharge after that. Yvonne looks like she has something up her sleeve as she takes a few precious seconds to focus on the rat being harried by Freddie and the spiders.

"True Strike!" she shouts before letting the arrow loose, right into the eye of the rat being ganged up on. It had taken a few other attacks from the others while she prepared, and that attack of hers finishes the first dire rat off. Over with Ragnar . . . I'm not quite sure how he's doing, actually. He's been bitten several times, and though he's bleeding, he's laughing, and I think swearing at the rat in Dwarven. He doesn't look too concerned about his blood slowly leaking out, and it looks like his HP, while below half, is pretty stable there.

Yvonne doesn't have another True Strike in her, apparently, but everyone's combined efforts soon finish the second one off as well. As the mana rolls in for me, I see Ragnar stagger, his HP dipping dangerously. I think he has some ability to let him put off damage for a bit? Aelara is on him quickly, however, and even with only cantrips, she gets him stabilized.

"Ach, that was a good fight," he says, taking a seat on the floor, not even both-ering with the chest. Speaking of, I make sure Teemo isn't planning a hit-and-run on whoever opens it.

I needn't have worried, though. Looks like he's in the maze, blazing trails for the thieving dire rats.

Yvonne nods, cautiously approaching the chest. "Good thing Aelara insisted we bring our guides. I don't think we could have handled that on our own."

The two kids exchange looks before Freddie speaks up.

"I . . . think you would have. Last time we were here, it sounded like a swarm was up here. And you guys haven't seen what's in the basement. This dungeon . . ." he trails off, uncertain of his dungeoneering knowledge. Rhonda, though, soon picks up the slack.

"It doesn't do normal dungeon things. The first time we were here, we went into the basement to get some spell spores. There was a huge swarm of spi-ders watching us the whole time, but they didn't advance. Well, not until I got enough spores for Old Staiven. Then the Spider Scion crawled out of the wall, and the swarm started to advance. We ran. I don't think they even climbed the stairs to come after us."

Freddie nods. "Yeah. They had us but let us go after scaring us half to death." He shrugs as Yvonne seems to decide the chest is safe and opens it. "This dun-geon's weird, but I don't think it wants to just kill people."

"It's generous with loot as well," adds Yvonne as she pulls out a nice shield from the chest, and the sound of coins sliding off it as she pulls it out can be heard clearly around the attic.

"That looks like a good shield for Mr. Ragnar," notes Freddie, and the dwarf chuckles and shakes his head.

"I'd never hear the end of it if I ever used anything but mah family shield, laddie. I think it's about enough to cover yer guide's fees, though, aye?" he says, looking to the other two adults, who both share a small grin and nod.

"I'm sure we'll find something in that chest to pay young Rhonda as well." She holds up her hands before the two can try to refuse. "It's nonnegotiable, young ones. Even if it wasn't guild policy, none of us would be comfortable with you two not get-ting at least some share of the loot after putting your lives on the line with us."

The two kids look a bit bashful about that. I guess they never really consid-ered that their lives could be on the line. I mean, they weren't. Even if I had to spend all my mana to call the rats off and loot myself for potions, I wouldn't let the kids get hurt. Still, I like this party. I hope they come back. Good role models for the kids.

They take their time looting and have a bit of a rest to divvy everything out. Rhonda gets herself a nice scroll of Frozen Armor, which Aelara says her master should be able to teach her how to transfer to her spellbook more permanently. Freddie, of course, gets his shield. The party gets most of the coins and potions, which the kids are more than fine with. They have full pockets from the other containers anyway.

They leave, and I send a few blackbirds after them on an expedition to see where they go. Looks like the longest expedition I've assigned yet.

I also have a huge pile of mana after all that, and my core is looking more like a softball now. I'm pretty sure it'll be fine in the chimney until about basketball size, so I have a fair bit of time left. Still, if people start coming back to delve, I'll finish the maze sooner than I thought.

Chapter 11

Alright, so, good news: delvers have returned! Herbalists can handle the occasional low-level thing, so I go fairly easy on them, especially since they tend to wander in solo. The bad news, however, is that nobody wants to try the hedge maze. It's grown enough that they can't directly see Tiny, but they can see the trees and webbing around his nest. He's even been working on putting a web roof over the whole maze. *Good thinking, Tiny. Don't need cheaters in my maze.*

Also, good news: Queen was able to identify what goes into a healing potion! Also, bad news: I need actual equipment to let her do her work. I've upgraded the secret lab a few times, and I'm pretty sure it's allowed to have equipment now, but I'm having trouble getting it.

I haven't been able to afford carpenter ants yet, but I might need to get on that. I've been trying to make at least some equipment for the lab, and . . . it hasn't outright failed, at least? If I had fire ants, it might be simpler, but I don't. I have lightning ants. I've been sending crows out on expeditions to try to get me some iron wire, but nobody has had any success yet.

With some iron wire, I could have the lightning majors zap it to make a heating element and use the empty potion bottle for the various processing that it looks like Queen will have to do.

The kids have come back, too. They're the closest anyone has come to checking out the maze. They looked inside from the entrance, but I think Lucas spotted one of the rat thieves, and the kids decided against looking inside. I'm pretty sure they've gained a level now, too. Low-level things aren't slowing them down hardly at all anymore. They even handled a regular dire rat on their own.

The gate opens, and I expect it'll be the kids again, but it's Elf Guy! *Heya, Elf Guy! Long time no see!* He glares at Poe as every single bird makes noise at him, and if I could, I'd give him a shit-eating grin.

"Dungeon clearly recognizes me. Avians making a racket. Not alerting other denizens, just making noise at me. No unusual staring." There's that mention of staring again. It must have been from when I moved the core and had everything on high alert. That's the only time I've done anything different.

"Still no obvious rooms. I see alchemical creatures, though, so it must have a secret lab somewhere . . ." He looks around before looking up to the belfry. "Perhaps in the belfry tower. Still no chests or anything up there. Acknowledged. Investigating."

Oh, Elf Guy is actually taking things seriously now. Doesn't mean I have to, though I do still have my dignity as a dungeon. I toss some various moderate encounters at him as he explores the house. He manages to trip one of the rotten floorboards to the basement and decides he doesn't need to get a closer look. Yeah, that level six lightning venom swarm is quite a thing. Pretty sure he could take it, but he's all business right now, no pleasure.

He obliterates the rat swarm in the attic, and I can visibly see him pause to ensure he gets his boss experience before he opens the chest. I'm not even sure he notices what he actually gets from it; he just stuffs it in a bag that should not be able to hold all of that.

"On roof. Raven Scion is observing me, but not making any moves. Bats appear specialized toward fruit bats, which helps explain all the herbalist nodes." He watches as a trio of crows land on the roof, one carrying a bit of iron wire. *Oh hey! Good job, guys! Recover a bit, then head out to see if you can find anything else interesting.*

"Confirm dungeon is sending expeditions. Must have a secret war room, too. Investigating belfry." *Psst, hey, Coda. Make sure everyone's awake. I don't think Elf Guy has violence on his mind, but still, be ready to bolt if it comes to it.*

I don't bother sending any encounters at Elf Guy while he's on the roof. Partially because my birbs aren't really focused on combat, and partially because . . . I kinda see the whole area as unfinished. Maybe I'll make the belfry into a garden or something later. It'd make sense to have it close to the ones that bring me seeds.

He cautiously peers up the stairs and goes, but doesn't seem fazed by what I would consider a pretty big anticlimax. "Confirmed belfry is specialized toward fruitbats. I can see seeds on the floor. Likely have been sent on expeditions at night. Sweeping for hidden rooms."

Yeah, I think he's gonna be there awhile. I make sure my bats will bolt if he gets twitchy and let him take a 20 searching for something that's not there. I look in to see how Queen's doing with the alchemy and with the new iron wire.

Right, I need to get that thing moved and shaped.

Hey! Who's my closest spider? Ah, there you are. Go get that bit of wire and leave it by one of the mole/snake holes. My sneks don't like being on the roof, and I don't want to just drop the wire off and lose it.

Fluffles, take that wire with you into the tunnels and coil it up as much as you can. I don't think my ants can bend that thing easily. Queen, make sure there's a big enough tunnel for the ants to move it to the lab, and get ready to start rotating whatever electric ants through as you need them. I want some healing ants, dang it.

By the time the coil is in the lab, it looks like Elf Guy is about done with the belfry. He doesn't look very happy. "Negative on secret room in belfry. I was sure it'd be hiding something up here." And that's why I'm not, bucko. Smart people look for areas being carefully ignored to wonder if that's important. And smart dungeons put their core in a place people walk past all the time. Who's going to look under every brick in a road?

Oh hey, he's looking at the maze.

"Confirm odd bramble patch. Looks like Spider Scion is in there, as well as several chests. They seem far lower level than they should be, though, especially with this dungeon. Acknowledged. Investigating."

Finally, someone to check out the maze! He won't be able to get the good stuff if he just picks a wall to follow, either. He carefully approaches the entrance and peers around before talking to his team back at the guild. At least, I'm pretty sure they're at the guild. I've found a few guild houses from my expeditions, but I still don't have specific names for them.

The adventurer delvers from the other day went to two different guild houses, so I can only assume one is a guild for delvers, and one a guild for . . . I dunno, dungeon inspection? At least I know which church is Freddie's and which magic shop is Rhonda's. I've been able to label things on the map, too, so that's good.

But back to Elf Guy. "Confirm Spider Scion in bramble. It's high enough level even I'll need to be careful. Also looks like lower-level dire rats in the area, but can't pinpoint. Rat Scion probably taught them a few tricks," he grumbles as he rubs his hand. Teemo does great work.

"Heading in." Yes! I just wish I could give a quest involving the maze. That'd be cool. Maybe one of the rooms would allow that? I'll need to check that later. For now, I watch Elf Guy as he stalks the maze. He can definitely tell where the chests and nodes are, but looks like he doesn't know the floorplan, which is good.

One of my rat thieves darts from the hedge, but Elf Guy has damn good reflexes. It doesn't get very close before a knife finishes it with a single stab. "Dire rats are rat thieves. Don't appear to be interested in combat. Spider Scion appears to be slowly tracking me, but not in any particular hurry."

Come into my maze, said the spider to the Elf Guy. Tiny was the best scion to put in there, since he can actually help change the layout a bit. If he webs an opening and tears down a different web, the whole maze basically shifts. And that's what Tiny is doing. I don't think he forgave Elf Guy like I did.

While Tiny slowly weaves his trap, Elf Guy explores the maze, gathering chests and nodes along the way. None of the thieves even get close to taking any of his stuff, and I feel like Elf Guy is starting to understand the maze a bit better. "Bramble is a different style of encounter than previously observed. Appears to be more of a race than a simple battle. Collect as much stuff as you can before the Spider Scion gets you and the thieves pick you clean."

As Tiny closes the drawstring and traps Elf Guy, he seems to notice. "Wait . . . something's changed." He frowns as he looks around before realizing what's happened. "I've lost this race. Extracting!"

That's what you think, Elf Guy. Tiny's webs aren't going to be fazed by your daggers, so no going up and over. Good luck trying to go through the hedges, too. I dunno exactly how much damage they do, but I don't think you have that many HP, my friend.

Tiny finally rounds a bend in the maze, the two able to lay eyes directly on the other now. Elf Guy dons his serious face and draws his daggers as Tiny slowly approaches. I can see his spinnerets slowly working on a web, too.

Yeah, he definitely still holds a grudge from when Elf Guy killed him.

"Sorry, big guy. You look too big for me to play around with now. Shadow Blade!" As Elf Guy melts into shadows, Tiny curls in a bit on himself, clearly remembering the attack that ended him last time. Several long gashes appear in his carapace, though not over anything particularly vital. As the attack comes to an end, however, Tiny tosses his web.

"Fu—!" is all Elf Guy gets out before the web envelopes him. *Tiny! You never told me you had a brain! I guess you really did remember the attack that ended you, and remembered when and where Elf Guy is when he finishes. Who's a good spider? You are! Yes, you are!*

As Tiny approaches Elf Guy, I remind the big lug about how the maze works. He deflates a little, but he did still win. Elf Guy looks terrified, though. *Don't worry, my dude. Good effort with the first run of the maze!*

Tiny moves one of his massive pedipalps over the delver, and Elf Guy closes his eyes, expecting a bite to finish him off. Instead, Tiny takes what I'm pretty sure is a bag of holding. He quickly weaves a larger bag, webbing Elf Guy up more in the process, and empties the magical pouch into the more mundane one. He drops that on the floor, and one of my rat thieves zips by to pick it up. I can see the indignation in Elf Guy's eyes.

With that, Tiny hauls him and his loot up and takes him outside the maze, depositing him unceremoniously just outside the entrance. Elf Guy gets to stew for a few minutes before Fluffles can come by and levitate him outside the gates. Hah! I only wish I could see the reactions from everyone!

Hey! Birbs! Expedition!

Chapter 12

So, birds are great at finding shinies, but not so great at understanding what people are doing. According to the expedition I sent to watch Elf Guy, he got a lot of odd looks from people before someone ran up to him. He wiggled and mumbled, and they eventually managed to get him unwebbed, then the two went back to one of the guild houses, which I'm now officially labeling the Office of Dungeon Affairs.

More importantly, however, the maze was a success! My core is now easily the size of a grapefruit! Elf Guy was worth *so* much mana, holy crap. I've got enough to do a few things, and I have a few ideas involving more public rooms.

First, I go ahead and actually set a garden in the belfry. Not a whole lot of herbalists seem to want to brave the attic boss, but with a garden up past it, maybe they'll bring along a friend or two to be able to see what neat things the fruit bats have managed to bring in.

The other thing is I've decided to make my porch a library. Why would I do something weird like making my porch a library? Because with a piece of paper and a bit of webbing, it's more of a bulletin board than a place for a bunch of books!

Come See the Maze!
Yes, the hedge maze! Can you brave the maze and exit with more than you went in with? Search for chests, herbs, and wood as you avoid Tiny and the rats that want your stuff! If he catches you, the only thing he'll give is a very secure blanket! Come brave the maze! Located just around back!

So yeah, I've basically got a flyer with that info webbed to my door now. I'm pretty sure it doesn't count as a quest, but it should at least get people curious and hopefully willing to check it out.

I've also decided to make a more public lab in one of the more normal rooms in the house. I was thinking about the spell Aelara showed Rhonda, and figured if people started making potions in a public lab, I could crib off their notes and make better stuff in the secret lab!

I'm really tempted to try to make a forge, but that's not happening until I expand downward. That's probably my next big project, but making the two rooms took about everything Elf Guy gave me.

"The nerve of that dungeon!" shouts the elven man for the fifth time today, pacing and scowling.

"For what?" asks the elven woman who is more permanently stationed at the guild building in this town. "For defeating you? For not killing you? For taking your bag of holding? For dumping you outside the gate?" She fights to keep the unprofessional smile off her face at the memory of finding him. At first, she had feared the worst, that the new local dungeon had truly gone murderous and used her associate to deliver a message.

In retrospect, she supposes it *was* sending a message, just not one anyone expected. It took all she had to not burst out laughing when the webbed elf started squirming and mumbling curses through the muffling web.

His snort at her snide question brings her back to the present, even if he doesn't actually give her an answer. Though his pride as an inspector may have been wounded, she knows it's not yet dead, and so she lifts the scroll and quill. "Are you prepared to give your official report?"

He sighs deeply and closes his eyes, taking a moment to compose himself. "You have my field notes to attach to the report as well?" When she nods, he takes another moment to organize his thoughts before dictating his report.

"Dungeon is not murderous, but in fact borders on actually playful at times. Unusual behavior observed by civilians was most likely from the dungeon moving its core, which it still keeps in a Secret Sanctum in an unknown location. Dungeon has been sending expeditions, so very likely has a secret war room. Dungeon has alchemical denizens, so certainly has a secret lab. Very likely has a secret library as well.

"Dungeon shows unorthodox behavior, but very little hostility. It has created a labyrinth of brambles inhabited by its strongest scion and thieving rats. Despite the power placed there, the maze is almost fully harmless, as I was defeated and simply dumped outside the dungeon instead of killed.

"Suggest higher-level inspector for next inspection, as dungeon has advanced quickly. I don't know what its next expansion will entail, but it will certainly cause major change no matter what it does. Inspector Tarl."

She nods as she finishes writing down his words then gives him the scroll and quill to sign. He does so and returns them to her, and she begins to apply a wax seal as she speaks.

"So, now that I know what you think of it professionally, what do you think of it personally?"

He considers it for a few moments before donning a smirk. "I think if I didn't have another inspection soon, I'd head back now and explore just for the fun of it. It's the strangest dungeon I've ever heard of, and I want to know more. And I want a rematch against that Spider Scion. It webbed me as soon as I got out of my Shadow Blade attack! I haven't even heard of Epic monsters planning like that!"

He shakes his head as he takes a seat in the lounge area of the guild. "Four-dock is going to become a much more interesting place soon—I can feel it—thanks to that dungeon."

Chapter 13

Business has been booming! The maze has become a huge success! I dunno if it was from dumping Elf Guy outside or from the flyer on the front door, but people are practically lining up to run the hedge maze! Most people literally run it, too, sprinting to try to find a chest or various nodes before sprinting out. It's about a coin flip for them to get out without losing anything to the rats like that, which seems to be the challenge most people are after. Tiny has taken to just ignoring the ones that don't go very deep.

The kids actually did a real run of the maze, though. They got two chests before Tiny caught up to them. Freddie took one for the team and got captured, but Rhonda got to escape with all her goodies. I told Tiny to take his shiny new hatchet instead of his shield. That thing's a bit of a memento, after all.

Rhonda actually followed Fluffles as he levitated Freddie out the gate, and I'm all but positive she helped him out of the webbing before they went off to do whatever they do. They're both looking healthier and stronger each time I see them, too. I swear Freddie's grown a foot since I first saw him, and Rhonda is much more confident, though still fairly quiet, seems like. I hope they're old enough for me to ship them because I definitely do.

The bulletin-board library was a great idea, too. Lots of people read the flyer to see if anything has changed, and I make sure to note things, like the new garden and lab in the house. The lab doesn't really need a warning, as I don't have anything specific in the way of anyone getting there, random encounters aside.

The garden, of course, has the warning of the boss in the way, though I don't say exactly what it'll be so I can change it as needed for various delvers. Sorry, herbalists. If you want to see what fancy stuff Coda's been growing, you need to bring a couple friends to help get you there.

Poe has earned himself a title, which is pretty cool. Marshal. I'm pretty sure it's not like a sheriff but more like someone who marshals the troops, gets them doing what they need to do and such. He's been practically handling my expeditions on his own now, too, which I think is also what a marshal would do.

The public lab has also been paying dividends. I've watched a bunch of herbalists whip up a few potions of this and that in there. I've written them down in the secret library, which I've upgraded a few more times, and Queen is happily working away in the secret lab.

Speaking of Queen, the healing ants experiment was a success! It's still pretty difficult to make the goo for it, but I now have a few medical ants stationed nearby the various high-threat areas, mostly the attic and basement. I've upgraded the lab a few more times, too, and have been slowly stocking it as my rats "borrow" little bits and pieces from the Alchemists in the public lab.

And speaking of the ants, one of my plans has fallen through. I had joked to myself about carpenter ants doing carpentry, and I was starting to wonder if it actually worked that way, but from the random ants the hill spits out, it doesn't seem to. They're just really big ants. Well, not *really* big, but I'm pretty sure they'd get there if I upgraded them. However, Tiny is all the big I need for now.

So now I'm looking to expand, but have no idea where to. Up is somehow still an option. I get the feeling it's for something later, once I figure out how to build more structures. Or maybe I can build on the clouds? Who knows.

Out is also somehow an option. It's easily the most expensive, but it's also very tempting. The war room seems to imply that I'd get the entire town if I expanded outward. That's interesting, but also concerning. It'd be cool to have truly intelligent denizens, but how would it work if I tried to tell them to do stuff?

And that'd be a *lot* of ground to cover to defend. I don't know that the townsfolk would appreciate suddenly having a severe infestation of roaches, flies, and mice, or the spiders and rats to deal with them.

No, I think expanding outward is something I'm just not ready for, and I dunno if I ever will be. What I do think I'm ready for, however, is to expand downward. I know there's stone down there. I mean, logically, there has to be.

There are also probably tons of cool new resources to gather, too, like ores and gems and stuff! I could make a smithy and an armory and actually be able to do stuff with them! And a jewelers, I guess?

Of course, there will also be new invaders. There always have been, whenever I expand. I'm pretty sure they'd basically have to come in through the basement, and the swarm I have there is serious business. Anything digging would be like the moles, so the vipers should be able to handle it, at least until I get whatever my new spawner is established.

I've been saving up more mana than I actually need to expand, wanting to make sure I'll have enough to upgrade my spawner and get my other denizens up to snuff for whatever awaits. I wish I could fit Tiny into the basement for when

I do this, but Teemo is a good replacement. He's not huge and tanky, but he *is* small and sneaky, and I've seen him do some serious damage to invaders that manage to get into the house. With him and Fluffles waiting under the basement stairs, I spend the mana to expand downward.

In Rhonda's lab—technically Old Staiven's, but she has a little section to herself—she prepares to put the finishing touches on a batch of Lightning Resist potions. With the dungeon being given the all clear and the sheer number of lightning-enchanted denizens in there now, it's second only to the classic healing potion as far as popularity goes!

She grabs the jar of ferromoss before Lucas gives a little hiss and hops onto her shoulder from atop a pile of books. "Huh? What's wrong?" Her familiar is usually so quiet, only hissing when . . .

Glassware starts rattling in their various holders, and Rhonda's eyes widen as she realizes what's happening. "Earthquake? Lucas, web what you can to keep it from breaking!" She's just glad her potions are at a point where she can rest for now.

Lucas literally jumps into action, webbing things that are wiggling too much for his liking. Anything that wiggles too much reminds him of flies or roaches, and he's all too happy to make them stop moving. His goblin is much different than the dungeon was, but he's pretty sure he's much different than he was now, too. Different isn't always better, but when it is, it's much better. And he thinks this different is pretty good.

"Master! The lab!" she shouts up the stairs, and he shouts back down at her, "You and that spider mind the lab! I'm keeping the shop from exploding up here!" Rhonda sheepishly nods, even though her master can't see.

The lab, ironically enough, is one of the most stable places in the store. The selling floor is just chock-full of enchanted things designed to help defend oneself. If they started going off from falling in this quake, some broken glassware would be the least of their worries.

Freddie meditates in his small room in the church. While part of him wants a bigger room with at least a window actually designed for looking rather than for just letting in a bit of air, another part of him reminds him that this is still a far better situation than being on the street. He has a bed. He has warm or cool clothing, depending on the situation. He has brothers and sisters to support him, as is only proper for followers of the Crystal Shield.

He also has Fiona, his spider. When he first got her, he thought she was some curse or test of his burgeoning faith. But now, he feels she was a lesson sent to teach him to look beyond simple appearances. Fiona has been much better of a companion than he could have possibly imagined. She's even helped him sneak a spare sweet roll from the kitchen on occasion. He knows he shouldn't, but if he were perfect, he wouldn't have much use for a god, would he?

As the floor starts to rumble, he nervously offers a quick prayer of apology. Surely a little bit of joking wisdom wouldn't earn him some smiting, would it? Sounds of alarm outside make him suspect it's not actually his fault, since other people are feeling the rumbling.

"Come on, Fiona," he says while he stands, grabbing his shield as he exits his room. He still hasn't had a chance to replace his hatchet after that huge spider got him in the maze.

"What's going on?" he asks one of the hurrying sisters. Though she seems busy, she doesn't seem to be panicking, so that's probably a good sign.

"An earthquake, young brother? Come, help me with my supplies. There may soon be wounded to tend to." He nods and follows her, and Fiona follows him.

Her orc is a good orc. He feeds her and lets her protect. He doesn't have a core or anything similar, but he's shown her she can protect all kinds of things. Sometimes, she misses the dungeon, but she can protect it and her orc at once now, which is nice.

In the Dungeoneer's Guild, the elven woman jerks up from her desk as things start rumbling. She was meditating and mentally processing her reports, not napping on them. It takes her a few seconds to figure out what's happening . . . and why.

She quietly swears to herself, glad the rumbling would mask it if there was anyone around to hear. "Where did I put that seal?! Ah, gotcha!" She snags a sealing stamp from among everything rattling and deftly plucks a brush and inkwell up as well. The last thing she needs is a scroll, and she knows exactly where it is.

Of course she does; it's not like any of the other dungeons have been behaving oddly. The rumbling starts to taper off as she paints the seal with ink, and everything is still by the time she unrolls the scroll and quickly stamps it.

Fourdock Dungeon
DEEP

Chapter 14

So, uh . . . I don't know exactly what I was expecting, but it wasn't an earthquake. The various delvers around looked really worried, and what encounters were happening, I just had my denizens run away. Tiny ushered a couple herbalists out of the maze and is now sitting at the entrance. Maybe I should make some more minor libraries at the various entrances to let people know when certain areas are closed.

Most of the delvers took the hint to leave, and the stink eye from Poe and the other ravens got everyone else away from the potentially dangerous spots. There's still some lookie-loos, but they're far enough back to ignore for now. Everything seems to be intact, and the expeditions I had out are returning and saying the town seems to be fine, too. I'm not sure how much I trust their definition of "fine," but nothing seems to have collapsed. It's not like I could do much to help, anyway.

The expansion definitely took, at least. There's now a ragged cave in the yard, and I have Poe and the unoccupied vipers keeping a close eye on it. I can still extend my senses into my new section, but I don't sense any new invaders just yet. I do, at least, have a new spawner.

Because there's always a ten-by-ten-foot room for jello.

Yerp, I got a slime spawner. I, of course, spend the mana to get a Slime Scion, too. She looks like someone took a mixing bowl and filled it with jelly, then just turned it out onto the floor. She's kinda cute, in an adorable blob kinda way. The more passive slimes are looking like they'll be more of an ooze, though, kinda like puddles and such. Maybe I'll get some other varieties as I upgrade it? I don't need *Dragon Warrior* slimes with eyes and a mouth, but an actual gelatinous cube would be cool.

As I take in my new expansion, however, I start to get a feel for how my new invaders might get in. There are passages I can't sense down, like how I can't sense much past my gate or my walls. So I guess there's an actual underground to be had.

I get basically every bat that's not of the fruit variety to fly down into the cave and set up shop, and get a bunch of my spiders in there, too. Roaches and mice look like they'll spawn pretty thick down here. I don't think moles will, though. Most of the caves are fully stone, which is pretty cool.

Fluffles and Teemo get to work doing their things down here, too. Teemo keeps finding little cracks and crevices to make into shortcuts for my denizens, which helps everyone get into position to deal with the new infestations.

New infestations are also why I'm not making any nodes just yet.

I remember how the herbs started attracting the mice. I don't want to make ore or gem nodes and attract . . . I don't know what. At least not until I'm better prepared. I need to get me a few more tough mobs to guard the various bits. The basement swarm I'll leave there for now, to help guard the chest. *Tiny? You can head back into the maze. I think everything here is covered, at least for now. Coda, I need you to make sure the bats sweep the new caves with sonar as regularly as possible, so your belfry is upgraded again now.*

Queen, keep doing your thing with the alchemy. See if you can manage anything to get through stone. My core is getting big enough that I'd like to move it again. Yeah, it didn't stay there as long as I had hoped, but I guess that just means we're growing at a good pace, right?

Oh, hey, Fluffles. Can you use your telekinesis and stuff to work through rock? I'm gonna need something if I'm going to get a new Secret Sanctum. I think the town mostly trusts me enough to make my Sanctum more public, but I want to make sure everyone still feels that way after the quake.

Most of the delvers wander off after we go back to DEFCON: *Normalcy.* I don't really blame them; sun's getting close to setting now, I think. I do get some nighttime delvers, but most like the day, probably because most of my stuff doesn't care about light levels very much.

Jello is just kinda wandering the caves right now, absorbing mice and roaches as she goes. I wonder what I'll do with her. She's kinda weird compared to my other scions, but maybe because I just don't know what to do with her. I know what bats do, what spiders do, birds, etc. I dunno how slimes do.

Oop, nighttime delver. Let's go see who it is.

Huh, they're not at the gate? And a second delver now, too. Where . . . *Oh!* They must be down in the caves! I focus down there, and I find them. I'm also not quite sure what's going on.

For just a moment, I worry one of the kids managed to get down there somehow, but they're not wearing tattered clothing anymore. Nor do they have a tail. Or scales. Or darkvision, I'm pretty sure. Whatever it is, though, it's bipedal and has clothes. Oh, and scales. And is running from . . . that thing.

What's that thing? I dunno. It kinda reminds me of an ankheg, which is basically a pincherbug that could go toe to toe with Tiny, although this is more reptilian, I think. Scales are a big tip-off.

I'ma call it a scythemaw until someone puts a book on cave critters in my library. It's big, scaly, and has two big mandible things at its mouth, in addition to the more usual sharp teeth for eating things that have an opinion about being eaten.

How the crap does that thing count as a delver?! The smaller one's screams refocus my train of thought. Questions later, action now!

Fluffles, Teemo, Jello! Go help the little lizard person! Queen, I'm gonna need medic ants on the double! Tiny, get your spinnerets down here yesterday! Coda, make sure everyone is doing what they should be doing! You're my Poe for pointing out nasty things down here!

Fluffles and Teemo make fast time toward the lizard person, with Jello . . . not making fast time at all. She's definitely going to be posted at one of the cave passages once I get everything better handled down here. She's not exactly a rapid responder.

Coda pings a little cave where the scythemaw shouldn't be able to fit into, and Queen gets the medic ants headed that way. I send a few rats to give them a ride, as they're way quicker than ants. Tiny is moving as quickly as he can, but he was near the center of the maze, so he'll be a couple minutes.

Fluffles and Teemo get to the lizard person first, which isn't much of a surprise. With Teemo's trails, the two can get basically anywhere in the dungeon within a minute or two, and they were already in the caves. What is a surprise, however, is that Fluffles just levitates the terrified person, then all three start dashing along Teemo's trails.

The rescued delver is screaming at the top of their lungs, but they're at least safe in Fluffles's magic. The scythemaw keeps running down the larger tunnel for several more seconds before it realizes its prey has vanished.

Uh . . . apparently, it's not going to accept that answer.

The thing starts tearing at my rock walls, either in frustration or because it thinks it senses its prey. *Well, that's not gonna fly, buddy. Say hello to Tiny.* He doesn't roar or anything like the scythemaw, but that tackle announces his presence pretty effectively, in my opinion. Fluffles sinks his fangs, too, before scuttling back out of retaliation range.

The hostile delver growls at Tiny, but I can see the venom has slowed it. *Just be careful, Tiny. I think all I can really support you with is some medical ants, and they're still en route.* I can see him working on a web, but it'll be a bit before he'll have it ready, and in a fight, seconds pass like eternities.

The scythemaw bellows and charges forward, lunging at Tiny's face. The big guy gets a leg in the way, which I think saves his life. The leg is bitten through, and the maw starts messily scarfing it down. With its mouth occupied, however, Tiny lumbers forward to deliver another envenomed bite. He leaves a thick web across the passage behind him as he scuttles past his foe, and now the hostile delver finds itself with its back against a wall. No, worse: a normal wall won't stick you to it if you press your back against it.

I don't think it is quite that smart, though. Or maybe Tiny's bites are slowing it down more than I thought. Come to think of it, a spider that big would be very bad news for anything of similar size if it got to bite it. The scythemaw might be resistant, but I dunno. I'm not an expert in giant lizards with swords coming out of their faces.

It finishes the leg and growls at Tiny again, and I see my spiderbro lift his front slightly. What's he up to? I don't get to ask any more silly questions before the lizard lunges forward again. For a moment, I worry Tiny will lose another leg, but he's a smart spider.

Just like he learned how to deal with Elf Guy's Shadow Blade, he has a plan for this thing's lunging attack. He tips himself over backward as it rushes forward, letting him bring all seven legs to bear. That's a lot of hydraulics to catch a lot of lizard, and it works. He grabs it around the neck to keep from losing any more pieces, his other legs curling under its belly before he flings it backward and into the web!

It crashes through, but I'm pretty sure that was the plan. It's not quite immobile, but with webbing and venom, it's not going anywhere. Tiny strolls up and bites it a few more times as he webs it more, and I let him enjoy his victory. Ah, there's my medic ants. *See what you can do for Tiny. I'ma go check on our other delver.*

In the little cavern, Fluffles has set the fleeing delver back on to the floor, where they promptly scramble to the back wall. As I focus in, I see that she is a girl. Uh, make that a *woman*, definitely. Is she a kobold? She certainly looks like it: long muzzle, red scales, cute little horns that jut backward. She also looks like she hasn't had a fun time, even before the scythemaw, judging by the dirt under her claws and the scratches in her scales. Fluffles and Teemo simply watch her from the only entrance/exit to the little cavern, not making any hostile moves.

I can hardly blame her for being terrified still, though. A snek and a rat snatched her up easier than the scythemaw did. She could probably hear the bellows and fight Tiny gave it, too. As the silence stretches on, broken only by her ragged breathing, she starts to slump to the floor. She manages to say something before she seems to pass out.

"Sanctuary."

Chapter 15

Thankfully, the rest of the night is much more boring, though a few other things happened that raised more questions. Not long after the kobold collapsed, I got a *massive* pile of mana, and I wasn't sure why. At least until I looked in on Tiny.

The scythemaw had officially kicked the bucket, though I didn't know why that'd give me so much mana. That's when I started to think about some of the other stuff the delvers have been saying.

I used to wonder why they'd think a dungeon would become murderous. I need delvers to make mana at any decent rate, so why would I kill them? Well, because they apparently give boatloads of mana, if this scythemaw is anything to go by. I can definitely see other dungeons taking the quick payoff instead of playing the long game. I mean, it'd still be murder, but it'd make logical sense, even if it doesn't make ethical sense.

So . . . I guess I can't really blame the town for being concerned. I'll definitely need to do the next move at night, or some other downtime. It's gonna need to happen soon, too. That big pile of mana has my core just barely fitting in the chimney now.

I also have a pending option with the kobold.

Resident Request. Accept/Deny?

It's not giving me any more details, either. What's a Resident? How's it different from a Denizen? Or a Delver? What happens if I deny? Well, best case is she eventually wakes up and just leaves, I guess? We both go our separate ways, even if only one of us is actually able to leave. Not really a fan of that option, to be honest.

And that's the best thing I can come up with if I deny her. The various other scenarios I can think of all seem to be various flavors of *she dies*. Honestly, her leaving is probably in that category, too. She doesn't have any gear; she barely even has clothes. She might have magic or something, but it was clearly not up to handling that scythemaw.

Hopefully, it's a rare thing to encounter in the far tunnels, but still. I don't know how I'd be able to help her if she stays, but I'll be able to do *something* at least, right?

Still uncertain, I accept her request to be a Resident.

At least it doesn't trigger another quake. In fact . . . I'm not actually sure what has changed, aside from the fact my counters now show Resident: One. Maybe I'll know more once she wakes up. I get some medical ants to check her HP, and see she's definitely had a rough time of it.

Not knowing what else to do, I try to anticipate some of her needs. She'll need food and water. Water isn't difficult, especially with the caves. There's a nice pond down here, so she won't dehydrate, at least. But what's she going to eat? I could try to send some expeditions to get her some bread or something, but I'm not sure that'll actually work.

I could have a spider web her a couple mice? Seems weird to me, but I don't know what else I could do.

Without any better ideas, I do just that. I also have Teemo keep tabs on her between blazing trails. I think he's taking Jello's slowness as a personal challenge/affront and wants to get her response time up to his standards, which I'm hardly against. With her being a slime, she should be pretty easily able to go anywhere he can.

With dawn comes the early delvers, and I update the bulletin board to show that the caves are currently empty. I'm also reminded to put up signs on my tunnels indicating where I stop.

You are now leaving the dungeon.

Simple and to the point. I have quite a few exits down there now, and I get the feeling I'll only gain more as I expand deeper. I also go ahead and spawn an ore node near the entrance, in the lawn. Looks like tin, so nothing too extravagant. I advertise that on the bulletin board, too, and see if anyone is interested.

As slimes spawn, I set them mostly to the various underground exits. I doubt they'd be able to handle something like another scythemaw, but they'd at least slow anything else down. They actually do a fair bit of damage if they catch something, too. I think I should be using them more like easily moved traps rather than wandering encounters.

As the morning progresses, delvers occasionally peek into the cave in the yard. I keep Jello just a little deeper than the tin node so they know they can get that ore fairly easily but that meaner stuff awaits deeper in. I'm pretty sure the early herbalists tell whatever smiths and/or miners they know about the cave, but none come check it out by the time the kobold awakens.

Teemo alerts me as she stirs, and I see her eyes slowly open before she jerks upright, the memories of last night returning to her waking mind. She stares around the cavern, her eyes wide, as she seems to look for the scythemaw. *Yeah, you don't have to worry about that thing anymore. I'd offer you a steak from it, but Tiny basically drank everything that wasn't the hide and the bones.*

Queen has been experimenting with the bones to see if there's anything interesting to them. I'm pretty sure there will be, but she's the Alchemist, not me. I've made sure she'll leave the two mandible things alone, though, at least for now. Those could be a neat trophy, or maybe weapons or something? I dunno.

But I'm getting off track. The kobold seems to calm down as she determines there's no threat in the room. She doesn't seem to spot Teemo, so that's why she thinks there's no threat. Soon, her eyes settle on the mice, and she carefully approaches the webbed rodents.

She picks one up and examines it before tossing the whole thing in her mouth. A crunch and a cut-off squeak signal to me that she recognizes a meal when she sees one. Probably not the fanciest meal she's ever had, but after encountering that monster, she's probably happy to be on the winning side of the food chain again.

As she starts to peer out of the cavern, I have Teemo quietly follow her while she explores. There's not all that much to see down there just yet, and it's only a matter of time before she discovers the corpse of her pursuer. Her eyes widen in fear when she first spots it, then they widen further in shock as she notices my various denizens working on the corpse. Rats and spiders work to extract the bones, dragging each out the mouth of the beast.

I don't want them to tear up the hide, and that's the biggest exit, even considering Tiny's bites. The ants are working on each bone, slowly chipping little pieces off to carry back to Queen. They're also working around the bite wounds, taking the damaged scales for experiments as well. Personally, I'm hoping for some earth-elemental stuff. The monster was tearing through the rock way easier than claws should be able to.

"It *is* a Sanctuary . . ." she whispers to herself, seemingly in awe. She mentioned that before she passed out, too. Does she know about dungeons?

Well, it's not like I can ask her, even if she does.

She cautiously approaches my denizens as they busily work, and they pay her no mind. She tries to take one of the smaller bones, but a lightning major zaps her to get her to drop it. I think she gets the hint to not bother ants at work. She watches for a time, and even helps pull what looks like a rib the rest of the way out of the mouth. The spiders and rats had managed to get it wedged between some teeth.

She doesn't stick around much longer after that, though. The denizens have it more or less handled, and there are more caves to explore. She eventually finds the little clear pond of water and eagerly slakes her thirst there. That's probably the biggest reason why she left the denizens to play with the dead scythemaw.

She grows very cautious as she discovers the entrance to the yard, and I'm pretty sure it's more due to the sunlight than Jello standing guard in the tunnel there. Or maybe she is nervous about the dwarf there mining the tin node. He spots her and pauses in his work, and the two just stare for several long seconds before he returns to mining.

She looks around a little before focusing on Jello and looking confused. I mean, Jello confuses me a bit too, sure. No sense staring at her, though. Might give her a complex. She's been growing in power quickly, however, which is both nice and concerning. I'm worried things like that scythemaw might not be as rare in the deeper parts as I would have hoped.

The dwarf eventually finishes mining and leaves, and my little resident cautiously follows to peek her head out to see the surface. If the mining dwarf was confusing to her, I get the feeling the surface is blowing her mind. Today's pretty busy. There are a few encounters in the yard, some herbalists are doing their herbalism thing, and it looks like a woodsman managed to run deep enough to get something decent before running out of the maze.

She takes in the whole scene, seemingly mesmerized by all the activity. She even spots Poe up on his perch over the chimney, calmly surveying the action and directing a few groups of expeditionary birds. She nervously slinks toward the house, and while the delvers give her curious looks, at least nobody thinks she's a new encounter.

She examines the flyer on the front door for a few moments before gingerly making her way inside. She steers well clear of the little party headed for the attic. I'm pretty sure they have a quest to go get some of the stuff Coda's growing, which would be cool. Quests give decent mana on top of the stuff they actually do to *do* the quest.

The kobold peers into the basement and seems to relax a bit as she sees the tunnel in the wall near the chest. I expect her to head back down, but instead, she heads up the stairs to the second floor. She seems very interested in the lab there, though she doesn't have anything to alchemize with. She surprises me again as she quietly climbs the ladder to the attic.

She's got good timing, at least, as the party has already finished the boss—a larger venomous spider—and continued to the roof and garden beyond. She looks into the chest just in time to see a packrat drop a coin off. She smiles at the rat but looks confused once again as she looks around.

She closes her eyes and slowly turns before she starts walking again. It's my turn to be confused for a few moments before I realize where she's going. She's headed straight for the chimney! Teemo prepares to attack her, but I tell him to wait. Maybe because she's a Resident? I don't think that's how she knows where my core is, though.

And she definitely knows. Her hand rests against the bricks separating her from my core, and she slowly opens her eyes with a peaceful smile on her lips.

"Sanctuary . . ."

Chapter 16

The Kobold

She slowly opens her eyes, feeling a little sore and cold. She supposes it's better than wet and warm in the belly of that tunnel horror. Her eyes shoot open at the memory, and she presses against the wall, looking for the monster she was fleeing from for . . . she doesn't even know how long now.

She replays the events from earlier in her head, piecing together what was and wasn't a dream. Being chased definitely was real, no matter how she wishes it wasn't. Being captured by some strange snake . . . probably happened? She remembers being levitated here, not walking. Is that snake still around?

She looks around and doesn't spot it, but she does spot three odd little bundles. She slowly approaches and sees they're mice. Her stomach seems to like the look of them, but why are they wrapped in webs? Shouldn't they be dead from spider bites? They're definitely still alive; she can see them breathing. Well, it's hardly the worst meal she's had recently.

She eats one and finds it tastes a little better than the mice she's had before. They're usually only little snacks and are a bit bland, but she finds she wouldn't mind eating more of these. Three is a good breakfast, though, and with her strength returning, she also finds her mind clearing.

Could this truly be a Sanctuary? She remembers the thought crossing her mind before blackness took her, but could it really be possible? The old legends speak of them being a haven and refuge for her people, but kobolds have been scattered and disparate for ages now. Those on the surface take them as simple monsters, and those underneath it take them as food or enslave them.

She needs to explore.

She carefully peers out of the little cavern and sees only more natural stone walls . . . and little else. There's not even glowmoss in here. She strangles her imagination before it can run wild with theories of a sealed Sanctuary. With her luck, there's something so vile in here, even glowmoss can't grow.

Pessimism firmly and reassuringly in place, she slowly explores barren tunnel after barren passage after empty cavern. Eventually, she can hear some kind of rustling, and only survival instinct keeps her from crying out when she finds the source.

The horror is sleeping, gathering its energy to resume chasing her!

No, wait . . . what?! She can only stare as she sees a bone start to protrude from its mouth before a rat wiggles out and finishes extracting its prize. Her eyes widen as she finally notices all the activity around what is now clearly the corpse of the tunnel horror.

Spiders, rats, and ants are all busily doing . . . something . . . to the body of the monster. She slowly steps forward as she sees signs of a higher intelligence guiding the actions of the simpler creatures. She's never seen anything like this! The only time she's even *heard* of something like this is . . .

"It *is* a Sanctuary . . ." she murmurs in awe, her pessimism evaporating. The rats should be eating, not pulling out bones. The spiders should be eating the rats, not helping them pile the bones! The ants should be more interested in the flesh, not in the bones of the creature.

She reverently walks around the work, wondering how such creatures could fell the monster, when she spots what defeated the beast.

Or at least, its handiwork. There are several pairs of large punctures in the tunnel horror's side . . . so the Sanctuary must have something mightier than the simple creatures now processing the body. Somehow, knowing the Sanctuary has something that could lay such a monster low fills her with peace, rather than terror. If it wanted to treat her the same, it easily could have. Does the Sanctuary accept her?

Feeling bolder, she walks to the pile of bones and selects one that she thinks could make a decent knife. She's not great with a knife, but it's better than nothing. Her delusions of grandeur are quickly snuffed, however, as one of the larger ants zaps her! She drops the club in surprise and pain, worried she may have insulted the Sanctuary. If even ants can call forth lightning, even at ant scale, what might does the Sanctuary keep secret?

Thankfully, the other ants and creatures return to ignoring her after she drops the bone. She supposes the Sanctuary has plans for it? *Do* Sanctuaries have plans?

Well, if they're intelligent, they must have some goals, right? The goals of something like that are surely unknowable to the likes of her, though.

She leaves the body of the monster behind her, glad of the fate it suffered, and resumes exploring. There are many passages deeper, with writing webbed to the walls. She can't read what they say, but she definitely doesn't feel the need to go any deeper right now. She knows what dangers lurk there, and only safety seems to lurk here.

She almost shouts for joy when she finds a small spring pool in a quiet cavern. The water is crisp and clean and wonderful on her parched throat. After taking a drink, she tries to consider what she should do next. She has food, she has water, she has safety. If the Sanctuary is going to offer her these things, she needs to offer it something in return.

But what? Offering it her life seems a bit ironic at this point. Well . . . if it has been sealed, maybe it could use someone to explore some more? She doesn't know what else she could offer it that it might actually find useful.

She wanders around, doing her best to go places she hasn't yet. She's encouraged when she spots a new thing that she's pretty sure is part of the Sanctuary: a slime! They're incredibly rare in the Deeps, and the ones there don't just sit in the middle of tunnels. Perhaps it's uncertain of the sunlight she can see at the end of the tunnel.

She's been on the surface once before and is in no hurry to repeat that experience. It's too bright, too open, and too . . . *weird* for her.

Her musings on the surface world are interrupted by the clear sounds of metal on stone. Does the Sanctuary have other kobolds serving it? That'd be wonderful!

She freezes as she comes upon what's making the sound. It's a dwarf! He's pillaging the Sanctuary! Why's he pillaging the Sanctuary?! *How* is he pillaging the Sanctuary?! It destroyed that tunnel horror; how is a simple dwarf beyond it? The dwarf spots her as she gapes, and though he pauses and looks at her, he soon resumes mining some kind of metal from the Sanctuary.

She looks back at the slime, wondering if it's going to actually try and *stop* the dwarf defiling its home, but it doesn't seem to care. Not that it's easy to get a read on a slime, but they usually head toward anything making noise to try to eat it. How long has it been watching the dwarf mine?

How long has she? The dwarf finishes his scarring of the poor Sanctuary and heads back to the surface. She doesn't want to follow . . . but this is the kind of thing she told herself she could offer. Nervously, she peers over the edge, wondering what the poor Sanctuary has been opened to on the surface.

It's . . . There's so many! Surface dwellers are practically *swarming* up there! She spots some wandering what looks like an ill-kept yard, gathering various plants. She recognizes ochredill as they pluck some from the earth. More defilers!

Over at a gigantic bramble patch, she can see a catfolk sprinting with a load of wood in his arms. What madness is that? Who sprints with their arms full of lumber? Who stops and takes a breather only a few steps beyond whatever they were fleeing from?! As she looks around, all she sees is activity! Even on the roof of that abandoned building there, she can see more defilers wandering around, fighting various things.

She's pretty sure she's still in the Sanctuary, but it must be overrun! Her eyes settle on a large black shape on the roof . . . and its eyes settle upon her as well. It . . . it's part of the Sanctuary. It's watching, observing, but not acting against the defilers. She can sense its strength from here; it could easily clear them out, but it doesn't. Why?

Perhaps the building holds some clue. The various defilers notice her as she nervously picks her way across the open ground, but none make any moves to hinder her, thank all that is good. She doesn't find any entrances until she gets fully to the opposite side of the building, where she sees a door with more writing webbed to it. She wishes she had been able to learn to read, but there's precious little time to learn for a kobold in the Deeps.

She cautiously tries the door, and it opens without fuss. Inside, she can see a multitude of rats and spiders attacking and devouring an endless horde of small creatures, mostly mice and flies. It's hardly a surprise the windows are so thickly-webbed if that many flies are trying to get in. Across the large room, she can see stairs headed up, as well as a small group of defilers at the top. They head into a new room before they can spot her, and she's glad for that.

She explores a little more, and soon finds the stairs heading down, which she is all too happy to follow. In the basement, she can see an opening back into the caves below, and she's relieved to be able to get back down there without having to brave the hustle and bustle of the yard. Part of her wants to return to the quiet of the cave system, but she made a promise to herself to pay the Sanctuary back! She's not going to run back to safety until she's surveyed everything she can!

Even if it seems the Sanctuary is fully aware of what transpires up here.

Still, she climbs back up to the first floor, and then up to the second via the stairs. There are quite a few large black birds perched on the railing now, but they ignore her as she scurries past them. This second floor seems full of random rooms, until she encounters something she's never been able to take a close look at before.

It's an alchemy lab. It doesn't seem the most well-furnished, but it is definitely still a place to brew potions and do whatever else Alchemists do.

She never thought a Sanctuary could have a lab in it. Is she not the first kobold here? She doesn't think the defilers would set up a lab in a random, abandoned building.

She leaves the lab behind, as she doesn't know the first thing about alchemy, and resumes her exploring. She doesn't meet the group she saw at the top of the stairs, and once she finds a ladder, she's pretty sure she knows why. She doesn't want to follow after those defilers, but this ladder seems to be the only way she hasn't looked yet. She sighs and steels herself before slowly and carefully climbing up.

At the top, she doesn't see the group, but she can hear voices coming from beyond a large window on the far side of the room, past an open chest. Curious, she moves to it and looks inside, just in time to see a rat drop a coin inside before scurrying off. She goes ahead and closes the lid, trying to process everything.

This place is still within the Sanctuary, but why are there so many defilers? Sanctuaries are supposed to fend off intruders that come to plunder and harm it, right? Is this not a Sanctuary, after all? There has to be some way to know for sure!

She closes her eyes as she tries to think back to the legends, trying to think of something to prove, once and for all, that this is a Sanctuary.

Creatures following guidance is one of the signs, but it could just be something a wizard or a tamer did? Surely, they'd want this place to themselves, though, instead of letting everyone muscle in on their riches.

Think, Aranya. Think!

Slowly, memories of stories being told resurface in her mind. She can practically hear the voice of her grandfather as he relays the stories of old. Legends tell of the heart of the Sanctuary, something truly vital to it. If you are part of the Sanctuary, you will know where its heart is, and you must protect it. That is a Sanctuary's true treasure, and one that must be safeguarded at all costs!

If this is a Sanctuary, she's pretty sure it's accepted her. She just needs to follow her heart, and she'll find the one that belongs to the Sanctuary. Her eyes still closed, she lets her feet guide her. She almost stops trying as she gets the feeling that it's very close, but that couldn't possibly be right, could it?

No . . . it is. She can feel something, and it's very close. It feels so warm and inviting.

Her hands brush against bricks, and she slowly opens her eyes. She can feel it. The Heart. It's here. She can't see it, but she knows it's there, just on the other side of the bricks. She can't help but smile and just bask in the presence of a legend from her people's past.

"Sanctuary . . ."

Chapter 17

I'm glad I can't have a heart attack anymore, as I don't have a heart. I certainly give it my best shot, though, as the kobold stands with her hand against the chimney. Thankfully, she seems to come to her senses before anyone else enters the attic, and she heads back down the ladder.

She searches the house for the rest of the chimney, and eventually finds the fireplace that's connected to it. I'm glad she simply nods to herself before going down to the basement and the tunnels beyond. I think my resident at least understands that my core is very important and should be kept secret. Otherwise, she'd have probably tried to climb up the inside of the chimney. She probably still will, but I'm pretty sure she'll be doing it at night, when basically nobody is here.

I need to get her something better to wear, though. To call what she has now *rags* would be a compliment. They only technically keep her decent, and she's gotta be chilly like that. I don't know how to get her some clothes, however. I can't exactly send Fluffles to the local tailor with her measurements and some coins.

Maybe I should have the rats try to steal some pants or something from the maze runners? I'm not a hundred percent sure how equipment works here, but I don't think I can just snag something from a slot and call it a day. The rats have only been able to get things that are easily grabbed. They might be able to tear some clothes off of people, but that'd hardly be much of an improvement. Maybe I could have the spiders repair anything that gets torn.

Wait.

Spiders.

I'm not an idiot, I swear. I just . . . overthink things and get focused on one path easily. Yeah, that's my excuse.

I don't think my spiders know how to make clothes; I don't either, really, but I can figure it out. If I was able to tell a spider to weave a heart, I can get them to weave clothes. It'll probably cost a bit of mana, but I seriously doubt it'll be enough to make any kind of dent in my income now.

I focus in on my secret library and upgrade it once more, wanting to make sure I have enough space to work on designs on my papers without messing up the alchemy stuff Queen's working on. However, this time when I upgrade it, my loose papers organize into an actual book! I leave it open to the alchemy stuff and start working on designs on the other pages. I can see between them just fine.

Okay, first . . . probably underwear. Uh . . . softer silk for at least the interior, tougher for the outside. Stretchier silk around the waist and legs . . . and tail, come to think of it.

I start to design the usual flap/hole/access thing before remembering that's a feature for male undies, not lady's. I briefly toy with the idea of using something similar for her tail, but I don't want it to be too restrictive for her.

Now, for her upstairs. Well . . . she's probably going to like support. She looks like she could use it. Softer inside, tougher outside, stretchier stuff for the actual support structure. Similar to the downstairs, really. Over the shoulders, underneath the boulders, make a comfy holder.

Oh, wait . . . how to fasten? I could try a hook at the back, but that seems a bit difficult. I don't have much metal to make a hook, either. Tie it in the front? I don't think I can make it a single piece that just slips on. Without any other ideas, I go with that, and take a mental step back to consider the designs.

And realize my secret library has basically become Victoria's Secret Library.

I almost erase the designs . . . but she really does need *something* better to wear. With a mental sigh, I call several different spiders down to the tunnels. Looks like she's returned to the little cavern Fluffles dumped her in last night. That's as good a place for her to claim as any.

I call a couple more spiders to bring a few more mice for her, and she gives the procession of arachnids a confused look as they slowly pile into her space. The caterers set a few mice not far from her, before everyone gets to work. She can tell I'm doing something, but definitely has no idea what. I can't really blame her. Who expects spiders to bring them dinner and then make them some silky underthings?

I work on some designs for other clothes as well, but after my first attempt at proper clothing looks like a bodysuit that'd leave little to the imagination, I move on to designing a simple robe for her. The bodysuit would be good under armor, which is what I designed it for, but I don't know if I'll be able to do anything like that with the scythemaw hide. And if I had her just running around in that suit, I'd be one distracted dungeon.

By the time I get a robe designed, it looks like the spiders are done with her first bit of clothing and present it to her. She seems confused at first, wondering why spiders would hand her a very thick bit of web. Once she looks over it, though, she seems to light up with realization, and seems happy to put them on.

Yeah, I'm gonna need the spiders to get that robe made, too. Thankfully, it's a much simpler thing than the bra and panties, even if it's much more substantial. I wonder if my spiders gained some tailoring skill or something, because they seem to crank it out much faster. The robe looks almost pearlescent white once finished, and I think it compliments her red scales nicely. It looks like she's almost tearing up as she accepts it and dons it, and I feel better knowing she's a bit more protected now.

It's getting close to sunset, too. The various delvers are mostly wrapping their stuff up, though there are still a few parties trying to do the adventuring thing a bit more seriously than the gatherers were for most of the day.

Oh, I think that group wants to try to get the chest in the basement!

I focus in on them to get a look at the daring group. Ah, looks like halflings are a thing here. He looks almost thick enough to be a dwarf, but no facial hair is a dead giveaway. He's got the classic sword and board and plate armor, so he's definitely their front line.

There's an elf with a spear and a little goatee. Makes him look kinda sinister, but his chainmail isn't exactly dark and brooding, though it's not unicorns and rainbows, either. It just looks well-used and well-maintained. He's probably some kind of melee DPS kind of class, if I had to guess.

I think that's a lady gnome under the goggles and knickknacks, but it's a bit difficult to tell. She looks like support to me, from how she's handing out bottles to the other two, but I can also see a different style of flask hooked into her belt loop. Looks like she can bring some boom when it's needed. Hopefully not *too* much boom. I did survive the quake just fine, but I'd rather not press my luck.

She talks as she hands the potions out. "So, we can all drink the Lightning Resist potions now, but antivenom only works after the fact. My first grenade should dissolve the webbing in there, and that usually will disorient a swarm of spiders, but not always, so keep your guards up. This salve will help your weapons actually harm a decent chunk of the swarm. The fumes will weaken or kill spiders that get too close to it."

The elf nods. "So more sweeping arcs than thrusts, got it. Anything else?"

The gnome considers for a few moments, then slowly nods as she hands them each a pill. "If something goes wrong and we have to flee, or if we can't, take the pill. It'll counteract this poison gas," she says, gingerly pulling a reinforced bottle from her pack. "I hope we won't need it, but that swarm down there looks mean, and this dungeon apparently likes to pull a few tricks."

The halfling shrugs but accepts the pill. "I hear the dungeon is pretty friendly. I don't think it'd drop something nasty on us out of spite. Still, better safe than sorry."

I wonder where these adventurers came from. They look almost as tough as Elf Guy, but with more numbers. I make sure my medical ants are around here, just in case the swarm is too much for them. It *is* level eight and both venomous and lightning enhanced. The group drinks the resist potions, apply the salve, and then it seems like it's game time.

They head down to the basement with the halfling in front, then the elf, then the gnome. The swarm hisses, bringing the encounter to an official start. While the spiders start to surge forward, the gnome hurls a flask into the middle of the room. It seems like it's some kind of corrosion bomb, maybe something like universal solvent wrapped around an M-80.

Whatever it specifically is, it does as the gnome said it would. The webbing dissolves very quickly, dropping the spiders from their home, and they have to try to reorient themselves toward the danger. The two melee fighters get a couple swings in before the spiders get their crap together and let loose a bit of chain lightning to hit the three.

I think it's a bit more potent than the party had hoped, but not as potent as they feared. While the party tries to recover from the bolt, though, the spiders are able to advance and start biting the fighters.

"Scirocco Blade!" shouts the spearelf as he spins his weapon, a bit of fire trailing as he moves. The heat either drives the spiders back or simply kills the ones that don't evacuate quick enough. The gnome tosses another flask and shouts a warning.

"Concussion!"

Clearly, they've practiced how to deal with that attack, as the spearelf moves behind the halfling and takes a knee, the butt of his spear on the ground. The halfling braces his shield just before a heavy *Whoomph!* blasts the swarm. It's scattered a bit, but still not finished.

The two fighters take the brief respite to drink their antidotes, and I can see the poison status wink out over both of them. However, it seems the recharge on the chain lightning is up, and the group suffers another blast.

The spearelf and gnome each take a knee, looking like they're almost out of the fight. The halfling sees this and bellows at the spiders as he charges forward.

"Deadblow Hammer!" he cries as he brings his sword down, which seems an odd name for a sword move to me. It's a pretty accurate one, though. I can almost see a huge hammer hit the swarm as an invisible force squashes a large number flat.

It seems that's enough to fully scatter the swarm, and the party sags from their hard-won victory. The gnome moves slowly, but she gets potions for everyone passed out, and soon, they're simply looking tired instead of on the brink of death.

They cheer at the loot in the chest, and I cheer for the mana I get from it. It looks like there are several different magical thingies in there, so good on them.

That chest has been cooking for a while, so I'm not exactly surprised it's got good stuff in it.

The party soon takes their hard-won loot and exits, and I think I'm going to leave the chest mostly undefended for a while, let it degrade a bit. That'll give the rat spawner room to breathe some, too. The basement isn't my biggest danger area anymore, after all. I want to get things a bit more gnarly underground.

Speaking of underground, I should see what my little kobold is up to.

Chapter 18

It seems getting the robe has filled her with determination. She's gone back to the corpse of the scythemaw. She's not after a bone this time, though. She's after a claw. Why would she want a claw? One of those big mandible things would probably be a better weapon.

Once she takes it over to where the monster tried to dig through my walls, however, I realize what she's doing. She gives a few testing scrapes and smiles as she sees the stone gouge for her. I'm pretty happy, too. I won't need to wait for alchemical ants to get some digging done!

Fluffles! Get down here! Use your telekinesis to see if you can smash a claw with a bone or with another claw! Once I get some chips the ants can easily pick up and use, I'll be able to have them start digging real rooms in the stone walls!

Speaking of the ants: *Queen! Get the workers to widen the tunnels from the secret rooms so we can get the stuff out of there. Don't break the surface on them just yet, but get ready. We're going to be moving shop soon!*

I design a quick handle in the secret library before telling the rats in the maze to get a decent knotted piece of wood and gnaw it into proper shape. I need a notch for the end of a claw to fit into, and then the whole thing can be secured with webbing. If the kobold wants to mine, I'm more than happy to give her a tool to do it with.

Next order of business, hmm . . . I need to move the spider spawner. The spandrel (yes, I wrote the word down after I heard Elf Guy say it) is too small for me to be able to upgrade it further. It has been for a while now, actually. I just didn't see the need to get stronger spiders before. Now that I have tunnels and stuff, though, I find myself wanting more things to handle the stuff down there.

In fact . . . that gives me an idea. *Sorry, kobold, but I'm going to be invading your personal space. Don't worry, though, I'll help you get more.* I have Teemo squeak at her to get her attention and lead her back to the little cavern. There's a crack in there that I think would be a good place to start expanding.

He squeaks at her again and gnaws at the wall. It takes a few repetitions before she seems to understand what I want. Once she does, however, her face lights up, and she eagerly starts chipping away at the little crack. My ants start swarming the rubble to break further down and cart off, and I have an idea for how to deal with that, too.

I don't need all these entrances letting something big and nasty wander in. I don't think I can just block them, just like I can't lock the front door of the manor, but I think I can mostly block at least some of them, only letting smaller things in. I have the ants and small spiders team up on one of the passages, using rocks and dirt and reinforcing everything with web.

It's hardly pretty, but I expect most big things would go around instead of trying to break through. And if they do try, I'll have time to move a response team into position. Between webcrete and slimes, most of the entrances will hopefully be too annoying to bother with.

The next several days are mostly spent with me focusing on digging. There's been a few more hostile delvers from the Deeps, but nothing like the scythemaw, thankfully. They give way more mana when I kill them than when I simply defeat one of the topside delvers, which just reinforces to me that a lot of dungeons must go after that quick payoff.

Still no new invaders, but I wonder if the new delvers are filling that role for the tunnels? At least nothing else intelligent has come in down there. Most of the critters run off when they spot a slime or something. The ones that don't tend to get got by a slime, and I get a nice bit of mana.

The kobold seems to be mostly nocturnal. She can be a bit of a night owl. Or morning dove? She'll usually be awake to watch the early crafters and such come in to do their gathering.

The first time they spotted her in her new robes, I don't think they knew what to do. It didn't take long for them to understand she wasn't going to harm them, and that she's not an encounter, either. They've been calling her the ghost, and she gave a few of them quite a scare until they realized she wasn't dangerous. So yeah, they mostly just ignore her, and she mostly just ignores them as she goes about her nights and mornings.

Soon enough, it's time to move. Midnight is the planned time for this, and it should hopefully be the last real move I'll need to make.

I get everyone to their various places. I've managed to choke down one of the cavern entrances, so small spiders and rats can watch that one. Poe and the ravens are to guard the surface; their increased alertness shouldn't make the people worry this time, since most of them are asleep.

Coda and the bats are keeping their eyes and ears on everything underground, and I have dire rats and spider swarms watching the other tunnel entrances. Fluffles and Teemo are on core duty, along with the kobold. I can't give her directions like I can my denizens, but she tends to follow Teemo when he squeaks at her.

First stop: the basement. I want to do a bit of a dry run, and moving the secret library seems like good practice to me. Kobold seems a bit nervous about what's going on. Spiders have been encroaching on the cavern a lot recently, and there's a flap of silk over the little tunnel we've been digging. She must know we're about to put something in there.

Teemo and a few rats quickly dig out the book that the ants moved to the basement, and Teemo squeaks at her to take it. She glances over at Fluffles, who simply flicks his tongue, and gingerly pulls the book out. She brushes a bit of the dirt off before realizing she's got something very important in her hands. With wide eyes, she clutches it to her chest, then follows Teemo down a trail to get back to the small cavern.

While the rats were digging out the book, most of my spiders were moving everything from the spandrel into their new cavern. She looks around but doesn't slow as she follows Teemo beyond the flap, which is now teeming with spiders.

The flap, that is, not what's beyond it. Beyond it is . . . well, an alcove at the moment. In one of the walls is a little nook for the book, and Teemo doesn't need to direct her for her to place the book there.

Beside the book nook is an indent for the alchemy lab, which already has a few rats bringing in various pieces. On the opposite side of the book nook is a divot, and the kobold's eyes widen when she realizes what must be going there. *Yeah, I'm gonna be bunking with you, hope you don't mind.*

I'll have a spider web the map up on the wall at some point, too. They're not going to be the greatest examples of their respective rooms, but they'll be safe and secret, and I can easily expand them. *Alrighty, Teemo. Get her pointed at the chimney. It's time to get the core moving.*

Kobold lady seems to understand what the next little quest I have for her is. She doesn't even need Teemo to guide her. He does, anyway, because that's his job and he's a professional. At the fireplace, she starts to take her robe off, but then reconsiders and leaves it on. I figure she wanted to keep it clean, but then decided she'd rather have the protection or something. Either way, she starts to shimmy up the chimney.

She doesn't get as dirty as I had expected. She looks more like she tripped into some dust than climbed up a sooty chimney. Probably because it hasn't seen use in who knows how long. Up at the core, the ants and spiders have been thinning the webbing supporting it.

The kobold wedges herself in the chimney with her legs, freeing her arms to reach toward my core. It's about a basketball in size now; much more, and it wouldn't be able to move without me having to tear the chimney apart. The ants and spiders start slowly lowering the core through the webbing. She reaches up and carefully extracts it, and then shows probably the real reason she kept the robe on.

She gingerly wraps it in the hem of her robe, creating almost a pouch. She still needs a hand to keep it secure, but it's better than using up both. It'd be pretty difficult to climb down with both hands occupied, I imagine. She also has her tail to help stabilize herself as she slowly descends.

Once she makes it out, she stares around, eyes wide. She definitely understands how important the core is. Teemo squeaks at her, and she's all too happy to quickly follow him down a trail. It only takes about a minute for them to reach the spider cavern, and then just moments to slip past the silk flap and into the safety of the secret base.

She visibly sags in relief before moving to the divot and carefully placing my core in it. *Good job, kobold lady. And good job, Teemo, with those trails.* This would have been a lot harder if we didn't have those shortcuts to abuse.

Chapter 19

Things have been much more relaxed in the dungeon these last few days. The spiders have been busy disguising the secret entrance as just a rock with a bunch of smaller egg sacs on it. I was first going to try to disguise it as the kind of egg you might expect a baby Tiny to crawl out of, but then thought adventurers might actually want to smash something like that. A bunch of smaller sacs on a rock is way less interesting.

In the secret base, the kobold and the ants have been hard at work digging, though the kobold basically spent the night after the move over by the spring, cleaning her robe. Which was fine by me. It gave me time to get the ants and spiders to make her a gift of a bed.

I don't know exactly what kobolds like to sleep on, but I bet they prefer something softer than just the floor. I had considered just making a little nest of webbing for her, but decided to make her almost a hammock. I say almost because it's not particularly high up nor is it designed to swing and potentially dump the occupant out on the floor.

It's more like a thick sheet of silk stretched over a divot in the floor. Because that's exactly what it is. I figure it should have enough give for her to be comfortable, and her confused look upon returning with her clean robe was worth the mana spent. When she figured out it was a bed for her, she even smiled over at my core. I like having a resident.

Oh, I've gotten my new form of invader now, too. I've been spending mana on getting more mining nodes growing. I've got copper, iron, marble, and a minor green gem. It says it's peridot, but I thought that was yellow? Whatever it is, the delvers love it. And so do the gremlins.

The gremlins are little twisted bipedal things; make me think of a scaled lemur or something. Thankfully, the slimes seem to love the things, and the dire rats like them, too. I don't know if the spiders don't like them or if they just have difficulty hunting them, but I've only seen a few spiders get one.

They love to go after the various mining nodes, and since I don't get any mana from them sneaking off with some, I do my best to keep that from happening. I've also had a few more delvers from the deep wander in, but they've all been less interesting than the first pair. They're mostly various critters that I can quickly defeat, and most run away from encounters then away from my demesne.

Operation: *Block the Tunnels* has been proceeding well, which also means Operation: *Bigger Secret Base* has been going well. Everything that gets dug out of the base gets taken to the various tunnels to choke them down.

The library is now an actual bookshelf in the wall, and I have a second book, too. The lab has become a full alcove now, and the ants are constantly expanding and adjusting the alchemical stuff according to Queen's will. She's been interested in iron since I wrote down a few examples of what steel looks like for its structure. I think she wants to either make some or extract some property of it.

I think steel ants would be cool, but I don't know if that's a thing. I don't hinder her efforts, though. She's definitely got the alchemy knowledge, not me.

Speaking of steel, now that the chimney in the house is open, I've turned the room with the fireplace into a little smithy-smeltery combo. Most of the miners don't bother with the place, but a few do avail themselves of it, and I eagerly take notes on how to actually process ore and how they actually use it.

I've also made a workshop on the second floor of the house, a few rooms from the public lab. A few of the woodworkers and masons, and even a jeweler, like to practice their craft there, which means I get even more notes on how to craft things. I've been putting the notes in the second book and making sure to illustrate as I can.

I don't think the kobold can read, but she likes to look through the book, and she tries to copy some of the crafting advice. She even mined a bit of copper and processed a small bar. I don't know what her plans are for it, but she was definitely proud of it.

Elsewhere in the tunnels, Jello has been growing by leaps and bounds. I wonder if she could somehow hear when I thought that gelatinous cubes are cool. She's hardly a cube, but she's definitely getting bigger and a bit more transparent. She's basically taken to just sitting at the smallest tunnel exit she can fit in and is practically filter feeding on gremlins and mice.

Works for me.

What doesn't work for me is some of the reports I've been getting from my expedition birbs and bats. They've been steadily expanding the map on the wall for a while now, and I've been steadily expanding the "war room" to fit it. If I can web a library to a wall to make a sign, I can do the same with a war room to make a map.

Anyway, the town is actually pretty big, and it looks like I would not be able to take the whole thing with an expansion, even with that massive price tag. But that's not what's not working.

They've found the wall and what looks like a bay to either a lake or ocean. I actually just sent an expedition to see if it's salty or fresh. And no, seagull invaders don't mean it's an ocean. Those pestilence birds will live anywhere with food, not just on beaches, but that's also not what's not working for me. I mean, it's *technically* not working for me, because seagulls suck and I want to know if I'm on a lake or an ocean, but no, what's not working is a new label on my map. I mean, it is working, but I don't like what it's saying.

See, I had never really stopped to wonder why people would be jonesing so hard for herbalism stuff, or for the mining nodes I have now, too. I just figured I'd have wanted to have some healing potions if they'd been a thing where I lived. Probably wouldn't have helped me with the semi-truck, but still.

There wouldn't be all that demand for my supply if people just wanted to put it on their mantles or in their medicine cabinets. And if I were the only supplier around, there wouldn't be Alchemists and such already here to use what I have. I had never considered that; though people seem to make a lot of healing potions at my workshop, people don't tend to drink a lot of them on my grounds.

But now I know why. The map doesn't lie. It might be vague at times, but it doesn't lie. And now, it's showing another dungeon on the other side of town. My expeditionists say people seem a lot more cautious around it than with me.

I'm not sure how far I'll trust a bird's word on how people act, no matter how many have heard, but still, it'd make sense. Elf Guy was very cautious the first couple times he visited, and he mentioned something about me potentially being murderous.

I thought he was talking about some other dungeons far away, but now, I wonder if it's a lot closer to home than I had originally suspected. For what the other dungeon seems to be, I wouldn't be surprised at all if it was murderous. I doubt there are many cemetery dungeons that are all sunshine and rainbows.

Chapter 20

I need information. I think the kobold could go out and get it, but I don't know how to ask her, and I don't know how the town would react to her wandering around. And, considering I need info on that cemetery dungeon, I wouldn't want her to head out without a weapon. No, the claw pickaxe doesn't count.

I do have an idea, though. I put a notice on the flyer on my front door.

Freddie and Rhonda, I have need of you. If you are willing to help, please wave and get the attention of Poe, my Raven Scion, and follow the next scion to approach you.

Yeah, a bit weird, even for me, but I don't know what else to do. I am, at least, pretty sure it counts as a quest, though. It cost me more mana than it usually does to write stuff.

Thankfully, the kids are pretty regular delvers, and they show up an hour or so after dawn to do stuff. I figure Rhonda is in constant need of herbalism stuff, and Freddie is more than happy to help keep her safe and get better goodies.

When the two read the flyer, however, they look very nervous.

"What do you think it means, Freddie?" asks Rhonda, looking about as sure of herself as the first time I saw her. I'm not sure I've ever seen Freddie look so concerned.

"I . . . I don't know. I mean, dungeons are supposed to be aware, but I've never heard of one that wants to . . . talk?" He looks up to Poe then around the house, like the answer will be on the grass. "Should we do it?"

Rhonda looks incredibly uncomfortable, and I half expect the two to simply leave, but she seems to come to a decision. I don't think she likes it much. "I think we should. Everyone knows this dungeon is weird, but nobody knows why. If we can somehow talk with it, maybe we'll learn something?"

Freddie nods at that, looking curious about what I could want, but also wary about dungeon danger.

Their decision made, they step out more into the grass and wave at Poe. He peers down at the two and caws, and I send Fluffles to go meet them.

While he's on the way, I get Teemo down to the secret base to try to relay some instructions to the kobold. Looks like she's simply perusing the crafting book, looking at the diagrams for various things. When Teemo squeaks at her, she practically falls over herself to stand at attention, and I can't help but smile to myself at her being so formal.

Alright, Teemo. I need her to get the map, and for you two to head to a random cavern in the underground. Maybe the spring pool room? That's a nice room, and the little glowing fungus has really taken a liking to it, so the kids should be able to see, at least. I'll need them to see, too.

Teemo squeaks at the kobold again and scrabbles at the wall underneath the map like he's trying to climb up to it. I'm pretty sure he could make it himself, but I need someone who can actually talk with the kids, so she might as well carry the map and project with at least some kind of authority.

She looks confused as she watches him pretend to fail to climb the wall before she looks up and sees the map. She slowly approaches, looking like she's worried she shouldn't, but she's interacted with Teemo enough to know he only squeaks when he wants her attention for something important. Once she carefully removes it from the wall, Teemo gives another squeak and heads for the flap. She follows, seemingly a bit baffled.

While they were preparing, Fluffles was heading up to meet with the kids. Freddie gives him a wary eye, remembering how he was transported from the maze to the gate when Tiny got him. Rhonda doesn't look too upset about him, though. She's never been carried around by him.

He leads them through the house and down into the tunnels, and the kids are very nervous as they walk through the basement. I'm just glad they followed Fluffles down that way. Yeah, it's the fastest way to the spring, but there's still some pretty strong stuff hanging out in there, giving the kids looks. I don't let them do more than just look, though. *They're practically guests right now, so be nice.*

The kobold has just gotten herself comfortable on the floor when the kids come in, and she looks at Teemo and Fluffles, confused. The kids, for their part, look at the spidersilk-clad kobold with equal confusion and a bit of awe. They've probably never seen a robe like that before; probably never seen a kobold, either. I haven't seen any others in the various other delvers, at least.

The kobold speaks up first. "Who are you two?"

"I'm Freddie, and this is Rhonda," pipes up Freddie, doing his tanky duty of taking attention when Rhonda doesn't know how to handle it. Girl is terminally introverted. "Who are you?"

"I'm Aranya, chosen Resident of this Sanctuary," the kobold responds with a bit of pride in her voice. The kids, though, still look confused and glance around the room.

"This spring?"

Aranya sighs. "Not just the spring. The manor, the tunnels, the maze, the yard, everything on this side of those walls; all are part of this Sanctuary."

Realization seems to light up Rhonda's face. "Oh, the dungeon!" She shrinks back a bit as all eyes in the small cavern focus on her. "It, uh . . . it asked us to come down here. It said it needs our help?"

The three look like they're uncertain how the kids could help me before Teemo squeaks at Aranya. The sound reminds her what he had her bring, and so she looks at him as she holds the folded map up, clearly uncertain if she should show the kids.

Fluffles, however, never learned to not be grabby with his not-hands, and so simply plucks the map from her hand with his telekinesis and spreads it on the floor for the three to see.

"Whoa . . . it's a map of Fourdock," says Freddie as he peers at the small map. "It even knows where we live?" he asks with a start, seeing his church and Rhonda's shop clearly labeled. Rhonda points out a few other labels.

"And the Dungeoneer's and Adventurers' guilds. And . . . a lot of stuff, actually." Fluffles lazily waves his tail over the map to get their attention before tapping the tip against the area with the graveyard dungeon. The kids' eyes widen as they realize where he's indicating.

"Neverrest Boneyard? You don't want us to go there, do you? The place is full of undead! It's supposed to be murderous, too, so guards keep people out as much as they keep the zombies and stuff in!" Freddie seems to know a lot about the place. It'd make sense, I guess. If your church is named after a crystal shield, you're probably expected to be able to protect people, so of course they'd be all over knowing about something dangerous like this Neverrest.

Aranya's eyes widen at the description of the other dungeon. "A Fallen Sanctuary? So close?" She looks deeply concerned, so I pay a bit more attention. She seems to know a lot more about dungeons than anyone else in this conversation.

Rhonda looks a bit confused at her reaction. "Why wouldn't it be? Dungeons tend to form in places on the outskirts of activity, so a graveyard or an abandoned building would make sense." She seems to pause as she thinks back to some of her lessons with her master.

"Old Staiven has mentioned this isn't the first time a dungeon has been in this spot, though. Nobody knows what happened, but none of the others ever seemed to become as established as the current one."

Elf Guy's cryptic warning about losing a good dungeon echoes in my memory, and I wonder if the various invaders are more of a potential threat than I had originally thought. I mean, I knew to keep them away from my core, but that was more instinct and wanting to keep creepy thingies away from whatever it was they wanted to get close to.

Aranya nods solemnly. "Fallen Sanctuaries are . . . well, fallen. They despise and destroy, instead of nurture and care. Legends say kobold society was shattered by a Fallen Sanctuary attacking its brethren. It was defeated and destroyed, but so too was the unity the Sanctuaries had created. Infighting and suspicion overcame camaraderie, and my people fled or were cast out of the Sanctuaries."

Dungeon wars? That doesn't sound good.

Oh . . . what sounds worse, though, is that Jello wants me to know she's found a new invader: a skeletal hand.

Chapter 21

Call me paranoid, but I don't like the fact that there's a graveyard dungeon on the other side of town, and now I've just gotten my first undead invader. This math is adding up in ways I don't appreciate, but I guess it's better than it not adding up at all.

Just in case, however, I should probably check my math. I tell Teemo to come collect the thing, once I'm satisfied Jello is done chewing on it. Aranya and the kids have a bit of story time while that happens, too. I'm bad with names and dates, though, so I mostly just pay attention to see if there's anything to give me more detail.

There's . . . not. It's an interesting look into kobold society, however, and the kids are enjoying it. According to the legends, kobolds were friends to the dungeons, and they had a symbiosis going, though it sounds like the kobolds basically worshiped dungeons back in the day. They seem to have gotten protection and friendship in return, at least.

Before they can ask much about kobold history after the collapse, though, Teemo comes back in and plops the skeletal hand down near the map.

Aranya looks disgusted, which is fair. A skeletal hand covered in Jello's jello isn't the kind of thing to parade around. Rhonda looks confused as to why the dungeon would bring a hand to them. Freddie, however, stares at the recently deanimated appendage.

"That was undead," he says with the certainty of someone who's seen pictures and heard lectures on this kind of thing. The other two immediately look more concerned, and Freddie leans down to get a closer look. "I've never been to Neverrest, but it's supposed to be crawling with undead. There might be some from other sources deeper in the tunnels, but . . . I think that other dungeon sent this."

Well, I was hoping it wouldn't come to that, but sounds like it has. I'm gonna need to increase the defense budget, looks like. The other dungeon probably felt the quake and has been sending expeditions into the tunnels to try to find me. I dunno if it has airborne stuff like I do to make expeditions, but I doubt the townsfolk would ignore zombies and skeletons like they do bats and birds.

Rhonda looks to Freddie. "Should we go tell the guild, then? I know they've been watching this dungeon closely and have warned people to stay away from Neverrest. This seems like something they should know about."

Freddie nods. "Yeah, I don't think their inspector has been back in after he tried the maze."

It seems it's Aranya's turn to be confused.

"Guild? There are surface people who monitor Sanctuaries?"

The two kids nod.

"Yeah, the Dungeoneer's Guild," replies Rhonda. "They keep track of dungeons and what's going on with them. They were worried this one had gone murderous, and nobody wanted that. Neverrest is enough of that for one town."

"Can you take me to them? All I know of Sanctuaries is from legends. If I'm going to help this one, I'll need the knowledge to do it properly." *Aw, I didn't know you cared, Aranya.*

"Can you leave?" asks Freddie. I'm glad he asked, because I don't know that, either. I'm also glad that it implies that the biggest hurdle isn't how the people will react.

Makes sense, I guess. I've seen all sorts of fantasy races come through here. Probably also explains why the delvers didn't think she was another encounter.

"I can sojourn, yes. The denizens do, so I can do the same."

Neat. Well, I consider this quest complete, so I spend a bit of mana to finish it. I don't gain any for it, but with all the new info and connections, I think it's well worth it.

With the meeting pretty much over, I have Teemo and Fluffles gather the map and vanish down a shortcut to get back to the secret base. I trust the kids, but it's a need-to-know kind of thing, and they just don't need to know. Freddie pulls out a rag I think he uses to polish his shield and picks up the hand to give as proof to the guild, and they all head for the surface and the gate.

Interestingly, when Aranya leaves, it doesn't list her as on an expedition but on a sojourn, just like she said. Well, while they do that, I should focus on the home front. Delvers are here, and they don't know about the plot thickening down in the tunnels.

Speaking of the tunnels, that should probably be my next order of business.

I've been mostly sending expeditions on the surface, but I should probably do something similar underground, too. I get various groups of bats, rats, and spiders to head out on expeditions down there, along with some healing ants to hitch a ride and provide support as needed. I pay special attention to the tunnel the hand came from, and make sure Jello stays blocking it up. She's happy with that. There's been all sorts of things to eat coming from there anyway.

Without knowing what else to do, I basically just start upgrading my various spawners. The spider spawner quickly takes over the little cavern it was moved to, so the little camouflage flap blends in even better. It's started spawning widows, too, which look plain mean. I order them around to the tunnels to make sure nothing can sneak in and to be able to provide support if something tries.

The rat spawner is starting to take over the basement, too, and has produced a ratling, apparently. It looks like a rat developed a hunch and started walking around on two legs. I can still give it orders, but I can definitely feel it's smarter than anything else I've spawned. Well, except the scions, but they're special.

Oh, I've also designated a warehouse. If I'm going to potentially be at war with another dungeon, I'm going to need a place to store stuff. And an armory. I think only the ratling and Aranya could actually use it right now, but better to be prepared. The ratling put Aranya's copper bar in the warehouse, then started making trips up to the maze to gather some wood, too.

It feels kinda weird to gather my own resources, but I make sure the ratling takes it slow with that. I still want most of it to be gathered by delvers so I can get mana.

I upgrade the snek spawner a few times, but nothing new has popped out yet. The vipers are looking bigger and badder, but I don't know how they'll fare against undead. I was hoping for constrictors or maybe even coatls, but no big nor winged noodles for me yet.

After an upgrade, the anthill starts occasionally spitting out fire ants, and Queen is all over snagging those to help with her alchemy. They really are fire-elemental, which is good. Undead don't tend to like fire, if videogames are any-thing to go by.

I don't upgrade my birds nor bats yet, mostly because I don't have the mana for it, but also because I don't know what I'd do with them. The surface and tunnels are pretty full with denizens, too. I think I'll have to actually take that upward expansion before I do much more with the avians. Maybe I'll be able to build a tower or something once I get some more ratlings.

I note in the alchemy stuff for Queen to analyze the mortar between the bricks to see if we can make some of our own. No rush on it, though.

Aranya

Aranya walks with the two defilers—no, *delvers*, she has to remind herself. They're not defiling the Sanctuary, especially if it specifically asks them for help. She supposes the other defilers should count as delvers, too. It seems strange to her that it allows them to simply pillage like they do, but the Sanctuary must have some kind of plan.

That's just one of the many mysteries that guided her to sojourn to this guild. The legends certainly have information, but certain details have faded over time. If this guild has more current answers, she needs them.

She looks at the two children, thinking her Sanctuary has an odd choice in help. Why these two?

"Why spiders . . . ?" she asks herself, though the two hear her and exchange a look. She probably didn't mean to actually ask, but telling the story would at least kill the awkward silence. It's not worth any XP, but it'd still be nice to be rid of it.

Rhonda speaks up first, as it was technically her idea to go get a spider.

"Well . . . I had just gotten apprenticed to Old Staiven, one of the local mages, and he told me to go get a familiar. But I didn't know what kind of familiar to get."

Freddie chuckles and inserts his two copper. "Something normal like a cat was too boring, I guess." Rhonda sticks her tongue out at him.

"I'm allergic to cats," she says matter-of-factly before continuing the tale. "Anyway, after thinking on it, I thought of our first adventure into the dungeon and all the spiders around. I just . . . like spiders, I guess, so I decided to try to get one."

Freddie laughs. "I think you wanted a spider just to mess with me. I used to be afraid of them," he explains to the red kobold. "Too many legs, too many eyes, venom. But . . ." he trails off, letting Rhonda continue the story.

"Anyway, we went and captured a few mice in a bucket, and some of the roaches, too, and tried to find a spider for me to make my familiar. Only, we didn't think about all the different spiders the dungeon would have."

"Rhonda wanted a jumping spider like Lucas there, and I just wanted to be done, heh. So we followed a couple into the kitchen, and she started enticing one with a mouse. Only, while we were both looking at the jumping spiders, there were net spiders on the ceiling."

Rhonda giggles at the memory. "We didn't know to look up at the time, so they just kept slowly plucking mice out of the bucket while we were distracted. And I guess that counted as feeding them, because Freddie tamed one without even knowing it was there!"

Freddie smiles at the memory, too. "Yeah, I about jumped out of my skin when I saw Fiona here on the bucket, happily munching away. In the end, though, we still had enough for Rhonda to take Lucas home, and I got over my fears and gained a great friend," he finishes, smiling at the spider with the huge eyes beside him.

She clearly wants to ask more, but they round a corner, and the kids point at a building that looks very similar to the other ones around, though it has a different sign. Aranya squints at it, resolving to somehow learn to read. With her Sanctuary apparently able to communicate in writing, she's going to need to learn to continue to contribute.

"That's the Dungeoneer's Guild building, Aranya," says Rhonda, and soon, she opens the door for them all to enter. Sitting at a desk in front of a shelf of scrolls, an elven woman eyes them as she sips some tea.

"Well, you're some interesting visitors. To what do I owe the pleasure?" she asks, looking amused at the odd little procession.

Freddie steps forward, setting the wrapped hand on the desk, and explains as he slowly uncovers it, "Well . . . the dungeon wanted to talk to us, and it showed us this."

The elf coughs into her tea when Freddie says the Sanctuary talked to them, and all amusement is gone from her face as she sees the skeletal hand in the rag.

She composes herself quickly, though, and grabs some paper and a quill and ink before looking at them all seriously. "If you all could explain what happened, please."

Aranya straightens herself and clears her throat before the kids can respond. "I am here on behalf of my Sanctuary. I need information to help it, and I will tell what I can to trade for it."

The elf gives her a considering look before replying in turn.

"You represent the dungeon's interests, then?" Aranya nods, and the elf continues. "Very well. It is a dungeon in good standing, and that hand is from one that is not. I take it your dungeon wishes to know how to protect itself?"

Another nod. "I don't know why, but it allows your def—uh *delvers* to enter and gather and fight, but I do not think it likes the idea of another dungeon bothering it."

"Very well. I am willing to trade information for information. I believe we both have a vested interest in the well-being of your dungeon."

Chapter 22

Alright, Neverrest, knock it off. I know those undead trying to get in are from you, not from other underground stuff. I know it's probing me, trying to figure out what's up with me, so I do my best to be inconsistent. I leave Jello in what appears to be the most direct tunnel connecting us, only having her move to let a few of my own expedition bats down the tunnel and back.

If I'm reading the map right, which is a big if, admittedly, that tunnel seems to run more or less straight toward Neverrest. I've seen a few other hands in the tunnels, though, so I know there's more than one route. I mostly let the slimes deal with them, not wanting to tip my hand too much about what I have available.

Some manage to get deep enough that I can have spiders get them. It's a bit nerve-racking to let them get that close to my Sanctum, but there's no real risk of it being discovered. There are just too many spiders around from the spawner for any hand to have a chance at getting in. I hope.

In an attempt to get a better idea of what I'm dealing with, I even decide to send Teemo on an expedition to scout what he can and return quickly. It costs a fair bit of mana to send him out, but I'm confident the little guy can sneak in better than the bats and get me more information than just where our borders sit.

While he, the kids, and Aranya are out, I try to keep myself occupied with running dungeon stuff. That doesn't take very much of my attention, however. Woe is me, I have *too* competent scions, and everything is running like a Swiss clock!

Coda is still minding the herbalism nodes, between organizing the subterranean bats. Tiny is doing his thing in the maze. Delvers have actually gotten brave enough to run multiple parties at a time, trusting in safety in numbers. One group of each set is practically guaranteed to be captured, but the total mana from them gathering stuff has increased, so I'm not gonna complain.

Poe has been keeping track of the yard and my birb expeditions, and has been helping map out Neverrest's borders and what can be seen from the sky. By all accounts, it's a typical large cemetery with gravestones and the occasional mausoleum. One or multiple of them probably have tunnel access, but we don't have any way to tell from the sky.

Jello is just happily eating whatever undead tries to get through her tunnel, and the numbers are slowly increasing. I don't like it, but there's not a lot I can do about it yet. At least they're feeding Jello nicely.

Fluffles is mostly wandering and practicing his magic. I think he's fully mastered that Protection from Elements spell, which will be useful, I'm sure.

And Queen is . . . actually, what *is* Queen up to? I know she's doing alchemy stuff, but I don't know exactly what. The ants are looking pretty excited over at the lab, though.

Alright, let me see . . . Healing goop is still being produced, and healing ants are being created with it, good. Bottled Lightning production also continues apace, excellent.

What's your third little setup doing, Queen? I see rough bits of iron and some coal from the forge upstairs, so I guess you're still trying to play with steel! Oh hey, I think you managed to make some. That little group there is looking very excited and pleased with themselves over the little bit of metal in their jaws.

I watch, fascinated, as the ants start to puke out a little puddle of liquid in a dish. At first, I think it's water, but it has a strange tint to it. Are her workers actually able to hold various chemicals for her? That'd be cool. I know normal ants can store water and food, and I know she's had some specialists helping her with the alchemy, but I didn't know they were storing chemicals. With an Alchemist queen, it'd make sense for her to have some that could.

Once they're satisfied with the amount of liquid, the ones with the steel come over and nudge the bit of metal into it. Slowly, it starts to dissolve, and the puddle starts to look more like mercury than off-color water. Did she somehow make liquid steel?

The ants are all very excited at the reaction, which is understandable, and a group of majors march up to the little dish. I imagine they might give a little speech in ant—or get a speech in ant from Queen—before they dip their mandibles in the liquid.

At first, I think they're just getting a coating of steel, which would be pretty cool. However, I take a closer look and see their mandibles are fully transmuting to steel! Or at least iron. I can't exactly zoom in far enough to pick out carbon in the iron atoms. They even make little clanking sounds as they test their new jaws. *Good work, Queen! See if you can get enough of that to transmute one of the mandibles from the scythemaw. That could be a really nice weapon for* Aranya.

Speaking of, looks like she's back! It also looks like the kids had other things they needed to do, because I don't see them. I send Fluffles to go greet her, and she smiles at him as the two head to the Sanctum. Once there, she sits on her bed for a moment to gather her thoughts before speaking to my core.

"Oh, Sanctuary . . . I bring troubling news. The Fallen One is truly a blight. Despite the efforts of the people of this town, it has destroyed several other Sanctuaries in its history. The people can't even expunge it, as only a Sanctuary can truly harm another. I fear it, my Sanctuary. I've only just found you, and you're under attack from an experienced foe . . . and I can do little to help," she finishes, seemingly ashamed of herself.

I have Fluffles curl up on her lap, since I can't think of much else to try to comfort her. I can't exactly just put an arm over her and tell her everything will be alright. At least it seems to help her some, and she gives Fluffles a small smile as she rests a hand on him. "Thank you . . ."

Before I can dwell much on what she's said, though, Teemo returns, and his report is pretty concerning. Unsurprisingly, there are at least two different spawners for undead: skeletons and zombies. Actually, make that three. The hands are their own thing, seems like. Neverrest also has plague rats, which thankfully only give diseases on bite, not from their fleas, so at least no bubonic plague to deal with.

It also has wasp spawners, which is especially obnoxious. It seems he's been harassing me for a while, though all he could bring to bear before the tunnels were the wasps. It seems to only have two scions, but they're apparently very powerful. One is a four-armed skeleton that seems to be wearing the best stuff the dungeon has gotten off of slain delvers. Teemo saw it practicing on a headstone, and there was no headstone by the time it was done just a few seconds later.

The other appears to be a lich, or some other form of fleshy undead with magic, so I'm gonna call it a lich. It seems to prefer a lab in one of the mausoleums, though it looks to be more an enchanting lab than an alchemy one.

I want enchantments. Looks like crystals are a big thing for that, so I make a mental note to look into that. Maybe Fluffles could handle duties like that?

Back to the report. It seems like it's gathering its denizens, too, as there were tons of undead feet for Teemo to hide behind and scurry around. He even managed to find its Sanctum! Sounds like it doesn't care about keeping it a secret, either, as it's simply in a large sarcophagus in the most central crypt. The Skeleton Scion guards it, so that's going to be a thing to deal with.

With his report finished, Teemo starts to resume his duties when he notices something, and so do I. Something feels off. I do a quick look around, but everything seems to be fine.

Aranya's gasp draws my attention, and I look at where she's focused. The map? Oh. Our borders are touching now. He's expanded his claim in the tunnels.

Chapter 23

Well, we're not at DEFCON: *Oh Crap*; at least not yet. Definitely at DEF-CON: *Caution*, though. None of the other tunnels seem to connect to him, but I'm still sending expeditions with my bats to make sure. The hands I found in other tunnels may have been able to sneak past Jello somehow. If I could find a way to sneak in closer to him without him knowing, that'd be great.

I tell Tiny to web the entrance to the maze, and send all my small spider swarms to guard it. I figure the venoms of the swarm spiders won't do much to the undead that will surely soon come to visit. I'm just glad the big guy fits in the tunnels still. I'm running out of large animals to compare him to.

Healing ants are all-tiny-legs-on-deck down there, though. I want to see if the healing will disrupt them like it does in just about any fiction with undead. The lightning and steel ants are also in the main tunnel entrance, but they're mostly on standby.

Jello is still my primary line of defense down there. As far as I can tell, Never-rest hasn't found any other paths in yet, either, and he doesn't have anything that can quite deal with Jello just sitting at the entrance. I figure he'll eventually move his lich down to do something nasty.

My various birbs are keeping an eye on the surface of the cemetery around the clock. There's more undead headed underground, but none that are any-thing especially new. Maybe he figures a bunch of zombies and skeletons will be enough? If I had expanded downward as soon as I could have, he would have been right, too.

But now I have ratlings. Still not very many, but they're starting to get kinda organized. They like to mine and use the forge/smeltery at night, and though they're still not very good at it, they at least have some armor and crude swords. They're probably going to be important for me later, but for now, I still have them mostly working on filling my little warehouse and armory.

Aranya is often in there, looking to see if anything is particularly good. She even spars with the ratlings sometimes, which helps her and them get better. I don't know how good they'll be able to get by the time Neverrest actually attacks, though.

I have also changed the sign on the front door. Now, instead of talking up the maze, it politely informs anyone who reads it that Neverrest has expanded its borders to be adjacent to mine underground, and that any delvers who would like to help should seek out Aranya, the kobold.

I'm pretty sure the kids are trying to rally the townsfolk, or at least the adventurers' guild. My birb lookouts say the guards at the gates of the cemetery have increased, which is probably why he's sending everything underground instead of trying to storm across the surface. He probably doesn't like his odds of having to fight through the town before even getting to me.

I've even sent a few probing slime attacks down the tunnel. They've earned me a nice bit of mana, too, but I don't know how much he gets from killing my puddles. I get a lot more undead than he does slimes, but from the mana cost and gain, I think it's about a wash.

Oh, I've also officially created a public war room. I might want to work with the townsfolk, but I'm not quite ready to allow them into my secret base just yet. Besides, it's not like Tiny can fit in there. It's in the cave next to the little spring, and the ratlings have slowly been making furniture for it. There's a rough table, now, and the ratlings are working on chairs, too.

I'm kinda reminded of that scene from *The Patriot* where Mel Gibson fails to make a chair and tosses the latest broken one onto a huge pile of failures. Except I don't think my ratlings are smart enough to get mad. They just take the broken chairs to the forge to burn as fuel.

Traffic has slowed considerably since I changed the sign. Some herbalists still come in to get the easy stuff, and a few miners as well, but practically nobody wants to fight anything right now. They probably don't want to weaken me. I mean, *some* fighting would still be nice, but I can hardly blame them.

Hey, speak of the devil: it's Aelara, Ragnar, and Yvonne! *You guys wanna beat some stuff up and train?* Hmm, from the way they're looking at the sign, I think they have something else in mind. I wonder if they got a quest from the Office of Dungeon Affairs? It seems like the kind of thing they'd make a quest for.

Yvonne is the first to speak up after looking at the sign. "It really is asking for assistance."

"Aye," nods Ragnar, stroking his beard in thought. "And it has a resident for us to talk with, too."

"Then let us go find this Aranya and see what the dungeon has to say," finishes Aelara, and the group starts to slowly wander, looking.

Teemo, go see if you can guide them to the war room. I'll have Fluffles get Aranya, and we can see about using the public war room for actual war planning.

I miss when I thought I wouldn't need it for that.

When Teemo squeaks at the trio, it seems even Yvonne didn't know he was there, and they all take a defensive posture. I think they can all tell he's much more than a simple rat. When he squeaks again and starts walking toward the basement, they look confused. A third squeak and a look over his shoulder, and they seem to get the hint to follow.

"Creepy . . ." mutters Ragnar, and the other two nod their agreement, but all three follow Teemo. With Aranya, it's much simpler. She's down in the warehouse, trying to get the ratlings to organize things a bit. They vaguely listen to her, but I think they're more interested in just getting resources in there rather than making it easier to actually use what's been gathered.

She turns to Fluffles when he hisses at her. "I'm trying to get them to organize! This place is a disaster!" He just hisses a few more times to get her to follow, and she reluctantly does. I wonder if she thinks she's in trouble.

She seems confused when he leads her to the war room, and her confusion seems to mount when Teemo enters, followed by the trio of delvers. Aelara is the first to speak up.

"Ah . . . Aranya, I presume?" The kobold slowly nods.

"Yeeesss . . . who are you?" she asks, trying to puzzle out why I've sent some delvers to talk to her . . . or sent her to talk to some delvers.

"I am Aelara, and this is Ragnar and Yvonne," she answers, motioning to the dwarf and birblady in turn. "And . . . well, the Dungeoneer's Guild wanted us to investigate what's going on, and it seems your dungeon wants the same."

"The sign said to talk to Aranya," adds Ragnar, and my little kobold sighs.

"So that's what it wanted . . ." she mutters to herself before gathering her thoughts and pointing at the map on the table. "Well, the Fallen Sanctuary you call Neverrest has made contact with my Sanctuary, and it's not friendly. Currently, much of the Sanctuary's resources are being spent to ensure the tunnels are secure."

As she speaks, I zoom the map to the tunnels, where everyone can see my various forces in the main tunnel entrance and the occasional zombie or skeleton scout trying to get past Jello. I then move the view of the map toward the war room, and to Tiny approaching. The party is stunned at the size of the spider walking into the meeting, then confused as he simply moves to the side. He's clearly part of the meeting now, even if he's unlikely to be doing much talking.

I get Teemo to squeak and Fluffles to tap the map again to get their attention as I do more shenanigans with it. I zoom out a bit, showing both my forces and the war room, then draw a few lines. My forces push into the tunnel, while the line representing the group heads up the stairs and out the front gate. I follow the line on its path toward Neverrest, having it go through the gate and beeline for the Sanctum in the crypt.

The party exchanges uncertain looks. Yvonne is the first to speak up. "I . . . I don't think we're qualified for this."

Aelara follows up. "Yes, Neverrest is very strong and absolutely murderous. We'd be utterly outclassed in there," says the elf with a bit of regret in her voice.

Ragnar, however, doesn't look as demoralized. "*We* may nae be able ta delve in there, but th' guild has stronger parties. We c'n tell th'dungeoneers what we've learned and try ta get the strongest in the guild t' help."

This time, Aranya speaks up. "The Sanctuary seems to want to help as well, and from what I've learned, only the Sanctuary can truly rid us of the Fallen One. Not only does it seem to want to send several of its scions to aid what delvers decide to go, but there are also alchemical ants that I'm sure it will send to aid as well. I've seen them heal wounds."

The three look surprised at that.

"Healing . . . ants?" says Yvonne, finding the concept beyond strange.

Aranya nods. "I know it sounds strange, but I've seen them in action." The party of delvers still doesn't look too convinced, but any help against Neverrest is good help. Aelara speaks up once again.

"Then we'll go deliver the information to the guilds, and hopefully get stronger adventurers to come." The four all look at the map again. They can see the numbers of undead slowly increasing as Neverrest continues to test my defenses. "And quickly, I hope. I don't think it will take its time in attacking."

Chapter 24

Aelara

Aelara, Yvonne, and Ragnar jog toward the Dungeoneer's Guild. They would run, but running adventurers can cause a panic. Jogging ones are surely simply training or eager to turn in a quest and be paid. And though they all would appreciate the coin, they all feel the pressure of time quietly bearing down upon them

"How bad do you think it is, Ragnar?" asks Aelara. Though they're all the same level, the friendly dwarf is probably the most knowledgeable about dungeons.

"Ah think we should join whatever adventurers from th' guild are available an' get back quick. Neverrest doesnae just refer ta not lettin' corpses sleep. It'll nae stop 'til one dungeon or th'other is destroyed, an' a stronger Neverrest is nae good for anyone."

Yvonne nods at the assessment. "I've peered through the gate at Neverrest before. The place is . . . evil. We can't let it grow stronger." Aelara nods as they round the corner, bringing the Dungeoneer's Guild within view.

"We're all agreed, then. We'll make our report quickly, then round up whoever at our guild is available." The three nod without their strides faltering, and soon enter the Dungeoneer's Guild.

Telar sits at her desk, two scrolls before her. One is for Fourdock Dungeon, the other for Neverrest. From the stats at last inspection, it doesn't look good for the new dungeon.

And judging by the looks on the faces of the adventurers that took her quest, things aren't exactly looking up. She sighs and speaks up as they approach. "How bad is it?" she asks, hoping she won't have to place the final seal on the scroll for Fourdock Dungeon.

"It's bad . . . but it could be worse," replies Yvonne, prompting a curious look from the elf behind the desk. Aelara speaks up to continue their report.

"At the moment, the dungeon seems to be keeping Neverrest at bay, but it also seems to know that a stalemate is unlikely to go well for it. It . . . has also directly asked for our help."

Telar's eyes widen in shock. "It asked for help? *How?!* Does it have a Voice already?!" If it's strong enough to have a Voice, Neverrest should pose hardly any threat to it, but it would also be much sneakier than anyone suspected.

Ragnar shakes his head. "Nae, no Voice. It *does* have signs. An' scions. An' a resident."

"Ah, yes, the kobold in white. Aranya, I believe. We discussed Neverrest when she visited not long ago. She's marshaling the dungeon's defenses, then?"

The party exchanges a look before Aelara speaks for the group. "No. The dungeon itself seems to be seeing to that. It even wishes to work with us to assault Neverrest."

Telar looks shocked. "Work together? How?"

"By walking through the gates of Neverrest rather than the tunnels," explains Yvonne. "It seems to want to take the Spider Scion, as well as the Rat and Snake Scions and whatever adventurers are willing, walk the streets of the town, and assault Neverrest from the surface."

The dungeoneer chews that idea over for a few moments, still looking like she thinks the party might be playing a trick on her. "If . . . if Neverrest is assaulting via the tunnels, it would expect a counter from the tunnels. It's never cooperated with us in the least, so would assume any attack on the surface would have to be fliers, since we specifically kill anything that it sends out."

She blinks for a moment after getting a grip on the tactical situation. "It could work. It could actually work. Most people don't know a scion at a glance, and if recognized adventurers were with them, nobody would even raise a fuss." Her professional look returns as she refocuses on the party. "When does it want to go?"

"As soon as possible. Neverrest will only increase its pressure the longer we wait," points out Yvonne, and Telar nods at that.

"Yes, it's very persistent. Give me a moment." Telar pulls open the scroll with the details of the party's current quest and signs it as complete before quickly starting another scroll. "Take this to your guild. It's an open quest for all comers to help assault Neverrest. If Fourdock can take the core, there will be a *substantial* bonus paid to your guild, and to all participants as well." She signs the new scroll with a flourish and hands both to Aelara, who nods.

"Then we shall go." Aelara accepts the scrolls, and the party makes its exit. They had been hoping to recruit members of the guild for this, and with a significant quest from the Dungeoneer's Guild, they'll probably have every adventurer in the guildhouse wanting to come along.

* * *

"Wha'd'ya mean *out*?!" shouts Ragnar at the balding and skinny orc behind the desk. He doesn't have the look of someone who could lead a guild, but it's a carefully curated facade he's kept from his adventuring days. It generally pays to be underestimated in this line of work.

The orc sighs and nods. "Everyone else is out on various quests at the moment. You lot were my emergency backup, and this is the emergency." He gets up from behind the desk and motions for them to follow as he leaves the office on the second floor of the house. He talks as he leads them down the stairs.

"And while it's not ideal, I get the feeling you three will be able to handle this crisis. Of course, that doesn't mean I won't be able to give you *some* help. Even without the quest reward, a chance to actually remove Neverrest would be a boon to this guild." He leads them to the basement, and toward a large door. He smirks at them as he opens it, revealing racks of weapons and armor, all clearly with potent enchantments.

"Those guild dues have to count for something. Whatever you see fit will be loaned to you for the duration of this quest, but do only take what you can use."

Even with that caveat, the three adventurers look like children on Feastday.

Chapter 25

Neverrest is a pain in my non-existent butt. I'm pretty sure I'm making more mana from this than he is, but he just keeps sending more and more undead at me. I get the feeling we are probably just not able to do too much damage to each other right now. I mean, undead get digested as well as anything else my slimes catch, but they definitely keep resisting longer than living things.

The healing ants do a number on them, though, which is good. Some swarming bites before the jellies get ahold of them speeds the whole process up, but I still get the feeling I'm guarding the pass at Thermopylae: holding my own, giving at least as good as I'm getting, but in a worse position as time goes on. I haven't had to retreat or anything yet, but I've been rotating my slimes as quickly as they can move. I've even upgraded the spawner and Jello!

Jello seems to love the taste of undead, too. She's actually earned a title from all the things she's killed: Purifier. It certainly helps, and it seems to make her less corrosive to living things, too, which is great for the ants.

I give a mental sigh of relief as I sense the three adventurers return . . . and then immediately wonder why there's still only three of them. They didn't seem very confident about their odds in the graveyard, even with me supporting them. As they hurry toward the war room, though, I can see why they are back. They're all decked out.

Aelara has what I can only assume is mythril mail of some kind. It sure looks like what Frodo had in the *Lord of the Rings* movies. She's also traded out her prismatic-styled staff for one that looks almost like a thin, living stalactite with a large bit of onyx or something on the flat top.

Ragnar still has his family shield, but I guess he didn't have family armor. If I didn't know better, I'd think he was a metal golem or something, but the beard sticking out under the helm kinda gives it away. That plate mail looks good on him, and I can only guess what kind of punishment he can take with it on.

Yvonne has some kind of black leather on. Not like Catwoman, but leather armor that is black. Looks pretty slick; maybe it'll help her with stealth or something? That new bow looks pretty cool, though. The, uh . . . main . . . bow . . . part? Whatever is usually wooden looks like it's made of cloud, and the string looks like a contained tornado. She has a regular quiver of arrows on her back, though, so I dunno how it'll actually work.

I'm glad Aranya's still in the war room. She's been mostly staring at the map and watching the battle unfold. I'm just glad she didn't grab a weapon from the armory and charge in, because that's what it looks like she wants to do. She recognizes her skills, however, and when to stay out of danger. I guess the deep tunnels don't suffer fools to live long down there.

She perks up when Tiny, Teemo, and Fluffles enter the room, and notices the three adventurers on the map. She seems to take a few moments to try to compose herself. She's basically my representative right now, so I guess her taking it maybe a bit too seriously is better than her taking it not seriously at all . . . or way *too* seriously. With the stories she's told to my core, I should probably be glad she's not founded a creepy cult around me.

She stands beside the table by the time the three enter, and seems surprised to see the change in their attire. "Nobody else would come?" she asks before looking like she realized how rude that could be taken. Aelara and the others look a bit awkward and shake their heads before the mage speaks up.

"Unfortunately, all the other adventurers are out on quests, but the guildmaster was at least able to lend us some potent gear." Aranya looks relieved to hear that.

"It does look impressive. Is it enough to change your minds about your chances against Neverrest?" she asks, and Ragnar nods.

"Aye! I'd wager I could go toe ta toe wi' th' big spider f'r a while in this!" Tiny doesn't look impressed, though. *Yeah, Ragnar probably forgot that you can weave . . . or he doesn't know you can in the first place. Either way, if you only swiped at him, that armor could probably take quite a pounding, big guy.*

"Are your preparations complete for your dungeon?" asks Yvonne, and Aranya can only give a slow nod. If I could, I'd tell her yes. Tiny has tons of my ants on him so they can distribute themselves on the walk over.

Speaking of, I have Teemo squeak and Fluffles tap the map with his tail, drawing everyone's attention back to the plan.

"Ah, yes. We believe your plan to walk through the streets to be a sound one. With the element of surprise and some luck, we should be able to destroy Neverrest's core before it can rally its troops," says Aelara, and the others nod. Tiny shifts from where he's sitting and extends a leg. It's only after Fluffles and Teemo zip up it that the others realize they're supposed to climb aboard, too.

Yvonne doesn't look like it's anything out of the ordinary. She's gotta be some kind of ranger or something to be so comfortable around Tiny. Ragnar looks amused at the idea, though he has a bit of difficulty climbing up, at least until Fluffles levitates him. Aelara looks uncomfortable with the idea, but steels herself and climbs aboard as well.

Once again, Aranya looks like she wants to join, but restrains herself. "Listen to the scions, delvers. The Sanctuary speaks through them without words. They will guide and protect you, but you must be willing to listen."

I wonder if she practiced that little speech in her head while watching the map. Either way, it's time to get this road trip started. We didn't pack any snacks, but I'm sure it'll be fine. *Tiny! Head 'em up and move 'em out!*

The party clutches onto Tiny's tarantula fuzz as he starts moving. Despite all the legs moving around, the body stays pretty level, and it seems like a smooth ride out of the tunnels. Once on the surface, I have Teemo squeak to get their attention. They all look at him with varying degrees of curiosity.

I have the ants swarm in front of him and have Fluffles levitate one of the healers for the heroes to inspect. Ragnar doesn't look too interested, but more from not knowing what he's looking at than from being disgusted by them or something. Yvonne and Aelara, though, each take an interest.

"The gaster is swollen and red," observes Yvonne, and Aelara gives her a curious look.

"Gaster?"

The birb chuckles and points a talon at the rear of the ant. "The butt. Normal ants will store food or water and swell from it, keeping it safe for the colony. These ones have . . . something else."

Aelara nods and speaks from her field of expertise.

"It appears to be concentrated healing potion, and I suspect these ants actually create it themselves. Nobody is quite sure how, but dungeons with labs will often create alchemical creatures. This is the first time I've heard of one making some with a healing element, though."

Once at the gate, I have Tiny carefully open it. I am a little nervous. If it's like the other expeditions, they'll all vanish from my awareness, which would be bad. I trust my scions, but I don't know what they'll do without me there to give them orders.

Well, it's too late to back out now. Tiny. Teemo. Fluffles. If we go radio silent, be safe, and keep the party safe, too. And be on your best behavior in town. We want to make a good impression.

Chapter 26

Whew, I can still sense them, and even give them orders! I can only sense what they sense, though. Colors are pretty washed out, but Tiny gives a pretty good view with his various eyes. Fluffles's heat sensing is great, and with him constantly tasting the air, I have a pretty good idea of what all's going on.

The townspeople are giving us curious looks, but they don't look very concerned. I feel like I'm in an impromptu parade—something interesting to look at, but nothing to really get excited over. I can at least fill in my map with some good details while I'm here. I should see if the delvers are interested in more field trips some time.

Speaking of, they all look . . . well, not *relaxed*, but pretty at ease. I guess this is kinda their job, so they're used to it. They're not used to getting to ride a huge tarantula with ants clustering on their backs, but the calm before a battle is definitely something they're familiar with.

And I'm not. I keep thinking what else I could have done or could do. In fact, I have a second part of the plan I'm supposed to perform. I tell my denizens in the tunnel to press forward, make Neverrest think I'm attempting to counter down there. He's gotta have most of his forces down there already, but I want to make him get everything else he can.

The undead get quickly overrun, at least at first. I definitely have the numbers advantage, but his zombies are much tougher than my spiders, rats, and snakes. I manage a good few dozen yards before his lines seem to solidify, and we're back to a mostly stalemate, if one much less organized. I fight carefully, doing my best to retreat wounded forces and get the ants to triage, not wanting to give him more mana than he's spending on undead.

I think it's still pretty even, though, which is less than optimal. I just hope he thinks that's all my strength, and so tries to push through to crush me. I mean . . . he might be able to; I'm not sure how much other stuff he has to throw at me. From here, however, I get the feeling he's not too concerned about what I can do to him. I kinda want him to bring one of his scions down here . . . but I also kinda don't. Jello could probably stand up to the skeleton for at least a bit, but she's my last real combat scion that's still at home.

I still prefer her chances against him than the party, though. The scions with them could probably team up and take it down, but I don't want to risk the party. My guys respawn; I don't think delvers do. Either way, we're approaching the gate. Teemo seems to have some good stealth options, so I send him off ahead to do his thing once the cemetery comes into view. With him scurrying off, the party seems to accept that this is go time.

Ragnar readies his shield and hammer, giving the approaching gates a wary eye. "Me'n th' spider'll keep their attention as we make our way t' th' crypt. We cannae get bogged down or we'll be overrun, so keep movin'. The scions'll do . . . wha'ever they're gonna do once there, an' we'll need t' make sure they c'n do it."

Aelara and Yvonne both nod, and I have Fluffles nod as well. It's more an outline than a full plan, but simple is good. Simple means more room to adjust on the fly. No plan survives first contact with the enemy, but I don't know any sayings about how outlines fare.

Meanwhile, Teemo has slipped inside, and it looks like he's not been spotted yet. At least he can't sense anything that indicates it. The main yard is looking much less populated, which is a good sign. I'm probably going to have a serious counterpush in the tunnels soon, which is exactly where I want all those undead to be.

Unfortunately, it doesn't look like the Skeleton Scion has taken the bait. Teemo can see him at what seems to be his post—standing in the doorway of the crypt. He also has a cape, which he didn't have last time. That lich must have made something new for him, and I have no idea what it'll do.

Well, it's not like we can back down right now.

I have Tiny stop right in front of the gate, to the suspicious looks of the guards there, but the party disembarking the spider seems to calm them. Aelara holds up a scroll for them to inspect.

"We're here on official business of the Dungeoneer's Guild. Let us pass." The guards look at the scroll for a few moments, then nod and step aside. Strangeness aside, nobody would be able to fake that seal. Fluffles slithers up Aelara's staff and settles himself on her shoulders, his tail pointing toward the crypt.

"Looks like things are mostly going well, for now," says Yvonne, nocking an arrow. I can see electricity arcing along the shaft, which is really cool. I want some kind of storm thing too.

The party braces themselves for a moment before we all charge the gate. Tiny bangs them wide open and hurries through, Ragnar right beside him. The huge spider could go a lot faster, but I don't want him leaving the dwarf in the dust.

A small group of zombies notices the party and moves to intercept, but Teemo darts from cover to nip at all three. I can feel he's done something, and the smile on Yvonne's beak confirms something has definitely happened.

"The Rat Scion can mark," she says simply before letting loose her arrow. It's not quite a lightning bolt, but it definitely does arc. It hits the first zombie and seems to turn in midair to pierce the other two, dropping the small group without anyone needing to slow down.

We definitely have his attention now. The rest of the undead on the surface start shambling toward the crypt, and they'll get there before we will. I redouble my efforts in the tunnels as well, sending in the ratlings now and starting to steadily push the hordes down there further back. Can't let him think he can ignore the tunnels, even with the assault on his core.

Ragnar is the first to hit the crowd of zombies and skeletons, and he does so like a meteor. I wonder if that armor of his is designed and enchanted along those lines. Either way, he bowls a lot of them over, and Tiny helps ensure few are able to get back up.

Aelara is confirmed as an Earth mage as she does her best to give the corpses a burial they won't be able to escape from this time. Fluffles does his best to push away any who manage to get too close. A few actually get into range to swipe or bite at her, but the mythril seems to do its job. Thankfully, Ragnar and Tiny are keeping most of the crowd away from the squishies.

Yvonne is shooting arrows as quickly as she can draw them, with Teemo darting and marking as many as he can. Unfortunately, it seems the Skeleton Scion isn't going to sit there and wait for us to get to him. He clashes his swords together before charging; I guess he can't exactly roar without lungs. He makes a beeline for Ragnar, who simply laughs maniacally. I'm pretty sure that's his thing to put off damage. I just hope that family shield of his fares better than the tombstone did.

Yvonne and Teemo try to focus some fire on the scion, but he dodges Teemo's teeth and maneuvers his billowing cloak to intercept the arrow. Looks like it's specifically enchanted against ranged stuff. That's gonna be annoying. I try to get Teemo to mark as many of the other undead as possible, hoping Yvonne will get the hint and shift her focus to the horde. I also have Fluffles point out the scion to Aelara, and the two try to shift from crowd control to singletarget.

"Meteor!" shouts Aelara, and I can feel Fluffles helping as the elf pulls a large rock from the earth and launches it at the skeleton. I can actually hear it break the sound barrier when Fluffles contributes his telekinesis. Block *that* with your cloak, jerk!

The apparent enchantment interposes the cloak between the rock and the skeleton, and his armor rings like a gong from the impact. Unfortunately, while the dent would have collapsed the rib cage of anything else . . . well, it probably did the same for him, come to think of it. He just doesn't have lungs to be inconvenienced by something like that.

He does seem a bit hampered by the simple physical shift in his structure, though. It drops two of its swords to wrap those arms around itself, while the other two arms swing at the laughing dwarf. Ragnar is able to catch both swords on his shield and grins like a maddwarf. With a wild laugh, he counters with his hammer, but the foe is still nimble enough to dodge out of the way. He's not able to dodge the upward swipe from Tiny, though, which sends the monster flying almost straight up.

Being in the air like that seems to give everyone ideas. Teemo and Fluffles team up for a kind of fastball special, launching the rodent at the scion to mark it. Aelara opens a yawning pit underneath it, which definitely won't be good for it once it lands. Ragnar and Tiny seem to refocus on the zombies, which are much less of a horde already. The dwarf charges once more, and Tiny tosses a large web over a lot of them. Yvonne takes her time nocking and drawing her bow.

"True Strike!" she shouts, and this time, it does look a lot more like a bolt of lightning, if a lot slower. I think the scion knows that's not going to be good for it, and it cocks an arm back to throw one of its swords. Teemo, gnawing on one of his legs, spots the action and jumps, putting himself in the line of the sword as it leaves the skeleton's grip. A moment later, the lightning strikes the scion, and the same thing happens to it as what happens to frogs that get struck by lightning.

Unfortunately, the sword is still in the air, sailing quickly toward Yvonne? Fortunately, Teemo is in the way! More unfortunately . . . impaling him doesn't seem to slow it down by much. It does seem to have thrown the arc off slightly, at least.

Even with Yvonne doing her best to dodge, it probably would have taken her in the throat, or maybe in the heart. With her turning and Teemo weighing it down, it takes her just above the floating rib. It can't go all the way through her, once again thanks to Teemo, but . . . judging by the look on Aelara's face, that's still not good.

Chapter 27

Yvonne!" yells Aelara as she rushes toward her fallen friend. Ragnar has stopped laughing, and that's somehow creepier than when he's having a good time in a pitched battle. Him and Tiny are handling the rest of the undead, giving Aelara a chance to tend to Yvonne. Not to Teemo, though.

He was a champ, but I can already see his respawn timer on the rat spawner. *Good job, though, little buddy*. I think Aelara can save Yvonne. Honestly, if she can get that sword out of her, the ants can help, too. Poor birbis lying down and trying to cough up blood. Or . . . she can't breathe. That thing probably got her diaphragm, come to think of it. *Get that sword out of her, someone!*

Aelara seems unsure what to do, but Fluffles is great at moving things around. I have him remove it as carefully as he can, and the healing ants swarm in. That seems to kick the elf into gear, and she adds her own magic to the mix. As far as I can tell, Yvonne is getting better.

What's not getting better is the situation in the tunnel. I think maybe Neverrest wants to make this a mutual kill or something, because that's definitely his lich down there now. It's not very concerned with aiming, either, and is tossing around all kinds of fire. I guess that when you don't need to breathe, you stop caring about burning things in a tight space.

It's pretty effective, too. The slimes boil easily, it seems like, and everything else I have still needs oxygen to function. Uh . . . I need to figure out something to stop him. Jello! No, he'll see her a mile away and just fireball her, too. Well . . . there are a few twists and turns down there. *Jello, fall back to a good kink in the path. Hopefully, you can grab him as he rounds a corner.*

Back in the graveyard, Yvonne seems to be getting better, but Aelara still looks concerned. Tiny and Ragnar finish off the last of the undead on the surface, and the dwarf sprints over to his fallen companion, with Tiny not far behind.

Fluffles. I need you to go to the crypt; Tiny won't fit inside. Just be wary of traps. In fact, levitate something and ride it if you have to.

"What's wrong?" asks Ragnar, doffing his helmet to look at the wounded birb. Aelara gives an exasperated sigh.

"I don't know! I've healed what I can, and the ants are helping, but something keeps hurting her!" The dwarf frowns at that and looks to the sword on the ground. He gingerly picks it up, and his frown deepens as he follows the runes with a finger.

His frown turns to a look of horrified shock as he finishes reading them. "Lifedrinking . . ."

Aelara's face turns ashen at that, and she looks down at her friend. "No . . ."

Yvonne, at least, is able to breathe again, even if she looks to be in a lot of pain. "Nnf . . . H-How bad is that?"

"Bad . . ." whispers Aelara. "It's an enchantment that fits this accursed place . . . and it's stronger than I can counter."

The lich spews fire as it stalks the deep tunnels, moving as quickly as it can. Its master demanded it reach and consume the core of the lesser dungeon. It is, of course, lesser. This new dungeon is not its master, and its master is the greatest by definition. These minions only reinforce that simple truth.

The filth may have caused trouble for the lesser undead, but the lich is a scion, and master of the arcane! Once into the lesser dungeon proper, it will be child's play to locate and consume the core. All it must do is—

Its world becomes white agony as it rounds a corner in the tunnels and finds itself enveloped by . . . *something!* The scion draws upon its well of magic to fight back.

Jello didn't like having to retreat, but she must listen to the voice. She likes the voice, and what it says has helped her a lot since she came to exist. She has enjoyed watching the delvers mine. She has definitely enjoyed eating everything that tries to come in at the tunnel she was assigned.

She has absolutely enjoyed all the weird food that has shown up recently. It wiggles more, but digests quicker. That's why she didn't like being told to retreat. Now she sees, though, that the voice is a smart voice. The tastiest thing she's ever eaten just blundered into her! She's going to need to remember to hang out in curves and stuff from now on.

Oh. Ow. The thingy is trying to burn her? How dare it! She is Jello, the Purifier! This tasty thing isn't going to kill her! She won't be able to eat it if it kills her! And she won't allow that!

The tombstone is not the best thing to try to ride, but it was the best option available. Fluffles grips it more in his coils as he levitates up the stairs, letting him see the interior of the crypt directly. He can see the open coffin with the glowing core inside, large enough that the lid could never hope to close around it. It's a more jagged and raw thing than the simple sphere of the Den Master.

He can also tell that's not the true core. The Den Master suspected that might be the case, but had hoped it wasn't. Unfortunately for the vile place he's in now, he can sense the true core not far away. Thermal sense is supposed to help him find prey, and he supposes it has done that job here as well.

It's behind a sealed grave in the wall. The scion doesn't know the technical term for it, but he knows he'll need to get in there. He also suspects he shouldn't touch the floor in here. As a snake, though, it's not difficult to grab onto some of the carved reliefs on the walls. It takes him a few long seconds to transfer himself from the tombstone to the wall, but once there, he smashes his former ride against the sealed grave.

He's not surprised when it explodes, and he's able to protect himself from the elemental fire before it washes over him. He's very glad he was able to practice that spell since the first time he saw the party of three. The Den Master is right about them being useful and worth protecting.

He levitates a line of rubble to slither across, and makes a little platform in the air, just before the evil core. It's large enough that it's practically right against the opening, so all he has to do is reach his tail for it.

"Please . . ." groans Yvonne, in clear pain. Aelara and the ants keep trying to help, but there's not much they can do. Ragnar takes her hand in his, trying to give her some comfort.

CONSUME

I mentally jerk back, shocked at the . . . what was that? *Fluffles? Oh, you touched the core. Do it again; I got a* bunch *of mana from that.*

DEVOUR

Screw you, Neverrest!

MINE

Nope, this is my mana now. It feels like that'll be my territory soon, too.

STRONGER

Hah, clearly not, bucko! Any last words? Feels like you're about tapped out already. No wonder my ants flipped their crap when that mole touched my core. I get the feeling a scion drinks a lot faster than just an invader, though.

GOT ONE

What? Wait . . . Yvonne!

I focus through Tiny and see the worst. Aelara is slumped over Yvonne, sobbing. Ragnar has his hand over her eyes . . . I think he just closed them. He seems to be murmuring a Dwarven prayer for her. Dammit . . .

Resident Request. Accept/Deny?

Chapter 28

Resident request? What? Who?

No.

Does it work like that?! Yes! Accept! Come on, be Yvonne!

Yvonne

This isn't how she expected everything to end, but she supposes everything must, eventually. All in all, she thinks there are worse causes to give everything for. She floats just above her corpse, and she thinks her greatest regret is the sadness she's caused Ragnar and Aelara. She can't help but smile at the corpse of the little Rat Scion, too. He tried. If not for that enchantment, he would have saved her.

As she contemplates, she notices The Raven circling above. She watches, curious. She was under the impression her soul would be pretty quickly escorted to the afterlife she'd earned, but . . . it's taking its sweet time. It notices her noticing it, too, and comes in to land atop her corpse. Not that the others can sense him.

"Yvonne Silvercrest," he says, and she nods. For good or for ill, she'll not try to pretend to be anyone else. Legends rarely go well for mortals who try. The Raven gives her a considering look before motioning a wing above her head. "Do you still mean that?"

She gives him a confused look, and he nods above her head. Looking up, she sees a floating, glowing scroll.

Resident Request: Pending

"What . . ." is all she can say, baffled. She did desperately ask the dungeon to help, but she didn't expect it would actually be able to do anything.

"Do you still mean it?" repeats The Raven, and she looks back to him in surprise before considering the question. When The Raven comes to collect your soul, it's wise to heed his questions. *Does* she still mean it? She's dead, so does it even matter? Well . . . it must, or he wouldn't be asking, and it probably wouldn't still be pending.

Would she actually be able to go back if she does mean it? She's followed the teaching of the Golden Wings her whole life, so she doesn't fear where The Raven will take her. But . . . if she could continue to live, would she?

She would like to keep exploring, keep adventuring, keep being with her friends and trying to make a difference in the world. Technically, she guesses her time has come, but she would like the chance to be able to do even more.

"It will not be easy," speaks The Raven once more in warning. She almost scoffs it away. Life isn't easy. But of course, he would know that. *There will be something else, then?*

Ah, right, *resident.* There'll certainly be strings attached, though the kobold, Aranya, seems to be doing just fine. Of course, she also seems to have come from the Deeps. It is arguable slavery is better than trying to live there. At least one's master has a financial incentive to keep one breathing.

Although . . . is she enslaved?

After some consideration, she chuckles at the idea. She seems to be able to come and go as she pleases. And there is royalty who would be jealous of that silk robe she wears. But . . . how far can she roam from her dungeon? *That* would certainly make things more difficult for her adventuring career, and for making a difference in the world.

Or would it? Fourdock Dungeon seems to be proactive in the area, and even better, proactively good. Or at least proactively cooperative. It certainly could, in theory, be playing an evil long game, but she doubts that. It seems like half of its spawners are focused on loot and resources rather than actual dangerous encounters. It'd have a lot of difficulty transitioning to being truly murderous.

So that's what it really comes down to, then: go to her final reward, or gamble on the strange dungeon. As she weighs her options, her gaze falls once again on the little Rat Scion. It tried to protect her . . . even when she wasn't a resident. And those strange ants, too. They tried to keep her alive. Why would it even *have* healing ants?

More of what little she knows about the dungeon flashes through her mind and strengthens her resolve. Whatever its true goals are, they are not malicious. She doesn't know what it actually wants, but she thinks she trusts it enough to want to find out and help it achieve it.

She looks The Raven in the eyes.

"Yes. I still mean it."

"Then it is done," quoth The Raven, and never more, as he flaps his wings.

In moments, he vanishes into the sky, and in watching him go, she can see the scroll change.

Resident Request: Accepted!

She feels herself drifting toward her body, and she smiles as things go a bit blurry. She wonders how this will actually work.

Did it actually work? My counter shows two residents now.

There! She's starting to move! *Welcome back to the land of the living, Yvonne! It's nice to see you're alive again.* She groans and sits up slightly, to the stunned faces of Aelara and Ragnar.

"Ugh . . . that was unpleasant—oof!" Ragnar and Aelara both hug her tightly, and she slowly hugs them in return. I guess she's still sorting her synapses back out. She gives a weak laugh at their crying happiness.

"It's good to see you, too."

"Yer alive! But how?!" demands Ragnar, pulling back slightly from the hug to smile at his friend, even as he wonders how she can be alright. Aelara seems to be taking a more practical route to identifying the cause, though, and appears to be doing a kind of magical scan. Yvonne, for her part, has the answer.

"The dungeon. In my final moments, I begged it for help. I'm a resident now, so I guess I respawn like the scions?" Ragnar looks confused at that.

"That's . . . nae how that works. Scions respawn. Residents dinnae."

Aelara gasps and drops her spell, looking at her friend with horror and pity. "You . . . you didn't revive, Yvonne. You're . . . you're undead."

Yvonne looks shocked at the news, and her beak runs with the first thing to pop into her mind. "That's why he said it won't be easy . . ."

Chapter 29

Undead?! I focus in on Yvonne to take a look at her stats . . . and yeah, right there, in bold print: **Undead, Intelligent.**

Well, it's better than just a shambling corpse, I guess? She seems to be fully fine, nothing like a lot of fictional undead who are in constant pain and such, so that's good, too.

The party all exchange awkward looks before everyone hugs once more. Ragnar and Aelara don't look like they're going to give up on their friend just because she doesn't have a pulse anymore, which is great. Nobody seems certain if she can leave me, though, so they decide to play it safe, and she stays behind while the other two head off to talk to one or both of the guilds.

Teemo's just respawned, too, so I tell him to go check on her. *No, actually . . . get Aranya to come with you.* I get the feeling that, out of all of us, she has the best idea of what's going on and how to help Yvonne. It's a pretty long walk through the caverns, though.

Man, I gained a *lot* of space, and a boatload of mana, too.

Uh . . . and a boatload of problems. Two undead spawners, a wasp one, another rat spaw—oh, three undead. I keep forgetting the hands. Whoof, Neverrest loved him some traps, too. There's all kinds of nastiness in that crypt he had his core hiding in. I guess I should work on cleaning things up while I wait for Aranya to go talk with Yvonne.

Well, simplest thing first: wasps. Screw wasps. What can I do to change them?

Oof, well, changing it is going to be expensive, for starters, but screw wasps. I also now have absolute proof that biology doesn't work here like it did on Earth, or the spawners don't have to make things that are related. I can change the focus of the wasps over to bees instead. For a significant chunk of mana.

But as I said: screw wasps. Besides, I think bees will be able to help take over the surface gardening while I focus my bats more underground. I've seen some of them trying to spread some little patches of glowing moss down there, but they've just been too busy on the surface to make much headway. My surface ecosystem is thriving, but underground is struggling.

I spend the mana but don't bother with a Bee Scion just yet. As far as I can tell, Neverrest never bothered with a Wasp Scion, either. Not that I agree with most of his choices in how to work, but broken clocks and whatnot.

Second: plague rats. I don't want plague rats. I figure I can't go wrong with more packrats. It's another decent chunk of mana to change those over, too, but I spend it anyway. I did get a *ton*, after all.

Now . . . what the *crap* am I going to do with all these undead? Sure, I can change wasps to bees and plague rats to packrats, but undead are still going to be undead.

Focusing in on the spawners, I can at least tell they don't actually need a corpse to animate something. They're all placed in a different mausoleum than the core was, probably for ease of protection. That's simple enough to, if not fix, at least sweep under the carpet until I get a better idea.

What undead weren't destroyed have fallen under my control, which isn't creepy at all, so I order them all back to the spawner, including the hands. That's . . . going to take a while, but I'll be able to tell the last one in to close the doors behind them. I figure, if nothing else, it'll have to stop spawning undead eventually just for lack of room. I'll definitely need to have Tiny web the door once they're all inside.

Actually, I should get this place cleaned up a bit, too. I have some undead close, and some pretty far in the tunnels. Until the stragglers get here, might as well have them clean stuff up. *Alrighty, you corpses! Grab a bit that's not moving anymore and get it into a pile. Poe and Coda! Get the bats and ravens to start bringing bits to the various plants and such for fertilizer. Anything that looks or feels weird, put it in this little cave here. Queen can take a look later.*

Yvonne, for her part, seems to watch the activity with confusion, and maybe a bit of awe? Probably closer to curiosity.

"What . . . should I do?" she seems to absently ask. Well, that's quite the philosophical question there, my little birb. I guess the simplest answer would be to do what feels right, but that's the kind of thing that can lead you in dangerous ways. I'm sure serial killers felt what they were doing was right. Probably not morally or ethically so, but in some way, I'm sure.

"Well?" she asks, speaking up a bit more and looking around.

Oh. She wanted an actual answer. *Sorry, Yvonne, but you're not a scion or denizen, so I can't seem to give you actual orders. Hopefully, Aranya can clear things up for you once she gets here.* Heh, she definitely looks uncomfortable slipping past all the undead in the tunnels, but at least she's following Teemo.

Well, Yvonne is looking a bit restless and/or frustrated; I should probably try to do something. *Hey, Tiny. See if you can get her attention and . . . I dunno, help with the cleanup? Oh, wait!* I dunno how much she knows about enchanting, but it'd be difficult to know less than I do. *Fluffles! Get her attention and lead her to the enchanting lab the lich had!* I wanna get a better feel for what's in there, and to know what that Lifedrinking thing is and if I can make something that counters it. It's kinda late for Yvonne, but still.

The birb jumps a bit as Fluffles's hisses, but she quickly recognizes the noodle scion. "What should I do?" she asks again, to which he replies with another hiss and starts to slither toward a different mausoleum. She looks perplexed, but she doesn't seem to have any better ideas than to just follow him.

I'm glad my residents, denizens, and scions can't trip my traps because *wow,* there's nasty stuff through his entire . . . workspace? I dunno what else to call it. There's the enchanting lab, a warehouse, an armory, a forge. None of them appear to be secret, but I'd be shocked if anyone breathing has laid eyes on what's down here before.

I set basically all the traps to wear off, which will take some time but is by far the cheapest way to deal with them. And it'll give me the time to organize and hide what needs to be hidden.

I bet that lich was involved in a lot of them, too, kinda like how Queen is involved in my alchemy and elemental denizens. I'm probably going to have Fluffles handle the enchanting, though.

Huh, wait a second. Why didn't I have the option to make an enchanting lab? Why didn't Neverrest have an alchemy lab? Do dungeons not automatically have access to everything? I wonder what else I could unlock.

I mentally shake my non-existent head and focus. Specifically, I focus on my secret area to see if I can make a secret enchanting lab. And I can. That was definitely not an option before.

I tell Queen to get ants working on digging out an enchanter's area, and designate an alcove for the purpose. We're going to need to get whatever research and such Neverrest had and secure it. I'm sure some of the people outside would use it to fight things like Lifedrinking, but I'm also sure some people would want that kind of thing to use.

I'm gonna need to grab as much of the library as possible, too, for similar reasons. For now, however, it looks like Aranya and Yvonne are going to meet up just outside the lab.

Aranya gasps as she lays eyes on Yvonne, and the birb seems to deflate a bit as the kobold speaks. "You're . . ."

"Undead. Yes . . ."

"No! Er, yes, you are, but . . . you're a resident now, too."

At that, Yvonne seems surprised, but I'm nodding to myself. She definitely knows what's up, or at least has an inkling. "What happened?" asks the kobold, stepping closer to look over her new fellow resident.

". . . I died. The dungeon tried to save me, but the Skeleton Scion had a Lifedrinking sword. In desperation, I pleaded for help from the dungeon. The Raven came to carry my soul to the afterlife, but landed and asked me a question. I realized I could go, or I could accept the help of this dungeon . . . so I stayed."

Aranya looks thoughtful at that information. "My people's legends tell of kobolds serving even beyond death. There are never too many at once, though, as they are a drain on the Sanctuary's energy." She smiles as Yvonne looks concerned at that. "Apparently, not too much individually, but too many becomes untenable. One legend speaks of a Sanctuary who wished to save every kobold in its demesne from The Raven, but the strain became too much to bear, and so Sanctuary and kobolds all went to see him at the same time." She shakes her head at her words while Yvonne still looks uncomfortable.

"So what should I do for the dungeon . . . or should I call it a Sanctuary now, instead?"

Aranya smiles at that question.

"I don't think the Sanctuary cares much about titles. I've tried various honorifics in trying to commune with it, but none seem to produce any different responses." She brightens as she gets an idea. "Oh, you must come see the core! It's magnificent! Surely, you can feel the warmth radiating from it?"

Yvonne looks a bit unsure, but Aranya simply smiles again. "Close your eyes and feel for it. It can be strange at first, but you'll know where the core is. As a resident, your prime duty to the Sanctuary is to guard its core. It triumphed over the Fallen Sanctuary because it was able to overcome its guardians and take its core. Should the same happen to our Sanctuary, it will be ours no longer. And . . . I don't think it would go well for you," she finishes a bit awkwardly, letting Yvonne work out the problem on her own.

Yvonne still looks a bit lost but seems to decide to try to close her eyes and feel for my core. After a few seconds, she tilts her head like she's heard something and makes slow sweeps as she hones in on me. Her head stops sweeping with her facing directly toward my core, even halfway across the city, and she opens her eyes with a small smile on her beak.

"I *can* feel it."

Chapter 30

"Come, let's go see it together!" exclaims Aranya, taking Yvonne's hand to start leading the way. *Aw,* she's made a friend and wants to share. I'd like to let them just relax and bond, but unfortunately, I have them outside the enchanting lab for a reason.

Teemo squeaks and Fluffles hisses, refocusing the two residents. Aranya looks at the two scions, wondering why they made noise. "What? You didn't want me to come take her to the core?"

In response, Teemo scratches at the door. "Ah, there's something in here it wants you . . . and possibly me, to see."

"You can understand the dunge . . . the Sanctuary?" asks Yvonne, looking like she is wondering if those robes bear more significance than simply covering the kobold's decency.

"Erm . . . not quite. The Sanctuary tends to not interfere with what I want to do, so long as it doesn't interfere with its plans. It communicates through the scions, most often Teemo and Fluffles here," she says, motioning at the two, then continues, "I think it mostly uses them because they're a lot easier to communicate with. Tiny is . . . not tiny at all, so he doesn't even fit in a lot of places. Poe and Coda are usually busy up on the roof. Queen is in the alchemy lab basically all the time. And Jello . . . is a slime."

Yvonne looks a bit lost at all that information, and Aranya can't help but giggle at the overwhelmed avian. "You'll get to know them all, I'm sure. Most of them have their areas they tend to focus on, but Teemo and Fluffles are most likely to be wandering around." She smiles at the new resident and gives her hand a reassuring squeeze. "You'll get used to it just fine, I'm sure."

Yvonne doesn't look so certain, but she seems determined to try to find her place here. She nods at the door. "So we should go in, then?" Aranya nods, and Yvonne cautiously opens the door.

Inside, they see the enchanter's lab, which looks a lot like a mundane work-shop, for the most part. The biggest difference from the one in the house, how-ever, is the number of crystals and various things inscribed with runes. There are tools for working with practically any material, even a loom over in a corner. I wonder if that'd make it more or less complicated for my spiders to make clothing.

In the center of the room is a table with a multitude of clamps, as well as a legion of lenses on swivels. That must be where the enchanting actually takes place. Aranya and Yvonne both look on in awe at the things before them. They each slowly enter and look around, carefully examining the various things strewn about. The array of lenses draws Aranya's attention first, and she takes several minutes to simply play with them, learning the magnification properties of the array.

Yvonne takes a look at the crystals before coming to examine the small shelf of books. She pulls one out and opens it, taking a brief look at a random page.

"It looks like a book on enchanting," she says, clearly able to read it but not able to get much out of it. I guess it'd be like handing a calculus book to an Eng-lish major; they can read it, but it probably won't make much sense.

Fluffles, go ahead and take that book, and as many others as you can carry, too. The secret library should be big enough to hold them, and if not . . . they can just be on the floor. I want that stuff secured ASAP.

I want the actual library down here secured, too, but I don't think that's in the cards right now. It's not a small library; I'll focus and examine everything later. Fluffles telekinetically plucks the book from Yvonne's hand, and after a few moments of consideration, reshelves it and simply levitates the small bookshelf. It'll be a bit crowded in the secret library for a bit, but I think it'll all fit.

With the stuff I needed them for done, Teemo and Fluffles head off; Fluf-fles to deliver the books, and Teemo to scout all this new territory and make more shortcuts. Aranya and Yvonne watch them leave, Aranya with a shrug, and Yvonne with apparent confusion. The kobold looks to her new fellow resident and speaks up.

"Looks like the Sanctuary is done with what it needed us for, for now."

Yvonne looks lost. "Then what do I do? It saved me, but . . . I don't know how to repay it."

Aranya takes a few seconds to consider, seeming to be thinking about her own start, before smiling at some of the memories. "It saved me, too, and I still don't know how to actually repay the Sanctuary. In some aspects, it's like it's straight out of my people's legends. And in other ways, it's utterly different and confusing.

"But I think this Sanctuary, at least in part, wants us to find our own path. It doesn't seem to just want servants or worshipers. It seems to be happy to provide what it can . . . but it is a young Sanctuary, and so can't provide much more than protection." She smiles and looks toward my core, and Yvonne can't help but follow her gaze, even if it's aimed at the wall of the enchanting lab right now.

"Yet, it's also a wise Sanctuary. It recognizes it can't provide everything for us. And as we learn to provide for ourselves, we can teach the Sanctuary to better provide, too. It knows how important knowledge is. It brought us here, to secure this knowledge, after all. I think, as long as we all learn, we can all improve."

Aranya's little speech really seems to give Yvonne something to think about, and apparently, she already has a question.

"What did you do when you first arrived?"

Aranya blushes a bit, embarrassed, but responds truthfully. "I mostly screamed and ran. I was fleeing a tunnel horror, and the Sanctuary saved me and killed it. After that . . . I slept. I was exhausted. But after it accepted me as a resident, I explored some."

Yvonne considers that and looks around the room, then at the doorway. "I'm a ranger, so I'm pretty good at exploring, at least. Perhaps we should explore some here, before going to the core? You mentioned safeguarding knowledge, like the books the snake . . . Fluffles?" She shakes her head at the strange name for my little telekine-noodle. "The scion confiscated. I doubt that's all the books Neverrest had. If there are more, perhaps we should look for them?"

Aranya looks a little uncomfortable at the idea, probably because she can't read. After a few moments, though, she seems to steel herself and nod. "You can read, then?"

Yvonne seems a bit put off by the question. "Of course. You can too, right?"

The kobold sighs and slumps a little, shaking her head. "There's precious little chance to learn down in the depths."

Yvonne blinks in surprise at that before stepping up beside her fellow resident and placing a hand on her shoulder. "Then I can help. I can help organize what information the Sanctuary can find." She smiles and kneels down to look Aranya in the eyes. "And I can teach you to read. We can both grow and learn, and help our new home."

Chapter 31

With my two residents full of resolve, they set about exploring the various other rooms around the workshop, and it doesn't take long before they find the library. It's not a gigantic library, but it still definitely deserves the title. It's got shelves on all the walls, several rows of shelves away from the walls, and what looks like a lectern or something to do your reading on.

Bleh, no couches or anything to be comfortable?

I suppose it makes sense. The lich probably wouldn't lounge on a couch reading a comic or something. Yvonne doesn't seem to care about the lack of comfortable reading spots, though, and simply grabs a random book off a shelf. She glances inside the cover before putting it back and grabbing the next book. She frowns when she looks inside, and sighs at the contents of the third book in line.

"They're not organized at all. The first was a book on trade routes from a century ago, then a book of poetry, and this one seems to be a cookbook, of all things." She gives the room a wary eye, and I have to agree with her body language. That's going to be a lot of work to transform into an actual, usable library. At least it means there's probably not much that's actually dangerous in here.

It looks like they're both going to be poking around the library for a bit, so I leave them to it for now. I still have a mess in the graveyard to sort out. I dunno if anyone is going to want to use the place for burying bodies anymore, but I want it in presentable condition.

I don't need no rubble and dismembered corpses littering the resting places of whoever's buried here. I don't need wandering corpses, either, so I set them all to the mausoleum and have Tiny web the door closed before letting him head back to the maze. I think he liked the field trip, but the big lug is definitely more of a homebody than a scion like Teemo.

Speaking of scions . . . I'm in a bit of a pickle. At the house, everything is running nice and smoothly because of all my scions. But I don't have any scions over in the cemetery or in the caves. I mean, I have Jello in the caves, and she seems to just be having a ball down there. It's hard to tell with slimes, but I'm pretty sure she's enjoying herself. At the very least, she's patrolling and keeping things from getting too far in.

But she can't handle both the caves and . . . I'm gonna call it the crypt complex for now. It seems like it was more or less the lich's stomping grounds. There's a bunch of rooms and such. Maybe I should try to move my ratlings in here? They're doing well enough in the caves under the house, but it's a bit crowded over there.

Additionally, there's still the whole surface cemetery. I never had much reason to think about how to care for one before I died, so I'm not sure what I'll actually need. The more I think about it, though . . . the more I think I'll need to unweb the undead mausoleum after all.

Alright. Let's take an actual look at what these spawners can do.

First: the zombie spawner. Technically, it's **Fleshy Undead**, because that's more comforting than just calling it a zombie spawner, I guess. Pretty much all the options are unsavory, in my opinion. Ghouls, ghasts, wights, skinwalks . . . I never thought *zombies* would be my best bet, but there it is. I'll leave it for now.

The skeleton spawner has a few options, but they boil down to different flavors of fighting or magic skeleton. I don't really want either. Though come to think of it, my scions basically grow into whatever role I assign them, so maybe it won't matter, at least for the scion? I do have an idea for what I want him to do. I'd love to not have an Undead Scion, but I think I have to work with what I'm being given. I'll check the other spawners before I do, though. I want to make sure I have enough mana for everything.

I had expected the bee spawner to act like the ant spawner, but it seems like it will let me produce a scion without much fuss. I wonder if any of the books in the library has info on bees. I thought they would form new hives like ants form new hills, but apparently not. I have an idea for what to use a Bee Scion for, and looks like it won't cost too much, either. Still, on to the next one.

The second rat spawner doesn't let me have a second Rat Scion. Lame. At least with packrats over here now, too, I can get loot running and so get more mana.

The hand spawner has all sorts of options for hands, which I wasn't expecting. There're the skeletal hands that seem to be scouts. There are zombie hands which seem to be ambush attackers, maybe similar to my spiders? And then there's just hands. They seem to be gifted with magic, but that's all the info I can get without spawning a scion.

I take a moment to make sure I have plenty of mana to spend on these, and I do. Neverrest really did give me a boatload of mana. I've been kinda burning through it, but I think I'll be able to slow things down a bit after getting my new scions spawned.

I go for the Hand Scion first, and I, of course, dub it Thing. It doesn't seem to have the cheekiness Thing on TV has, but that's fine. I send it to the enchanting lab to get acquainted with the tools there. I had considered having Fluffles be in charge of my enchanting, but I like him being able to wander around and deal with trouble. Besides, I'm not in any real rush to get magic stuff, so I can let Thing take its time. I'll need to spend more mana later to upgrade the secret enchanting lab, but that can come later.

Next up is the Bee Scion, who I'm calling Honey. I send her and her little swarm to the library. Looks like Aranya and Yvonne are exploring around the complex by now, so they don't get to greet the new scion. I tell Teemo to prioritize a few trails from the library to the surface when he gets a chance. Honey is going to be a busy bee, but if Queen can handle leafcutter-ant stuff *and* alchemy stuff, I'm sure Honey can handle a library alongside bee duties.

The last scion, however, I have a unique plan for. I'm glad the ratlings can kinda make things, because I'm going to need some. I need my spiders to help with this, too. Thankfully, it doesn't cost much mana, since it's not really anything they haven't done before. Well, except for the dye, but that's just coal and water. Not exactly a complex process.

My skelly exits the crypt and closes the door behind him, not seeming to be bothered by the odd task I have for him. From the tunnels come a few ratlings carrying what I asked them to make. First, a long black robe. Even if I'm in good standing, I get the feeling I shouldn't parade around naked undead. Insert boner joke here. Also insert joke about inserting boners here, too.

The second thing is a scythe. My ratlings don't seem to have mastered steel just yet, but they can handle iron. It's nice and sharp, and he looks nice and sharp in his getup. I'ma call him Grim, the Grounds Reaper, and I set him to his first task: using a scythe for its intended purpose. The grass here is way too shaggy.

He barely gets started before I have two delvers, and I'm pleased to see it's Aelara and Ragnar. They're back in their regular duds now, too, so I think things are more or less settled. They give Grim wary looks, which fade to confusion as they see him mowing the lawn. Ragnar seems to be the first to gather his thoughts about what they're seeing, and he laughs.

"Ach! This dungeon 'as a sense a humor!"

Aelara can only shake her head and chuckle in agreement. "Indeed. Come, let us see if we can find Yvonne or a scion to lead us to her. We need to talk about the guild's response to what's transpired."

Grim

Existence. A mausoleum. The skeletal figure lies still for a few seconds, concepts forming in his skull, certainties and suppositions muddling together. The known is accepted: he is a scion. He is a skeleton. He will serve and protect the Master for his existence, and do its bidding. The supposed are left for later: what does the Master wish of him? Will he be able to serve his duty properly? What duty does the Master have for him?

The last question, at least, has an answer. He can feel the attention of the Master on him; the hurricane's eye focused on his skeletal form. Purpose quickly follows. Wear. Wield. Protect. Rebuild. A name is formed for the skeleton: Grim.

He can feel his bones resonating with his purpose and with his unofficial title, gifted from The Master: Groundsreaper. The Master takes amusement from the title and name, but the nature eludes Grim. He exits the mausoleum to see The Master's demesne.

A graveyard, as is proper for a skeleton. The area is disturbed by recent conflict, and Grim somehow knows it was wrested from the grip of one who would harm the Master. He can only nod at the destroyed undead, noting no denizen corpses of other types. His Master is strong and wise to be able to crush the former keeper of this place. His purpose to protect and rebuild are obvious, but he must wait to begin.

Wear. Wield. His Master has gifts to bestow. Denizens approach with something made of pitch-black cloth and with a large scythe. Ratlings? Perhaps the Master used their cunning to achieve victory? He shakes his head, dashing the pointless thought against the inside of his skull. He has his purpose to fulfill.

He takes the cloth and finds it to be a robe. He pulls the hood over his bleached skull and accepts the scythe, feeling something resonate within himself. Wear and Wield are fulfilled . . . now, he must Protect and Rebuild.

He is uncertain how to start. The Master impresses an idea upon him, and it is a strange one. As he looks around, though, it has merit. Much of the carnage is being dealt with by the taken undead, and it is a job for more than just his two bony hands.

The graveyard is overgrown. It must be tamed. The scythe The Master gifted him will work perfectly to bring it into line. As he moves to fulfill this purpose, an image from the Master sticks in his head. It is a field of grass, trimmed low and tidy. Trees ensure privacy among the rows and rows of tombstones. The living walk among them, paying their respects.

Yes . . . this is what the Master wishes him to build. It is strange to give an undead such a task, but it resonates with his purpose. He will be honored to build such a place for The Master to watch over. It is not the existence of battle that he had expected, but it feels as if it could be even more fulfilling to build than destroy. And if the resonance he can feel is any indication, he will have the strength and power to ensure tranquility reigns in the graveyard. Any who try to disturb it will simply have to be laid to rest here.

Chapter 32

Yvonne sighs and hangs her head a bit under the shade of the tree where she and her friends meet to discuss what happened. "I probably shouldn't be surprised I'm out of the guild . . ."

"Well . . . only technically," speaks up Ragnar, to the confusion of my latest resident.

Aelara continues. You see, while you have technically fallen in duty to the guild in the completion of a major quest, there's technically nothing keeping you from rejoining."

Yvonne looks confused. "What? Undead aren't barred from joining?"

Ragnar grins. "Not technically! Y'see, th' normal r'quirements keep undead out anyway. No zombie c'n sign a contract, fer example. But nothin' in the charter nor in any o' th' bylaws specific'ly excludes smart undead!"

"So . . . I could come back? But . . ." Yvonne looks a bit rudderless, while her friends continue to try to help walk her through what's going on.

"The guildmaster is fully aware of your unique situation and new obligations, and he asked us to remind you that, even as an adventurers' guild member, you're technically not obliged to take on any quests you don't wish to. If you feel a quest is too far away or at cross-purpose to the dungeon, simply don't accept them." Aelara gives her friend a gentle smile.

"And while you would need to find a party to join, it just so happens the guild has a party who is tragically shy of a member after their latest quest. You would technically be back on the bottom rung, but the guildmaster has set a new quest to return the property that was tragically lost in the conquest of Neverrest."

Ragnar grins again. "Guildmaster dinnae miss a trick, aye? If ya rejoin an' just come back wi' th' fancy gear ya borrowed, he said ye'll basically be back to where ya were in guild standin' an' have a big payment for completin' th' quest!"

Yvonne, for her part, still looks lost. Teemo wriggles out of a crack in the ground nearby, and she looks at him. "What should I do? Can I truly be an adventurer *and* a resident?" Teemo looks at her for a few seconds before giving a squeak and continuing on his way. Those shortcuts don't make themselves.

She turns her gaze back to her friends. "And can I even leave, even if I *do* accept the offer?"

Aelara nods. "While nobody seems to be absolutely sure, it seems highly likely you'll be able to leave for at least some period of time. Neverrest could send its undead denizens out beyond its borders. Additionally, Miss Aranya is also able to *sojourn*, as she puts it. If undead can leave, and residents can leave, undead residents should be able to leave," reasons the elf.

Ragnar looks around, watching Teemo vanish down the start of another shortcut. "An' it seems t' me yer dungeon isnae opposed t' ye rejoining, too."

Yvonne slowly nods. "Aranya did say it seems to want us to do more than just be here." Her resolve seems to slowly firm, and she stands with a nod. "Yes. I would like to rejoin the guild, then."

Her friends smile, and all three grasp hands. They've been through much together, and they all intend to get through much more in the same way.

I can only half pay attention to the party's warm reunion right now, though. After Fluffles took those books to the secret base, I lost track of him. He's not out on an expedition or something, either. I scour my various places and get a bit of an appreciation for just how much I've grown since I got here.

Used to be, it'd take me just a few moments to scan myself and bring the little vague feelings of what's happening to the forefront of my mind. But now I have the house, the garden, the maze, the tunnels, the cemetery, and the crypt complex.

He's not in the complex; that's the first place I checked. I thought maybe he came back to look at the workshop or look at other books, but no, Thing is still all on its own in the enchanting workshop. Looks like it's getting ready to head to the secret base to look over the magic books and get an actual idea of how to enchant things.

He's not up in the cemetery, either. The whole graveyard is pretty quiet and peaceful now, with Grim's mowing being the only real movement up there. I wonder if the local churches will want to come consecrate the place or something. I don't even know if that's a thing.

He's not down in the tunnels. Jello is doing Jello things, eating gremlins and other invaders. I kinda get the feeling she misses eating the undead, but she seems to be going for quantity of other stuff rather than the quality of roaming corpses. The ratlings are helping mine various new tunnels and caverns, too. They're still not especially good at it, but more room means more room for encounters. I'll probably try to design an actual tunnel complex beneath the house soon. I'll probably need Coda's help. Sonar will help to plan and make sure the ratlings mine where and what they need to.

It's strange, but I feel like most of what I mine off the walls almost vanishes, while the nodes seem to never lessen. Must be some part of the weirdness of this reality, or just the weirdness of dungeons. Either way, I'll probably need to designate a few more mining nodes if I want to fancy the place up.

Anyhow, back on the hunt for Fluffles. He's also not in the house. Business has been slowly picking back up; seems like most delvers are content to wait for the official all-clear from the Office of Dungeon Affairs and Elf Guy. I wonder when he'll be back. It's been a while since he took a look around.

He's not in the maze, either. That's still just Tiny and the dire rat thieves. Tiny seems to be planning out a new layout for the maze, placing webs and such and almost sectioning parts off. Looks like he's got an area up to the first chest that's a fairly straight shot, probably for the people who try to just sprint through. The deepest chest, though, is starting to get pretty good. It's no longer a Least or even a Lesser Chest. Big guy knows how to try to lure stronger adventurers deeper.

Fluffles isn't even in the yard, and that's the last area to look! The herbalism nodes were getting a bit overgrown, thanks to the lull in delvers while dealing with Neverrest, but now, they're getting pruned back by the more daring herbalists. The anthill is still spitting out ants. It started occasionally producing carpenter majors who are the size of mice, and Queen has been taking a few to help move her larger experiments around, while the rest are helping spread the different fungi around in the tunnels. I don't know how, but there are some new types popping up in a few nooks down there.

Fluffles isn't even in the snake spawner! Oh . . . wait. He is. Why is he in there? *How* is he in there?

Ascending? What?

Chapter 33

Telar smiles as she places the final seal upon the scroll.

Neverrest Boneyard
Subsumed

"Couldn't have happened to a better dungeon," she says, glad to have that pain in the neck finally dealt with. Fourdock will certainly be doing something weird again soon, but she'll drink her inkwell if it's anything even remotely as dangerous as Neverrest would have done.

She gets a second scroll and magically copies the contents. The main guild will want to have the full account for the records. She almost does the same for the Fourdock Dungeon, but refrains for now. It will be best to wait to update the rest of the guild on that once the inspector can get a good look around. The details as she has them now are vague and sparse at best, and the guild was formed to combat that kind of poor understanding of dungeons in the first place.

No, that wouldn't do at all. So she simply places the copied scroll aside and the other two scrolls back on the shelf; one in the section for former dungeons, and the other on the section for active ones, right next to the other two.

Karn

Karn the Slight smiles as he takes a step back, appreciating the latest trophy for his guildhouse. Sure, it's just a scroll with a seal at the moment, but the Dungeoneer's Guild should be making a proper trophy plaque for the destruction of Neverrest. As with all things with large organizations, it will take a while, but even the placeholder scroll deserves a place of pride among his guild's achievements.

There is, of course, the trophy case of ribbons and true trophies from the various Adventurer tournaments. His own party even came in second place in the Iron Barony Reliquary Hunt! Though that was a while ago. But the latest accolade is one of the rarest ones as well. It's not often a dungeon even earns the ire of the dungeoneers so much that it needs to be destroyed, and rarer still that it's actually accomplished. Rumors abound about how the dungeoneers actually remove hostile dungeons, and the only ones that are well documented are from established dungeons helping and subsuming the offender.

But that small party, and that *new* dungeon proved up to the task of actually subsuming Neverrest! Karn knows a lot of people will assume it was mostly the party's doing, but a lot of people know practically nothing of dungeons. He knows it was Fourdock that was able to destroy Neverrest, not the party. Still, they hardly did nothing.

The report he got from Ragnar and Aelara was concerning, then tragic, then confusing. Yvonne, not only a resident now but undead as well? Intelligent still, too, which for most people is only something theoretical or nightmarish, depending on how the theory goes. He had sent the two to go turn in the quest at the Dungeoneer's while he pored over guild bylaws, as well as kingdom laws.

Guild law doesn't actually mention undead anywhere, probably because there's never been an undead who could meet the other requirements for membership. Kingdom laws *do* mention the undead, but there's also a lot of wiggle room there. While a perpetrator being undead will impose harsher penalties for most crimes, it seems nobody ever actually put quill to parchment to specifically outlaw being undead.

That discovery put a smile on Karn's face. While he sometimes misses going out on quests, it's things like this which remind him why he's here. Sneaking around and slipping daggers into what needs them may solve immediate problems, but sneaking through legal codes and finding loopholes is more satisfying and lucrative. It's a small wonder that so many rogues retire and go into law. The skillsets overlap so nicely.

Tarl

"I hate inspecting the Southwood . . ." grumbles Tarl as he moves through the forest. It's not that the Southwood is a dangerous dungeon. Far from it, in fact. It's practically the poster child for toyboxes! Well, if it weren't for how bloody large the place is!

Where a dungeon like Fourdock can be inspected in an hour or two, Southwood takes close to a week! And everything is so spread out! The elf sighs and shakes his head as he continues, trying to keep his focus. The White Stag's clearing shouldn't be too far from here, and the core is never far from it.

He focuses his mind by speaking to his voicecatcher. Closer to a guildhouse, he'd be able to magically transmit a copy directly to someone like Telar. In the outskirts of the Green Sea, though, he'll have to actually make it back to be able to give his report.

"Southwood remains mostly unchanged since last inspection. Various nodes appear to have moved, which is typical for its behavior. What few denizens there are appear to still be focused on growing and nurturing the various herbalism and hunting nodes. White Stag's clearing appears to still have antler markings on the trees from the Stag." The forest starts to thin, and he can make out the form of the Southwood's only known scion. "Spotted the Stag. Expect to need to barter information to be able to check on the core, as usual."

He gets closer, and the large stag peers down on him with those solid blue, softly glowing eyes.

"Outsider. You come to gain information, and know you must offer information in trade. Speak."

Tarl manages to not roll his eyes at the Great Scion and Voice of the Southwood. If he manages to upset it, he'll have a far worse fight on his hands than with that big spider back in Fourdock. For all the Stag's apparent majesty and grace, it basically only wants gossip on other dungeons. If that's all he has to pay to be able to confirm Southwood's core is still more or less the same, he'll happily pay it.

"The Harbor remains unchanged. It still viciously defends its waters, but it shows no interest at all in expanding them. Neverrest appears to be slowly building up again. It must be able to tell Fourdock has a new dungeon, so it will be wanting to consume it as it's done the others that formed there.

"The new Fourdock Dungeon has created a maze of brambles guarded by its mightiest scion. The price for failing the trial is not death, however. If captured, delvers are webbed, and an item of value is taken before they are removed from the bramble and eventually the dungeon."

The Stag tilts his head at that, possibly listening to the core's response. The silence continues longer than usual, and the inspector starts to wonder if something has gone wrong before the Stag finally speaks once more.

"My Lord suspects more has happened since you last frequented Neverrest and Fourdock. The number of wasp invaders has lessened dramatically in the last day. My Lord bids you return with news of what transpired, and you will be graced with news of transpirings deeper in the Green Sea."

The scion shakes his head, sending a faint series of chimes from the points of light hanging from his antlers. "For now, the accord is met, and you may gaze upon My Lord's Heart and behold there is no flaw nor blemish to be found."

The elf nods and gives a careful bow to the White Stag as he steps aside, entering the clearing. "Clearing entered. Core appears unchanged. Clearing appears unchanged. Quest offered and accepted to give Southwood updated information on Neverrest and possibly Fourdock dungeons. Info on the Green Sea Forest has been offered as payment. Extracting. Should return to Fourdock itself in about a week."

Chapter 34

Man, Ascension takes a while. There's a little progress bar under Fluffles's portrait in the snake den, but it doesn't give a percentage or anything. From the slow rate of filling, though, it'll probably take a few days before he's done doing whatever Ascension does.

At least I have a vague idea *why* he's Ascending. He's finally earned himself a title: Conduit. All I can think is that it's because he was how I got Neverrest's mana. It'd make sense that it'd do something to the noodle. That was a lot of energy being moved.

I haven't had too much else to do, though. Yvonne is on her sojourn to the guild to return the stuff she borrowed and renew her membership. I told my spiders to go ahead and make her a set of silk clothes and a hammock/bed thing for her in the secret base, too.

I also make sure they stay quiet. Aranya has been up way past her bedtime and is sleeping soundly in the secret base. I'm pretty sure she gave my core a little prayer of thanks or something before going to sleep, too. I wish I could tell her she doesn't need to do anything like that, but I get the feeling she wouldn't really listen, even if I could.

I'm . . . actually kinda bored. I don't have the mana right now to start any actual projects. Delvers have been slowly trickling back in around the house, but it's nothing like it was before dealing with Neverrest.

I poke around my various things, just kinda letting my mind wander, until I notice something strange with the rat spawner. It's well and truly taken over the basement, and I even have a few dozen ratlings wandering around doing their things. I was wondering if I could upgrade the spawner further, and it looks like the answer is complicated.

Rat Spawner: Max Level!
Enclave Available: 1/1

Upon investigation, it asks me to designate an area for an enclave. I mean, I had been considering moving the ratlings over to the crypt complex. Seems there's a ton of room over there, and if they get to digging, there will be even more. It'll take a fair pile of mana, but not as much as I would have expected. It'll be basically everything I have at the moment . . . but why not! If another Neverrest attacked or something, I wouldn't have the mana to mount a decent defense right now anyway, and mana sitting there is mana not doing any work.

I designate the furthest part of the crypt complex for my ratlings. It might have been a barracks or something when Neverrest was using it, but it should be plenty of space for my ratlings to have an enclave, whatever that actually means. The space itself doesn't change at all when I spend the mana, but all my ratlings sprout a progress bar.

Advancing

Looks like that will take a while, too. The ratlings are already acting a bit different, though. Pretty much all of them head to the warehouse and grab wood and tools and head for their new enclave. A couple even grab a few larger spiders to bring, which the spiders don't seem to object to.

Once at the new enclave, they start cleaning up, removing the rotten and decaying bunks. At first, they just pile them outside the area, but a few start taking long trips to the forge to use the things as fuel. They'll probably make terrible fuel, but it's better than just letting them sit around and rot.

While a few see to the rotten old bits, most of the others see to getting their enclave started. Crude wooden tools are gnawed into shape and then used to make larger things.

Looks like they're making a crude wheelbarrow. Or a couple. The first is commandeered by the ones clearing out the trash to more easily get stuff to the smelter.

The next one is trundled up to the graveyard surface, and Grim points them toward a spot near one of the outer walls. At first I think they are somehow trying to escape, but they actually just want some dirt. I suppose that large box down there will be for growing some kind of crop. Probably mushrooms.

Others work on making a few cages for the spiders, weaving their silk into a simple lattice to spread over framed boxes. The spiders don't seem to mind, especially since the ratlings keep feeding them mice and roaches. No taming bar appears, though, which is kinda strange.

Come nightfall, they have about six caged spiders, most of the trash has been burned in the furnace, and their mushroom bed looks about half filled with dirt. They haven't tried to make any beds or anything yet, and more or less just get comfortable in a big pile to sleep. From the progress on the bars, they'll need about a week to finish this.

Oddly enough, I've had a few more ratlings spawn, but they don't have progress bars, and they don't seem to have any interest in the enclave.

Even more strange: looking at them and the ones in the enclave, I can already see some differences.

Chapter 35

So, this last week has somehow managed to be both interesting and kinda boring at the same time. I don't mind some boring after all the excitement with Neverrest, but still!

My new scions have been adjusting and growing into their new niches. Honey has started slowly working on organizing the library, and I do mean slowly. It takes a ton of bees to move a book, and it takes her a while to read it to know where it should go. I'm not sure if I should be surprised that she can read or not.

I gave her what vagueness I could remember of the Dewey decimal system, and she's been working on it. Aranya sometimes goes in there just to watch her work, too, when she's not busy.

Thing has picked up at least the rudiments of enchantment, and it looks like most of the application for me is in trapmaking. No wonder Neverrest had so many traps. I had been avoiding the things a lot, since all I had access to were either so minor that the mana gain didn't make much difference, or were potentially lethal.

Magical traps seem to be a lot more versatile. The first trap Thing's managed to make is a slowing trap, which is very helpful around the entrances in the tunnels. He takes a crystal, a bit of honeycomb, a ball of web, wiggles his fingers around, and I have a little slowness trap. I can get behind traps like this. Jello loves them, too. She's taken to wandering from entrance to entrance to catch whatever's been slowed. I hope Thing figures out an entangling trap, or something similar. That'd be even better for Jello.

Grim seems to enjoy tending to the graveyard, and I've even seen him coming over to the yard around the house to keep the lawn a bit more managed. The enclave ratlings have been gathering the cuttings, too, to feed their little mushroom farm and weave a few rough little baskets.

Aranya's been spending a lot of her time in there with them the last week. Her eyes seemed to light up when she noticed the enclave, and she's been trying to help them get their society started.

Yeah, a society. They've been changing a lot over the week. They're still listed as ratlings, but the advancement bars are almost full. I bet they'll get a different name once it does. They only have a passing resemblance to the ratlings anymore.

They've also started wearing clothing. It's a lot rougher than what I made for Aranya and Yvonne, and they seem to have used a bit of the grass cuttings as reinforcement and/or decoration. It keeps their modesty, at least.

They've even gone on a few small expeditions on their own and returned with some dead critters from deeper in the caverns. My little ratlings are getting along just fine, it seems, and I think I have Aranya to thank for that.

As for my other resident . . . well, she hasn't been around very much the last week. She comes back in to rest, changing into the silk robe and such once in the secret base, and gives Aranya her reading lesson for the night before she is off again in the morning. She doesn't sleep, though. The first night she tried, but after tossing and turning for over an hour, she got up and wandered. I get the feeling that she can't sleep anymore. She's taken to helping Honey organize the library instead, which seems to help clear her mind. I hope she can get some more hobbies eventually. The library won't be able to keep her forever.

She's also mentioned that most of the quests she's been getting have been from various mages and clerics in the city wanting to study her. It's apparently been a bit awkward, but she wants information as much as they do.

She seems to be almost stuck in the state she died in, which makes her a pretty intact corpse. From Thing's studying, it seems Lifedrinking basically just sucks the HP out of someone. Since Aelara and the ants healed her as well as they could, she's in as good a condition as she's ever been.

She's also not breaking down like most undead do, which is weird. I think it's because of the upkeep I pay in mana. The experts say she's been suffused with different energy than what powers other undead. They even did a little test with a pinprick and healing spells.

That would have hurt a normal undead, but she said it felt a lot like getting healed before she ever became undead. There was a lot of technical talk that she didn't understand, but she was at least able to get them to stop nerding out long enough to tell her that she's in no danger of becoming a rotting, walking corpse.

Her mind also seems to be unaffected, which makes both of us relieved. She doesn't want to lose herself, and I don't want to have done something like that to her. It's still something to keep quiet, though. Nobody wants to learn there's an intelligent undead walking around. That's the kind of thing that draws crowds with torches and pitchforks.

Chapter 36

Today is looking like it'll be pretty eventful. Still not much delver activity, though Yvonne was able to confirm that most delvers are waiting for the inspection before returning. She also said the Dungeoneer's Guild (or the Office of Dungeon Affairs, as I like to call it) expects him within the next few days to do the much-anticipated look around.

No, the activity will be coming from Fluffles and the enclave! Looks like both will be finishing up sometime today. I can't wait to see what my favorite noodle will be with the Ascension finished. The ratlings in the enclave are also much different than my normal ratlings. I think Aranya is going to do some kind of ceremony with them once she wakes up tonight, so that'll probably finish that up.

I can feel my gates opening, which is a bit of a surprise, and I smile to myself as I see Elf Guy! As is tradition, Poe and all my birds start squawking, cawing, tweeting, and generally making a racket. He grimaces and looks up at Poe as two more sets of feet join him.

Rhonda and Freddie? He can't be planning to bring them on the inspection, can he?

I tell the birds to shut up for a second, and the three delvers look around.

"Why'd they stop?" asks Freddie, looking pretty good in what looks to be fairly worn ringmail. He has a tabard over it with a crystalline shield, so I can only assume he's getting further with becoming a paladin.

"Why'd they even start?" follows up Rhonda, wearing the most classic black mage robe and hat, and a short staff with a carved swirl on top. Elf Guy just sighs.

"The dungeon knows and seems to approve of me, and shows it with the birds making noise when I show up. They stopped . . . because I think it knows you two are coming along for the inspection."

Uh . . . Poe? Would you kindly flap down there and get an explanation for this? Elf Guy likes to play with the more dangerous stuff, and I don't think the kids are ready for that.

The group freezes as Poe gives a louder caw and spreads his wings, casting them in shadow as he takes off. He circles a few times before gliding in and landing before them, the big bird much larger than any ordinary raven—or *any* bird back home, for that matter. He's able to look the inspector directly in the eye as he caws again at Elf Guy, who looks quite unhappy.

"I know! They're kids! But they're also the most experienced delvers in town! The guild hasn't sent anyone to back me up for this inspection, yet it requires I not inspect solo after what your big spider did!"

"Tiny," corrects Rhonda and Freddie at the same time. Elf Guy just points both hands at the kids in exasperation.

"See?! They even know your Spider Scion's name!" The kids exchange awkward looks while Poe continues to eye Elf Guy. He's got a point, but . . . I don't want the kids trying to get around the traps over in the crypt complex. Yvonne hasn't left for the day yet, though. Maybe she can help.

I mull it over a few more seconds before giving Poe the clear, and he caws at the kids once more. Elf Guy deflates a bit and nods.

"Yeah, I know. They're my responsibility. I don't want them getting hurt any more than you do." Poe nods and takes off to land back on his nest, letting him observe the yard and beyond. The kids look to Elf Guy with wonder.

"You can understand the dungeon?!" exclaims Rhonda, looking like she's about to nerd out. The elf holds up his hand to stop her.

"Not in so many words. It doesn't have a Voice yet, so it has to speak with actions. It takes a bit of practice, and you have to get to know the dungeon a bit before you can interpret with any kind of accuracy," he explains before pulling out his little talky thing . . . which appears to be a magical rock?

"Have entered Fourdock Dungeon via the main gate at the mansion. Dungeon recognized me, but seemed to want to know why I am not solo this time. I explained the situation, and it seems to accept. Proceeding with inspection."

I let them check out the yard and the manor while I have Teemo get Yvonne's attention. She's probably a bit bored, what with not being able to sleep anymore, so she follows him without much prompting. I wonder if liches delve so deeply into forbidden magic just because it's something to do?

Back with the party, they take a quick look around the yard. The kids point out the new cave to the underground area, which he notes into his rock. I don't send anything too mean at them, mostly because I don't have much mean in and around the house anyway. I have some plans for some stuff for later, but I need to get my mana production back up and running with that sweet, sweet delver income. At least they do their part on that front by fighting encounters and gathering herbs and stuff.

The inspector spots the snake den and stares for a few moments before pulling out the rock. "Snake Scion Ascending; looks like it'll finish any minute now. Conduit title, so it was the one to drain Neverrest's core. Consider this preliminary confirmation Neverrest is subsumed."

Inside the house, it's mostly the same: fight things, loot things. I let them fight a nice swarm in the attic with lightning enhancement, and it goes pretty smoothly for them. Rhonda knows how to protect from lightning pretty well, and Elf Guy is some serious DPS. Freddie keeps the swarm's attention, and their spiders give what support they can.

I still get a lot of satisfaction from Elf Guy visibly waiting to get the boss XP before opening the chest.

Out the window and onto the roof, they get a few more encounters and poke around the belfry. Rhonda spots some seeds she seems to like before they head for the basement.

"Basement stairs contain multiple rotten and squeaky floorboards. Rat warren has overtaken basement entirely. There appears to be an entrance to the cave system, but there is too much rat activity to make it a viable pathway. Possible location of Secret Sanctum, but too much activity to confirm."

They head up and out, and the inspector starts paying more attention, as this is new territory for him. "Fresh cave system from the earthquake reported from the expansion. Many various mining nodes observed. Minor gremlin activity drawn by the nodes. Dungeon appears to maintain focus on eliminating invaders quickly and efficiently. Oozes abundant in caves, as well as more bat activity. Dungeon appears to be still working on fully utilizing the tunnels. Likely was distracted by encroachment of Neverrest."

He chuckles and pockets his rock. "I wish I had been here for the fight. If Fourdock hadn't launched that surprise attack, it would have been in big trouble. I wonder if Neverrest actually knew most of the adventurers were gone that day."

"It couldn't, though . . . right?" asks Freddie, suddenly worried that the Boneyard had been more informed than anyone had thought. The elf just shrugs.

"It's hard to say, but Neverrest was pretty determined to cause trouble. It had wasps, too, to send on expeditions. They wouldn't be the best at gathering intel, but even they can tell when a guildhall is empty." The kids don't seem to like that, and Freddie speaks up again.

"Do you think Fourdock keeps tabs on that kind of thing, too?"

"Probably. That Raven Scion is a Marshal, so he's been managing a lot of expeditions." He chuckles at the kids. "I wouldn't worry, though. This dungeon doesn't strike me as the type to actually spy on anyone. Besides, birds aren't the best at that kind of thing. Better than wasps, but they still don't pay attention to the right things." *You're telling me, Elf Guy.* I feel like half the things the bird expeditions want to tell me about are various shiny things they spotted, even when I'm pretty sure they're almost all just shards of glass.

Rhonda points down the tunnel they're traveling in. "We should be coming up on the spider lair soon. You . . . can handle a widow, right?" The inspector nods and pulls out the rock again.

"Approaching spider lair. Guides warn of widows. It will probably be spawning aranea soon, too. The rat warren was maxed out and spawning ratlings, so I doubt this one will be far behind. Widow spotted. Engaging."

The kids' eyes widen, and they turn to face the threat. Freddie and Fiona keep it distracted and slowed with webbing, giving Rhonda a chance to freeze a few of its legs to the ground. A Shadow Blade from the elf, and soon, they're raking in the XP, and I'm raking in the mana. Definitely going to need to get tougher delvers in to beat up more of the widows.

They only take a peek inside the lair before moving on, as there are a few more widows wandering around while they decide which tunnel they want to patrol. Further down the tunnel, Freddie points out the public war room.

"Public war room confirmed. Even appears to be furnished via ratling craftsmanship. Table is rough but stable. Chairs similar. Large map of the surrounding area and dungeon on top." He takes a few seconds to look over the thing. "Secret Sanctum not included. Likely other details missing as well."

From the entrance comes the voice of my new resident, who seems slightly amused by the party. "Is this an inspection or a field trip?" she jokes with a smile, seeming to understand why Teemo led her here. The kids are a little embarrassed, but the inspector is all business.

"An inspection, good resident. I take it you're to help with the more dangerous areas of the inspection?" he asks in a formal tone, and my birb nods.

"Yes. The crypt complex has a multitude of dangerous traps from Neverrest. The dungeon seems to intend to let them wear off, but it does take time."

The inspector nods. Once he notices Teemo, his official demeanor falters a bit. "Ah . . . and the Rat Scion. Still no Voice, but it's smart enough to communicate at least somewhat." He turns his focus back to Yvonne. "Would you be willing to give information on the various scions?"

Yvonne glances at Teemo, who nods before climbing up to rest on her shoulder, officially joining her to chauffeur the group. She returns her focus to the elf and the kids, and nods. "Yes. It seems the dungeon isn't against sharing that information."

She doesn't continue. I don't know if it's because she wants them to ask specific questions, or if she's distracted by Fluffles finishing his Ascension. She definitely looks up that way, at least. Elf Guy follows her gaze before his eyes widen in realization.

"I suppose I'll start with asking about the Snake Scion, then."

Chapter 37

Wingnoodle! Yes, Fluffles's Ascension has brought with it a pair of feathery wings, officially making him a coatl. He's gotten a bit bigger, too. He was around six feet long before, but now, he's pushing ten. It'll be a tighter fit for him in some of the snake tunnels now, especially with those wings, but he should still be able to get around with ease.

His MP bar also looks different . . . in that it's not there anymore. He seems a little curious about that, too, as he levitates a couple nearby rocks. I can feel the tiniest trickle of my mana being used when he does. He uses my mana to cast stuff now? That has probably made him my most dangerous scion by far. If he has my full pool of mana to draw on, the snek could probably levitate things all day without breaking a sweat. I wouldn't want him to waste my mana like that, though.

He seems to come to the same conclusion, and I tell him to head down to the public war room to introduce himself. In the meantime, Yvonne answers Elf Guy's question as best she can.

"Fluffles is, as you know, the Snake Scion. He's a magic user; mostly force, I think. I'm no mage. He and Teemo here both tend to wander the dungeon and tend to various tasks, though Teemo is usually blazing new trails."

She smiles at the Rat Scion on her shoulder, and even gives him some little pets before continuing. "Teemo is the Rat Scion and Scout. He's always exploring the dungeon and creating shortcuts for the denizens, and even the residents. He, Fluffles, and Tiny were all involved in the raid on Neverrest. He tried to save me when the Skeleton Scion threw a Lifedrinking sword at me. If not for the enchantment, he would have succeeded in that, too."

"So you're actually undead?" asks Freddie, looking confused. "I've heard rumors, but nobody actually believes them." Yvonne sighs and nods.

"I am. The dungeon was able to help me return. The Raven gave me the choice of returning or going to my final reward, and I chose to stay."

Nobody really has a reply for that, which I find kinda interesting. I would have thought Freddie would want to grill Yvonne about what the afterlife was like or about this Raven or something, but no. I guess the Crystal Shield Church doesn't really deal with ferrying souls? Either way, that seems to have answered his question so thoroughly that it just leaves a bit of an awkward silence behind. You can't just follow up someone telling about how they died and came back with asking how their day was.

Thankfully, Fluffles shows up not long after, and Elf Guy's professional demeanor gets things rolling again.

"Snake Scion has Ascended to be a coatl. Has Conduit title, so at the very least, Fourdock has subsumed *a* dungeon. Scion is named Fluffles, but despite the unassuming name, the scion should not be engaged in combat. If it was able to reach any dungeon's core, let alone Neverrest's, it was a strong scion even before Ascending."

Fluffles likes the praise, and coils into a very satisfied position as Elf Guy makes his voice notes or reports to someone, or however the rock actually works. The kids just look at my wingnoodle with definite looks of awe, which only make Fluffles happier.

All right, you snekbirb, that's enough basking in adoration. Jello's been running around as quickly as she can to try to keep the tunnels clear of invaders. She could use your help down there. He nods to the nothing that is me, then nods at Yvonne and Teemo as well before flapping his wings and gliding down the tunnels. I think he's looking forward to actually putting his new abilities to the test.

They all walk through the tunnels, and Yvonne gives what basic information she can about the other scions, which gives me an idea for something to do once I get delvers back and making me mana. Elf Guy just continues speaking notes into the rock and asking questions, most of which I have Teemo nod to.

The only real thing I flat-out refuse to give him info on is my core location and the other secret rooms. That's for residents only. I don't think Elf Guy would do anything nefarious with the info, but I don't know every single person in the Office of Dungeon Affairs. Even in a fantasy world, bureaucracy will get corrupted. I dunno what a normal delver would be able to do with my core, but I'm in no hurry to find out.

He stops trying to wheedle that kind of info out of Yvonne—between encounters with slimes—once they reach the crypt complex, and he starts taking notes on the surroundings again as Yvonne leads them around the various deadly traps.

"Confirm that Neverrest had numerous potent and deadly traps in its catacombs. Also confirm they all appear to be wearing off. This corroborates the resident's claim Fourdock has no interest in those traps and has set these to expire. Recommend catacombs be off-limits for approximately a month, and recommend scheduling the next inspection for that time."

They get close to the enclave, and Elf Guy and the kids all seem surprised to see the ratlings standing guard at the doorway.

"Ratling Enclave encountered. Appears advancement will be finishing shortly." He looks to Yvonne to see if she has anything to add, which she does.

"Aranya said she wishes to do some ritual with them later, once she awakens. She tried to explain it to me, but I'm not sure what it actually entails. I only understood that it should finish the advancement of the ratlings and make them a true enclave." The inspector nods at that and speaks to the rock again.

"Enclave will likely finish advancement tonight; much more quickly than any other enclave I'm personally aware of. Likely due to guidance of Resident Aranya. Recommend delvers stay away from enclave unless specifically invited. There are guards posted, and though they have made no advances toward us, I doubt they would be so passive if we actually wanted to enter. Looks like ratlings will be ratkin dwellers."

You what? Everyone else seems to think that explains everything, but I don't!

Thankfully, I have a library not far from here, and a bunch of bees to deliver a message! I'll just spend a little mana and write—why can't I write? I did it before! Maybe if I make it a quest?

I try to focus harder on the little scrap of paper in the library, but all I feel is a weird equivalent to a headache as it feels like something else talks to me? It's just a concept in my mind, a quick bit of information, but I'm pretty sure I didn't put it there.

Dungeons may only communicate via their Voice.

What was that?!
And what's a Voice?

Chapter 38

After a bit of totally-not-panicking, I try to figure out what's happened. I can still do some stuff with signs, mostly formal informational things, but I can feel a bit of lag between when I decide what I want to write, and it actually being written.

I . . . I think I just got patched? And maybe have a moderator assigned to my signs now? That's concerning. I still need to ask about the dwellers the inspector mentioned, but how do I do that now?

Elf Guy has mentioned a Voice a couple times, but he hasn't elaborated on what it is.

I check my core, wondering if it might be an option there, but it's not. That's just where my various expansion options are, and a few more detailed numbers on things.

I grumble to myself and make a mental note to try to figure it out later. For now, I really should keep paying attention to the inspection. I almost want to pull a few undead to toss at Elf Guy and the kids, but I don't want to go opening that can of worms. Or that crypt of corpses, as the case may be.

"Encounters significantly diminished in the catacombs. No sign of undead. Neverrest would have certainly assaulted us by now, and Fourdock should have access to undead if it's subsumed the boneyard."

Yvonne speaks up. "The dungeon does have the undead spawners. They're located in a crypt on the surface, which is sealed. There are the two Undead Scions, though. Thing, the crawling hand, and Grim, the Grounds Reaper."

The whole party all look a bit surprised by that, and the elf speaks up first. "Can you take me to see them, then? Undead Scions tend to make the guild anxious." Freddie nods at that, looking unhappy at that development. I have Teemo nod, and so Yvonne nods as well.

"Thing should be in the enchanting lab not far from here. I believe the dungeon intends to use it to enchant things, just as it uses the Ant Scion for alchemy.

Come." She has to lead them around even more traps, as the enchanting lab was one of Neverrest's most important rooms. I'm just looking forward to the traps wearing off so I can look over the shoulders of whatever enchanters come delving.

Elf Guy and the kids definitely seem a bit more tense now, which I can't really blame them for. Undead Scions kinda imply an intent to use more undead, which not many would like to see happen. I do actually have a plan to use more undead, but that will come later.

I give Thing a heads-up to expect visitors, *so don't get into anything that would require too much focus.* I don't want him to blow himself and/or the lab up because the inspection interrupts him. Looks like he's doing a few minor testing enchantments along some lines I asked him to pursue, which is good. That project has been on the backburner for long enough.

Yvonne opens the door and steps inside, and Thing gives her a wave before scribbling a few notes and turning to a different page in his studies. Elf Guy and the kids cautiously peer inside, and Thing waves for them to either come in or go away. He's got his hand full and can only juggle so much.

They come in, cautiously looking around the room as Elf Guy takes notes. "Confirm Crawling Hand Scion. No Enchanter title yet, but looks to be well on its way. Enchanting lab is well furnished but seems low on books."

Yvonne nods at that. "Neverrest had extensive tomes on enchanting, which Fluffles took to the secret library. I assume on orders from the dungeon itself." Elf Guy sighs at that and resumes talking.

"Fourdock has sequestered Neverrest's notes on enchanting in its secret library. Fourdock has shown a pointed interest in information and controlling what information is made available. Can't confirm definitively but seems most likely Fourdock doesn't wish knowledge of Neverrest's more odious enchantments to be made public." He glances toward Yvonne and lowers the rock as he addresses her.

"Though if it does find something to more easily counter Lifedrinking, I hope you'll be able to convince it to share?" She stiffens a bit at the mention of that enchantment and simply gives a tight-beaked nod. Elf Guy may be a professional, but he's not the most diplomatic, I guess.

While that's been going on, Rhonda has been watching Thing's experimenting and taking notes, whereas Freddie seems to be watching Thing itself. Both seem fascinated in their own way. Rhonda is definitely watching Thing's technique, and I think is trying to copy his motions to remember with her own magic weaving.

Freddie is watching Thing's movement and seems to be growing more confused. "It's not acting anything like a crawling hand should," he finally says to himself, though Rhonda can obviously hear.

"What do you mean?"

He gestures at Thing as he hops off the table to grab a few reagents, tossing them from their various jars and bottles and onto the work surface. "Crawling hands are supposed to be grasping, crushing undead. They instinctively seek to restrain victims so stronger undead can get them. This one has no interest in us at all." Thing swats at Freddie's ankle to get him out of the way before hopping back up onto the table.

"Well . . . no interest except when we're in the way, I guess," he adds, having moved his foot. Rhonda thinks on that for a few moments.

"Well, the other scions don't act like normal denizens, so why should a crawling hand be different?"

"The other scions are fully and naturally alive," points out Freddie as he watches Thing measure out the various reagents on the scales. Rhonda watches as well, even pulling out her own little book and a charcoal stick to note the measurements before she speaks up to Elf Guy.

"Mr. Tarl? Do other Undead Scions act like normal undead?" Tarl, huh?

He nods.

"Every other Undead Scion I've personally seen has been part of a Belligerent dungeon, at best, and so combat oriented. With this hand, though . . . it would seem their behavior has more to do with what the dungeon wants of them, like with other scions." Yvonne can only chuckle as she gestures toward the door.

"If you think this one is odd, you should see Grim, the Skeleton Scion and Grounds Reaper."

Chapter 39

Tarl, Freddie, and Rhonda all seem a bit uncertain about going to meet the Skeleton Scion, probably all of them remembering the old Skeleton Scion that Neverrest had. The inspector stifles a sigh and nods to Yvonne.

"I take it it's up in the graveyard somewhere, then? I need to inspect there as well."

Freddie nods and speaks up too. "I also need to look around some. The church has long wanted to consecrate the cemetery so it can be used for proper burials again. There are catacombs under the church, but they were never intended to house the remains of all of Fourdock."

Yvonne glances toward Teemo, and I have him nod at that, too. I like the idea of the graveyard being used for proper graves again. It also reminds me of something I noticed about the undead I have, but that can be dealt with later. For now, Yvonne leads them up to the surface, exiting the mausoleum in the east.

"To the west is the sealed crypt with the undead spawners, and the former home of Neverrest's core is to the north. Grim is . . ." She looks around but can't spot him, so she looks to Teemo. He nods toward the west and squeaks.

"Grim appears to be doing some work beyond the sealed crypt."

"To the west, then. I'll take a look at the sealed mausoleum before examining the Skeleton Scion, then the former home of Neverrest's core, and that should more or less finish the inspection."

"I can get a good look around the graveyard while we do that, too," says Freddie, already looking around. I can't tell if he's relieved or disappointed at the lack of wandering undead.

It's not long before they all stand before the crypt, which I could have honestly sealed better. I never got the chance to have Tiny actually web the doors closed again, but thankfully, undead don't seem to know the difference between a door and a wall. I did put a warning on the double doors, though.

"Don't undead open inside?" reads Tarl, confused. Freddie and Rhonda look confused as well.

"That seems . . . fittingly cryptic to put on a crypt," says the orc with a shrug before the inspector walks toward the doors. He reaches for them when Rhonda gasps.

"Wait! You read one door, then the other!" She points, and Freddie's eyes widen as he sees it, the inspector blocking their view of one of the doors. Tarl takes a step back to reread the warning, and he nods.

"Don't open, undead inside. Fair enough. I do need to take at least a peek, though. Stay back, kids. They shouldn't notice me this close, but they might notice you." The kids don't look too happy about that, but they listen. He goes sneaky mode, and even I have to pay attention to keep track of him now.

He cracks open the doors and peers inside, seeing the wall-to-wall zombies and skeletons. He manages to not panic, at least, and quietly and quickly closes the doors before sneaking back a bit. Nearer to the kids, he pulls out the rock again.

"Zombie and skeleton spawners are located in the west mausoleum, which has a warning on the doors: 'Don't open, undead inside,' and it's not wrong. There's very little room to move in there, and the undead seem to be in torpor with no stimulus available. Highly recommend delvers stay well away. Moving on to the Skeleton Scion."

Grim is actually touching up some of the stonework around the mauso-leum. He's hardly a strong magic user, but he has time to spare, and he seems to be Earth elemental in his magic, which helps a lot with his duties. Tarl and the kids about crap their pants when they walk around the corner and see him, hand against the wall, hood up, and scythe in his other. I don't think they have a concept of the grim reaper here, but he's been an icon back home forever for a reason.

Grim just ignores them as he continues fixing cracks and chips in the masonry. It takes a few seconds before Tarl slowly brings out the rock.

"Encountered Skeleton Scion. It's . . . it's a groundskeeper. Currently, it is performing maintenance on the west mausoleum. It's an imposing figure in a black robe and a scythe, but it has shown zero interest in me and my guides. Recommend delvers ignore it as it goes about its business." Notes made, all of them quickly move on. Grim watches them go. *Yeah, I don't know either. Maybe they're just anxious to be done. The inspection's been going on for a while; they're prob-ably hungry.*

It doesn't take them long to get to the northern mausoleum, and it takes even less time for them to notice the damage from the tripped explosion trap. The inspector looks at the shards of false core before looking at the former resting place of Neverrest's true core.

"Confirm Fourdock has subsumed Neverrest. There appears to have been a false core made of glass, with the true core hidden in a crypt in the same mausoleum. Fourdock appears to have spent much of the mana gained from it on changing the wasps to bees and plague rats to packrats, as well as various scions. Guards at the cemetery gate are no longer needed.

"Manor appears optimized for new delvers. Bramble labyrinth suitable for all levels; prior notes on dangers seem to still apply. Tunnels are for low- to mid-level delvers; appears to be mostly strong spiders and various slimes, with occasional bats. Catacombs appear underutilized at this time. Will likely change as delver activity returns. Church of the Crystal Shield appears free to consecrate the graveyard and resume normal operations in that respect.

"Scions should generally be left alone. Most are prioritized toward support and upkeep rather than combat. Those who are combat focused are more interested in invaders and monstrous delvers from the Deeps. Doubtful the scions would slay groups who attack them, but it seems likely they would be dumped outside of the dungeon, bereft of all their gear.

"Still no designated Voice. Still no indication of location of core, nor of various secret rooms. Interestingly, it has several public rooms which likely have secret counterparts. Suggest attempting negotiations with the upcoming Ratkin Enclave to establish friendly relations. Delvers should stay well away from the enclave for now, until relations are made."

He considers for a few more seconds before he's seemingly satisfied and puts the stone away.

"Do you really think it'll let the church consecrate the grounds?" asks Freddie, and Tarl nods.

"I'd be surprised if it doesn't. Dungeons do see benefit to having a proper burial ground in their borders. The Royal Cemetery is actually a dungeon, in fact. Its only known denizens are small fey, as is its scion and Voice. It has no known income aside from the prayers and respects offered to those interred there. So I wouldn't be surprised at all if Fourdock decides to dip its toes in those waters. It seems to have a lot of plans, and it needs mana for them."

Chapter 40

From the moment she opened her eyes tonight, Aranya looked . . . excited? Nervous? Proud? Let's go with complicated, yeah. She ate her traditional breakfast of a couple webbed mice, and she definitely did a little prayer and stuff before tucking in to her meal. She went and cleaned herself up a bit, and now she's about to enter the Ratling Enclave.

The guards at the entrance give her respectful bows and allow her to pass, and she gives them each a smile and respectful nod before heading inside. The place has changed a lot over the last couple days. Their little farming area is coming along great. They've got a good half-dozen stacked racks of mushroom plots now. Nothing is making mushrooms yet, but the mycelium is growing rapidly through the dirt and detritus.

They've been making beds as well, in a very similar style as what I made for my residents. Much like the clothing, it's a bit rougher, but still seems to work just fine. They all piled together the first night, but they've actually been more or less pairing off with their beds since then. It seems like each bunk bed is a couple. They haven't done the nasty yet, but I get the feeling they're just waiting for the right time before bumping uglies.

The leader ratling is somehow older than the others. He's hardly hunched and withered, but his muzzle definitely has a bit of gray to the end of it. He also has . . . it's larger than a walking stick, but it's not exactly a staff, either. The end curls a bit, starting a little above his head level, and comes back down in a crook, ending at the height it started. In the center hangs a small orange gemstone, ground by hand into a rough sphere.

He smiles as he sees Aranya, and opens his arms wide. "Ah, Chosen Aranya! Sanctuary smile upon you!"

My kobold in white smiles back and embraces him. "Larx! Sanctuary smile upon you as well! Is everyone ready for the ceremony?" He smiles and nods before rapping the butt of his stick against the floor. The guards head inside, and I move Fluffles to guard their entrance. I don't think anything will actually interrupt, but if this goes how I think it will, I'm going to be having some extra responsibilities here very soon.

The ratlings gather around the back, and Aranya and Larx stand in front of the rear wall, which now has a simple orange circle drawn on it. The two can see Fluffles coiled in front of the doorway, facing outward for any potential threats. Larx looks to be fighting being awed, while Aranya smiles and gestures for the other ratlings to look. "The Sanctuary approves. It guards us as we prepare to commit ourselves, ensuring our safety for this ceremony."

There are murmurings as they look at Fluffles, and he adjusts his wings to get a bit more comfortable and totally not to just show off a bit. *Right, Fluffles?* Larx raps his staff against the floor again to get their attention before he speaks.

"The Sanctuary blessed us with this gift, this chance to be more than mere denizens. There are challenges and trials with this blessing, but also gifts. The gift of will. The gift of choice. The trials of sustenance. The trials of our mortality. The Sanctuary does not simply brush the trials aside, for it knows the trials bring strength. We, all of us, have changed, but we all remember our earlier times. We all remember bringing ore to the smelter, watching the intense heat transform the odd rocks into purified metals. We all remember the effort to shape that metal into useful form, and how much more useful it was than the odd rocks they came from.

"We are odd rocks no longer. We have been forged, purified, and shaped by hands more refined than the ones we used to have, and more than the ones we've been gifted with now. And we have been guided by one chosen by the Sanctuary," he says before stepping aside slightly, letting Aranya step forward.

She still looks a bit nervous to me, but she's putting on a pretty strong face. Public speaking is never the easiest. "I've been proud to help guide you. The Sanctuary gave you the same blessing kobolds received so very long ago. Our legends say we were much simpler before being blessed with our own will. It was terrifying to be given the blessing, but our Sanctuaries guided and helped us, and when they gave the blessing to others, we guided and helped them as well.

"It has been my great honor to serve the Sanctuary and guide you through the terror that is understanding. Would that I could give you direct missives from the Sanctuary's Voice, but it is quiet. But that does not mean it doesn't communicate." She opens her arms wide to indicate all around them.

"It leads by example! Defend yourselves, but do not needlessly kill. Do not be afraid to try something new. Be clever. Outsiders are not automatically bad. See the opportunities to help, and so to *be* helped in the future." She gives a small bow and steps aside, letting Larx retake the center stage. He raises his staff high before continuing.

"We all remember the glory of our Sanctuary's Heart, even as the memory of its location has faded. We remember the gentle and warm glow, the slow swirling of its depths, the mesmerizing presence it has. We give it thanks as we step forward, and will continue to give it thanks as we can, and follow its will as we can."

He raps his staff on the floor three times before raising it again, outward instead of upward. He slowly sweeps it over the little congregation as he continues. "We are ratlings no more. We are ratkin, and we dwell in our Sanctuary. It is our home, our Sanctuary, and we will do all we can to please it."

One last rapping of the staff on the floor, and the progress bars wink out. Just like he said: they're ratkin now, and are dwellers instead of denizens. I can't give them orders anymore, either. I technically could, up until the bars finished, but it was getting more and more expensive to do so. I hadn't told them to do anything since the bars started, but still.

Aranya is changed, too. Not physically, though. She's still a beautiful little red kobold in a white robe. But now she also has a title: *High Priestess*. She and the ratkin start to sing a little song, and I can feel my mana flow increase. I thought they might give me some mana, but that's pretty good. Their small congregation gives me the kind of mana generation I'd get from a fairly slow delver day, which is nothing to sneeze at, especially once I get delvers returning.

I tell Fluffles he can go back to wandering and helping Jello as the guards return to their posts. They watch him glide off with wonder before taking their position on either side of the door. I watch them all for a few more minutes, trying to collect my thoughts on my new dwellers.

I always worried Aranya might start a cult around me.

It's not a creepy cult, thankfully. Kinda embarrassing, but I at least seem to be providing a good enough example that they aren't trying to sacrifice anyone, but still . . .

What do I do now?

Chapter 41

Yvonne sits in the secret base, idly petting Teemo and reading a book from the library. Those two have had a special bond since the raid on Neverrest. They both still do what they need to do, but when their leisure time overlaps, they're together.

I think it's kinda cute, and it makes sense. Teemo and her have very complementary skillsets, and he even tried to save her life. It's not surprising they get along well. Yvonne very specifically didn't want to go join the ceremony with the ratkin, and I'm not really surprised about that, either. She definitely has her own religion to follow, and I doubt Aranya will get her to convert.

Which I think is why she's sighing and putting her book aside to look at me and at Teemo. "What do you think of all this, Teemo?" He just squeaks and noses her hand, wanting more pets. Pets are clearly more important than potential drama about a cult.

She chuckles and gives him a bit more of what he wants. "You don't care, hmm? What about you?" she asks my core, like I can actually answer her, and she huffs out a small laugh at herself.

"Still no Voice, of course. Well, Aranya always says to read your will in the scions." She smiles at Teemo, who wants his belly rubbed, and she can't help but indulge. She looks over to Queen in the alchemy lab, ants swarming over everything and not seeming much different. She looks over to Thing, obscured by the book he's perusing in the nook that is the secret enchanting lab. I need to get that more dug out soon, but I still have plenty of time before the public enchanting workshop will see any actual use.

"Do you not care what they're doing, perhaps?" she asks herself, thinking out loud. She's monologued to me before; I think just to have the comfort of having some thinking being know her thoughts. She doesn't really do it in front of Aranya, though. I guess she doesn't want someone interrupting her musings.

She smiles after a few moments and shakes her head. "No . . . I doubt anyone could have no opinion at all about being worshiped. I doubt you like it, though . . ." she voices her thoughts, continuing to chew on the situation. "You never seemed to have any inkling that you'd want it . . . so why not stop them?"

Teemo squeaks and looks her in the eyes before giving a little ratty shrug, and she works on interpreting that. "Uncertainty? Hmm . . . why *not* stop them . . ." she asks herself, actually considering the question instead of leaving it rhetorical. She sighs as she seems to come to an answer.

"I suppose why isn't the question, but how. If you tried to punish them, they'd just think they upset you," she says, trying to wrap her head around the idea of being a reluctant object of adoration. She chuckles and takes a light hearted tone of admonishment. "You really should have expected something like this when you gave them true intelligence, you know."

Yeah . . . I probably should have. I've never been much of a planner, though. I'm just pretty good at improvising. I have my goals and work toward them, and deal with problems that pop up, and try to head off ones I can think of. And then improvise to deal with what I didn't think of.

"I wonder who you'll make your Voice?" asks Yvonne, looking into the depths of my core even as she continues to idly pet Teemo's belly. "I wonder what they'll actually have to say?"

Yeah . . . me too. I've finally figured out how to get a Voice, but as for who . . . Well, I'm about as sure of who will get it as Yvonne is, which is to say I don't know. I'll need to figure it out soon, however. If the dwellers keep this rate of mana going for me, I'll be able to afford the upgrade for one of my scions soon. And if I'm going to be the center of a cult, I need to get some actual dogma set down sooner rather than later.

What should I actually tell them, though? Getting to the pearly gates wasn't exactly a surprise to me; I am a Christian. But it's not like I can quote the whole bible for them to write down. I can get the core points, but book and verse will always elude me.

But I don't think I was sent here to do that. Sure, I'm pretty sure an angel could easily descend and drop a bible in my metaphorical lap, but that didn't even happen to Moses. He got ten sentences. Sure, he got to talk with Him a lot, but only those were written in stone.

And I don't even remember all of those! I'm pretty sure the "No Idolatry" one is going to complicate matters the next time I die, but I don't know what to do about that. That's part of why I'm saving everything for a Voice. Even if I don't know what I'll even say!

"Be excellent to each other" might have worked for Bill and Ted, but it's not exactly informative. *Alright . . . calm down and think. Goals. Improvise.* My goal in this: don't screw up and accidentally make a cult like how most people think of a cult. So how?

Keep it simple, for starters. People will always try to complicate things, sneak in edge cases to try to ease their consciences. Ten commandments in stone, thousands of pages. Sure, it's history and all important to understanding the whys of a lot, but the ten are the explicit, stated things.

And even those can be condensed. I might not remember all of the commandments, but I remember the greatest commandment: To love. Love thy neighbor, thy parents, thy God, and all the other commandments will follow.

Seems like a good place to start. Love truly, and evil will have a hard time getting a foothold.

Chapter 42

Ah, the pitter-patter of delver feet. I used to think pitter-patter was a quiet sound, until I watched my sister's kids for an afternoon. Now, I know it's more like what a herd of elephants sounds like.

Whatever the volume, delvers are back! And they are trying to make up for lost time, seems like, which is fine by me. I need mana to designate someone as my Voice, and they're handing it over like it'll expire soon. They even tried to be extra cheeky and run a bunch of people through the maze at once, thinking Tiny couldn't get them all. He didn't *quite* get them all, but I think he's made his point about playing by the unofficial rules.

And "defeating" those delvers has me *very* close to what I need for my Voice, so I should probably sit down and actually have a think about who it will be. I'll start with the easy ones that I won't be doing that with.

None of my newbies will be my Voice. Honey, Grim, and Thing are all still getting used to the roles I've given them already. I don't need to complicate things for them even more and try to have them talking to people, too. Besides, they'd all have their hands full even if they'd spawned as experts in their fields, which they aren't.

It also won't be Jello. While she's friendly enough and seems to like the delvers, she's about as metaphorically sharp as the roomful of jello that she is. I think I want my Voice to be one of my smarter scions.

Coda is also out of the running. While he doesn't have too much work to do right now, especially since Poe took over the underground expeditions, too, I have some plans that will be eating up his time soon. One or more gardens is the least of what I hope to put him in charge of.

Definitely not Queen. She's sharp as a tack, but the only people who even know what she looks like are Aranya and Yvonne. While I do want to talk with them, I also want to have the option to talk to whatever delvers I need to.

Also not Fluffles. Some people like to min/max and pile all their bonuses on one thing, but I've never really liked putting all my eggs in one basket like that. Besides, he's still ironing the kinks out of being a Conduit.

Which leaves three: Teemo, Tiny, and Poe.

Poe's on the bottom of my list, mostly because the expeditions keep him busy. Aside from that, however, he'd probably be a good Voice. You don't Marshal the troops well if you aren't smart, after all. He's also in a good location to talk to people, and maybe even people well outside my borders. And he can fly, so it'll be easy to avoid or ignore anyone I don't want to deal with.

Teemo would be a good Voice just because he's basically everywhere. He's practically my Voice already, just with ratty miming instead of words, because he's the most convenient to send pretty much no matter where someone is. He's also sneaky, so he can ignore people I don't want to deal with. But his sneakiness also kinda plays against him being a Voice. Scouts aren't generally the most talkative, at least not publicly.

I like the idea of Tiny being my Voice just for the theme and how he works. Wanna talk to the dungeon? Step into my parlor, says the giant spider to the flies. I also feel like he's my smartest scion, which seems like a good idea to have for my Voice. The biggest problem is that he's . . . well, *big*. If he gets much bigger, he won't fit inside the house anymore; even some of the tunnels are a bit cramped for him already. Feels kinda weird for my Voice to not be able to get everywhere.

While I mull over the decision, I feel the cemetery gates open. Freddie walks in, looking mostly confident, and about a dozen people in robes come in after him. I guess he wasn't joking about the church wanting to consecrate the cemetery quickly. The robed people all look at least a little nervous, even the one with a little crystal scepter thing.

"You're certain the dungeon won't attack us, young brother?" he asks Freddie. The orc nods.

"We should be fine, Head Acolyte. I've been in this dungeon a lot, and Mr. Tarl said it probably won't have any problems with us consecrating the graveyard."

"But it has Undead Scions! Several!" I can practically feel Freddie's restraint as he doesn't roll his eyes.

"It does, but they don't act like undead. After the consecration ceremony, we might be able to find the groundskeeper, if you want? It looks intimidating, but it never made any hostile actions."

The head guy just suppresses a shudder at the very idea of getting close to Grim. "Perhaps some other time. The ceremony will likely leave us all drained, and I'd rather not face an undead that strong at anything other than my best."

Freddie just shrugs, and the group cautiously walks to the rough center of the graveyard. As they go, there are some long looks at a lot of the graves. I'm pretty sure I got everyone who's supposed to be in one into one, but hard to tell if they're all in the *right* ones. Still, the fresh-ish graves seem to make the priests or whatever their technical ranks are a bit confused.

Not long after they reach the center, Larx actually exits the mausoleum that leads to the crypt complex and makes a beeline for the group. Freddie points him out, and they all just kinda awkwardly stand around while the ratkin approaches. Elf Guy was saying people should leave the ratkin alone for now, but I guess he never expected them to be proactive.

Imagine that; stuff in my dungeon being a bit weird.

The older ratkin peers at Freddie before smiling like he's a grandkid. "Ah, you must be young Freddie!"

The orc is a bit taken aback at that, uncertain how to respond, but respond he does. "Uh . . . yes? That's me. How do you know me?"

Larx laughs. "Chosen Aranya has talked about you and your friend, Rhonda. The Sanctuary surely approves of you two and your growth!"

"Thanks?" Freddie replies awkwardly. I guess the boy never put any points into diplomacy . . . or hasn't had a chance to yet. Paladins don't exactly get a lot of skills, at least if we're on DnD rules.

"What are you and your friends up to, young Freddie?"

"Well . . . we're going to consecrate the graveyard. Mr. Tarl said the dungeon would probably not object, and the Church of the Crystal Shield has been running out of room for proper burials for years now."

Larx seems to absently take the tip of his tail in his hand, idly playing with it. Kinda like twiddling his thumbs as he looks around. "I do believe Mr. Tarl is correct, as none of the scions have made themselves known to interfere. May I watch?"

Freddie shrugs and looks to the Head Acolyte, who seems more impatient to get started than worried about any trade secrets getting out.

"You may, but please stand back and do not interfere. We take this very seriously." Larx simply smiles and steps back, taking a seat on the steps to one of the mausoleums, resting his staff across his lap as he watches.

"Oh, Crystal Shield! Light of Purity! Bulwark against the dark! Defense against the unspeakable! We beseech you to bestow your blessing upon these defiled places of rest! Let them be tormented no longer, and grant all who would spend their eternal rest here the eternal rest they have earned!" The head guy raises the scepter as he speaks loudly while the others bow their heads and murmur quiet prayers of their own. When he finishes, a little alert pops up for me.

Form Pact with Crystal Shield? Yes/No?

Hmm. I don't mind the shield helping keep those corpses in the ground, but I don't think I'm up for any pacts just yet. So . . . no, but thanks.

The head guy frowns when the alert vanishes, and raises his voice. "Place of darkness! Begone! Flee from the Light of the Crystal Shield and cower in your dark places! This will be a holy place of peace, not your home to desecrate those who have earned their rest!"

Resist Geas? Yes/No?

Definitely resist. This one actually costs a little mana, too. But I don't need this guy trying to muscle in on my home. The acolyte, however, doesn't seem to like that answer. He takes a deep breath, preparing to shout even louder, I'm sure, before Larx's voice cuts him off.

"Would you mind if I try?" he asks, giving the best kindly grandpa face I've seen in a while. Freddie looks a bit surprised, and the head guy looks pissed. He looks ready to give Larx an earful, but stops himself.

"Very well. It will give me time to prepare the censer and a few other holy reagents."

Larx smiles and steps forward, giving a wink only Freddie can see before he raises his staff and speaks. "Sanctuary, please hear my plea. Let these fallen keep the rest they have earned and be troubled not by the woes of this world ever again."

Consecrate Graveyard? Yes/No?

Huh . . . that doesn't cost me any mana.

I accept, and a faint wave of orange blooms from his staff, washing over the entire graveyard. It crashes against and around the mausoleums rather than through them, probably because there aren't any normal corpses in there? Either way, that gave me a *lot* of mana! And I can see it ticking up now as well, thanks to the Consecrated Graveyard. Larx smiles and rests the butt of his staff on the ground, looking pretty pleased with himself. Freddie looks impressed.

The head guy looks like he's gonna blow a gasket, though. "How dare you!"

Larx still wears that sweet grandpa look. "Dare? You gave me permission, my good priest," he points out, which only angers the guy further. He starts yelling and swearing and making a scene while the other priests slowly distance themselves from him for being so loud in a graveyard. Or maybe they notice Grim silently making his way over.

He walks up behind the screaming elf and raps the butt of his scythe on a rock, drawing his attention. The head guy simply sneers and raises his scepter. "Begone, creature of darkness!" He swings at my scion, scepter glowing with a soft blue flame. Grim casually blocks it with his scythe, and the blue flames bloom out, much like the orange wave with Larx.

Grim's robes aren't even ruffled from the display, and the flames die with nothing to fuel them. The acolyte's zeal is gone in a heartbeat, and he looks absolutely terrified as Grim leans closer. He raises a finger to his mouth and presses them to the lips he doesn't have, giving a quiet hiss before straightening and simply walking away.

Only Larx's voice and the sound of Grim's steps can be heard. "The scion is right. This is a cemetery. Show some manners and lower your voice, please."

Chapter 43

Freddie and the other Crystal Shield guys don't stick around long after that. The head guy looks pretty cowed, Freddie looks a bit confused, and the priests just look kinda embarrassed. I can't really blame them. The silence after Grim left was the kind that makes someone reevaluate the choices that led them to where they are, and nobody looks really proud of what they did.

Well, except for Larx.

Either way, that little kerfuffle tipped me over the threshold to designate my Voice! And . . . I think I'm going to offer it to Teemo first.

Hey, bud. So, uh . . . wanna be my Voice? Nah, I'm not exactly sure what it entails, aside from talking to people sometimes. Probably not very often, no. For the most part, I want to keep letting my actions speak for me, which is great for broader things, but there are more complex ideas I'd like to communicate.

. . . Yeah, and I need to tell the ratkin about the love stuff if they're determined to put me at the center of their cult. Yes, I would like you to keep doing your Scouting. I'm pretty sure you'll still be able to. I mean, look at Fluffles. He still can do what he did before he became a Conduit, so it'll probably be the same with being my Voice?

Heh, no, you won't need to greet everyone who shows up. You'll probably be talking a lot with Yvonne and Aranya, probably a bit with Freddie and Rhonda, some with Ragnar and Aelara, and probably with Elf Guy, too.

You're only saying yes because you want to see the look on his face when you talk to him, aren't you? Well, I guess it can be for multiple reasons. So, you want the job? Cool.

Teemo

The boss is an odd one. It's not like Teemo has been a scion in any other dungeons, but he was created with some expectations set in his little rat mind. Some expectations the dungeon met and exceeded with ease. Some expectations never seem to be on the dungeon's mind at all.

It's difficult to tell, sometimes, what's actually on its mind. It speaks clearly enough, but a lot of the concepts go way over Teemo's head, and even over Tiny's. The big spider takes a pretty stoic look on that fact, saying the dungeon's odd behavior has certainly been working well so far.

Teemo would like to argue that point, but he really can't. Especially not after their victory over the rival dungeon. He still feels a little bad about not being able to save the tall birdwoman, but even that seemed to work out well in the end. Besides, the Skeleton Scion cheated with that enchantment anyway.

But now, the dungeon has actually *asked* if he wants to be its Voice. Asked! Who does that?! A really weird dungeon, that's who. It even talked with him about it, at least as well as it can right now, instead of just dumping the responsibility on him.

Honestly, his first instinct was to just do as ordered, but he wasn't ordered. Then he was going to decline. But . . . the dungeon really *has* been doing amazing things with its nonsensical decisions. Maybe having a simple rat like Teemo as the Voice will also do amazing things? He doubts it, but he also doubted the maze would work.

Either way, those doubts are a bit moot at this point, as he's already accepted. All he has left to do is head to the ratnest so the bar can start filling. He just hopes it doesn't take him as long to Ascend as it took Fluffles.

Freddie

Freddie didn't expect the consecration to go like that. He thought it'd be a simple matter, things would go off without a hitch, and the church would be able to start transferring the interred to the cemetery.

He's pretty sure the last part will still happen, but Head Priest Torlon has been slowly talking to everyone individually about what happened. The gnome is usually very genial, but he's clearly unhappy with how it went. He first talked with the Head Acolyte, and then the attendant priests, and now he's waving for Freddie to come into his office.

Freddie hasn't actually ever been in there before. Even when he took his initiate vows, they were done in front of the entire church, so he can't help but look around as he enters the office. Shelves line the walls, filled with various books on various subjects. A chipped crystal shield hangs on the wall behind the desk, put there after Torlon retired from his days as an adventurer.

He smiles as he sees Freddie's eyes lingering on it. "I've been asked why not get a new one to hang up, but I think it's very fitting. The Crystal Shield does not require perfection. Life will leave its mark on everyone, and you can't be a proper protection if you pretend it doesn't. But please, have a seat, Freddie."

The young orc nods and takes a seat, waiting a moment for the Head Priest to climb up onto his own behind the desk. "Can you tell me what happened today, Freddie?"

He just looks a bit confused. "Didn't . . . didn't everyone else already tell you?"

The Priest smiles.

"They did, but I want your perspective. People can miss things or have their own perspective on the events. You know the dungeon best of all the ones who went today, so of course I want to hear your perspective on what happened."

Freddie still looks uncomfortable, but he can't really argue that logic. "Well . . . uh, we all got ready to go this morning. The others were nervous about going, and I did my best to reassure them that the dungeon's safe. Some were, uh . . . more reassured than others, but everyone had enough faith we'd all get through this safely.

"We walked through the gates to the cemetery, which felt a bit strange. I don't think anyone has walked through those gates since before I was born! At least none that weren't breaking laws. Um . . ." He pauses to collect his thoughts before continuing.

"We got to the center of the cemetery without seeing any undead, though we did see some fresh graves. I wouldn't be surprised if the dungeon did its best to try to put people back in their proper graves."

Torlon smiles at that. "Some of the priests said the same thing. They've seen graves that had been burst out of, and graves that were freshly filled, too. The dungeon is an odd one . . ."

Freddie smiles at the understatement, then continues. "Before we could get the ceremony started, one of the dwellers wandered out of one of the crypts. I guess it connects to some tunnels down there? He acted like a friendly grandpa and asked to watch, and the Head Acolyte agreed.

"He just sat on the steps to one of the mausoleums and watched. The Head Acolyte invoked the Crystal Shield and tried to consecrate the cemetery, but I guess it didn't take? Then he tried to exorcise the dungeon, I think? He was getting ready to prepare a full ritual when the ratkin spoke up and asked if he could try."

Freddie chuckles for a moment before trying to hide it. "Uh . . . I don't think the Head Acolyte was paying attention, and he just told him sure. And . . . he consecrated the cemetery. The Head Acolyte was uh . . . displeased. He started yelling and threatening and carrying on, which got the attention of the Skeleton Scion.

"The Head Acolyte tried to Turn Undead, but . . . it failed. Utterly. Like it had no power over the scion. Not that it resisted, but that it didn't even *need* to resist!" Freddie trails off at the memory before remembering he's in the Head Priest's office.

"Uh . . . and then we left. The dungeon didn't kick us out or anything, but we all kinda felt like we should go before we could do anything else like that . . ."

Torlon nods, his subtle smile never wavering. "Did the scion threaten the Head Acolyte?"

Freddie looks confused at that, then concentrates as he thinks. "No? It leaned forward and shushed him, but that was it?"

"Did the ratkin interfere with the rituals?"

Freddie shakes his head without even needing to examine his memories. "Nah, he just watched. Er . . . as far as I could tell, anyway. I could feel when he consecrated the area, but never felt anything from him when the other attempts failed." He thinks about the odd ratkin before remembering something.

"Oh! He knew who I was! He said the dungeon knows me. And Rhonda, too!"

Torlon simply nods at that as well before giving Freddie a crooked smile. "I'm not really surprised. You and your friend seem to spend much of your spare time there. We're all fortunate it's a friendly dungeon." His smile slips slightly at that before settling back into his usual friendly look.

"Well, if that's all you can think of, I believe we're done with this matter for now?" Freddie scrunches his face as he tries to remember anything else important, then nods.

"Yeah, that's all I can think of, sir." The gnome motions for him to lean forward, and Freddie does. He gives the younger a simple blessing before letting him leave. As the door closes, the friendly look collapses into one of exhaustion.

Torlon

"I knew I shouldn't have sent the Head Acolyte . . ." he grumbles to himself as he falls back into his chair. The acolyte means well, but his zeal can lead him to forcing awkward situations . . . like with the dungeon. He just *had* to invoke the Crystal Shield in the consecration rather than the simple generic purification rite. And then to attempt an exorcism on the dungeon itself! The Crystal Shield itself must have been protecting him for the dungeon not to simply destroy him on the spot!

Possibly even more worrying, though, is that Turn Undead had no effect on the scion at all. The way everyone described it, a simple breeze would have had more effect on the undead scion! And then it just shushes him like a librarian? He sighs and looks up to the hanging shield over his head.

"I miss how straightforward things were when I was an adventurer," he laments, enjoying the catharsis of wallowing for a few moments. Still, he can't just wallow while there's a potential problem to ward off.

He takes a moment to recite a prayer, strengthening his resolve to do what he knows he has to do. The Head Acolyte will need to be punished in some way, likely starting with no longer being the Head. And the rest . . . will depend on the dungeon.

He grabs his quill, ink, and some parchment, and gets to writing. If anyone can help him make amends with the dungeon, it'll be the Dungeoneer's Guild.

Chapter 44

Teemo's Ascending looks like it won't take *too* long? Just a couple days, I think. It doesn't give a time, but I can guess from the progress bar.

I wonder how much I can change before Teemo wakes up? I hadn't realized how much I was spending on spawning things when fighting Neverrest. Now that I have my delvers back but don't have that threat looming, my mana is starting to pile up quickly.

First thing, hmm . . . I need to get the tunnels into gear. There's that glowing moss in most places now, so I'm pretty sure I can actually get delvers down to adventure in there, too.

I upgrade the slime spawner a few times, and it actually starts spitting out little blobs occasionally instead of the bigger pools that are the oozes. Thankfully, still no little faces on them.

I figure they'll be good for general encounters, and they move a lot faster than the oozes do, too. With faster slimes, I think I can actually maintain some more mining nodes, so I start sprinkling them around through the tunnels instead of just being mostly near the surface.

I also upgrade the spider spawner, which actually maxes it out! That big ol' spider lair sure looks the part now. Good luck to anyone trying to find my secret base. The spider spawner also spits out . . . something kinda ugly.

It's an aranea, and it makes me think of a pug with too many limbs: ugly, but kind of in an endearing way. It also has little grabbers on the pedipalps, so it looks like it'll be able to manipulate things, too. It's about the size of a large dog, so it'll probably be able to do similar things as the ratlings.

It takes a few minutes to collect its bearings before skittering off, and I let it. I have things I need to do over in the crypt complex, and I actually need Coda's help, along with the ratlings.

I know what I want to do with my undead. While my manor is more for noobs, and the tunnels are being set up for more mid-level groups, I want the crypt complex to be for higher-level adventurers. But I also don't want my undead to just be marching across the grass to the mausoleum to get into the complex. So I'll need to dig.

And that's where Coda comes in. Well, kinda. He's not exactly going to be good at digging, but he has his sonar to make sure the ratlings dig where they need to and don't collapse anything.

They start off a bit awkwardly as he learns how to listen for the higher pitch of areas that are bearing loads, to be able to tell the ratlings where to dig, but I'm confident in him. It's a long way to burrow, but I'm not in any specific rush.

I doubt they'll finish the tunnel before Teemo's done Ascending. That's a lot of rock to get through.

Right, speaking of Coda's job, I really should upgrade the belfry and the garden there. I made it a garden a while ago, but it's about as much a garden as my little signs are libraries. The bats just drop seeds all over the place, either from eating or from the inevitable aftermath of eating, and delvers just pick up what catches their eye, with or without some free fertilizer.

I want to get a good underground garden running soon, too, but I figure I should make sure I know how a normal garden goes first. The upgrade costs a decent bit, but not really that much with how much mana I have coming these days. Planter boxes line the walls of the belfry now, and there are even some on the outside of the different windows and what have you.

Nothing else changes yet, but that's fine. The bats are still asleep at the moment. Coda was sleeping too, but I woke him to get him to at least have some preliminary sonar scans going. I let him go back to sleep and keep a bit of an eye on the ratlings. They're making pretty slow progress, so I doubt they'll be able to get into trouble before Coda can return and check with more sonar.

I decide to go see what my aranea is up to. Once I find it, I'm still not sure. It's managed to make itself a little hiding space above the front porch in the crawlspace there, and it has a plank of wood and a bit of charcoal. It stares at the board for a few minutes before crudely scrawling something on it, attaching a bit of silk, and dangling the thing down to be seen from the porch.

Kil fiv ratz

What?

Chapter 45

Rhonda

R atkin dwellers? Interesting." Old Staiven strokes his narrow beard as he finally gets some free time to ask his young apprentice how being an official guide in the dungeon went. A ratkin himself, he can't help but be a bit prideful that his kin are the first dwellers in the strange dungeon.

Rhonda nods vigorously, excited to be able to finally tell her master about the trip! Lucas, her spider, is less excited about the nodding, as it forces him to cling onto the large hat or be thrown off. He chitters at her once she stops, and she bashfully doffs her wide mage hat and sets it aside.

"But that's not even the best part! The dungeon has a scion it's training to be an Enchanter!" She starts digging through her pack to find her notebook as her master raises an eyebrow.

"An Enchanter? Already? Which scion is it? Maybe that coatl, or the bat?" Rhonda shakes her head, despite it being mostly obscured by her pack, and speaks. The words are muffled, but clear enough to Old Staiven. He might look old . . . and he is, really, but his ears still work just fine.

"It's a crawling hand! Freddie said it was acting weird for a hand, mostly ignoring us except for when we were in its way in the enchanting lab. Ah-ha!" She pulls herself from her pack, her notebook held high in triumph.

Old Staiven is glad he's had practice with apprentices, or else he would be grinning at the goblin for her excitement. Her growth has been remarkable. She's still a bit shy around people she doesn't know, but get her interested in something, and she's quite excitable. He just has to play the long-suffering master to help her temper that.

He speaks up as she starts searching through the notebook. "Ah, so you saw it at work? And it wasn't hostile? Crawling hands usually cause no end of mischief.

Why, one time, one managed to get into one of my bags of holding while on an adventure. I think I still have that bag around somewhere. I never did get the nerve to check what actually happened in there to produce that kind of noxious smoke . . ."

Rhonda shakes her head, still looking through her notes. "No, it mostly ignored us! Hehe, it slapped at Freddie's ankles when he was in the way at one point, but other than that, it was just working on something. I was hoping you could tell what it was . . . here!"

She smiles up at him and offers her notebook. The notes catch Old Staiven's eye immediately. He accepts the book and starts slowly looking through the notes. "Interesting . . . It looks like some kind of Spatial enchantment." He holds the book for her to see and points out the various reagents that were on the table at first.

"These, and a few other reagents and formulae, can be used to make a bag of holding and other demiplanar items and magics. I wish you could have gotten ahold of its actual writings. It changed its focus once you started watching. See these?"

He again points out the list of reagents she noted down. "These are usually used in various movement magics. These three, and a bit of honey or web, will get you a slowing spell. Those ones there, and some oil, will make a greasing spell." He squints his eyes at one of the noted ingredients.

"'Unknown yellow fluid'? You should know the difference between direwolf piss, frog bile, and lemonade, Rhonda," he admonishes her, a bit surprised at her failure. She shakes her head.

"It wasn't any of those! It had a simple cork, so I would have been able to smell if it was the bile or urine, and it didn't have the little floating pieces for lemonade. I was hoping you'd know what it was?"

Old Staiven strokes his beard again as he mentally goes over yellow fluids used in movement enchantments. "You didn't mention any glowing, so probably not fermented sunbeam. No bubbles, so not a sulphur elemental . . . Heh, you'd have been able to smell that anyway . . ."

"Oh, it did have a faint glow. Not much, but a little," she offers, trying to remember anything she didn't write down. In fact, she quickly takes the notebook back and puts that in before giving it back to her master.

"Only a slight glow? Could be distilled moonlight, but that's a pretty advanced reagent to get ahold of . . ." He looks out the window, just barely able to see the spire of the belfry for the strange dungeon. An even stranger idea starts worming its way through his mind.

"You said it's quite the peaceful dungeon?"

Rhonda slowly nods. "Yes? I mean, Freddie and I fight a bunch of things every time we go, but it's not actively trying to hurt us, I think. Mr. Tarl said it's 'cooperative,' but not a 'toy box.'"

Old Staiven smiles at his apprentice. "I think we should go visit together, then. It has either already figured out how to distill moonlight, or it has some component I haven't heard of. Either way, I think it will be enlightening for the both of us!"

Chapter 46

I really hope I can teach my aranea how to write better. Or rather, I really hope Honey can teach my aranea to write better. She sure seems like she's going to try, at least. I had her send a few bees over to read the sign, and what she saw clearly upset her. I did my best to calm her down and told the spiderpug to head to the library.

Not before someone managed to accept the quest, though. So yeah . . . the aranea are giving out quests. If this was an MMO, I'd say they're something like a daily quest. They're not very complex, but it does net me extra mana, and I assume it nets the delver extra experience.

While the first one makes its way to the library to learn how to write properly, the spider lair spits out another aranea, who immediately heads for the little crawlspace. I'm just glad it doesn't try writing another sign.

Actually . . .

Aw, can't bypass the ban on general talking with people through anything but Teemo. I wanted an Eat at Joe's sign. The attic aranea doesn't seem to think of any new quests by the time the delver returns, though it does toss down a sock woven from silk as a reward.

The delver looks pretty confused at the singular sock, and seems to wait for a second one, but it soon becomes obvious one is all he's going to get. He just shrugs, pockets the sock, and heads back to town. I'm not sure what his actual business was, but he seems satisfied.

Once he goes, though, the aranea slips out of the crawl space and out into the yard. I guess this one is more of a trapdoor spider than a ceiling spider because it digs a little hole and puts a simple camouflage cover over it. And then it goes and gets a stick with a bend in it, and another plank of wood. It plants the stick and scribbles on the plank before hanging its new sign and hiding in the little hole it made.

Git sum erb

I think Honey is going to be even busier than she was. And speaking of busy, I need to get busy with my undead stuff. I don't think I'm actually going to be able to get the new path from the mausoleum to the complex finished before Teemo finishes Ascending. Who would have thought digging through stone would be so difficult?

It's probably a good thing, though. I want to get my zombie scion at least a little settled in before the rest are unleashed. And he'll need some gear to do the job I need. I'm not sure where I managed to get some leather, but I know what I'm going to use it for.

I get my spiders working as I spend the mana on my new undead scion.

Uh . . . maybe?

The mana is spent, and he exits the mausoleum as quickly and as quietly as a zombie can be expected, but he's listed as *Undead(?)*. Yeah, with a question mark. I check on Thing and Grim, and they both have question marks now, too. I'm pretty sure they didn't have that before. I can't check on Yvonne at the moment; I think she and her party are off doing some kind of adventuring elsewhere, but they should be back in a day or two. They seemed to want to test out how far she can go from me, and how much time she can stay out, too.

But back to my zombie scion and his role. I want him to be my first actual Boss scion. I like the idea of being kind of a training dungeon, helping delvers prepare to go deal with murderous dungeons like Neverrest and whatnot. If I'm going to be helping delvers prepare for nastier stuff, they're going to need to actually *face* nastier stuff. But that also doesn't mean I'm going to just sic a super stronk ghoul or something on them. I have my own pride and creativity to consider, too.

So, with that in mind, my spiders and a ratling come to give my zombie scion his gear. Red padded gloves slip over his hands, and a roughly carved bit of wood goes into his mouth. He's understandably confused by this but seems to enjoy chewing on the mouthpiece. I don't try to stop him; I'm pretty sure most boxers like to play with their mouthguard when not in a fight.

Okay, Rocky. I don't have any montage music for you, but let's get them dukes up. A bit more . . . that looks good. I'm not sure you actually need to protect your head, but form is important for boxing. So is footwork, so no more just shambling around, got it?

The Dungeoneer's Guild, AKA: The Office of Dungeon Affairs

Telar enjoys her job as the accountant for this area of the country. Last couple months aside, it's a nice and boring job. Even with the advent of the new dungeon, it's been more interesting than hectic. Well, mostly. The issue with Neverrest had her worried, but the Fourdock Dungeon handled itself with aplomb. As long as it stays cooperative, her job shouldn't get much more difficult.

With the new developments, she absolutely hopes it stays cooperative. It has a Conduit now, it has dwellers, it will most likely have a Voice sometime soon. It's also going to keep doing weird things; she has no doubt about that. Cooperative dungeons are always a bit . . . eccentric. Some behave like toyboxes but still have strong denizens to enforce whatever rules they fancy. Some are almost belligerent, but their monsters and traps have pathetic strength.

With Fourdock being cooperative, it'll need to be inspected more often, whenever possible. Hullbreak Harbor still shows no interest in expansion, and with it being mostly open water, there are few adventurers who care to delve. It hardly needs a yearly inspection, just enough to make sure the status quo is maintained.

Even the Southwood doesn't need inspections often. It seems pretty satisfied with its current situation . . . or at least it had. Something in Tarl's report makes her suspect something is going on, but she doesn't know what. If it weren't for the dwellers and likely impending Voice from Fourdock, she'd have sent him back out to deliver the information it seems to want. But it'd be a poor exchange to give information that will be out of date before you even open your mouth, so he's taken the week off to do whatever he wants.

She's also taken the chance to research the cooperative dungeons that are known, as well as how to handle dwellers. It hasn't been as helpful as she would have hoped, with how different cooperative dungeons tend to work, but it does at least give her *something* to go on instead of pure guesswork.

Her tea and musings are interrupted by a changeling entering the guild. While some people find the shapeshifters to be disturbing in their normal forms, their strangeness doesn't even register to her anymore. Once you've accepted you're overseeing large swaths of land and/or sea that have opinions, you grow an appreciation for how relatable problems are for entities with legs.

He nods at her, and she sits up a bit straighter, getting the feeling this is not simply a social visit.

"Uh, hello. The dungeon is . . . kinda being weird," he says, uncertain how to actually talk about a dungeon. This is why they have inspectors. She just gives him a professional smile and motions at the chair on the other side of her desk.

"I take it you mean Fourdock Dungeon? I'd almost be more concerned if it's *not* being weird," she says with a small smile, which gets the delver to smile as well, before she continues. "But please, what is it doing now?"

"Well . . . I'm not an adventurer, so maybe it's normal? See, I wanted to try to get some pelts and whatnot. I'm a tanner and leatherworker. Anyway, I checked the notice board at the front there, and noticed a little rough wooden sign hanging down from the rafters. It wanted me to kill five rats," he explains, and Telar takes notes.

"So I go ahead and decide to do that and accept the quest. Like . . . an actual quest. Not a complicated one, but still a quest!" Telar simply nods like it's nothing out of the ordinary. It *is* unusual, but acting like it *is* tends to make non-adventurers a bit nervous.

"So . . . I killed and skinned the rats. Rats make nice slippers, actually. Then I returned to the porch. And this dropped down from the rafters." He reaches into his pocket and pulls out a simple silken sock. "Yeah . . . just the one."

Telar looks at it like the puzzle that it is before returning her focus to the changeling. "While that is unusual, it's not especially concerning. I'd need Inspector Tarl to confirm, but it sounds like the dungeon has likely maxed out its spider spawner and gotten access to aranea." She leans back as she explains.

"The max rank for any spawner gives access to semi-intelligent denizens. The ratlings the dungeon has, for example, are more interested in gathering and stockpiling than they are in fighting. I wouldn't be surprised if the aranea have decided the best way to help the dungeon is to give quests."

The leatherworker still looks a bit confused. "Doesn't that mess with the dungeon?"

Telar shakes her head.

"As far as we understand, dungeons gain even when their denizens are killed by delvers. This is partially why inspectors are instructed to defeat whatever encounters they come across, as well as gather whatever resources are available, too. This is also why Neverrest was locked down. If delvers don't go inside, they can't beat the denizens and so help the dungeon. But killing anything that leaves the dungeon will actively harm it, as it doesn't gain anything."

"That seems weird."

Telar just smiles. "That's dungeons."

Chapter 47

Office of Dungeon Affairs

The perplexed leatherworker soon leaves the guild, and Telar puts away her notes to give to Tarl once he's done with his short sabbatical. Her door opens again, and she's surprised to see a certain gnome walk in, though his orc companion is much less of a surprise.

"Head Priest Torlon! And Freddie! To what do I owe the pleasure?" she asks, before remembering. "Ah, right. The consecration. How did it go?"

The gnome and orc exchange a look before the Head Priest speaks. "Well . . . it's consecrated. But I worry we may have insulted the dungeon." Telar looks confused at that.

"Insulted? How?" She sighs and digs out a scroll. This sounds like it's going to be complicated.

Torlon looks to Freddie. "You were there, son. Go ahead."

"We went to do the consecration, and the Head—er . . . the acolyte in charge tried to consecrate it in the name of the Crystal Shield, but it didn't work. Then he tried to force it, and that didn't work either. Then one of the ratkin who lives there tried, and it worked. And the acolyte started making a scene because of it. Grim, the skeleton scion, came up and shushed him, and the acolyte attacked, but it had no effect. Uh . . . then we left," he explains, giving a quick summary of what happened.

Torlon speaks up next. "The former Head Acolyte has been punished and is no longer afforded even the small position of power he had. He's a good lad, but headstrong, not thinking things through. I told him to do a general consecration, but . . . I fear his zeal may have made things difficult for us all. Is there any way to make amends with the dungeon?"

Telar tries not to groan at the potential mess they've put on her desk. "Well, you're correct to demote the one who tried that. Consecrating an area in a dungeon in the name of any deity forms a pact, which could have been even more of a potential mess if the dungeon *had* accepted. And then trying to force the matter . . . I personally would suggest against him going back into that dungeon for a long time, possibly ever again."

She sighs. "And as for making amends . . . that's complicated. If it was a toybox, a simple gift and apology would usually be enough. If it was belligerent or murderous, there'd be no real point in trying to apologize. But Fourdock Dungeon is cooperative. That doesn't mean it's a pushover; that means it's willing to cooperate if it can get something."

She takes a few moments to gather her thoughts, glad she's been reading up on cooperative dungeons, and letting the two fidget in discomfort. She turns her eyes on Freddie.

"You said you left? Not that you were chased out?"

He nods. "Yeah, after Grim shushed him, the skeleton simply turned and left."

"And the ratkin wasn't hostile either?"

The young orc shakes his head, and Telar relaxes at least a little. "Well, I don't think it directly took insult, but a proper apology of some kind would be a good idea. Most cooperative dungeons respond well to an expenditure of effort and will."

Freddie gives her a confused look. "A what now?"

She chuckles and continues. "Effort and will. Dungeons allow delvers to fight and loot because they expend effort and will, which vitalizes the dungeon. The precise mechanics are still unknown, but in short: go delve. Maybe offer it a gift of some important or powerful item, too."

This time, it's the priest's turn to look confused. "That's it? Just go and be a delver?"

Telar considers for a moment before speaking again. "Well, follow the implied rules of the dungeon. If you just go in there and start wreaking havoc, I doubt it'll be pleased. But if you wander around, maybe accept and do a quest or two for it, fight some, gather some, just show it you are not there to try to tame it. And do so in your full capacity as a priest of the Crystal Shield. It needs to understand that the church as a whole doesn't want to rule it."

Torlon looks a bit conflicted. On the one hand, that would be no problem for him to do. He actually would very much enjoy at least a small chance to stretch his adventuring muscles again. But then again, that's the problem. One usually doesn't get to *enjoy* apologizing. "You're certain that would work?"

Telar laughs. "With Fourdock, I'm not certain of anything! But I do think that's your best bet if you want to try to smooth things over."

The priest can't help but chuckle at that. "I'll see what I can do, then. A gift, and do some delving . . ."

Rocky's training is . . . going? I don't know if it's going *well*, but he's doing a little better. All I've been able to have him do is shadowbox and get him to practice punches. I think I understand the difference between a hook and a cross. Maybe. A jab and uppercut are simple enough, at least in theory. I just have documentaries and movies to remember the theory, and it's up to Rocky to put it to practice.

At least he seems to like it. I'm just glad his form looks closer to what I'd imagine a beginner human would have, rather than the flailing of a rotting corpse. So I guess there really is progress being made, after all.

I'm also drawing up designs for various equipment and even a boxing ring for him. A heavy bag will probably be the simplest thing to make. I don't know where I actually got the leather from, but I'm happy to have it. Maybe a mix of sand and web would give it the right feel . . .

The gates opening at the cemetery side draw my attention away, and I see a new delver . . . and Freddie. From the looks of things, this is Freddie's boss. Looks like the two are having a bit of a disagreement about something.

"Are you sure? It seems kinda . . . important to just give away," says the young orc, and the gnome decked out in chainmail, a scepter, and crystal shield nods.

"And that's why I'm giving it away, Freddie. I'll miss it, of course, but it doesn't do much just hanging on the wall over my desk. Now, you said the skeleton scion is around here somewhere?"

Freddie still looks uncertain, but he nods. "Yeah, every time I've seen him, he's over here somewhere, doing groundskeeper . . . or grounds*reaper* things, I guess?" Huh. *Hey, Grim! You've got company! Go see what they want.* I'm pretty sure they're not here to start trouble, at least. The skeleton stands from the small flower patch where daffodils have been growing and makes his way toward the pair.

Freddie and the priest head for the center of the graveyard, and the priest looks around approvingly. "It *is* sanctified, as you said. And seems to be well cared for, too. It broke my heart how Neverrest treated this place. I'm glad it's in better hands."

The two mostly wander for a few minutes while Grim makes his way over, the living quietly appreciating the work and the rest of the dead. The priest notices Grim first, which isn't surprising. I'd wager this guy is even stronger than Elf Guy.

"Ah, the skeleton scion. You said his name is Grim, Freddie? He does cut an imposing figure, doesn't he?" Said imposing figure stops before the two and waits. It takes almost a minute for the two to realize Grim can't speak, so it's on them to start any conversation, one-sided as it may be. The priest clears his throat and takes a step forward.

"Greetings, Grim. And greetings dungeon, as well." Grim gives a nod, and the gnome continues. "I'd like to apologize on behalf of the Church of the Crystal Shield for the behavior of one of our acolytes. He was asked to do a general consecration, not one in the name of The Shield, and he certainly was not asked to attack your scion," he says, raising his voice like I can't hear him. That's fair, though. He probably hasn't talked to a lot of dungeons.

"So I've come to make amends, if amends can be made. I offer you my shield as part of the apology." He holds the shield toward Grim, who tilts his head in question. "Yes, I mean it. It is yours to do with as you will. It protected me through my days as an adventurer and is important to me, just as a peaceful relationship between you and the church is important to me, too."

Well, I'm glad he's taking it seriously. I probably would have just let him be, but he seems to genuinely want to try to make it up to me. It's a little awkward to take his *shield* from him, but I'm not getting any notices of pacts or whatever, so I tell Grim to go ahead and accept it.

The gnome smiles in relief once he does. "Thank you, dungeon. I've also been told a good way to try to make up for the mistake is to do some delving? Would you be amenable to that?" Heck yeah, I would be! I even know what I want him to do . . . or at least try to do.

Grim nods and points past the gates, where the belfry of the house can just be seen over the rooftops of the town, and Freddie speaks up. "Over there is where most of the fun stuff is, sir. This side is still a bit of a mess, from what I could tell with Mr. Tarl."

The gnome smiles and gives Grim a small bow. "Thank you, Grim. I'll go delve where it's appropriate to do so, then." The two turn to leave, and once they're out of sight, I tell Grim to take a shortcut. I know exactly where I want that shield.

By the time the two enter the typical delver gates, I have things prepared. Freddie is looking excited, and he directs his boss to the porch to see what information there is to see, then stops and stares at the little wooden sign dangling from the rafters.

The priest, though, simply smiles at the sign. "That's it? That doesn't seem like too difficult a task," he says, peering at the sign. They're much more legible already, thanks to Honey's help.

Loot Tiny's Chest.

Chapter 48

If I still had ears, I'd be grinning to both of them. Freddie's boss has no idea what he's getting into. At least his relaxed smile falters a bit when he turns and sees the look on Freddie's face.

"What's wrong?" he asks the younger before looking around. Nah, there are no traps around. Well, aside from that quest, heh.

"Uh . . . you remember the big spider that Yvonne's group rode to go fight Neverrest?" asks Freddie, unsure how to actually explain what this quest entails. The small big guy nods.

"Ah, yes, Miss Yvonne. I wish I could have given her more insight to her unique condition."

"Well, that big spider is Tiny."

He blinks. "That's not tiny at all."

Freddie smiles. "Yeah . . . I think the dungeon named him that just for that kind of reaction. Tiny is also the boss of the maze," he says, motioning for his boss to follow.

At the hedge maze, the scene is now a little different than usual. I had Fluffles clear the maze while the two were walking from the cemetery, and he's now coiled at the entrance. The usual runners are all standing around chattering, confused at the change.

Freddie sees everyone and raises his voice for them all to hear. "The dungeon has a quest in the maze for Head Priest Torlon. To loot Tiny's chest." The crowd goes silent for a moment before they start murmuring about the news. Torlon looks like he's starting to understand the magnitude of the quest now as Freddie turns to face him.

"See . . . there are a couple chests in there which people try to get, while Tiny tries to catch them before they can. Oh, and there are dire rats who try to steal your stuff sometimes, too. Anyway, Tiny has his lair in there, and some people have said there's a chest in there, too, but nobody's been able to get it yet. Even Mr. Tarl hasn't been able to get it," he adds.

To his credit, Torlon looks more intrigued than concerned. "And if Tiny catches you, he webs you, and you get carried out? I remember hearing something about you losing something to a spider Guardian?" He thinks for a few moments before speaking up again. "Are we allowed to fight Tiny?"

The young orc scrunches his face in uncertainty. "Uh . . . kinda? I think just about everyone has taken a swing at Tiny, but he doesn't seem to take it personally. He tends to take weapons away after webbing people who try to attack, though."

The gnome smiles and seems to start warming up; hopping in place, wiggling his fingers, just getting the blood pumping. "Maybe if I was more of a fighting class I'd try my luck, but I'm not. Did you know, Freddie, that I wasn't always an adherent to the Crystal Shield?"

"Uh . . . I mean, you had to be a kid at some point, right?" he replies, clearly having no clue where the priest is going with this.

The gnome laughs as he starts casting little sparkles over his head, I guess to get his mana pumping, too. "I used to be an illusionist before I took up the Shield. I was pretty good, too, even by gnome standards," he says with a bit of pride. "So I think I'll just have to try to stay out of the way of this Tiny!"

With that, he seems to be ready, turning to face Fluffles. "I'm ready to brave the dungeon's challenge." My noodle nods and slithers to the side to let him pass. Freddie looks like he wants to go, too, but he's a bright kid. He can see that his boss wants to do this on his own. And it'd probably be more difficult for him to use an illusion to keep them both hidden from Tiny.

Not that I expect Tiny will be fooled. He's got thin webbing all over the place, so he can feel where people are. Unsurprisingly, the gnome vanishes as he enters the maze, and the hunt is on. Tiny doesn't seem too concerned, however, and does his typical thing when actually pursuing someone. He starts webbing certain intersections closed, opening others, and patiently weaving his trap.

I notice one of the other chests being opened, and the potion and coins vanishing.

Looks like he's going to try to do a proper run of the maze. I think he's going for each chest, not just the big one at the end. More mana for me, so I'm not gonna complain.

At the second chest, I get the feeling he's realized his invisibility isn't working, as I can hear him tapping the lid of the chest after he's looted it. Probably trying to think of a way to beat my big leggy-boi.

The gnome reappears and crouches down. Looks like he's spotted the webbing. "Ah . . . that complicates things." He soon smiles, though, and starts creating . . . shoes? They sure look like shoes. Probably illusionary shoes? How's that going to help him against Tiny?

He jumps and lands with the shoes at the same time, and I understand how that'll mess up Tiny. They're not just illusions of sight but illusions of touch, too. He laughs before they all scatter, and he takes off in a different direction.

Tiny pauses as he feels the change, and I keep an eye on the real gnome. I don't tell Tiny anything, though. This is supposed to be a fair chase. My big guy seems to think for a few moments before changing his tactics as well. There are two other chests before the main one, and Tiny knows he wants them both. So he doesn't need to know where the gnome *is*, just where he's going to be.

So Tiny has to play the odds and hope he gets lucky. Or be patient. Tiny picks a chest and stakes it out while Torlon makes his way to the other. He's even subtle enough to wait for several shoes to get there before he opens it, and he doesn't leave until they all get there.

He appears to be planning while he waits for his illusions to converge. I'm not sure how, but he can definitely sense the other chest, and also the main one. He seems to look from one to the other before making up his mind. "Play by the rules . . ." he says to himself before he starts to pick his way toward the last of the simple chests.

He fleshes out his illusions as he makes for it, and I only know which is him because I've been paying attention with more senses than Tiny can bring to bear at a distance. They're some pretty serious illusions, too, as one trips over a big web snare and is hoisted up as the trap closes around it.

The gnome lets it dissipate with a little pop, and the others start moving in. Tiny seems to be enjoying himself, at least. He throws webs, he throws illusions into webs. He actually lassoes and hog-ties one of the illusions, too. Then I notice I've lost track of the real Torlon. There are only three illusions running around now; at least, I'm pretty sure they're all fake. It's getting difficult to tell.

It's not until I feel the chest being opened that I know where he is. I can't even *see* the chest being opened; it looks untouched still. No wonder he's proud of his illusions.

I give him a couple seconds to get away before telling Tiny only the last chest remains, and the big guy is surprised and impressed.

He takes one of Teemo's shortcuts to his lair while Torlon weaves his way through the maze to the goal. Tiny gets there first, of course, and has enough time to weave a tangle around the last chest. No more sneaking up to take it while his back is turned.

The priest/illusionist comes to a stop as he sees Tiny's lair, and Tiny guarding the last chest. The trees make a dense canopy overhead, giving some room for vertical movement but not much. Sunlight filters through, leaving it bright enough to still see clearly, but also producing shadowy areas to potentially hide. A thicket to the north is Tiny's actual spawner/lair thing, and the chest and spider are more or less in the center.

Torlon surveys the area before his eyes land on Tiny. "It'll take more than a simple Phantasm to distract you now, hmm?" he says with respect in his voice. Looks like he's been having a harder time than I thought he might be, which is great. His fight so far with Tiny has been making me some good mana, but I get the feeling that will be a drop in the bucket compared to whatever happens next.

He raises his hands, and a large shape starts to form overhead. "Simulacrum!" he shouts, and it suddenly comes into focus: a giant wasp. I'm . . . pretty sure it's an illusion? The leaves seem to be rustling from the beat of its wings, and dust and detritus from the ground is being blown around too, so it's difficult to tell. If it *is* fake, Torlon's pulled out all the stops to fool every sense he can think of.

"Blur!" he shouts, and his form becomes hazy, indistinct . . . and multiplies. There are four of him now, as well as the big wasp.

But Tiny hasn't been idle while Torlon prepared. A large web flies at the wasp as Tiny tries to deal with the major threat first. Its stinger sweeps through the air and slices the web in half, though it can only dodge part of it. The wings are entangled, forcing the angry thing to land with a puff of dust. Its feet even leave marks on the ground as it charges Tiny, and the two grapple.

The blurry Torlons, meanwhile, all take wide routes to the webbed chest and start slowly working through to it. I'm pretty sure all he has to cut through is some knife or something, but I still don't know which is the actual Torlon.

Tiny and the wasp tumble and wrestle, trying to web or sting their foe into submission. My spider knows to keep the two ends of the wasp from getting too close to him, but focusing on defense like that makes it difficult to get any offense going properly. And he's against the clock, as well as the wasp. It doesn't need to even hurt him; it just needs to keep him busy long enough for Torlon to get the chest.

Looks like Tiny has a plan for that, however. As they wrestle and roll around, he manages to slowly steer them toward the other half of the large web. He manages to land the wasp on its back, sticking it to the ground for just long enough to get his spinnerets into gear. Just as he gets it restrained enough to no longer be a problem, the wasp vanishes . . . as do the other illusions.

The initial webbing was never cut in half. Tiny stands over a pile of restraining web, and the large one he threw. Over at the chest, a single Torlon stands, breathing heavily and leaning on the freed chest.

"I hope . . . this counts . . . as a win . . ." he huffs, wiping sweat from his brow. It sure counts in my book. Tiny agrees and walks forward. Torlon stiffens as he approaches, but the big guy just waves a leg at the chest, and the gnome gives a tired smile.

"Whew . . . heh. That took everything I had. Well, let's see what's in here." He smiles and hefts the large lid up, coins spilling as the seal is broken. Once he gets it fully open, he stares at what lies atop the pile of coins and gems: his battered shield.

Reaching over, Tiny plucks it from the pile and brings it to his mouth, giving it a solid bite and a new chip before offering it to the stunned priest. He accepts it, his hands tracing each ding and nick, each scratch and chip, memories clearly filling his head. A tear falls, and he smiles at Tiny.

"Thank you."

Chapter 49

Teemo's done Ascending!

He's not even crawled out of the rat's nest before I'm nudging him with what I want him to say first. *Come on, say it! Please?*

My rat Voice gives a sigh.

"Captain Teemo on duty. But I'm not a captain . . . I think?" I'm pretty sure he brings up his status to look at while I'm silently celebrating at the top of my not-lungs. I calm down by the time he's done looking, and he looks a bit confused.

Honestly, I kinda am, too, but I'm not concerned. Fluffles became a coatl, but Teemo is still just a rat. Not a dire rat or a ratling or some crazy spirit rat or something. Just a rat. Who can talk. *How do you feel, Teemo?*

"Faster? And I can hear you more clearly."

Oh? What did I sound like before?

"You . . . didn't really *sound* at all. Just feelings and flashes of intent."

Ooohh, like an empathic bond. That's kinda how I hear you guys, too. Anyhow, do you have any questions for me before we get to work?

He manages to look a bit bashful. "Yeah. Uh . . . why me? I know you were considering Poe and Tiny, but why me?"

Well, there are a couple things. One is the cult. I had a feeling my Voice would be kinda influenced by who I chose, instead of just regurgitating what I say. Poe would be a bit too . . . regimented. He likes things ordered and planned. Tiny would probably give me an air of mystery and wisdom, but after the cult really got started, I started thinking that'd be a bad idea. So I wanted you, Teemo, to keep me grounded.

The second thing is that you're the best one to get around to actually talk to people. With your shortcuts and size, you can basically get from *anywhere to* anywhere *in less time than it'd take Tiny to even get out of his maze.*

And you'll be a bit of a test for delvers who want to talk to me. If they can't give you the respect you deserve as my Voice just because they think you're a normal rat, then I don't have anything to say to them except goodbye.

Teemo takes a few minutes trying to process that. I felt his uncertainty before he Ascended, so I'm not really surprised he needs a bit of time to come to terms with everything.

"What should I call you?" he asks suddenly, and I regard him curiously. *What do you mean?*

"Everyone has a different name for you. Tiny calls you the Weaver, Poe calls you Lord, Fluffles calls you Den Master, Jello just calls you the Voice . . . which is kinda ironic, come to think of it. Grim calls you Master. Queen and Honey both call you Emperor."

Huh. What do you call me?

"Boss," he says with certainty, and I take a moment to think. What should I be called? Most of the scions just have a title for me, not a name. I could give him my name, or even an internet alias or something, but that feels . . . weird. But what else should I be called? I was never any good with names.

Maybe a title, then? Yeah, because I was totally a noble before getting hit with a truck.

But there were things I earned. I got my degree in engineering, for one. That feels weird too, though; being a dungeon called Engineer.

Hmm . . . that does give me an idea.

It's a pretty fitting one, too, as I think about it. I've played a lot of tabletop RPGs, DnD, and such, and even ran a bunch of games. That's probably why I run my dungeon like I do, or at least partially. Death traps are boring—to run and to play—so I never tried to do that. And the whole, you know . . . real-people-dying thing.

I focus back on Teemo, and his eyes are a bit crossed. *You okay?*

He shakes himself before replying.

"Yeah, sorry, Boss. You think . . . weird. I can hear it all, and know what it all means, but it doesn't make a whole lot of sense. The meaning of a lot of those words feels like a whole book!"

I chuckle at that. *Sorry. Hopefully, you can learn to ignore me when I'm just thinking to myself, or I can learn to not think in your ears, heh.*

Anyway, I have a name. You can call me the DM.

"Thedeim?"

What? The DM.

"That's what I said, Boss. Er, Thedeim."

Huh. How'd you get that? You know the meaning of what words I use, right?

Teemo shifts a bit on his little ratty feet. "Yeah, but the meaning is way too long to call you. The word you used sounds like Thedeim."

Weird. Phonetic? Oh man, I knew we weren't actually speaking English! Is it some kind of translation magic or something?

"I . . . maybe? I've only ever been in this dungeon."

Right, right, sorry. You don't magically have the answers any better than I do. Though speaking of magically having the answers, I think the first official thing I need you to do, my Voice, is to go talk to Larx and Aranya. I'm still uncomfortable with the cult, but I get the feeling they won't just stop if I ask them to. Aranya is a High Priestess now! And Larx sanctified the cemetery! It kinda rings hollow to tell them I don't have any power or anything.

Teemo nods at that and gets moving to gather them up to talk. Thankfully, the only difficult part is in making sure it's only Larx and Aranya. They both wanted to have him address all the ratkin, which neither of us really wanted to. So Teemo put his tiny foot down before the two could go try to gather everyone.

"No! Now, are you two gonna listen to what Thedeim has to say or not?" he asks with a glare, and the two slowly deflate before they both realize what he said. He doesn't let them get a word in yet, though.

"Yes, the Boss's name is Thedeim. You can call him that, or Boss, or Sanctuary . . . just don't call him late for dinner? What?" He looks toward my core despite being over in the ratkin enclave before shaking himself and continuing.

"Anyway, he only really has one piece of advice for how to live. Love." Larx and Aranya both look confused at this, but at least they seem to have learned to be quiet while my Voice is talking.

"And not lust. He's not a sex sanctuary. He's a love sanctuary, so don't go organizing big orgies or something to try to make him happy. Just . . . love. Genuinely care for others without needing anything back."

Aranya looks overjoyed, and Larx smiles like he's been given some great nugget of wisdom. When Teemo doesn't continue, Larx speaks up first.

"A wise and caring Sanctuary . . . Thedeim."

Aranya looks about ready to explode and starts talking a mile a minute before Teemo gets her to quiet down long enough to get a word in edgewise.

"Settle down! The Boss knows you want to talk, Aranya, but we've got stuff to do." When she looks like he just ate her puppy, he hastily adds, "But we can talk in the morning, before you go to sleep, okay?"

The red kobold perks up significantly at that, and I mentally smile at the three before directing my attention elsewhere. Teemo's not kidding about me having stuff to do. I got a very nice pile of mana from the priest's battle with Tiny, and even more once he looted the chest.

It's enough for me to at least finish the first part of what I want for the crypt complex. The ratlings haven't broken through to the crypt just yet, but it should be close. I've also been upgrading the zombie and skeleton spawners, and they're both ready for me to choose their specialization.

I take a closer look at my options, and notice ones I didn't before: fungal zombies and green skeletons. At first, I wanted to ignore the fungal zombies, but I actually think they'll be safe. The plague rats that Neverrest had never actually started a plague; they just could infect delvers with stuff with a bite. So I don't think I'll be accidentally shrooming the city to destruction. I'm pretty sure they'll just have chances to drop mushrooms when beaten, which is kinda cool.

The green skeletons are a bit more vague. I don't think they're just gonna be a recolor of a normal skeleton. Maybe they'll be kinda mossy?

Whatever they are, they're more intriguing than the other skeleton options, so I go ahead and upgrade the spawners. The zombies don't change much, except for growing a little mushroom on the top of their heads. It's almost cute. The skeletons actually do start developing moss, so yay for guessing!

Now, all I need to do is wait for the ratlings to break through, and they can start populating the crypt complex.

Chapter 50

Teemo's off making more shortcuts and catching up with the other scions. He's understandably confused when he meets Rocky.

"Uh . . . Boss? What's with the zombie scion?" I chuckle to myself. *He's a boxer! Which is a kind of martial artist who specializes in punches. The gloves are to help them not kill each other when they fight. I want him to be my first actual fighting scion. I named him Rocky because I expect he's going to be knocked down and get back up a lot.*

Teemo just gives the zombie a weird look as it chews on its wooden mouthguard. "Well . . . he calls you Coach."

Hah, that's great. Is he happy with what I've been having him do?

My Voice nods. "Yeah, he seems to enjoy it. He seems a bit more on the ball than I'd expect a zombie to be. I mean, he's about on the same mental level as Jello, but zombies and slimes aren't really known for thinking, Boss."

Glad he's enjoying it. Maybe it's my weird thinking that's making them have to adjust? Who knows.

Teemo continues on his way, and Rocky continues to practice his punches and footwork. He's still pretty awkward, but I'm not disappointed. He still hasn't gotten a title for being a boxer yet, so I can hardly expect him to be in top form.

The other scions all seem to react similarly to Teemo being my Voice. They chat, and I can only get impressions of what they're saying, though Teemo can translate. They all want to know if they're doing well, and I assure them they are. I ask if they like their roles, and they all do. Coda is especially happy to be working in the mines, too. He was worried I had forgotten or abandoned him, so he's glad to be able to contribute. He's also apparently started calling me the Foreman, which is kinda cool.

Eventually, morning rolls around, and Aranya returns to her bed near the core. I ask Teemo to go hang out with her like promised. She starts off laying on the worshipfulness pretty thick, but Teemo's pretty quick to shut that down. She's my High Priestess; she doesn't need to bow and scrape. Not that I want anyone else to, but if I'm supposed to be in charge, I get to decide how my direct underlings act toward me.

She asks about the mysteries of creation, of my grand plans for the world, that sort of thing. Teemo's a bit too happy to burst her bubble about that, but I *did* ask him to help keep me grounded. He tells her I don't know any mysteries of creation, which I kinda do, but only in laws of physics that may or may not still apply. He tells her I don't have any grand plans, which I don't. The closest thing I have to a plan is that I want to get the tunnels and crypt complex in better shape, then probably expand downward again. There are a lot of connecting tunnels, so there shouldn't be another earthquake . . . I hope.

She asks about me, and I'm honestly not sure what to tell her. She asks why I saved her, which is at least easier to answer. She was in trouble, so I helped. She asks about the delvers and why I treat them like I do, which leads to a technical discussion about mana income, some basics of economics and psychology, and her recollections of the legends of her people. Teemo is looking a bit overwhelmed by some of it, and when Aranya interrupts herself with a big yawn, I tell Teemo to go ahead and tell her to sleep. We'll have plenty of time to talk about stuff.

I'm glad Teemo and the other scions don't seem to need to actually sleep . . . nor do my denizens, which is convenient. Sure, they sometimes do anyway, but that's more about them not having anything to do rather than an actual need.

While I let my attention wander, I feel a familiar pair of feet at my manor gate.

Hey Teemo. Elf Guy's here. The rat perks up at that, and he grins. *Now, be nice, Teemo. Or . . . at least don't be mean.* I like him, but that mostly means I'm comfortable ribbing him some, heh. Looks like he's not talking into a rock, either. Maybe he's here on a normal delve?

While I muse, Teemo moves. I even get an idea and tell the rafters aranea to prepare a special quest for Tarl. He looks almost relaxed yet eager as he approaches the porch, though he looks a bit confused at the rough wooden sign hanging near the bulletin board. His confusion only peaks when he hears a voice.

"Well, well, well . . . if it isn't the only delver I've ever attacked. Hello, Elf Guy," says Teemo, hidden under the boards of the porch. Tarl has his dagger out in a flash, looking around. Looks like Teemo has gotten better at hiding because it doesn't seem like Tarl knows where he is.

"Who's there?! Are you one of the ratkin?" he demands, his eyes darting around.

Probably should dial it back a little, Teemo. I get the feeling he's had some bad experiences with dungeons surprising him. My Rat Scion actually giggles before speaking again.

"Settle down, Elf Guy. I only took one of your HP, anyway. A small price to pay to remember to make sure the encounter is over before looting, right?" Tarl looks even more confused before he puts together who's talking. His sharp look quickly falls flat. He keeps looking around, but there's a lot less urgency to it now.

"Ah . . . the Rat Scion. I probably shouldn't be surprised you're the Voice." With a laugh, Teemo hops up on the porch railing, letting the elf get a good look at him. "Probably the most practical choice, really," continues the delver, peering at my rat. "I doubt there's anywhere in the dungeon you can't quickly get to. And you'd get people to drop their guard . . . or at least get fools to drop their guard." He straightens himself and sheaths his dagger.

"I'm here as an ordinary delver, dungeon," he starts, only for Teemo to interrupt.

"Thedeim."

"What?"

"That's the Boss's name. Thedeim."

Tarl's eyes widen at that. "It's already chosen a name for itself?"

"Himself, and yeah."

The elven delver absently reaches into his pocket before remembering he doesn't have his little note rock. He shakes his head to clear it. "Right, normal delver. On vacation, not on a quest . . ." he says almost to himself, then focuses on Teemo again. "Does the dun—er, *Thedeim* have anything he wishes to say?"

Teemo simply smiles and nods at the rough wooden sign. "He thinks you might like that quest."

Fight Rocky.

"Who's Rocky?"

Teemo laughs again. "Go to the central mausoleum in the graveyard. He'll meet you there."

With that, my Voice vanishes down a shortcut, leaving Tarl to try to decide what to do. I'm pretty sure he'll go do it. I haven't done anything to actually harm him before. Tiny has beaten him in the maze, but that's about it. With a sigh, he nods, though he doesn't immediately head for the graveyard. Instead, he heads around back to gather a few herbs, and once he notices the garden in the belfry has been upgraded, he enjoys himself through the house and the boss fight to get to the roof to look at what's up there, too.

He gathers a few clippings, but he doesn't seem interested in getting a full plant for himself. I imagine he's probably traveling most of the time, so he can't exactly keep his house plants watered. I wonder if he makes potions, or maybe even poisons.

Either way, he's taking his time and enjoying a delve, and I'm enjoying the mana. I can throw my strongest stuff at him in small numbers and keep him busy enough to have fun but not in any real danger of being overwhelmed. I feel like I'm a thrill park, but you stab the attractions instead of riding them around whipping corners and massive drops.

I'm not worried about him taking his time, though. It gives Rocky the opportunity to get into position and practice his ducking and weaving some more. Eventually, however, Tarl walks into the mausoleum, and Rocky spots him. My zombie stops chewing on his mouthguard and instead slots it between his sharp, rotten teeth like he's supposed to. He hits his gloves together and does a few jabs to declare his intentions while Tarl just looks confused.

"A zombie scion? What did you . . . you actually want me to fight it?" Teemo's not there, but Tarl is smart; he can figure it out. After a few moments, he shrugs and draws his blade. "Alright. Let's see what weirdness you've come up with this time."

He approaches slowly, and Rocky keeps his attention on him. He's got his dukes up as proper as I can tell, but this'll be the first real test of not only how well boxing theory translates into boxing practice, but also how well Rocky can actually work in this role.

Tarl is wary. He doesn't know what kind of fighting style Rocky is using, and he's been in enough fights to know a new style can really throw you for a loop. He tries a simple slash, which Rocky jukes to the side to avoid and counters with a decent body blow.

Tarl takes the shot with a grunt and backs off, but Rocky quickly moves forward. *Atta boy, Rocky! Float like a butterfly, sting like a bee!* Of course, Tarl is way more agile than my boxer, so he gets away, but it takes a bit more effort than he seems to have expected.

"How's a *zombie* move like that?!" he grumbles before moving back in. The two exchange blows, and I can see the flaws in Rocky's defense, though I'm confident it'll work well enough with practice. He can handle slices on his arms as he protects his body, and his counters are nice and quick. It's almost like the boxing stance is a time-tested way to fight.

Tarl backs up again, sporting a few bruises now, and Rocky has some decent cuts and stabs. "Did you actually make a zombie monk? Well, he's good in melee, but how does he handle ranged? Windblade!" Rocky ducks to the side and weaves to the other to avoid a second attack. Then he grunts with an uppercut, and a line of embers trails behind his gloved fist, blocking the third Windblade.

"With Fire affinity?"

Uh, yeah, I'm with Tarl here. Where'd you get Fire affinity, Rocky? No, you're not in trouble, I'm just surprised. Maybe I can start thinking a bit more *Street Fighter* than "Eye of the Tiger."

"Shadow Blade!"

Rocky hunkers down, protecting himself as best he can, but I think all three of us knew who was going to be winning this fight from the start. *Ya done good, Rock. That's just round one. Take a breather, and we'll work on how the fight went once you respawn.*

Tarl is looking pretty pleased with himself. I wonder how much XP he got from that?

"Your first Boss scion? I'd have never expected something like this . . . which I probably should have expected from you. I'll be done with my vacation next week, and then it'll be time for another inspection, I think. The guild still needs to make official contact with your dwellers, too."

He heads for the cemetery exit, and even nods at Grim as he spots him, then pauses before leaving. "Keep surprising me, Thedeim. I had a good feeling about you from the start."

Chapter 51

Tarl's dramatic exit is a bit ruined when he comes back to the manor to turn in the quest. I've been trying to convince the aranea that socks should come in twos, but the idea of giving two items for completing one quest is utterly anathema to them. I'm not too upset, though. I find it kinda adorable that they have a primitive sense of fairness.

The spider lair has spawned a few more, and while a couple have taken up places in the tunnels, it seems like the new ones are focusing more on delivering stuff from the warehouse. My ratlings still aren't great at smithing, but knives and little shields have joined the potential quest rewards. I've even seen a few rough gems get handed out.

I've also discovered where the leather came from. It's from my ratkin. It seems like making leather is a lot simpler here than back home. Here, you basically just skin a thing and get thing leather. On Earth, tanning is a lengthy and disgusting process, so I'm not exactly going to be crying about how easy leather is to get.

As for how *I* got it, since my ratkin dwellers are their own thing? They've set up a little . . . I guess offering area? It's not far from their enclave, and they just place part of whatever they make or hunt or gather there, then my aranea pick up whatever they like, though I think *like* is a bit strong. I watched what they decided to take and what they decided to leave in exchange, and it seems almost more like osmosis than any actual barter system. High-concentration gets taken to a low-concentration area until they're roughly equal.

Which works for me. I think the ratkin will figure out how it works eventually and probably try to tailor their offerings to what it looks like my warehouse needs. I even had Teemo tell them it's not required but it is appreciated.

I've also realized something else: I haven't looked at my traps in a while. Like a *while*. I think the last time I even thought about traps, I didn't even take up the entire house. I have a lot more options in there now.

There are the expected pit traps, spike traps, rockfalls, even quicksand, none of which are really interesting to me. There're also things which are more mechanical than what I used to have access to; things like poison gas, darts, blades, trapdoors, and the like. Then there are, of course, the magical traps that Thing has been working on. He finally got a breakthrough with the Spatial magics from examining the bag of holding, so he's been experimenting a lot to see what he can come up with.

I've asked him and Queen both to try to figure out something for sleep traps. Alchemical or magical would be fine, or even both; I think it could be an interesting thing to keep delvers on their toes with. Instant-death things are boring, but that doesn't mean other dungeons won't try to spring them, so I need something to emulate that. I think sleep will do well for it.

I've also been getting an idea while looking at the various traps. I wonder if I could do a *Ninja Warrior* thing, or emulate one of those embarrassing gauntlet shows that always have annoying voice-overs on TV. Could be another good non-combat thing for people to do.

I tell Coda the basic plan for something like that and point out what I think will be a good area to dig to set something like that up. It'll take a while, but Coda and the ratlings are both getting a lot better at digging.

They need a new digging goal now that they've broken through to the mausoleum. The undead flood out at first, fungal zombies and green skeletons sweeping through the crypt complex, but the place is big enough that they soon thin out enough to not be a death trap. A few aranea even set up in the tunnels and the graveyard to hand out quests to go beat them up, too.

As I sketch plans in the secret library, I feel familiar and unfamiliar feet at the graveyard gate. I see Rhonda with Lucas riding her hat, and for a moment, I think Larx is with her. Only for a moment, though. While Larx almost seems to be playing at being old, this guy is *definitely* old. His robes are thick, with pockets everywhere, and he leans heavily on his staff. Something about the way he moves, however, makes me think of a certain king earthbender. I hope he's not here to start anything. He's with Rhonda, though, so it's probably fine.

His eyes look over the cemetery, just taking everything in as he speaks up. "So, this is what's become of Neverrest?"

Rhonda thinks for a moment, then gives a slow nod. She's been learning to not move her head around too quickly. Lucas doesn't like having to suddenly hang on for dear life. "Kinda, Master. Fourdock Dungeon subsumed it and is in charge now. The church has even been bringing bodies to be buried properly!" I get the feeling Freddie's happiness at them getting proper interment has rubbed off a bit on his friend.

What'd they say the name of her master was? Old . . . something? I know she and Freddie have mentioned him several times, but I don't remember what his name actually is.

Whatever his name, he seems satisfied with looking around the graveyard and smirks as he spots the mausoleum with the sign on it.

"Don't Open, Undead Inside. Direct and to the point. Now then, Rhonda. Where did you say this hand was?"

She points toward the mausoleum that leads to the complex. "That leads to a lot of tunnels, and he's in there somewhere. Or at least his workshop is. That's also where the nasty traps are."

The old ratkin nods and waves that off. "That's fine. If the dungeon wants to be rid of those traps, I'll be more than happy to clear them out as we go. Maybe by getting some goodwill from it, it'll be more willing to talk about that reagent you saw." I can see his eyes twinkle as he mentions the reagent, but I don't know what he's talking about.

Thing, have you been making unobtanium without telling me? Well, either way, you're going to be having guests soon, looks like.

Teemo, would you come meet these two in the complex? The ratkin seems pretty confident he can handle the magical traps, but I'd like you there to make sure they don't get in over their heads.

The wizened ratkin takes his time walking and seems to enjoy the peace of the graveyard. "It's nice to see it like this again. I had actually seen it before Neverrest took it over, you know." I can believe it. He looks old enough to have had a pet dinosaur as a kid. Huh . . . I wonder if dinosaurs were a thing in this world. Maybe they're even *still* a thing in this world.

"Now, Rhonda. I don't want you getting near the magical traps, but I *do* want you to pay attention while I work. You may be more Ice aligned than Metamagic like myself, but you can still learn to spot the weaknesses in a spell. I'll be picking those apart to let the spell collapse in on itself. If you don't know what you're doing, trying that can set it off, or even focus all that energy on yourself. So I expect you to take careful notes!"

"Yes, master!" she replies with a gleam in her own eye. She grips the straps for her pack a bit tighter, and I'm sure she has a bunch of magical stuff in there, as well as her little notebook and charcoal stick. The two get into the complex without any issue, and Teemo gets to them well before they get to any of the traps.

"Hello, Rhonda. Who's your friend? No, not you, Lucas. I know who you are."

"Eep!" eeps Rhonda when Teemo speaks, and she looks around in surprise. Her master gives a wary eye as well, but neither can see Teemo. After a few moments, the young goblin speaks.

"U-Um . . . this is my master? Old Staiven?" Staiven! Right!

Teemo steps out of the shortcut and stands in the tunnel for the two to see.

"Ah, so you're her teacher. Thedeim says you're doing a good job with her." Rhonda fights a blush while she also fights confusion at the talking rat, and I think she's losing both battles. Her teacher, however, looks at Teemo calculatingly.

"The Voice? The dungeon is called Thedeim, then." He takes a few moments more to think before giving a smirk. "Tell Thedeim he's doing a good job with the cemetery." Heh, I think this guy is going to be tough to impress.

Teemo returns the smirk before nodding behind himself. "The Boss says you're here to get rid of the traps and talk with Thing? You're sure you can handle them? Neverrest had a lot of nasty stuff enchanted down here."

Old Staiven nods with the confidence of someone who is a master of their craft. "If they were fresh and actively upkept, I might have some problems, but I can see the fraying of the spellcraft from here. If they weren't so dangerous, I'd have Rhonda practice on a couple."

Rhonda looks nervous at that idea, but her master ignores her as he continues. "Thedeim is fine with me dispelling them?"

Teemo nods. "He is, if it can be done safely. He doesn't like aggressive traps like these."

With that, Old Staiven gets to work. Rhonda takes notes as he talks about spellcraft and rune design and all kinds of technical things. I take notes in the secret library, and even copy Rhonda's notes, too. Thing's going to have a field day with this stuff. The first couple, he takes his time with, making sure Rhonda understands what he's doing, and he even has her try to explain how to unravel one before he does so himself.

He corrects her a few times when she works through it, but he does soon collapse it like she suggested. It makes a loud snap instead of the quiet *whump* when he does it himself, but she is still a novice.

After that, however, he starts unraveling them much faster. If he took his time to explain with each of them, they'd be here all day. Watching him work, I doubt Neverrest could have done much to stop him strolling around however he pleased down here, aside from burying him in undead. I'm just glad for the mana and for the place getting cleared out. If I can give him whatever reagent he's after, I'll probably do it. The complex is basically ready for business now that he's cleared the traps.

Teemo leads them to the enchanting lab, and Thing is there, patiently waiting. Old Staiven's eyes immediately settle on the disembodied hand before he lets them wander the room.

"That's quite the impressive enchanting lab. Especially that lens array." He looks ready to get lost in exploring the shop of a fellow magic user when Rhonda gently tugs on his robe to get him focused. "Ah, yes. Business before pleasure.

My young apprentice here noticed an odd reagent the last time she was here. A yellow liquid."

Yellow liquid? I peer through the various cupboards as Thing taps a finger in thought. I'm seeing a lot of yellow liquids, and while I technically know what they all are, I have no more idea what they all do than I'd know what a shelf of chemicals in a more traditional lab do, despite being able to read the labels.

Thing waves himself to try to get him to give more details, and Teemo speaks up. "What kind of yellow liquid? There are a lot in here."

The enchanter holds out his hand, and Rhonda places her notebook into it. "Let me see . . . Ah, yes. Judging by the other reagents, it has properties pertaining to movement?" he says, looking to Thing and Teemo to see if they can confirm. Thing thinks for a few more seconds before snapping, seeming to know what it is. He hops off the counter to get it.

Oh, you've been keeping some Bottled Lightning in here? I probably should have figured it'd be something that could be useful in enchanting instead of just something to give my stuff Lightning affinity.

Thing levitates it to the table before hopping up himself. He immediately has the ratkin's full attention. "What is *that?*" he asks like a kid who's seen a candybar for the first time. As my Voice, it's on Teemo to respond.

"The Boss calls it Bottled Lightning."

"How do you make it?" comes the immediate response. "I've never seen anything quite like it before."

"Queen, the Ant Scion and Alchemist, makes it."

"Can I meet her?"

Teemo grimaces and shakes his head. "No. Her domain is the secret alchemy lab."

Staiven still stares at the small bottle. "I'd almost pledge myself as a resident just to get to talk to her . . . but that wouldn't be reasonable," he says as he tears his eyes from the vial with visible effort. *Hmm.*

Hey, Thing, Queen. Do you two think it'd be a bad idea to let him have a small sample? I don't think it will work the same on delvers as it does on us, but you two are the experts.

Unfortunately, neither of them appears to have any actual advice to give.

Well, I'm pretty sure it's something that can only be made in a dungeon, possibly even only *by* a dungeon, via scions and such. It wasn't exactly a complicated recipe or used anything especially rare to make. Pretty sure I made the first bit in a literal hole in the dirt with a couple ants just chewing and spitting.

Alright, Thing. Prepare a little sample vial for him. I really do want to thank him for clearing out those magical traps.

Teemo speaks up as Thing gets to working on what I asked. "Thedeim says you can have a small sample as a thanks for clearing the traps. He's not sure what it'll do to you guys, but you look like you know what you're doing."

Elsewhere

A small purple light forms atop a mat of mycelia. Something primal tells the fungus to protect the tiny shard. Soon, wide-capped mushrooms block it from sight, and spores get produced in more quantity.

Usually, the fungus would be happy to let spores travel, or even get lucky and kill a small insect well away from the main biomass . . . but now it's different. Working that slowly could endanger the purple source of light. It can't have that.

Chapter 52

Yvonne's back from her questing with her friends, and she looks glad to be able to relax for a bit. Teemo, in contrast, is pacing in one of the shortcuts, mumbling to himself. I think it's equal parts adorable and touching.

After all, it's pretty awkward to just say "Hey, sorry you died. I tried my best." Well, when not talking to a gravestone, at least. I am starting to get a bit concerned about him, though. I guess survivor's guilt is a thing, even when both parties are technically alive.

Hey, Teemo. Settle down, man.

My Voice squeaks in surprise. "Boss! I'm sorry. It's just . . . what do I say to her?"

Well, you can always start with hello. I don't think he appreciates my advice.

"And then what?!" he snaps at me before remembering I'm technically his creator. He sighs deeply and deflates a bit. "Sorry, Boss. It's just . . . what do I do? What if she doesn't like me, now I can talk?"

Why wouldn't she like you? Seems like every moment she's not actively doing something while here, she's relaxing with a book and petting you.

"But she didn't know I could *think!* I think? What if she blames me now that I can actually talk to her? What if she doesn't want to pet me anymore?"

Teemo, she doesn't blame you. If anything, she appreciates how hard you tried to save her. As for petting you . . . Well, just ask her to. I don't think she had any problems petting you before you could talk. Just don't make it weird, heh.

"How do I do that?" he asks with genuine concern. All I can do is mentally shrug. *I dunno how to do that. I've never really been petted. Humans are more built to give the pets rather than receive them.*

Teemo looks confused. "What's . . . ?"

What?

"What's built to give pets but not get them?"

Oh, humans?

"Yeah, that. That doesn't come through. It's like . . . I dunno what it's like, but I get no meaning at all from it."

Huh. That's weird. I'd have expected it to have almost a crippling amount of meaning behind it.

I mentally shake my head. While interesting, humans—or lack thereof—isn't the point of the conversation. *The point is: go talk to her, Teemo. Not an order, just advice. She's not going to be upset with you.*

He still looks uncertain, but he knows he can't just dodge her forever. Well, he probably *could*, but he shouldn't . . . and he doesn't want to, either.

He starts heading for the secret base, which is where she's headed, and I go ahead and focus my attention elsewhere. I feel like he'd be embarrassed if I was deliberately listening in while they talk.

Instead, I watch my various delvers doing their delving. The house and maze are always relaxing to watch for me. The newbies and crafters are . . . well, I get the feeling most dungeons don't really cater to them. Most of them really are terrible at fighting. I'm hardly an expert, but even I can notice when they unbalance themselves with a swing or put themselves in awkward positions to defend.

But the ones who gather show their skill there, which is interesting to watch. Gently handling herbs to get them gathered without messing up whatever properties they need, chopping at the trees to quickly and efficiently get enough wood to cart out of the maze, or the intricate measuring and mixing in the public lab for making potions. I still pay attention to the people who make stuff in there, but Queen actually has ants in there watching, and she'll ping me if she sees something she'd like me to write down.

I'm just glad my handwriting is way better as a dungeon than it ever was when I still had hands.

I shift my attention to the caves and tunnels, and am glad that things have been smoothing out down there nicely. The fruitbats and ants have gotten that glowing moss just about everywhere down there. I probably wouldn't want to try to read by the light in there, but it's bright enough that just about everyone can see and fight properly.

The occasional widows from the spider spawner are almost like wandering minibosses, which helps keep the lower-level groups on their toes. I've had to save a couple groups with the healing ants, but most are prepared enough to either fight or run away. Thankfully, the lessons of being beaten seem to stick, and I haven't had to save any particular group more than once.

The nodes down there are getting good use, too. Plenty of metals and gems that the delvers love. There's actually a group of dwarves and gnomes who seem to be trained for mining in dungeons. Their picks have two sides, like I picture a normal pick, but they have one side which is designed for digging, and one side designed for fighting. I'm always happy to see them show up, since they make me a bunch of mana.

Jello has also acquired a bit of a fanclub, it seems. After Torlon ran the maze, other Crystal Shield folks have come to do a bit of delving. Most of them are newbies, but there are real fighters in their ranks, too. They wouldn't be able to train Freddie to be a paladin if they didn't.

Anyhow, one of them noticed my Slime Scion's title, and now I sometimes get a small group who will follow her around while she's patrolling, and they'll help her as they can. One of the aranea even sometimes gives out a *Help Jello* quest. Jello, of course, is over the moon to have delvers helping her.

The tougher Crystal Shield folk have been more focused on the crypt complex. The fungal zombies and green skellies are actually resistant to being turned, probably because of all the plant/fungal life that's part of them. They seem to be a great way for them to practice their stuff, and they also help spread herbalism nodes in the crypt complex, as well as often dropping alchemy ingredients for the delvers when defeated.

Rocky has been having plenty of action, too. Like Grim, turning just doesn't seem to work on him, and he's tough enough that the occasional party who wants to tangle with him has their work cut out for them. I haven't been able to get him to throw a fireball or do an actual dragon punch yet, but he has been getting very good with his boxing. My spiders are working on making a speedbag for him to practice on, to go with the heavy bag.

Elsewhere in the complex, Coda and the ratlings have been making quick progress on the gauntlet, and I've been setting traps in there. Technically, the entire thing is going to be a water trap. The description more talks about the potential for soaking clothes and people, making them chafe and such for the entire delve, which yeah, it will. It will also be a lot better to fall into the water than just onto stone.

The traps to knock people off are all a bit of a mishmash, which is fine by me. Some are more like *Ninja Warrior*: tests of strength and such, though I do my best to keep them from all being overcomplicated pull-ups. I don't want my delvers to skip leg day. There are tests of balance, and even a few simple puzzles. And, of course, various padded things to surprise and push people off the platforms, just to keep people on their toes. Well, planned, anyway. It still needs to be dug out more, and I have to spend the mana for all the traps.

The ratkin have started to head into the town to trade, too. It's been small scale so far. Most businesses don't want to do official trading with my dwellers until after the Office of Dungeon Affairs makes official contact, but commerce waits for no bureaucracy, no matter how it complains.

I peek in on Teemo and Yvonne, and smile at the two. Yvonne is on her bed, a book in hand, and Teemo on her lap, her other hand idly rubbing his belly. *See, Teemo? You were just overthinking it. Enjoy the break, you two.*

Chapter 53

A couple days later, Elf Guy is back, and he seems to be all business. He walks up to the front porch and speaks clearly to nothing. "Dungeon Thedeim. The Dungeoneer's Guild would like to officially declare your intention as we understand it, and treatise with your dwellers. Please bring forth your Voice so it may be heard."

Fine by me. *Teemo, if you would?* My Rat Scion nods from the shortcut he's in, and soon scurries out from under the porch.

"Okay, I'm here. What do you need?" he asks with his typical lack of decorum. The elf simply looks at him with enough solemnity to make up for it and speaks.

"The Dungeoneer's Guild does hereby declare you to be a Cooperative Dungeon. We recognize the benefits you can grant, as do we recognize they are not for free. Your mercy has been noted, and in appreciation, the guild will attempt to inform delvers of the rules as we know them."

Teemo just grunts at the flowery language. "Okay, what's that actually mean?"

Tarl smiles and squats down to be more on Teemo's level, dropping the formal act, his declaration apparently finished.

"It means that as long as you don't just kill delvers because you can, the guild will do its best to make sure they behave and don't make a mess."

My rat nods at that. "Good. That's pretty much all the Boss wants." I mentally nudge Teemo, reminding him of a question I've had. "Oh yeah, he also wants to know what would happen if he expanded into town?"

Elf Guy gives him a confused look. "Is he planning to?"

"Not exactly," he replies, shaking his head. "It's just one of the options, apparently. Part of why he expanded down a while ago was that he didn't know what would happen if he tried to expand out more."

"Ah," says the inspector as he takes a seat on one of the stairs. "As I'm sure Thedeim can guess, it'd be complicated. Everyone would technically become dwellers. Some would approve, some wouldn't, and some wouldn't care. The mayor would probably be upset, and it'd cause political ripples throughout the kingdom." He shrugs. "I'd recommend against him expanding outward, at least on the surface. He'll be stepping on a lot of toes if he does."

Teemo just nods at that. "That's about what he figured, yeah. Anyway, you wanted to talk with the ratkin, too?"

Tarl nods and stands. "Yeah. I have a formal treaty to normalize relations with them and the guild, and by extension the kingdom and even the world. They're sovereign, technically. Dungeons are their own territory, which is why expanding outward would be complicated at best. The treaty basically just says they're recognized as such and offers trade deals."

Teemo sticks out his ratty tongue in mock disgust. "That sounds like politics, bleh. Better them than me. You can head to the enclave on your own. That ratkin enchanter came by the other day and cleared the magical traps out." He pauses for a moment before speaking up again. "Actually, I'll escort you. The Boss is also working on a new challenge."

The elf's eyes light up at that. "Oh? After the labyrinth, that sounds intriguing." The two talk as they head into the house, and Teemo hops on Tarl's shoulder to make it easier on the both of them. He explains the concept as he guides the inspector, who seems confused at my sudden embracing of traps. I notice Tarl looking around the rat nest in the basement, trying to be subtle as he walks. I should see if I can't leverage that desire to know where my core is to get something out of the ODA . . . though I have no idea what I'd want.

Before I can get too deep into thinking what I'd want, however, I feel new feet at the manor gate. Why are most groups trios? Maybe it gives the best balance of versatility versus splitting loot too many ways. They look a bit . . . off, though. I think I've seen most of the local delvers before, and these three don't look local. Their armor and clothes look like they've seen a lot of miles and are expected to see a lot more.

The leader seems to be a troll of some kind—kinda tall and lanky, rough purplish skin, beady eyes. He has a pair of shortswords crossed over his back, with chainmail underneath. I'm thinking another melee damage class like that one elf a while ago, but with swords instead of a spear.

It looks like their designated mage is a druid? And a halfling, too. I'm pretty sure she's a druid, at least. She's riding a wolf and doesn't have weapons like I'd expect a ranger or something to have. She has a gnarled staff with bones, teeth, scales, and feathers hanging off it. I would say it looks hand made, but I get a good sense of power from it. And, come to think of it, probably everything is technically handmade. I don't think there are magical factories around.

The last member is an olive-skinned elf, which is interesting. Is that a wood elf? Or is that a regular elf, and the other elves have been eladrin? Maybe he just has a good tan? Eh, I'm going with wood elf until told different. He's dressed in hide armor, and he seems to have a bunch of boomerangs, of all things. Taking a closer look, however, they're metal and look to be really sharp. He wears thick gloves to protect himself. I would think that'd mess with his aim, but with how his eyes move, I get the feeling that's not going to be a problem.

The wood elf speaks up first. "So this is the new toybox?"

The halfling shrugs. "Looks like. Unless you think big creepy mansions have infestations of adventurers to go with the spiders and mice?"

The elf glares at her, but the troll speaks up before they can get a proper bicker rolling. "Cram it. I heard that gnome priest got one hell of a prize from beating one of the scions." That gets the other two to shut up, and also makes me squint at the small party as he continues. "So we just gotta find a scion to beat up. Not the spider. I want a fresh chest. You spot anything, Hark?"

The elf, apparently Hark, looks around before looking up. He grins as he spots Poe up on the chimney. "Raven Scion up there, Vnarl." The troll looks up, using a hand to cover his eyes, and grins.

"Perfect! Mlynda, help him draw it down here. I don't want to fight it in its lair." The halfling and elf nod. Hark tosses one of his boomerangs while Mlynda summons a thorny vine out of my nice lawn and has it throw thorns at my Marshal.

Poe just looks at them with contempt as their attacks either fail to reach him or are easy for him to duck without even getting out of his nest. As they continue to try to draw him out, I wonder if they're very stubborn or very stupid. Almost none of their attacks are actually on target, thanks to the distance and the height. Poe has the high ground, and there's not a whole lot they can do about it.

Except get frustrated. Which they do. I wonder if the ranged barrage is their main tactic. The boomerangs always come back, so their ranged fighter never really runs out of ammo, and the druid seems to be able to coax an infinite amount of thorns out of that vine. The troll, however, is getting bored *and* frustrated, but soon spots something to take it out on.

One of my ratlings has an armful of wood from the maze, and Yvonne is helping it. I guess she wanted to get up and do something, rather than just read books all day with her down time. Vnarl, however, seems to just see two walking sacks of experience. He darts forward and cuts down the poor ratling, much to the surprise of Yvonne. She gives him a glare before speaking up.

"What do you think you're doing?!"

He just grins and slowly steps forward. "I heard you died, Yvonne. Looks like it didn't stick. Let me help you with that . . ."

While the raven had been content to ignore the pests when they were just bothering him, he doesn't appreciate them hindering the ratlings in their duty. He especially doesn't appreciate the threatening tone and stance their leader has toward Yvonne, and neither do I. *Stop them, Poe. And try not to kill them.*

The caw Poe gives as he spreads his wings is otherworldly in its menace, and I can practically hear a certain evil red genie declare that you'd be surprised what you can live through. It draws the attention of the other delvers around the manor, and the unwelcome party all grin as they finally get a rise out of my Raven Scion. Ravens and crows circle around and blot out the sun over them while Yvonne takes the chance to slip away.

Poe is looking significantly more badass than I expected. I check his status and see something I hadn't before.

Poe, Raven Scion
Lord of Unkindnesses
Marshal of Murders

. . . When did he become a raid boss?

Chapter 54

The trio (and wolf) seem remarkably calm about the avian apocalypse brewing overhead, which has me a bit concerned. Are they that stupid? Or are they that strong? I feel like delver isn't a career where stupid gets to live for long, but I also feel like the attacks they were trying to use to lure Poe down were kinda pathetic, too.

Whatever the reason for their confidence, go time is truly upon them all. With a caw and a powerful flap of his wings, Poe sends two groups of birds at the trio. The flying blackness moves gracefully like a swarm of fish, advancing at his command.

The halfling raises her staff and stands tall on her wolf's back as she shouts, "Enthrall!" Power bursts forth and sweeps over the ravens and crows as they near the group, but not a single bird falls out of line. The three notice quickly, but not quickly enough to avoid the incoming pain.

They all hunker down as best they can as the mixed unkindness wreaks its namesake upon them. The mass of black feathers soon soars back to the sky, leaving the trio covered in scratches and slashes. The wood elf growls at his teammate.

"Yeah, that worked great! Got any other fancy spells to do nothing with?"

She shouts at him in response, "I didn't see you do anything! How was I supposed to know that scion would make them immune? It worked on the wolf!"

"Shut up, both of you! If you haven't noticed, we're still in a fight!" The troll glares at the two, who glare at each other, but soon have to focus their attention back on Poe. "Mlynda, tornado. Hark, fill it with pain," the leader orders, and the two quickly follow.

Mlynda raises her staff again and quickly summons a small tornado while her favorite person to yell at starts throwing his boomerangs into it. It reaches some kind of tipping point as the next attack from Poe comes in, and the two shout, "Razor Winds!"

They do their best to keep the uncontained blender between them and the birds, but all three still take further scratches. The two who love to argue are looking like they decided to wrestle with barbed wire, but the troll seems to be regenerating through the small wounds, mostly.

The tide of feathers ebbs once more, and before they can get a look at the aftermath, the wood elf is screaming.

If he wasn't afraid of heights before, he probably will be once Poe decides to release him.

Poe

Poe had never understood why Aranya used to call the delvers "defilers," but now he gets it. If these had been the first delvers Lord Thedeim encountered, how different would he run his demesne? The screams of terror coming from the delver in his talons brings his focus back. Deal with the threat first, ponder theoreticals later.

He would have been happy to continue to ignore the three until they got bored, but then their boredom found a new target. The ratling will be fine once it respawns, but then they decided to threaten his Lord's second resident.

While Lord Thedeim is still an enigma to all but Teemo, the other scions can still sense his moods. While his presence is most often soft and warm, a thermal to uplift, it became a storm-swept cliff when the troll advanced on her.

It warmed slightly once she escaped, which is the only reason he'll soon be releasing the arms of his unwilling passenger rather than testing how high he can fly with such heavy prey.

He snaps a sharp turn and releases the wood elf to gravity, watching the sloped roof rush to meet him. Belatedly, he sends a blunt gale to adjust the fool's orientation. Lord Thedeim prefers to not kill thinking delvers. Poe isn't so sure these ones match that description, but he'll err on the side of mercy. It's much easier to be less merciful to the living than it is to be more merciful to the dead.

The elf grunts from the rough righting of his tumble, and Poe feels the attacker should be glad to only be likely to break a limb rather than his neck. He watches, taking satisfaction in the pained sounds, as gravity introduces its new friend to all the interesting hard things the roof has to offer before reuniting him with the ground. The elf lies in a groaning heap as Poe takes a moment to inventory his state.

Alive. No limbs broken but possibly a few ribs. And a lot of other injuries besides. He doubts the elf will be available to be introduced to any more of gravity's friends for a while. That just leaves the other two.

Thedeim

The other two watch as Poe takes off with their . . . well, I would say *friend*, but I think that's a bit strong. The Lord of Unkindnesses has a claw wrapped around each of his biceps as he takes off after having used the cover of the flocks to slip in and snatch him up.

I'm worried I'll have to remind Poe not to kill him, but he releases the jerk barely before clearing the roof, not that he gives him a simple straight fall. He hurls the guy at the slanted surface and slings a dense bit of air at him as well, slapping him around a bit before he bounces off the roof, the gutter, and several thick branches before landing in a pile on the ground.

I'm actually impressed. That was a pretty thorough beating Poe laid down without killing the guy. From the groans, he might have preferred that, but this group isn't getting off that easily.

Speaking of the group, it looks like they aren't finished yet. While Poe rallies his birds, the troll and halfling hatch their own plan. She summons two of those thorny vine things, and the troll uproots them, letting them sink into his forearms. That's gotta sting, but troll regen makes things like that an option, I suppose. Mlynda has the vines take his swords, wrapping around the handles and leaving Vnarl looking like a purple Kratos.

Poe's attack is different this time, too. Instead of two wings of blackness sweeping in from two sides, it's more like a single river of black going at them. I don't think he's going to give them the chance to recover between attacks this time. That formation looks long enough that it can loop back in on itself and keep the pain going until the other two are as incapacitated as the first.

The troll meets the onslaught head-on, swinging vine and sword like this isn't his first rodeo. The halfling is crouched behind her wolf now rather than standing proudly on top, shouting over the din of caws and ordering the vines to unleash their thorns. Between the thorns and the steel, the river of black soon becomes just a stream, then a trickle, before it peters out entirely.

The two stand, grinning and exhausted, though not unharmed. The halfling and her wolf are bleeding from so many scratches and slashes that I'm pretty sure they're both actually in danger of bleeding out. And they both look better than the troll.

Where they have scratches and cuts, he has deep gashes and slices. They're deep enough that even his regeneration looks like it's not going to be up to the job of keeping him in the fight for much longer.

He and the halfling laugh defiantly at Poe as he lands atop the porch to look at them. It takes them a few moments to realize two very important things. One, they haven't gotten their boss experience yet. Two, they can still hear a *lot* of cawing.

The nearest wave of ravens and crows on expedition have been recalled. The grins vanish at the realization, and Poe takes off once more, the Marshal of Murders not finished with his prey just yet.

He flaps his wings, sending blades of wind to sever the vines, and the tired duo can't protect them in time. The cawing changes as Poe looks down on them, my Raven Scion opening his beak to clarify the chant from his lesser kin.

"Again!"

The duo can only stare at the oncoming wall of blackness and deafening tide of "Again!"

Vnarl quietly says as they get closer, "But . . . it's a toybox . . ."

The halfling punches him in the hip before the blackness of feathers consumes them and quickly leaves them in the blackness of unconsciousness.

Chapter 55

Well. Now that I have these three handled, what do I do with them?

Taking their stuff is a given. My free ratlings and aranea are more than happy to relieve the trio of all that heavy stuff. My healing ants stabilize the three and the wolf, but don't do anything to wake them up just yet.

Hmm . . . I could just web them up by the entrance with signs reading *Free Candy* and a pile of sticks nearby. But while amusing, I don't think I should just let people beat them up . . . even if I kinda want to. They threatened Yvonne! They deserve a good beating!

Which they kinda already got. Still, I'm not letting them off that easily . . . but what else can I do with them?

Then I get an idea.

A wonderful idea.

I get a wonderful, *awful* idea.

Tarl

Negotiations with the dwellers are going well. Elder Larx is sharp and shrewd but doesn't have a malicious bone in his body . . . Well, maybe a maliciously compliant one or two. The elf mentally shrugs. Whatever the malevolence of the ratkin's bones, he's a good negotiator. The boring process of a political power recognizing another exists is done rather quickly. The dwellers understand they're hardly a powerhouse, but being connected with the dungeon helps ensure that nobody will bother with the hassle of trying to subjugate them.

Not the *most* flattering appraisal of their situation, but an accurate one, at least. The more interesting negotiations are for trade agreements. His guild is interested in information first and foremost, and though the dwellers are reluctant to give much information on Thedeim, they are willing to trade their maps of the deeper tunnels, and what they know of the threats.

He's been authorized to offer coin for the knowledge, which Larx is happy to accept. The ratkin understands they have a lot of goods to offer to delvers and even ordinary people, but they have little cash on hand to leverage further. They *could* go delve, and some of the ratkin like to do just that, but most don't want that kind of life.

He's in the middle of suggesting they attempt to sell herbs or other ingredients to Cobble Bread, just across the road, when he notices Teemo's ear twitch. Several emotions flicker across his face before settling into a look of growing confusion.

Larx notices as well, but Tarl speaks up first.

"Is something wrong, Teemo?"

The unassuming Voice takes a few more moments to respond. "Uh . . . it's complicated. A trio of delvers showed up and tried to egg Poe into a fight. He ignored them, until they threatened Yvonne."

Tarl groans at that. "Can the Dungeoneer's Guild negotiate for the bodies?"

Teemo smirks. "There aren't any bodies." He lets the inspector's imagination run for a few moments with that statement before clarifying. "They're alive. And the Boss is singing a weird song."

That raises a few red flags for Tarl. "What kind of weird song?"

The look of confusion returns as Teemo answers. "About over-the-top insults to an even more over-the-top bad guy?"

Tarl relaxes slightly at that, though he's still not fully put at ease. "What's he doing with the delvers?"

"Hey, Boss? Boss! What're you doing with the delvers?" The confused look makes a comeback before understanding takes over, only to be crushed by the weight of an evil grin. "Cool. Enjoy the song, Boss." He looks back to Tarl and straightens himself a little.

"Thedeim has captured three delvers who displeased him. He has claimed their equipment to do with as he sees fit, but that is simply what happens to those who challenge one of his scions who does not wish to be challenged. For the crime of threatening a resident, they are to be jailed until such time as their guild pays an appropriate ransom or they can pass a trial to earn their freedom. Or until Thedeim decides they have learned their lesson. So says Thedeim, through his Voice."

Teemo looks pretty proud of himself for the declaration, and Larx looks interested and thoughtful about it. Tarl fights not to sigh, and opens his mouth to reply.

"Then, as representative of the Dungeoneer's Guild, I thank Thedeim for his mercy, and will be attempting to contact their guild so they may attempt to make the proper amends." The elf relaxes a little before continuing. "So what's that actually mean?" he asks with a small smirk, able to throw the rat's own words back at him.

Teemo smiles wide. "You remember the gauntlet we passed on the way here?"

". . . Yes?"

"The Boss is attaching a jail to it, and is making it a lot less fair."

Elsewhere

The mycelia can feel something wriggling through the mat of its biomass. It is long, with jaws and legs; a foe and an ally to the fungus. The things have long helped break down what needs breaking down, but they also will sometimes eat the mushrooms or nutrient stores.

It starts to increase spore production as the thing gets closer to the shard of purple, but something stops it. The fungus is a good protection from detection, but it is a cloak, not a shield, nor is it a sword. But the long things could help fill those roles.

Cautiously, it lets the thing through, and is relieved to see the long insect will be helping the small light. A spark of understanding runs through both fungus and insect, the two knowing they will be rivals no longer.

Tarl

He watches with rapt attention as the jail is built and upgraded. It's rare to get to see something like this, and he quietly murmurs into his note stone as he watches.

"Ratlings and aranea are bringing materials from the warehouse to facilitate room formation. Jail bars started as simple stone columns that bent out of the way for the Snake Scion to levitate the prisoners inside. Poor steel bars were brought, and the formerly-stone bars transmuted to the material, consuming it and likely some energy as well. It must take less energy to upgrade if proper materials are provided.

"A small, separate chamber has been created for the wolf. Dungeon seems uncertain what to do with it. Other delvers have been stripped down to mundane clothing. Certain classes may be able to bypass the bars at the moment, but the Voice has indicated there will be magical and even alchemical precautions taken."

He lowers the stone for a moment before looking at Teemo. "Does that mean Queen will be leaving the secret alchemy lab? I'd like to meet her, if only to be able to provide a description for the records."

The Voice nods. "She's on her way. She said she wants to personally test a few things. She'll be a bit slower than Thing, though. He wants to get a look before actually enchanting anything, but Queen has a few ideas for what she wants to do already."

He looks at the occupants of the cell before continuing. "Do you know them?"

Tarl shakes his head after only a few moments.

"No. I think they're from one of the larger guilds to the south. I'll check with Karn to be sure, but I don't think he'd let any of his adventurers go delve with what seems to be such poor intelligence."

Teemo smirks. "Yeah, they don't seem very smart." The elf just rolls his eyes.

"You know what I mean. They didn't bother coming to the Dungeoneer's Guild for the latest information, or they would have known not to attempt something like this."

"Think anyone will raise a stink about this?" asks the rat, looking a bit wary about the idea. Tarl just shakes his head.

"Nah. These three are fairly big fish for our small pond here in Fourdock, but they're small fry back home. Probably wanted to prove they could handle themselves; maybe that they didn't need to pay for information on a dungeon to be able to beat it." He shrugs before continuing. "Whatever the case, their guild shouldn't raise a fuss. Most dungeons would have just killed them, so this is still better for the guild, even if they have to pay a ransom."

"Do you think Thedeim's idea will work like he wants it to?"

Tarl taps his foot as he thinks. "I don't know, and I don't know if I *want* it to work or not. In theory, delvers overcoming—or failing to overcome—traps should generate energy for the dungeon. I don't think any have tried tying a jail to a gauntlet of traps." He sighs and regards the rat. "I'd actually suggest making the jail and the gauntlet secret rooms, if Thedeim can. I doubt most delvers who earn their way inside will talk much about it, out of shame, but other dungeons might try using something like this as a waterwheel if they learn about it."

Chapter 56

I consider Tarl's suggestion on making the punitive gauntlet secret. On the one hand, I want to be able to humiliate these delvers for being jerks. But on the other hand, especially if this works, other dungeons could cause a lot of trouble with this. Imagining Neverrest having a mana farm is just . . . no.

I sigh and get to working on hiding the entrance to the jail and gauntlet. At least I didn't make the exit for it yet, so that can be hidden from the start. It looks like Coda can help with that, which is great! Him and the ratlings have been progressing quickly with the mining or stonework or masonry or whatever it technically is. All I know is I can get them to work on it, and it'll probably be better than what I can make.

It's not like I can make another eggsac-covered rock to hide behind. It'd be kinda obvious. I think Coda is looking into some kind of sliding wall, or maybe a hinge. He's the Architect, so I leave him to it.

Which leaves me with two more things to handle with this mess. One: I need to talk to Yvonne about what happened. Two: I need to talk with that wolf if I can.

Thankfully, Yvonne doesn't seem too shaken by the ordeal and is back to helping the ratlings gather some materials. Looks like she's going to try mining some iron, now that I've used some steel on the jail, and might be using some on the secret gauntlet.

I know Teemo wants to go talk to her, too, but I think talking to this wolf is the priority. Tarl has left, or at least returned to the enclave to make a better farewell. I'm not the only one going to be busy from this incident, after all.

I tell the healing ants to get ready to heal the wolf enough to awaken, but don't have them actually do it yet. *Teemo, you can talk to the wolf, right?* He looks uncertain before replying.

"I think so? It sounded like he came from another dungeon somewhere, so I should be able to talk."

Cool, I just wanted to make sure before healing it . . . or him, I suppose, to consciousness. It takes a few minutes for the ants to get the wolf looking healthy enough to just be asleep rather than in a coma. Teemo starts tossing little pebbles through the bars to wake him up. It takes him aiming one right into a nostril and forcing a sneeze before the wolf stirs.

He slowly looks around, regaining his senses, before it looks like the fight comes rushing back to him. He jumps to his feet and backs into a corner, growling and looking around.

"Easy there," says Teemo, trying to calm the wolf down. "You're safe—from the birds and that halfling. Enthrall doesn't sound like a fun thing to deal with." The wolf locks eyes on Teemo through the bars, and while he calms slightly, he doesn't stop growling, nor does he lower his hackles.

Teemo winces and nods. "Yeah, that's about what I thought. She's not dead," he starts, which makes the wolf bark and gnash his teeth, getting a good frothing rage going. Teemo sticks a few little rat fingers in his mouth and whistles, high-pitched and loud, to get the wolf to focus.

"Thedeim's not going to let her enthrall you again, don't worry. Heh, and she's not getting off easy, either. The Boss is—" I mentally clear what passes for my throat and remind Teemo that's knowledge to keep away from dungeons who aren't me. Yeah, the wolf isn't a dungeon, but he's from one, it seems. In fact . . . what's he listed as?

I look and see he's an invader, which is interesting. I'm pretty sure he wasn't that when he was enthralled, but I didn't think to look at his status before Poe had to lay a beatdown.

Teemo talking draws my attention before it can wander too much further.

"Well, let's just say the Boss might be getting more out of leaving her alive." The wolf still doesn't look happy, but he's not looking rabid anymore, which is a good start. He growls a bit more, and Teemo replies.

"Uh . . . that's a good question. Hey, Boss? What're you gonna do with him?"

Um . . . does he have any suggestions? I don't think I can make him a resident. Teemo relays my words and listens to the ensuing growls.

"Huh. He says a jail is usually used to try to get information out of invaders, or even try to turn them. His home dungeon is leagues away, so information on it probably won't do much. So I guess you can try to turn him to your side?"

How's that work? I don't want to try to break him or something like that. The wolf growls before Teemo can ask, and I get a pop-up.

Transfer Request: Wolf
Accept? Yes/No

Oh. That's simple enough. It costs a decent bit of mana, but not enough to put much of a dent in anything.

New Denizen Type Found
Designate Scion?

Oh? That's what it tells me when I get a new spawner. It costs about the same as it did to turn him, so I might as well, right? What to name him, though. Big Bad? Nah. Lobo? Nah. Lupine? Nah, I only have one of him anyway. Moon-Moon? Heh, nah. Let me see . . . try more obtuse. Sparta was big into wolves, I think, so I could call him Leonidas. That's a bit of a mouthful, though. Shortening it would be . . . *yes*.

Leo. The wolf named lion.

I watch his name change from Wolf to Leo, and I can feel his confusion. *Heh, get used to that feeling, Leo. You're under new management, and I get the feeling I run my dungeon differently to others.*

Wolf Scion Found
Wolf Spawner Not Found
Designate Wolf Spawner

You're just causing all kinds of alerts, Leo. I hope you're proud. I actually hope you're proud—new spawner! I can actually place it, too! Where, though? The manor grounds are kinda spoken for. I might be able to squeeze it in at the side of the maze, but that would be a bad spot for it. It's not like I need more encounters in the yard.

The cemetery has a fair bit of space, though I don't want encounters in there.

Looking around, I see a good spot, actually. Back behind the mausoleums, near the outer wall could work. The graveyard's north wall has wilderness on the other side, not more town. The ratkin might be able to domesticate some of the wolves, too, to help them with their underground hunting.

I might even be able to send some wolves on expeditions. The crows and ravens can get a literal bird's-eye view, but the wolves have the endurance to go *way* farther out. Or at least they should. Part of why man and dog are such a good pair is that dogs can actually keep up with moving all day long. Most everything else tires out.

I nod to myself and place the spawner near the wall. I'll see about having Coda or maybe Grim make a staircase or something for over there later. For now, I unlock Leo's cell and ask Teemo to give him the tour. My Voice hops on Leo's back, and the two set off while I tell Teemo to ask him about the job I'd like him to do around here.

I need someone to keep an eye on the prisoners, and also someone to manage any future wolf expeditions out into the wilderness. They might sound unrelated, but I think a Warden can handle both.

Chapter 57

Alright, with Leo getting himself settled, I need to prepare a few things to talk with Yvonne and Aranya. I mean, I knew there had to be jerks around; I had just hoped to be able to be a bit more prepared first. Locals are always easier to keep friendly. Nobody wants to go rocking the boat if they have to actually *live* on the boat after.

So if that group had some idea about me, others will eventually, too. I can't force people to not be stupid, but I can prepare so I don't get any of it on me and mine. Aranya and Yvonne definitely count in that group, so I'll be giving them something a little before it's perfectly ready, but the finishing touches can come later. Really, they just need to be filled up, which is something that will take time.

The other thing, though . . . is I'm probably going to be doing the isekai hero thing of introducing new crap. I don't have the internet, so I can't just give a schematic, but I *do* have my secrets of creation in the form of an understanding of engineering.

I just hope reality isn't just magic, and that magic doesn't just override my understandings.

I get to making some notes in the secret library while I wait for the sun to set and Aranya to wake up.

Leo

What kind of dungeon had he signed on with? There are so many *outsiders* around. Why does his new Alpha let them just run around?! The tour with the Voice only raises more questions, especially with how many other scions there are. It actually has a scion for everything. How does it support that kind of cost? Letting the outsiders live is so much less mana for the dungeon!

As the tour progresses, he starts to see how. This Alpha doesn't focus on just felling a few big elk. No, it understands how to get enough rabbits to more than make up for it. This new Alpha may still be a pup, but it's got some interesting ideas.

Like the maze. After meeting the scion in charge of it, Leo is glad they decided to try to tangle with Poe instead of Tiny. Poe at least was a straight-up fight, more or less. Tiny would have simply incapacitated them, one by one, without ever presenting a target.

He's pretty sure Poe could have, too, but the Marshal wanted to play with his prey before going in for the kill. Or the knockout, thankfully.

He growls at the memory of following that group . . . that *halfling!* Enthralling him instead of the proper taming process! He couldn't even abandon her because of that! Not until she stopped paying the upkeep, anyway. With her knocked out, the spell wore off, at least.

The other scions all seem surprisingly powerful, too. Most of them don't even fight! They should be masters and mistresses of their lairs, ready to defeat any delver stupid enough to test them! But instead, they're busy doing practically everything *but* fight!

Then again . . . they're kept busy. A steady stream of rabbits, not the occasional elk. Even seeing the results, Leo still finds it hard to believe. He didn't believe the claim of the pup of an Alpha subsuming Neverrest, not until the tour got to the graveyard and the mausoleum.

His old dungeon knew of the blighted cemetery and was just glad it was so far away. But Alpha Thedeim was able to subsume it, and has the Conduit Fluffles as proof. He shudders at the idea of having encountered *him* instead of Poe, or even Tiny. Even the large spider would have expended some effort. Fluffles could have done . . . practically anything to them, without even moving a muscle!

Seeing the wolf den in the back of the cemetery helps calm his mind, though. It looks basic but comfortable. If his new Alpha can keep this kind of mana flow going, the den will be seeing upgrades soon, and Leo can have a true pack once more.

Although, after meeting the other scions, he gets the feeling he's a lot closer to having that already.

The Office of Dungeon Affairs

Telar fights the overwhelming urge to hit her head against her desk as Tarl gives his report. She somehow manages to resist, but can't stop the groan that escapes her.

"They *seriously* thought Thedeim was a toybox? *And* threatened a resident?!"

Tarl shrugs. "That's what Teemo said. They hadn't recovered enough to be able to give their side, but I can't think of anything else that would earn that kind of reaction. At least the townsfolk aren't worried about Poe acting like an avatar of the Raven?" he offers his coworker.

She doesn't look very comforted by that. "I got a lot of them checking in that everything was fine after that display, too. Did you know Thedeim's scions were that strong?"

He shrugs again. "I had an inkling. Recall that I suggested a higher-level inspector a while ago. Though with the new crypt complex, as Thedeim likes to call it, I might be able to go get me a couple levels. I still doubt I could take any of the scions besides Rocky, even with some extra experience. I think even Head Priest Torlon would have trouble if the dungeon decided to get serious."

"So you think it will be more serious from here on out?" she asks. She's pretty sure Thedeim won't change just because of one party, but Tarl is the experienced inspector here.

She relaxes when he immediately shakes his head. "No, he's smart enough to know people like that exist. Heh, and smart enough to have come up with a good punishment for those who try. He's probably going to do a few new things, however. His resident got a good scare, but I don't think he's going to react like Hullbreak did."

They both grimace at the memory of what happened there. Telar continues first. "What do you think of the jail and gauntlet combination?"

He sighs at that. "I think it'll work, which is concerning. I asked him to make it secret, and he seems to be working on that. He might have it hidden, or at least secured, by the time that group wakes up. He might even specifically be keeping them unconscious until it's all ready. He does have that Alchemist scion. Leafcutter queen ant, Alchemist."

She nods at that, adding the information to the packet. "I take it you won't be telling the Southwood about the combo? What did Thedeim authorize you to share?" While technically they could share any information they acquired, certain dungeons liked their privacy. It wouldn't do to upset the dungeon in the center of their town.

Telar's musings on dungeon relations drift to a halt as she realizes Tarl hasn't spoken up.

She turns to see him looking off into the distance, thinking, before slapping both palms to his face.

"Ah. You forgot to ask."

Chapter 58

I've got my notes as prepared as they can get. I still don't know how magic works, which can be a *big* wrench in my plans. I have a couple gues—I mean theories on some of it, but I'll need to talk to my two residents to get any actual information. I probably should have tried to talk with Old Staiven about this, but if any of my ideas actually work, it could be way more dangerous than a dungeon with a mana battery.

Dungeons don't get up and walk around, after all.

When Aranya wakes up, she can feel the anticipation in the air, and even looks over at my core. Teemo just tells her to have breakfast, and that I want to talk to everyone after. Well, to her and Yvonne, at least. I would include the other scions, but I'm paranoid enough about this to want to keep it in the secret base, at least for now.

After a period of time somewhere between a blink and an eternity, it's time to have a chat.

"Thedeim wants to know about magic," says Teemo simply, and my residents look confused at that. My kobold speaks up first.

"Neither of us are mages. I don't know how much we can teach him?"

Yvonne nods before Teemo speaks up again.

"He says he doesn't know anything about magic. *Anything.* He says he needs baby's first magic talk," relays my Voice, giving my core a weird look at my choice of phrasing. No sense in sugar-coating how little I know. I need the basics of basics here.

Yvonne slowly speaks up. "Well . . . everyone has magic. At least a little," she starts, looking to Teemo to see if she's managed to insult me. She hasn't. She's confirmed one of my theories, even. Teemo smiles and nods for her to continue.

"Everyone has an affinity that is part of who they are. And their class can give them an extra affinity. Some dedicated casting classes even have a minor affinity for all magics."

I mentally smile at that, relaying my reply through Teemo.

"So most dedicated casters, like Rhonda and Aelara, focus on their innate affinity and use the class broadness to give them more utility with protections, healings, and such?"

The residents nod, and Aranya speaks up. "Most classes that use weapons will give Kinetic affinity, which they use to help land and avoid blows." Yvonne nods and continues.

"Ragnar actually has Life affinity as his innate, and Kinetic from his class. If a foe doesn't take him out in one strike, it'll have difficulty taking him out at all. I've seen him handle some ridiculous hits."

"What are the affinities?"

The two look unsure at that, but Aranya forges on ahead. "Well, there are the more classic staples: Earth, Air, Fire, Water, Dark, Light, Lightning, Thunder . . ." she trails off, looking to Yvonne to see if she's missed any. The birb picks up the thread.

"And a lot of others that represent the physical natural world." She smiles as a memory comes to mind. "Lava and Magma are separate affinities, and Ragnar will gladly go on and on about the differences if you let him." Lost in the happy memory, Aranya continues once more.

"Then there're the . . . weirder ones? Life, Death, Kinetic, Spatial, Time . . . I know I'm forgetting a lot more," she finishes awkwardly, and I take a moment to consider the information.

There are the classical elements and friends. All physical things. I wonder if it's a Nature affinity, or if it tends to be broken down into Animal and Plant affinity, or even finer? Or does that count as Life? I have Teemo relay the questions, but the residents don't really know. That's fine. The other ones are more like forces to contrast the masses of the first set, or maybe verbs compared to nouns.

It's a good place to start from, at least. Before I set about giving them information in return, I have a few more physical things to give them. Teemo pulls two strange swords out of a shortcut.

My residents are confused at first, but Aranya recognizes the shapes first. "The tunnel horror!"

Yvonne looks confused, and I have Teemo clarify.

"The Boss has been calling it a scythemaw because of these things. You didn't think he'd just thrown them out or something, did you?" he asks with a smile, motioning for them to pick up the swords.

They are curved and sweep back nicely, with sharp spikes on the back of the blade. The handles are made of wood and have enough length to use one or both hands to swing. The pommels have a decent knob to them, to help with the balance and to be able to whack someone with if you don't want to cut them.

I think Aranya will need both hands for hers, but Yvonne should be able to treat hers like a bastard-scimitar.

"But tunnel horrors don't have metal pincers?" says my kobold, gingerly holding the weapon like she's afraid she'll somehow break it.

"Queen has a metal infusion formula. I dunno how it works, but she was able to transmute them both to steel. But not before making a few modifications. Those spikes on the back have little holes in them, and Queen had her smallest workers burrow channels through them. There's a cavity in the handle, and the pommel can unscrew to get access to it. You can fill it with venom. Boss has some of the paralysis venom from the widows in there right now, and there's a little jar in the lair for them to milk into."

The two look at the swords with wonder as Teemo continues. "Thing even expanded the cavity with Spatial magic, so they can hold a ton of the stuff. You should be able to just imagine the venom, and it'll start coating the spikes. Thing also reinforced them, made them sharper, and better balanced, too!"

"An artifact . . ." says Yvonne with reverence, and Aranya can only nod slowly.

"Thedeim was going to give them as normal gifts to you two as something cool to have. But after that trio today . . ." Aranya looks confused, and Yvonne sighs, the fun of a new toy slightly soured by the memory of the day.

"A group of delvers showed up and picked a fight with Poe. Then they tried to pick a fight with me. Poe . . . didn't appreciate it," says my birblady with a grin at the end. "Thedeim has them in a cell right now, and has an interesting punishment for them, too."

Teemo nods as Aranya looks concerned. "The Boss wants you two to be able to defend yourselves, and those swords are part of it. He doesn't know if you two are very good with swords, but he would ask you try to train with them, at least a little."

Aranya quickly nods. "Of course! I'll never be a master of a sword, but I can at least get good enough to hit someone. If one hit with the spikes can paralyze, I don't have to actually be all that good with it for it to work."

Yvonne nods as well. "I'm better with a bow, but I had been meaning to get better with a sword or something else in melee. Arrows are terrible for stabbing with."

Teemo smiles at that, my relief showing in his relief. "Good. The Boss just wants to keep you two safe. Which brings me to the next thing he wants to share." He gives Aranya a sideways glance. "You asked if he knew the secrets of creation. He says he does . . . in a way."

The red kobold gasps and focuses entirely on my little Voice while he tries to pop her enthusiasm. "He says he doesn't know the whys. That falls under philosophy and such, and he says you need to mostly find your own answers there. What he *might* know is *some* of the hows."

The residents look confused at that, so he tries to explain. "The Boss knows a lot of weird things, but he's not sure if they translate. But if they do, he says he should be able to expand a lot of affinity things. He says Fire and Ice are the same thing, and Kinetic is closely related, too. Space and Time are closely related, and a lot of other things that honestly go right over my head. He's going to start explaining them to Fluffles, since he has Kinetic affinity, and he says even my Spatial affinity could let me do Fire and Ice stuff."

He looks at my residents. "So, what are your affinities? He's pretty sure he can help you expand on them once he knows."

Yvonne replies first. "Mine is Fate."

Aranya starts at that, causing Yvonne to give her a confused look. "What? My True Strike lets me feel the best moment to release an arrow for maximum effect."

Aranya speaks up. "Mine is Fate, too. When I first found Thedeim, I was desperately following the feel of my affinity." That earns a look from my ranger, but my High Priestess continues before she can comment. "And as Thedeim's High Priestess, I know what his Primary Domain is. It's also Fate."

The three all exchange glances, and I wish I had eyes to join in. None of us are exactly masters of magical knowledge, but it doesn't take a genius to understand three Fate affinity people probably don't just accidentally get drawn together.

Chapter 59

We talk a bit more about Fate affinity and how it works, and it seems to me like *Luck* might be a little more accurate, though that might be splitting hairs. I always felt like luck was basically quantum stuff, but if that's actually how it works, it destroys my working theory on how magic works.

I was thinking it was basically controlled quantum observation: observe the wave-form just right, and collapse it exactly how you want. Could be a fireball, or it could be a coin flipping heads when you need it. That sort of thing. Sounds to me like, if it *is* related to luck, it's not the foundation for magic. Or maybe it is. Non-causal stuff is even weirder than most people think it is.

The other option for how magic works is for it to be a fifth fundamental force. If I remember right, there's the strong and weak nuclear forces. I forget exactly what they do. I think one is what makes it so mass doesn't overlap, despite most mass having a ton of room between the atoms, and the other . . . keeps protons and electrons and neutrons from collapsing together? I just remember those two don't do a ton outside of atomic scale.

The other two forces are gravity and electromagnetism, which do all kinds of fun stuff. I swear, it feels like potential energy is just a kludge to get around how those two almost cheat. A gravity well will make a moon or a pebble fall at the same rate if there's nothing in the way. And, of course, magnets work via friggin' miracles, as everyone knows.

Teemo

The rat grunts from the weight of the thoughts of his dungeon. His Boss *might* know *some* secrets? He grimaces at the thought there could be even more!

Yvonne notices the change in her small friend's face and stance.

"Is everything alright, Teemo?"

He answers, some strain coming through in his voice, "Well . . . I don't think the Boss was joking when he said he knew some of the secrets of creation. He's not even telling them to me, more like just talking to himself, but the weight of some of these ideas is . . ." he trails off, uncertain how to even explain it.

Thedeim

Musings on the so-called secrets of creation I only half remember and half understand aside, I can work with what my residents are talking about even without knowing where magic actually fits. Well, I hope, anyway. If it *is* Luck magic, it's time to try to explain bell-curves and standard deviations and ways to actually cheat at luck. There's not a game of chance out there that can't be rigged or cheated somehow. Card counting, loading dice, aces up sleeves; Lady Luck is not the pure maiden some people like to think she is.

Teemo's Spatial magic allows for all kinds of shenanigans when it comes to defending himself and others, too! Those shortcuts of his are bigger on the inside than out, so he's got some serious non-Euclidean geometry going on. He could make terrain that *looks* flat actually be incredibly unstable, or the opposite. If he gets *really* good, he could just make there not even be a path to himself, or be able to hit someone from anywhere, or allow an ally to do the same!

Rocky's Fire affinity should allow for him to at least double-dip with elements, and potentially get to Kinetic, too. If his Fire affinity lets him move around and manipulate heat, not only should he be able to produce fire by turning the heat up, but create ice by turning it down, or create *both* by *moving* that heat energy instead of brute-forcing it.

Teemo

Teemo wavers and sits down, the two residents looking more concerned. "Can we do anything to help?" asks Aranya, a bit unnerved at the state of the Sanctuary's Voice.

"Talking . . . helps, I think. It's . . . it's like he's thrown open vault doors of knowledge. Talking helps to keep me from trying to follow. Just hearing him think, it's just words. But if I try to understand, it's like I'm being crushed!"

"Then don't try to understand?" offers Yvonne, unable to think of any other suggestions. Teemo gives a pained chuckle as something his Boss said a while ago suddenly makes sense.

"Heh, try not to think about pink elephants, especially with them stomping all around you."

Thedeim

Tiny and Fluffles's Kinetic affinities are going to be even more fun. I always liked solid mechanics: levers, fulcrums, pulleys, ramps, and so on. The simple machines that make up what a lot of people think of when they hear the word *engineer*. For Tiny, I think he'd be better to try to make into the proverbial immovable object, show him how a truss actually functions to be able to take the kinds of immense loads they can, and how to abuse angles to deflect kinetic forces away, instead of just absorbing them.

And Fluffles would be the unstoppable force, especially with him using *my* mana. I don't know exactly how much a delver usually has, but I'd be surprised if I don't have at least an order of magnitude over all but the strongest of casters.

It's also interesting that the affinities I feel I can best abuse are the ones my residents think are the most esoteric. I have no idea how Poe's Wind affinity would fundamentally work. Is it some kind of mastery over the gaseous state of matter? If so, is Fire affinity mastery of plasma, rather than thermal energy? Coda's seeming Thunder or Sonic affinity—is it only sounds? Is it any potential wave? Maybe it's pressure control, instead?

And even if I have everything understood properly, all of this is easier said than done!

Before I can sprint my way deeper down this rabbit hole, a pained squeak pulls my attention.

"B-Boss . . . s-slow down!" my Voice gasps, a little bit of blood leaking from his nose. My thoughts, which had been running a mile a minute, suddenly lock up. I bite back the mental shout to Queen to get him some healing ants, and take a few moments to try to calm myself.

I can feel Queen directing the nearest healing ants to look over Teemo. Calm. Focus. Stop hurting your friend. Just because he can respawn, doesn't mean he doesn't feel pain.

My Voice sighs in relief from the ants working on him, and hopefully from me not thinking my way down the paths of tech and science that probably haven't been seen in this world yet.

"What *was* that?" asks Yvonne, alternating between looking at Teemo with concern and at my core with a different kind of concern.

Teemo pushes himself to his feet with visible effort. "That was just some of the Boss's knowledge. I saw things . . . some just numbers and weird drawings of numbers, and some as huge things that actually exist! But . . . they don't exist?"

He stiffens when I give him the simplest explanation and tell him he can tell my residents.

"He . . . he says they don't exist *here*. They exist where he's from."

My two residents both look confused at that, and Aranya manages to speak through the confusion. "Like . . . in the realm of the gods?"

"No . . . a realm like ours, but also nothing like ours." He grunts and holds his head for a moment before shaking it off. "I don't even know how to begin to describe it, either. I can get some of what he says about it, but there are also huge gaps. He'll talk, but I don't get any meaning at all about it. It's like putting together a puzzle, but some pieces just stop existing when you reach for them."

I mentally nod, remembering when Teemo said that the word *human* had no meaning for him. My mind starts to wander down the paths of what that actually means, but I reign it in for now. I can wildly theory-craft later. Maybe after experimenting a little to see if it's better if I'm "zoomed out" when I do it, or if it's better to be focused somewhere away from Teemo.

And speaking of experiments, there's a very simple one I can have Teemo explain to my residents. Flipping a coin is one of the oldest games of chance out there, at least as old as coins. I'd expect just trying to look at the result before it happens—while the coin is in the air—would be a good, repeatable, low-effort way to hone that skill. So, if I have them call coin flips to practice, we can get a baseline. And then, when I have them try to call a bunch of flips before tossing the coin, it'll be a good introduction to how odds actually work.

Calling one coin flip is 50/50, but accurately calling five flips from the start is only one in thirty-two, even if the odds of calling each individual flip as they happen is still 50/50. Mathematically, it's pretty simple, but conceptually, it's really weird. With any luck, the mana costs will scale in a way to make it easier for my residents to grasp.

I keep myself from thinking too far down that path just yet, not wanting to hurt Teemo, but I can't help a little nugget of an idea getting stuck in the back of my head. There's a system here, reminiscent of a video game. If we can keep running down the numbers of how luck actually works, we might be able to do some actual RNG manipulation.

Chapter 60

The rest of the night I mostly spend with Teemo, confirming the affinities of my scions. Unsurprisingly, looks like everyone has Fate affinity, probably because of me. It makes me wonder if we could actually avoid accidental kills. I've been wondering about when it would happen. Yeah, I know, doesn't seem like something I'd worry about.

I'm not exactly *worried* about it; more like I thought it was kinda inevitable. Parks and stuff back home have more safety measures than I do, and don't tend to involve any actual fighting, yet people still accidentally die, right? I've had a few close calls, but the medical ants have been able to get people at least stabilized so someone with better healing magic can actually save them.

I had thought I was just lucky . . . but now, I wonder if it's that Fate magic. I don't think I've ever used it, but if my scions have it, maybe my denizens have at least a little? Either way, it makes me hopeful that I won't actually need to make a memorial or something for the fallen. I'm still going to leave some room in the graveyard, maybe even use the central mausoleum, but I don't designate anything just yet. I can still hope.

Anyhow, back to my scions. Pretty much everyone's affinity isn't a surprise. I had actually expected Grim to have Death affinity, but I guess Grounds Reaper comes with Earth, rather than Death. Maybe he'll get something weird like Burial or something later, if that's even a thing.

Man, I desperately need more information on how magic works.

I do my best to explain some of the basic ideas to my various scions without using Teemo to relay it. For one, I don't want to hurt him again. For two . . . I don't know if specific concepts will actually work as an explanation. I worry it'd be like Teemo when he got overwhelmed if I tried to just explain every detail. Instead, with the empathic bond, I think they'll be able to figure things out a bit on their own.

And I'm not in a rush, which helps. I know I'm not simply fabricating a new thing; I'm practically having to *invent* stuff here. Making something new, whether it's an idea or a physical thing, takes a lot more time than a lot of people think. It's like getting flat-packed furniture. You have everything you need, you even have instructions, but it's going to take a lot of time to actually put it all together.

Except here, only a few things are labeled; there are a few extra pieces that won't fit, but we won't know that until we get into it, and the guy with the instructions has to try to mime them out instead of telling you.

So yeah, my magitech Rome isn't getting built in a day. Still, there's already progress. Everyone has been testing things, seeing if any of the concepts feel right. Tiny, for example, has started playing with his webbing and integrating his Kinetic affinity. Tension is a concept spiders understand instinctively, or else they couldn't build webs, and Tiny's pretty bright besides. He's been using a few sticks and branches as pulleys and just seeing how things work. I have no idea if it'll be applicable to his magic, but he's still interested.

Coda has been devouring every bit of engineering concept I can get through to him, even if I'm not sure it'll work with his Sonic affinity. Yeah, everyone else calls it Thunder, but I'm calling it Sonic. Anyhow, it might work for him; it's hard to say. If his affinity is more for pressure than waves, it could help him a ton. Pressure is just a distributed force, and engineering is all about forces in their forms.

Rocky has been the biggest surprise in all this, though. I dunno if he's a savant or what, but he's been able to move thermal energy around. I don't think he's quite crossed the threshold into what anyone else would consider Ice affinity, but he's been able to do a lot with his fire just from that bit of advice.

I'm not sure if I should be relieved or disappointed that he still hasn't managed a hadouken yet. Either way, I'm still proud of his progress.

Teemo, I'm also proud of, though his progress is a lot slower than the others with the concepts. I can't blame him, either. Non-Euclidean geometry is a difficult enough thing to grasp without me trying to pile on the relations between temperature, pressure, and volume. Besides, he's a natural with the odds-calculation stuff. The Fate affinity seems to come naturally to him, which is great. Aranya and Yvonne are having more difficulty with it, so he's happy to give them pointers and what help he can.

Queen and Honey are both Knowledge affinity, which seems to be a bit of an ironic mystery. The only thing my residents could really say with any confidence is that it's the opposite affinity to Illusion. That makes me suspect they're two sides of the same coin, but I can't really think of anything to test those two. I might be able to ask Torlon about it, but I don't know how much he'd be able to explain. He's kinda busy what with running a church.

Dawn approaches, and even with all the theorycrafting distractions, the first iteration of the gauntlet is ready to go. With it ready, I tell the healing ants to go ahead and heal the jerks to full before clearing out. I also tell Leo he should be there when they wake up, and Teemo too.

My Voice entertains them both with throwing pebbles at the trio to try to get them to wake up. He finally gets one to awaken when he tosses a pebble right into the troll's mouth when he starts to inhale a massive snore. He wakes with his eyes bulging for a moment before he coughs up the small rock. He looks around for a few moments, adrenaline clearly coursing through his veins, before he kicks his companions.

"Wake up!"

The wood elf yelps and curls up from the kick before groaning and looking around with bleary eyes. I don't think he's a morning person. Or he's still a bit sore from being bounced off the roof. The halfling grumbles something that would probably make her little thorn plants wither, and sits up to glare at the troll. The leader doesn't meet her glare, though. Instead, he's still looking around the cell they're all in.

"Where are we?" he demands of his underlings.

The elf shrugs. "Jail?"

The halfling just growls at him. "Who uses a dead-end cave as a jail cell, idiot?" She turns her vicious look on the troll. "We're still in your *toybox*, Vnarl."

The troll rounds on her with a snarl. "I get it! It's not a toybox!" I wonder if the two are actually going to throw down, but Hark speaks up before they can.

"So . . . what do we do?" They both turn to him to shout their ideas, but it seems like neither can actually think of anything. There's not a whole lot of options for them to do stuff. There's no clear door. They're in regular clothes. There's not even dirt for the halfling to grow her vines.

At this point, Leo decides to make his entrance, stepping in front of the bars so they can see him. All three notice the movement and relax a little in relief. Mlynda speaks, authority in her voice.

"Ah, you escaped, wolf. Get us out of here." Her smug look fades when he takes a seat and lets his tongue hang out of his mouth, giving his best wolfy grin as Teemo speaks up from his shoulder.

"You're not in any position to order him around, Mlynda."

She shrieks, "That's what you think! Enthrall!"

Teemo and Leo continue to smile at her. "That's adorable that you thought that would work." She shrieks a few more Enthralls at the two. "Less adorable now. Anyway, welcome to the Punitive Gauntlet!"

Vnarl and Hark look a bit confused, and everyone ignores Mlynda as she wears herself out trying to Enthrall my two scions.

"Uh . . . this looks more like a cell than a gauntlet," points out Hark, to which Teemo nods.

"Thedeim wanted to give you three a proper chance to prepare yourselves before having the challenge presented to you. I think you're going to need all the help you can get."

With that, the back wall slides down, and the three get their first look at the challenge I've made for them.

Chapter 61

Rather than looks of terror or concern or even excitement, the trio wear looks of confusion as they get their first look at the gauntlet. Maybe they were expecting swinging blades and gouts of flame? What they're getting are a lot of platforms, ropes, netting, and other things that look like a random jumble with even less of an obvious way forward than if I went with the blades-and-fire option.

"If you all want to escape, you all need to get through the gauntlet," says Teemo simply, which seems to get the jerks to focus. They still look pretty confused, which is fine. I'm not going to tell them how to do any of the obstacles.

Vnarl smirks as he starts to understand the first section. "Just a couple little steps for the first challenge? I hope your dungeon isn't feeling too proud of itself for this one!"

The first obstacle is a twist on the classic stepping stones. I have them set at different levels, so it'll be very difficult to go quickly through, but I also have them set up so they can pivot and rock. To get past them, they'll have to minimize their forward momentum. Otherwise, as Vnarl demonstrates, the platform will tilt, and that momentum will send you into the drink with a surprised look on your face. It also gives me a nice bit of mana.

Hark laughs at his leader while Mlynda sits on the edge, smirking at him as he tries to figure out what happened. "When are you going to stop underestimating this place?" she asks, still blaming him for their predicament. Not saying it's wrong to blame him, just saying she still is.

He grumbles and curses as he climbs the ladder back to the cell area. "Yeah? Let's see you two do better!"

With a shrug, Hark steps up.

"You gotta learn to be lighter on your feet, Vnarl," he says before jumping. While he sets himself to land with minimal momentum going forward, his foot lands well off-center of the small platform. It swivels away, giving him no purchase, and now Vnarl is the one laughing. I'm pretty happy too, with more mana in the bank.

"I thought you were light on your feet, Hark!" guffaws the troll, and Mlynda titters as well at his misfortune. Hark doesn't look too upset at failing, and even swims forward a bit to try to get an idea of what the next obstacles will entail. He can't get a good angle from the water to really see, though.

He climbs back onto the home platform and gestures for the halfling to try her luck. "Well, your turn to show us how it's done, heh."

Vnarl grins and nods, taking a seat. "Yeah, show us how it's done," he challenges.

I'm looking forward to collecting my mana from Mlynda too, as her companions challenge her to do any better. "Hmph, it can't be *that* hard. It's just a couple jumps," she says. She talks a big game, but I'm not sure how well she'll actually be able to do on the rocking stones. She gets a bit more of a run up to jump, and I'm practically counting the mana already.

She surprises me, however, by curling up a bit in the air and using her hands to grab the small platform as she lands. She actually manages to cling on, giving the other two a wide grin of victory. "Hah!" They look surprised for a few moments before grinning back at her.

"Hah!" shouts Vnarl in triumph as he points. There are several more stones to cross before she can truly claim victory, and without having a run up, there's very little chance for her to actually make the distance.

She tries anyway, the other two heckling her, but she only manages to flop into the water with a splash. Vnarl goes next, though he doesn't manage to get any further just yet. His landing looks a bit better, but he still can't manage to get a good jump to the next step.

I also notice I get less mana for him failing the trap a second time. It's about twenty percent less, looks like. I'm a little sad I can't get infinite mana, but I'm probably not the first dungeon to come up with the idea of sending delvers across a single trap multiple times. Some other dungeon must have tried sending delvers in a loop over some trap before, after all.

Ah, well. It's still extra mana for me, just not as much as I was hoping. I ask Teemo to head over to the enclave and let Leo keep watching the group try to get past the first challenge. I'll have to talk with him later about organizing some wolf expeditions, but that can come later. I let him enjoy his schadenfreude as Teemo slips down a shortcut.

Larx is tending to the mushroom beds when Teemo gets there, and he greets my Voice with a smile and a small bow. My rat has tried to get him not to do anything like that, but Larx insists. "Ah, Teemo. Have you come to try and find an early mushroom to harvest?" the ratkin asks with a smile and twinkle in his eye.

Teemo shakes his head. "Nah . . . well, not really. You know those delvers

Thedeim captured?" Larx nods, so my Voice continues. "They're probably gonna be there for a while, so they're going to need some food. Can you guys provide them with something to eat? Nothing too fancy, but Thedeim's gauntlet is going to take a lot of energy for them to get through."

Larx smiles at that and nods again. "I should be able to convince the others to help with that. They may get treated as taste testers for new recipes, too. Arthul has been wanting to try his hand at something more complex than stew for a couple weeks now."

Teemo chuckles. "That should be fine, as long as it's edible. Do you guys need anything in return? Thedeim doesn't want to just impose on you for this."

Larx considers that for a few moments. "Could you ask him to send a few more thorough expeditions down our main hunting tunnel? The caverns down there are very interesting and great for hunting, but they're nowhere near fully mapped yet. Some of the hunters say the air has been feeling different down at the outskirts of our hunting range, too. I don't think it'll be anything too concerning, but perhaps he could check and put our minds at ease?"

"That sounds good. Leo needs to get some experience organizing expeditions anyway. It'll be a good way for him to get used to it before he has to try to send his wolves out on the surface."

"Then we have an accord," says Larx, holding out a finger, which Teemo shakes.

Elsewhere

Fungus and centipede work in conjunction to safeguard their little purple source of light. Neither would usually care about light, nor would they always work so closely toward a goal, but things have changed since the tiny fragment coalesced.

Ever since they started working together, *others* have been trying to reach the little piece of purple. Roaches were the first, but have made little headway. Spores and mandibles make quick work of them, and their small mutual master wants more to feed upon.

The second outsider is much more difficult, but makes a worthy tribute for their master. Fur, teeth, and grasping claws, the beast felled a full dozen centipedes before finally succumbing. The guiding force fed well and made *two* dozen centipedes to prepare for the next beast.

The presence of their master slowly spreads through the cavern, unaware of its purpose. It just knows it must grow.

Chapter 62

I think Leo could watch the terrible trio fail at the gauntlet all day. They've actually started getting a couple stones through, but haven't managed to clear all of them. I don't think it'll be too long before they get through that first challenge, however. Probably tomorrow, after they rest up a bit.

I impress upon Leo the need for him to send a few of the lesser wolves down the ratkin's hunting tunnel. At first, I thought the lesser wolves were cubs or something, but they seem fully aware and mobile. They're just more sized like coyotes than wolves. I guess that's why they're called *lesser*?

Whatever the reason or relation to actual wolves, Leo starts heading to the roof, wanting to talk to Poe. Makes sense to me. Poe has been in charge of everything sent outside, so it'd be a good idea to get tips and tricks from him.

He takes a shortcut without much haste, and I notice a familiar person enter from the gates. My birds all make a racket, and I smile to myself as Elf Guy shakes his head at the greeting. He walks up to the bulletin board and speaks to it.

"Dungeon Thedeim, please bring forth your Voice. The Dungeoneer's Guild wishes to discuss a matter," he says formally, and I poke Teemo to go see what he needs. It doesn't take my Voice long to get there.

"What's with the formality, Elf Guy?" greets Teemo with a smirk.

Tarl can only chuckle. "The guild prefers it."

"Well, me and the Boss don't. Knock it off and just talk normal."

The inspector smiles at that. "Fair enough, heh. Each individual dungeon has to be dealt with differently. Which is why I'm here, actually. The Southwood is another dungeon, one the guild classifies as a toybox. It has few denizens, and none specialized toward combat."

"Ah, that's why those knuckleheads were talking about a toybox. I thought they were just trying to insult the Boss."

Tarl snorts at that. "They might have been. Anyway, the Southwood allows the guild to check up on the core on one condition: that it be given information on the other known dungeons in the general area."

Teemo perks up at that. "Yeah? Does it know about us?"

"A bit. It knows you're a manor in the city and had a conflict with Neverrest, but my information was out of date even when I talked to it. Its Voice actually told *me* that you may have destroyed Neverrest. It felt the wasp invaders lessen with your victory."

"Huh."

Tarl nods and continues. "So I wanted to know what information you're comfortable with sharing with the Southwood. Ordinarily, we'd simply give it the basics, but it has specifically asked for information about you, and offered information about the Green Sea in return."

"What's the Green Sea?" asks Teemo as he absently scratches his ear.

"It's a massive forest to the north of here. The Southwood is actually named that because it's the southernmost tip of it. There are theories that it's a massive dungeon, or even a network of dungeons, but it's so remote and the trip so arduous that none have actually been able to confirm anything. And the Southwood implied something is happening there."

"Which could be a big pain in the rear for all of us. So . . . you want to know what to tell it? Will you tell us about it in exchange?"

Tarl nods. "The Southwood likes to keep tabs on other dungeons, but it isn't too concerned about other dungeons knowing too much about it. The only real restriction is on information about its core, but every dungeon is at least a little cagey about those details."

Teemo and I huddle up to discuss what to give out, and he focuses on Tarl after a few minutes.

"The basics should be fine: where we are, how big we are, spawners and monsters and stuff. You can even tell it about the Punitive Gauntlet if you want." He holds up a tiny hand to stop Tarl before he can even say how bad an idea that could be. "The Boss says it has diminishing returns. The group woke up this morning, and the mana they're making is already down to a trickle. He says other dungeons have probably designed themselves to send adventurers over the same trap multiple times before, too. He says the extra mana is nice, but not exceptional."

Elf Guy actually pulls out his little note stone and repeats that information before looking back to Teemo. "Then that should be more than enough to satisfy the Southwood. I don't think I'll tell it about the gauntlet, mostly because I don't think it's really feasible for it to try something similar."

Teemo perks up as he remembers something. "Oh, we also have a wolf spawner now, too."

Tarl looks confused at that. "Did you expand out past the cemetery?"

Teemo shakes his head. "Nah. That druid halfling had Enthralled a wolf from somewhere, and when she got knocked out, the spell broke. The wolf didn't want to go back to her, so Thedeim offered to let him stay here. And then made him a scion, which then also let him make a wolf spawner."

The inspector looks fascinated by that. "I've heard of dungeons being able to produce spawners without expansion, but the details are always sparse."

Teemo nods. "The Boss says maybe keep that fact from the Southwood. He says turning invaders into spawners could be a dangerous thing to let get out . . . though he doesn't know if all dungeons have access to a jail."

Elf Guy taps his note stone against his chin as he thinks. "Jails are fairly rare to find in a dungeon, though secret jails may be more common. I think most dungeons are just not smart enough to use a jail when they're young, and don't really need it when they're older and have the mana to just straight-out pay for a new spawner. Still, I'll keep how you got a Wolf Scion and spawner quiet. It's not something I think the Southwood would actually try to do anyway."

Leo

Watching the group fail to get across the least of the challenges of the Alpha fills Leo with a deep sense of happiness. The Voice called it schadenfreude, which is a strange word . . . but not an inaccurate one. Still, the duties of his new title gnaw at his tail like a teething pup, so he can't just enjoy the show forever.

Alpha Thedeim wishes to ensure the safety of the lands and people outside his borders, and that job belongs to Leo now. The Alpha wishes him to cut his teeth on some simpler expeditions down in the tunnels in aid of the dwellers, and Leo is happy to have something simple to build his understanding on.

He's just a little confused as to why he's expected to do it, rather than Poe. The Marshal has had command of expeditions above and below the ground for quite some time, so why would the Alpha set his newest scion with such a similar task? He could go and ask. The Voice is happy enough to explain what needs explaining, but Leo has a different target in mind.

You send a new pup with an experienced hunter for their first hunt. So he should go see the experienced expedition leader for advice, and see if he knows why Leo has this duty instead of him.

Taking a shortcut is an interesting experience. His old dungeon never had a Scout, and so only had a few actual secret passages, and they were all fully mundane. These, however, let him squeeze into a crack even a mouse should have difficulty with, and then walk with ease toward a different one to slip out of. Honestly, these things are probably why the Alpha doesn't worry about crowding delvers. If there are too many denizens in an area, they can easily move without just rolling over any delvers, and if there are too few, more can be easily moved into position.

He hops off that particular train of thought as he exits the shortcut to the roof and makes his way toward Poe. He tucks his tail in submission to the large bird, who immediately waves it off.

"That is not needed, Warden Leo. We both serve Lord Thedeim, and so need not bow and scrape to each other."

"That's easy for you to say after having a go at my belly," grumps Leo as he remembers how the fight went.

Poe just nods. "If not for Lord Thedeim, I would have happily sunk my beak and talons into your belly, but he urged mercy, and his wisdom in doing so now stands on the roof with me. He has a new scion and a new spawner because of you. You should not think lesser of yourself for the method it was achieved."

Leo shakes his head. His new Alpha has some weird Betas. "The Alpha has asked me to mount some expeditions, but I don't know why. And . . . I don't really know how. I was just a regular wolf at my old dungeon; I never had to be in charge of anything."

Poe nods at that as well. "While only Voice Teemo actually knows the thoughts of our Lord Thedeim, he has a reason for treating us as he does. As for the expeditions . . . while my flocks can detail the maps with ease, they can't detail what lives on those maps. On the wing, there is little care about those moving along on the ground, be they mice or bears. I've tried to get them to understand the need to pay attention but . . . it is difficult."

Leo sits and lets his tail idly swish back and forth as he absorbs that. "So . . . you know the land, but the Alpha also wants to know the *life*."

Poe fluffs his feathers in happiness at that. "Indeed! There is far more to understanding the surroundings than in simple topography. As for expedition advice . . . I'd suggest making sure your denizens know to flee rather than fight, should the need arise. Lord Thedeim does not wish undue death nor harm to anyone. The expeditions we send beyond his borders should follow this as well."

That makes sense. Why change policy drastically when outside? Though that also reminds him of something else. "Why does the Alpha have so many scions? *How* does he have so many?"

Poe caws in laughter before turning amused eyes on the wolf. "I can only guess as to Lord Thedeim's secrets, but I do have an idea for that. Your old dungeon; did it give you direct orders to do things?"

Leo nods. "Of course. Denizens would get all kinds of orders."

"How many times has Lord Thedeim given you an order?"

Leo opens his muzzle to answer, but slowly closes it as he thinks. ". . . Being made a Warden was the closest thing to an order he's given me."

Poe fluffs his feathers again. "I believe that is why Lord Thedeim can support so many of us. I'm honestly uncertain if he's noticed our upkeep costs, partially because I'd expect they pale in comparison to what he spends his mana on."

"Like the gauntlet."

"Indeed. So he gives us directions and lets us pursue them as we see fit, trusting we will do the job to the best of our abilities. He doesn't need to constantly spend mana to give us orders. He challenges us to grow, and so he grows with us, and us with him."

Leo is quiet as he thinks about that as well. He never thought being a scion would involve so much *thinking!* In his old dungeon, he just had to be strong and fight, after all. His old dungeon also progressed a lot slower. Even in the short time he's been here, he's seen more change than in a month at the old dungeon.

Poe interrupts his thoughts as he speaks up again. "Now then, as to how to actually run an expedition, I should be able to help with that. Let me see, where to start . . ."

Chapter 63

The terrible trio have finally managed to get past the rocking stones. The diminishing returns for a trap also reset at dawn . . . I think. They reset at *some* point, at least. It might be midnight, it might be dawn, it might just be from them not triggering the trap for a while because they're sleeping and I have the wall up. Whatever the actual reason, my new mana source is stable, if not especially large.

The public gauntlet will probably be a great hit, though. Even the trio seems to be . . . well, not exactly *enjoying* the challenge, but also not exactly hating it either. They're getting stuck on the wave log right now, however.

I have a log roll thing set up, with the ends stuck into the wall for a track. It follows a bit of a wave shape, going up and down a few times before getting to the next platform. The log is also fairly rough, which the trio seem to think is to give their feet grip as they try to walk on it while also making them be careful about tripping.

None of them have realized they need to just hug the thing and not drop off yet. It's pretty funny watching them get stuck in the first dip, however. Fluffles is keeping an eye on them down there at the moment and is using his telekinesis to reset the log once they fall off. None of them are actually all that adept at log rolling, so I think they might be stuck on this one until someone thinks outside the box.

Speaking of outside: Leo's expeditions are coming back with all kinds of interesting details? The bats that Poe would send underground had the same kind of intel issues the birds do, except bats don't even care about shinies. I know a lot about how the ceilings are, but that's not exactly useful.

With the lesser wolves, however, I get great info! This cavern has some glowing mushrooms instead of the moss stuff; that cavern has some old claw marks, probably from a scythemaw; this other cavern has a little stream and pool, and so on. Nothing is especially concerning just yet. Even the scythemaw marks have moss and such growing over them, so if they were marking territory, that maw is long gone. It might have even been the one that chased Aranya!

The lesser wolves have also started noticing the weird something the ratkin have been noticing too, but haven't been able to quite put their paw pads on what it is just yet. With both the lesser wolves and the ratkin feeling something weird, I've decided to slow down on the public gauntlet—for a moment, at least—and upgrade the wolf spawner a few times to get it to start making actual wolves.

I also get access to specializations, but I don't specialize it just yet. I think I might actually go for something offensive with the wolves, but I'm not sure what. Dire wolves aren't a specialization, which isn't surprising. I figure that will probably be one of the later things the spawner will make, maybe even the last. Some of the specialization options might make Cerberuses instead, but I still haven't decided on what to take.

I almost take timberwolves, just because I can taste the pun, but I have enough plant-related things right now. I'm leaning toward either Orthruses or tundra wolves, which seem to be physical and magical specializations, respectively. An Orthrus is just a two-headed doggo, which is why I expect they'll probably end up with Cerberuses at the end . . . unless I can get some kind of wolf hydra.

The tundra wolves are Ice aspected, which could be cool, pun only kinda intended. I'm just not sure which to take. Orthruses would lead to very cool denizens, and with Cerberuses, I'd have some great guards. On the other hand, I don't really have much in the way of denizens that cast spells and such. I dunno.

Although . . . I could take the multi-puppers and just get a new spawner and set that toward magic. I've been thinking of the other invaders and catching some to make my own, but most of them aren't really tempting. The roaches are just no. Even if they're a viable option, I don't want giant roaches wandering around.

Mice are also a no because they're basically just weaker rats. I wouldn't be surprised at all if they just *become* rats if they join me, too. There are still some wasps around, but I don't need them. I already know they're the same thing as the bees, even if I also know they're about as unrelated biologically as flying, striped, stinging insects can be.

The seagulls are also a no. I'm pretty sure they're just a different specialization for birds, and I already have my ravens. It might be interesting to see a gull turn into a raven, but I don't want to convert one just to have a show.

There are two invaders which might have some potential, though. The first are the moles. I know they can't dig through stone, at least not as normal moles, but I'd be shocked if I can't at least specialize them into something that can. That'd make expanding deeper go so much more smoothly. The ratlings are doing a good job, especially with Coda's help, but I think they're better at doing basic crafting than mining.

The other invaders that could be an interesting denizen are the gremlins that are always after my mining nodes. They're quick, sneaky, and at least strong enough to dislodge a bit of ore or a gemstone from a node. They might make good miners, too, as well as potentially being good to send on expeditions.

Either way, I think I'm going to wait before trying to get a new spawner. I could probably fit one or two around, but I want to get more space before trying. I was originally going to start expanding down the tunnel Aranya came from, but recent stuff has made a few other options interesting.

I could expand past the cemetery walls and get a taste of the wilderness. I'm sure there are all kinds of interesting things I could get, and tons of room for more herbalism or lumber nodes. I wonder if animal nodes are a thing. It'd also give me a better foothold to try looking into the Green Sea. That's a pretty long-term project, though, so no real rush on it.

The other option is to expand down the ratkin's hunting tunnel. It'll help secure their hunting grounds, and maybe I can even get a spawner for whatever is giving everyone that weird feeling. I'm kinda in the business of weird, after all.

Chapter 64

The public gauntlet is getting close to being finished. I've made it a lot simpler and easier than the one attached to the jail. Once the trio finally free themselves, I'll probably open that one up to everyone, too. The mana gains are decent, but with the investment I put in, I don't think it's especially dangerous for other dungeons to try something similar.

It might even encourage other dungeons to capture instead of kill delvers, who knows?

The trio has also managed to get past the wave log. The troll tripped and managed to cling to the log, doing a few spins before it stalled out on him. So now they know to just grab on from the start.

It's funny seeing them look so unstable when they get off. Nobody has fallen into the water because of it, though. They all just take a seat to let the world stop spinning and try to figure out the next obstacle: my own take on the salmon ladder.

If I had left the stick free, they'd have just taken it and probably tried something stupid. So instead of a little ladder of pegs they have to try to climb, I have it set in a track with the most basic of ratcheting systems. It's basically a bunch of hinges. They'll let the stick move up past them, but when gravity puts its foot down, the hinge blocks it from falling further.

And the trio has no idea what to do about it. I'm pretty sure Vnarl and Hark could do pull-ups with enough vigor to climb, but I don't know about Mlynda. None of them have actually figured out how it works yet. It's not exactly an intuitive thing to try if you haven't seen the show. So far, they've just been jumping to it, climbing on top of the bar, and looking around confused.

If they don't figure it out in a day or two, I'll probably have Teemo tell them what to do.

The expeditions in the tunnels are getting closer to whatever the weirdness is. They've been taking it carefully, making sure the weirdness isn't just from them going deeper into the tunnels. The regular wolves seem to be a lot better at getting info than the lesser ones, so I've been having the lessers come join in my encounters.

Freddie and Rhonda have been enjoying them a lot, and the kids are actually starting to go and encounter my undead, too. They've even gone a couple rounds with Rocky, though they haven't won yet. I've been keeping him from practicing his magic on them too much, just going with his basic fire and ice punches. Once he gets better at it, I'm going to explain to him thermal shock. He might even be figuring that out on his own. He likes to alternate hot and cold punches, though that might just be because he alternates his hands to actually throw them.

Elsewhere

Giants stalk in the unknown. Mushroom and centipede have valiantly fought off the soft invaders of teeth and claw, but outside has much more terrifying things in store. The perceptions of the purple shard have encompassed the cavern, but there is a void in one of the sides. And outside that void lurk giants.

Centipedes have tried to brave the outside, but it is disorienting and confusing beyond the safety of the influence of the shard. Sounds can be heard, rumbles can be felt, shadows can be seen . . . the beasts of teeth and claw are among the least of the threats from outside.

So what can be done?

Leo

The prisoners are behaving . . . at least as well as can be expected. They eat the stew the ratkin provide and attempt the gauntlet, bickering the entire time. Leo still enjoys watching them fail, but to be honest, managing the expeditions is so much more interesting.

The new wolves are eager to prove themselves to him and to the Alpha, and they've been working well with the ratkin. Leo is pretty sure they're going to be taming many of the wolves properly, rather than being like that *halfling* and Enthralling them. It's good for both of them, really.

The wolves have way better senses than the ratkin, and the ratkin have thumbs and pockets to bring things back. One of the first wolf expeditions tried to bring back a few mushrooms, but what wasn't accidentally swallowed was too slobbery to be useful, and the wolf that swallowed his had a very unpleasant time.

The next expedition returns as scheduled and makes their report. They've been tracking the scent with the help of the ratkin, and believe they've actually found the source! Leo's excitement to accomplish this for his new Alpha is quickly tempered when the wolves tell him what the source is, though.

It's a dungeon. A pup who hasn't even opened its eyes yet. They had considered destroying it, but that would be a fight, and Leo had made sure to impress on them Poe's advice to avoid fights. Leo would have told them to just end it before it could be a threat . . . but he gets the feeling Alpha Thedeim won't do that. He can't imagine what his Alpha will *actually* do, but he won't need to even try.

He mentally tucks his tail and gives his report through the empathic bond. He can feel the mild disapproval at him showing his belly like that, but Poe says the Alpha isn't likely to act on it. He doesn't like to stand on protocol often, which only encourages him and Poe to keep doing it. They want to show their respect, after all.

Alpha Thedeim seems intrigued by the news, and many emotions and concepts flitter through the bond, too quick to comprehend, before it settles down. Leo is to send expeditions to keep the pup safe, but not to enter its domain.

He can also feel the Alpha reach for the Voice, and actually send him on an expedition, too.

The Office of Dungeon Affairs

Telar works at her desk, industriously transcribing Tarl's reports to go into the official record, and preparing to transcribe from the official record regarding both Hullbreak Harbor and the Southwood. Thedeim expressed interest in information on them, and while she'd prefer to keep Hullbreak's details quiet, they might be able to barter at least some information to at least get a look at Thedeim's core.

Most dungeons have some form of trick to keep their cores safe. The most obvious is a dedicated scion to attack any who get too close, while the second is to simply hide it. Most do both, like with Neverrest. Sure, its true core was close to the false one, but an effort was at least made to keep it hidden.

"Where's Elf Guy?" asks a voice from nowhere, and Telar only just manages to not upend her inkwell over the papers in her surprise. She looks around the small room which is the public face of the Dungeoneer's Guild but can't find the source of the voice. A whistle calls her attention to the top of a shelf of pamphlets, and she sees a rat?

"Yep, it's me. I'm Teemo, the Voice of Thedeim." Telar stares for a few moments, her mind racing to try to remember the protocols for talking to a dungeon's Voice. Teemo, however, doesn't let her get her legs underneath her, and repeats his question.

"Where's Elf Guy? You know, the inspector? Tarl?"

"Er . . . he's off to the Southwood to give it the information it requested," tries the elf, wishing she had gotten more training in how to actually talk to a dungeon and its Voice. She's supposed to be directly dealing with people, not dungeons! At least, she doesn't seem to have offended it yet.

Teemo nods. "Right, right, didn't think he'd be off so quickly. You're part of the ODA, right?"

"ODA?" she asks, confused.

"The Office of Dungeon Affairs. That's what he calls you guys. He knows you're the Dungeoneer's Guild, but that still doesn't stop him from calling you that."

That raises so many questions, Telar doesn't even know where to start. She latches onto the one thing he said that makes any actual sense. "Yes, I'm part of the Dungeoneer's Guild. I am the guildmistress for this particular branch. How can the Dungeoneer's Guild assist you, Voice Teemo of Thedeim?" Oh, sure, *now* her training kicks in.

"Well, the Boss found a dungeon in the deep tunnels. A baby one, apparently. He wants to know what to do about it."

"He found another dungeon?!"

Chapter 65

It feels kinda weird to watch through Teemo's eyes while he talks with the ODA lady. I've gotten so used to just *knowing* what's going on around me that just having the directed senses of a rat is strange to me now.

"The Boss is pretty sure it's a dungeon, at least," says my Voice. "The expedition can taste it, but it's really small. The Boss was most of the entire manor when he started, but the little cavern this one is in is barely bigger than the main entrance room."

The lady's eyes widen slightly at that. "You really did find a nascent dungeon, seems like. What have you done with it so far? What do you plan to do with it?"

"Well . . . the Boss isn't sure yet. He doesn't want to just eat it like Neverrest, but he doesn't know if that's even an option. And if peace can happen, he has no idea how to start."

She nods and starts digging through her desk. "Dungeons can peacefully coexist, though it's usually more a matter of them being too far apart for attacks to be viable. I know I've heard of ones coexisting, but I don't know if I have any of those records handy . . ."

Cool, so we can give peace a chance. But how? I'm almost positive any denizens I send in will be labeled as invaders, and probably won't make the dungeon trust me much. And sending a scion could be even more dangerous. Teemo might be alright; a Voice is for talking, after all. But sending someone like Fluffles would probably be a declaration of war.

I don't even know if my dwellers would count as neutral parties or as delvers for the little dungeon.

Teemo listens to me thinking to myself while the lady digs through her stuff, then speaks up. "Would the ratkin be fine to send inside? The Boss hasn't asked anyone to go in yet. In fact, he's been pretty explicit that everyone stay out."

She nods as she digs through a cabinet. "Good. Dwellers count as invaders in other dungeons, as they are at least implicitly on the side of a foreign dungeon. Keeping everyone out of it is a good idea for now. Ideally, we'd wait for Inspector Tarl to return, but he's likely to be gone for at least two weeks, probably closer to three."

"Yeah, that's a lot of time to just let the thing sit on the Boss's doorstep."

She sighs as she seems to accept she doesn't have the references she's been looking for, and she sits back in her chair. "We'll need to get some delvers to go take a look."

"How about Rhonda and Freddie? They seem to be pretty interested in dungeon stuff, and that one seems pretty weak, so they shouldn't be in much danger," suggests Teemo.

The elf considers that for a few seconds. "That could work. If I give them a quest to check it out, that should keep them listed as delvers, even if you help them get down there. They'll need to check it often, every few days at the worst, daily if they can manage."

"Alright. You make the quest; I'll go see if they're interested." With that, my Voice hops off his perch and heads out. He doesn't have any shortcuts outside my borders. That was one of the first things he tried, and while he can, they're a lot harder for him to keep hidden outside. I don't think my outside friends will appreciate shortcuts into their homes, so it's the long way for us.

Thankfully, Teemo is still a rat, so it's not exactly difficult for him to move around unnoticed, even without him actually using his various stealth tricks. Closest to the ODA is Old Staiven's shop, so he heads there first to check in on the nerdy little goblin.

"Is the dungeon doing some delving of its own now?" asks Staiven with a grin as Teemo enters. My Voice is a bit surprised the old ratkin noticed him, but he probably shouldn't have been. I bet Staiven has enough wards and stuff on his shop that he'd even notice a fly entering without his explicit permission.

"Actually, the Boss wants to talk with Rhonda. We found something, and the dungeon guild people thinks she and Freddie might be a good fit to check it out."

"Ah, interesting. Rhonda and Freddie *have* taken quite the interest in dungeons . . . She's down in the lab right now, taking inventory. There are a few things in there she probably hasn't seen yet, so it was going to be a bit of a test, but it can wait for her to look into this thing for you."

"Er . . . it'll probably be a daily thing for her to look into," informs Teemo, but Staiven just waves that off.

"If it's something dungeon related, she can do it on her off time each day. Goodness knows she'll make any excuse to go delving in her free time anyway." He inhales and raises his voice. "Rhonda! Upstairs! You have a visitor!"

A muffled, "Coming!" comes from the open hatch behind the counter, and soon follows the goblin herself, hat and spider on her head. She looks around the shop, confused for a few seconds, before she speaks up. "Where's Freddie?"

Staiven just smiles at his apprentice. "I didn't say it was Freddie. The dungeon's Voice is here for you."

She gasps and looks around. Teemo has mercy on her by hopping up on the counter and squeaking.

"Right here, kiddo. Thedeim found a nascent dungeon in the deep tunnels and wants to make peaceful contact. The dungeon folk say that pretty much anything he tries to send will be treated as an invader, though, so he needs delvers to do it, and suggested you and Freddie."

Rhonda's eyes shine with curiosity at that. "A *nascent* dungeon?! Why us? Shouldn't Mr. Tarl be sent for that?"

"He's off on a quest to the Southwood, so he's going to be a while. So, you want the job?"

"Yes!" she shouts, before blushing and calming herself. "I mean, uh . . . Master? May I?"

He rolls his eyes and chuckles at the goblin. "That's fine with me, Rhonda. This will be on your own time, though. I'll not have you skipping your lessons to go gallivanting down dangerous tunnels."

She whoops and thanks him, and Teemo speaks up after she calms down a bit. "Alright, let's go talk with Freddie, then, and see if he can go, too."

She nods vigorously, and her hat doesn't move as much as I'd expect. Lucas, her spider, is looking happy with himself, so I think he's webbed it to her head. Doesn't seem like she minds, at least.

Teemo hops on and nods to Lucas, who gives him a little bow in return. "Alright, to the Church of the Crystal Shield!"

It actually takes a few minutes before they can go, as Rhonda needs to mark her spot in the inventory process. Once Staiven is satisfied she'll be able to pick up where she left off, he lets them all go.

It's much faster riding Rhonda than Teemo walking on his own. A rat on his own needs to be stealthy. A rat on a girl's hat whom she is actively talking with is just another curiosity that the townsfolk chalk up to the dungeon being weird.

At the church, Rhonda walks up to one of the priests who's sweeping the steps and asks if her friend is available. It seems Freddie is in the barracks behind the church, doing some training. She thanks him and heads there.

Inside, a shirtless Freddie holding a wooden axe and a training shield is facing off against one of those spinning wooden dummies. He'll hit one of the arms of the thing and it'll spin, so he has to put his shield up to block the counter.

Rhonda takes a few seconds to enjoy the show before Teemo speaks up.

"Hey, Freddie! You busy?"

The orc stops and steps back, looking over his shoulder at the trio in confusion for a moment, before recognizing his friend. His look of confusion returns quickly, however, as he doesn't spot my Voice. "Did you learn a new spell to change your voice, Rhonda?" he asks. She giggles and shakes her head, pointing to the rat on her hat.

"Nope! Teemo's here! He has a quest for us!"

"Actually, I don't. Technically, if me or the Boss gave you the quest, it'd mess the whole thing up."

Freddie looks a bit lost. "You have a not-quest for us?"

Teemo chuckles as Rhonda walks to her friend, who is moving to towel himself off and have some water thanks to the break in his workout. "The Boss found a nascent dungeon, which is like a baby or something." Teemo shrugs. "He wants to try peace with it, but anything he sends would be an invader. So he needs delvers, and they need to be not technically working for him. The lady at the guild says she'll make a quest for it."

"Why not send Mr. Tarl? Isn't that his job?" asks Freddie as his own spider descends from the ceiling and plucks Lucas from Rhonda's hat. The kids don't seem concerned about that, so I guess the two spiders will just do spidery things together when their masters hang out.

"He's off to the Southwood, or we would leave it to him, but the dungeon is too close to just let it grow on its own."

"Hmm. Let me check with the Head Priest. I'd be happy to explore, but I want to make sure it won't mess with my training." Rhonda and Teemo both nod at that, and Freddie gets his shirt back on while Teemo hops back onto the hat. It looks like the spiders are busy chatting or playing, so they get left to their own devices in the rafters.

Getting to the Head Priest is pretty simple. He runs a pretty chill ship, seems like, and nobody tries to stop the group from knocking on his door. Maybe they just know Freddie and Rhonda well enough to know they wouldn't bother him for something silly.

I can't help but smile to myself as they're let in and I see the battered shield above the gnome's desk, who smiles warmly at the two over some paperwork he had been working on. A bit of surprise crosses his expression once he notices Teemo on Rhonda's hat.

"Rhonda and Freddie, how're you two doing? And the dungeon's Voice too?" he asks jovially, glancing above himself at the shield with its new chip.

Freddie takes the lead. "Well, sir, Thedeim has found a nascent dungeon, and the Dungeoneer's Guild would like us to check it out and keep an eye on it. Mr. Tarl is out on business, so he can't do it."

"It'll pretty much be a daily thing, too," adds Rhonda.

Head Priest Torlon nods at that. "Ah, I see." He taps a finger against his desk as he thinks. "I don't see any problem with that. You go delving often enough in your free time, so I don't think it'll interfere with your training, Freddie. It'll need to be on your free time, however."

The young orc nods at that. "Yes, sir. I'd like to try this, sir. Dungeoneering is . . . interesting."

Torlon smiles at that. "Good! Maybe you and Rhonda will be able to join the Dungeoneer's instead of the adventurers' guild when your apprenticeships are done. Paladins are encouraged to go out into the world and spread the word rather than sit in the temple all day and do paperwork," he says with a wink before waving the two off. "Away with you two, unless there's something else? This sounds like a great opportunity for you two, so no sense delaying."

The kids nod and bid their farewells, getting a quick blessing from him as well, before making their way back to the barracks to collect their spiders, then to the ODA, which has changed slightly.

Instead of only the lady's desk, there are now two smaller ones pulled out as well.

The kids exchange a glance before the guildmistress speaks up.

"Have a seat, you two. I don't mind sending you off to investigate the dungeon, but I refuse to send you off without at least some basic training."

Rhonda eagerly takes a seat and pulls out her notebook and charcoal stick. Freddie whispers to her, and she giggles before giving him a few loose pieces of paper and his own writing implement. I get the feeling it's not the first time he's come to class without the proper tools. I wonder if they'd have been so interested if they knew they'd be in school for a bit before getting to go look at the shiny new dungeon.

Chapter 66

I only half pay attention to what the lady tells the kids, though I do at least catch that her name is Telar. I kinda already know the basics of dungeons just from experience, and from how Elf Guy behaved in those early inspections: beat up a few things, gather a few things, take a look around . . . That's about it.

It's difficult to pay too much attention over there when the terrible trio is making unexpected progress in the gauntlet. They still haven't figured out how to do the salmon ladder properly, but they seem to have an idea that will probably work . . . in theory, at least. They're formulating and practicing in their cell area right now.

"Do you two have any better ideas?" asks Vnarl, though without the usual snarl. Hark shakes his head, and Mlynda just sighs.

"I know there's more to it than just a bar. It goes into the wall weirdly. I just can't figure out what it does," she says, and Vnarl shrugs.

"If you figure it out, maybe we'll try something else, but this is our best bet right now." The halfling wants to argue, but she knows she doesn't have any other ideas at the moment. Hark is looking more relaxed than the first day they were all put in here. He's probably glad mommy and daddy aren't fighting as much anymore.

He carefully positions his feet, almost taking a low horse stance, then nods at Vnarl. "Well, let's get to work. Once we can do this on normal ground, we can try doing it on that bar."

The troll nods and climbs onto the elf's shoulders, taking a similar squatting stance. The two look really unstable, and Hark has to adjust his feet a couple times before he stabilizes. Vnarl is still a bit wobbly, though. They decide that's good enough for the moment, and he motions for Mlynda to climb up. She still doesn't look like she likes this plan, but she climbs her two party members and squats on Vnarl's shoulders.

The trio compares notes, starting with Hark, as they all try to keep their little pyramid/tower going. "I think getting Vnarl into position is going to be the big hurdle." The troll glowers a bit, but grudgingly nods.

"Yeah . . . Mlynda climbing up isn't much of an issue with how light she is, but me climbing onto Hark is . . . awkward." The halfling thinks for a few moments before speaking up.

"Try it closer to the wall, then? It'll give you something else to try to use for support," she suggests, and the guys consider that.

"That could work," confirms Hark, and the three get their feet back on the ground before moving to the wall to try the suggestion. With a hand on the surface, Hark is *much* more stable, and Vnarl has a much easier time climbing up, too. The halfling scurries up and plants herself on the top, and the three smile in triumph before Vnarl speaks up.

"And then we stand, I lift Mlynda as high as I can, and she just has to hang on until Hark can climb up!"

"Easier said than done . . ." grumbles Mlynda, but she seems on board with the plan.

Not the intended way to get past it, but if they start actually working together as a team, rehabilitation might really be an option. It's actually the *next* obstacle that's supposed to teach them to start working together, but I'm not going to complain about them getting their act together a little early, even if they're overthinking the salmon ladder.

The next obstacle for them is a cargo net conveyor belt. I have a cargo net that loops around two free-spinning things, letting it move like a conveyor belt when someone tries to climb. I think someone could, theoretically, climb it fast enough to get to the top on their own, but have you ever seen someone try to climb a cargo net with speed? It's hilarious. The solution for that one is simple: just have someone hold the net to keep it from moving.

I had expected that one to take them a couple tries to figure out, but now, I think they'll barely be slowed down by the challenge. After that will come the last of the ninja challenges. I had considered a warped wall kind of thing, but that'd put the shorter races at a severe disadvantage. Instead, I came up with what I'm calling the wedge climb.

It's kinda like a spider climb, where there are two walls close enough that you have to wedge your arms and legs to keep yourself from falling, but the walls aren't parallel. It looks like a big wedge has been taken out of the wall, which will also make it harder to actually wedge yourself into it. That one will probably also take them a while to get through.

The next couple hours, I busy myself with working on the public gauntlet. People could probably run it now, but I want to get a bit of polish first. It's looking pretty rough right now. The aranea have been pretty interested in it lately, too. They haven't given any quests for it yet, but they have woven a few large pads and placed them around the platforms.

I need to figure out some kind of waterproofing if I don't want them having to constantly replace the things. Maybe Queen can do something? Or Thing? I poke them both with ideas and suggest they look at the library for more. Honey has finally cataloged everything, and has been wanting to send expeditions to get more books, but I haven't let her. I don't need her to go and steal a library. I'm hoping I can get Telar to get me a line to a book dealer eventually.

Not right now, though. Looks like she's done teaching the basics, so the kids are ready to go take a look at the little dungeon. A couple of the ratkin are going with them, so at least nothing nasty in the tunnels should be able to surprise them.

Elsewhere

Giants stalk at the bounds of perception. The soft invaders could be crushed underfoot of the titans who lurk outside. The master of the fungus and centipedes is wary. It's vulnerable. But how can it hide better? It's already hidden behind many caps. What else can it do?

The giants are content to lurk no longer. The first enters, and it towers over everything. It is green and has a wide mushroom cap. Could . . . it actually be friendly? Mushrooms are good. What follows the enormous mushroom is definitely *not* a mushroom. While it is also green, it has no cap, and it *towers* over the walking mushroom.

It rumbles, and the walking mushroom rumbles back. Uncertain, the master of fungus and centipede sends a wave of defenders to stop the intruders. They don't feel like an existential threat like the invaders, but they should still be driven back.

The centipedes answer the call and move to assault the titans, but they are destroyed by ice. The master gets a lot of energy from that, and so starts to send waves of valiant centipedes to assault the intruders. They only rumble at each other as they walk around inside, and it's not long until the titanic walking mushroom finds the shard of purple. It was plucking its smaller kin and happened upon the fragment.

It rumbles and the not-mushroom comes and looks. In desperation, the master sends all its forces, but to no avail. However, the two don't harm the shard. With the energy gained, it regrows the mushrooms hiding itself, and the outsiders leave it alone and leave.

What are those enormous outsiders? The master is stronger after their visit. It must strengthen its denizens. Stronger mushrooms, stronger centipedes. Should it kill the invaders if they return? The fragment is much stronger after their visit, so should it try to get them to return many times? Mushrooms use outsiders to spread their spores without needing to kill. Can the master gain from the outsiders without destroying them? Are they truly friends? But only fungus and centipede are friends . . . right?

Chapter 67

As far as I can tell, the baby dungeon hasn't gone nuts. It tried to attack Rhonda and Freddie, but they're strong enough to deal with anything it might try to pull. Leo's been sending more wolves to keep an eye on it, and as far as they can tell, it hasn't really changed its behavior.

It's still making centipedes and mushrooms, which is interesting. I thought it somehow had the mushrooms as herbalism nodes, but the wolves say the fungus is what's dealing with the smallest invaders. That's cool. I want active mushrooms.

Its borders are still slowly expanding, which I think is a sign it's a baby dungeon. I could only expand in leaps and bounds, not the slow but steady way this one is going. Maybe different dungeons expand differently? I know not all get the same rooms, but what if not all expand in the same way?

Also, I'm tired of calling it "the baby dungeon." The kids say the core is purple, so I'm calling it Violet. Violet's a cool name. I considered trying to give Violet one of my denizens, but there are a couple problems with that idea.

For starters, Violet definitely doesn't have a jail yet, so it's probably not even an option right now. Beyond that, it might not be a good idea to give it denizens anyway. What if it takes a page out of my book and does something really weird, but it's not as peaceful as I am?

I wouldn't mind stealing its denizens, but I need more room for that, and more room is expensive. Coda and the ratlings have been working on helping me use the volume underground, but the going is slow. Plain old rock isn't the worst building material, but it only really supports stuff when it's in compression, rather than tension.

See, different things work under different loads. A string can handle tension, but it does nothing if you try to squeeze it. Stone is great for squeezing/compression but abysmal for tension. Steel is great at both, which is why people build with it. But I don't have access to that much steel. So Coda has to take things slow and plan to make sure everything stays in compression.

Making everything arched helps, but there's still only so much that can be done. I think I'll be able to expand the current caves to be comfortable with slimes, wolves, and spiders, and expand the catacombs to be better able to handle the undead, but I'm going to need more room before I get any more spawners.

Right, I should also make Rocky an actual boss room. He's pretty much just been hanging out in the central mausoleum, but that's a temporary solution at best. I want to give him an arena, maybe even a proper squaredcircle of a boxing ring, but I also want to have spectator seating. I don't have room on the surface for something like that, and building it underground will be difficult.

Hmm . . . magic might be able to help, though. I've been meaning to upgrade the secret alchemy lab for a while now, and Thing's secret enchanting lab is also in serious need of upgrades, too. I could ask Teemo to pull some Spatial shenanigans, but I feel like that's a bit of a long shot. He's still having trouble pulling Spatial shenanigans apart from his shortcuts, and I don't want to put something this important on his tiny shoulders if he's still figuring out how to do what I want.

I'll probably need to settle for Queen using the steel transmutation to weave reinforcements into what will have to be a dome over the ring and stands, and probably have Thing reinforce it with some enchanting stuff, too.

Can I manage an actual boxing ring? The ropes and turnbuckles are relatively simple, but I don't know how the floor is handled. It has some kind of give to it, but not too much. It's a ring, not a trampoline, so it has to be more than a thick bit of cloth under a ton of tension.

I make a note in the secret library to brainstorm it a bit later. All the ring stuff is in the future. It's maybe not incredibly *far* in the future, but still far enough away I have time to plan a bunch. Queen's going to need her lab upgraded a ton to be able to make the steel transmutation in the quantities I'll need, anyway.

No, the more immediate thing I should probably spend my mana on is in specializing my wolves. In seeing how my delvers deal with my encounters, my lack of magic denizens is becoming more and more obvious. The lightning stuff is nice, but the lab's level still makes it difficult to produce enough to make it particularly common. But with my wolf spawner making tundra wolves, that'll not only make my delvers have to think about the ice element too, but give more magical things in general they'll need to deal with.

Besides, I'm starting to feel the seasons change. From Poe's expeditions, it's been plain to me for a while now that I'm in a bit of a temperate forest kind of climate. If we were much more south on Earth, it might count as the kind of thing that makes giant redwood rainforests.

I'm pretty sure I showed up sometime in spring, and the weather has been mostly warm, and things have been growing. But now, I can tell the leaves are changing colors and the air is getting a bit cooler. I dunno how quickly winter hits around here, but I can tell it's coming. So if I'm in a cooler climate, my new ground-expedition guys should be well able to handle cold, and maybe even deep snow.

And the other wolf options just don't capture my imagination. I seriously doubt the wolves with multiple heads will *actually* give me a wolf hydra, so I go ahead and spend the mana. The spawner starts making tundra wolves to go with the normal ones.

I wonder if anything interesting would happen if I gave a tundra wolf some of the go-juice? Would they have Ice and Lightning aspects? Or would it just overwrite the Ice aspect?

I'll need to do some experiments once I have more of both wolves and go-juice. Or I could experiment with the couple fire ants Queen has gotten from the anthill. She doesn't have enough yet to just experiment all willy-nilly, but the little ants are more expendable than the wolves.

I go ahead and poke her with that as an idea, and let her organize and prioritize it as she wants.

With the lab getting expanded soon, she'll probably want as many of her fire ants as she can so she can actually make the go-juice in the first place. We can't go and cripple her ability to do her work just for idle curiosity, after all.

Chapter 68

I watch the terrible trio as they balance precariously on the salmon ladder bar. They still haven't figured out they can do pull-ups to raise it, so they've been working on their terrible trio tower technique. They're actually at a point where they can all get on the bar, so now they just need to finish the maneuver and cling onto the ledge.

They all take a deep breath and start counting to three together.

"One . . ." says Mlynda, her eyes locked on the ledge that's currently out of her reach. She shifts her feet only slightly, confirming to herself that Vnarl has her properly in hand.

"Two . . ." continues Vnarl, feeling a bit awkward as the center part of the tower, but he's the best suited for it.

"Three!" finishes Hark, and they all three stand and start falling toward the ledge, which Mlynda manages to catch this time!

"I got it!" she exclaims with excitement. She has her hands in place and is clinging as best she can, but it will get a lot harder once they start the next part of the plan. She'll have to support Vnarl and Hark at the same time. It shouldn't be for too long, but it's still going to be quite a strain.

Vnarl adjusts his grip on her feet as Hark carefully prepares himself. The elf speaks up once he's ready.

"Let me know when to start, Mlynda!"

She takes a few more breaths to calm herself, then tightens her grip on the ledge. "Ready!"

With that, Hark steps off the bar, and the trio swing to the wall, hitting it with a dull thud. It's not too much of an impact, but they need to work quickly if they don't want to end up in the drink again. Hark quickly climbs Vnarl and reaches the ledge. He transfers his weight there instead of on the troll before climbing up. He grins in triumph at being on top before turning and hauling up

Vnarl. The troll gives Mlynda a shove to get her up onto the ledge before Hark gets him all the way up, the leader seeing the smallest member struggling to keep her grip.

As I thought, the cargo net conveyor barely slows them down. They take a few minutes to recover before Vnarl goes and tests the cargo net. Once he sees it move, he just holds it, and Hark and Mlynda climb up then hold it for him.

They all just kinda stare at the wedge wall for a few moments before Mlynda voices what's on everyone's mind. "What are we supposed to do with that?!"

Vnarl looks just as lost, but Hark squints as he gazes upward. "I think we climb it."

Mlynda rolls her eyes as a bit of her venom from before seeps into her words. "Oh, really. How?"

Hark doesn't rise to the barbs, instead pointing at the wall. "You wedge yourself in and climb up like that. I've had to climb a few trees like that before. Here, watch." He steps forward and jumps at the wall, splaying his limbs as he gets inside, wedging himself in place. He wiggles a bit to get himself into a comfortable width for climbing before looking over his shoulder with a grin. "Then you just climb!" He demonstrates, and the other two look impressed.

Mlynda goes next, and though she almost flubs the landing, she manages to keep herself from falling. It takes her a bit longer to get into a comfortable position, but she starts going up. Hark helps her as she nears the top, and I can see her arms are looking pretty weak. I don't think she'll be getting back up there today.

Vnarl follows suit and wedges himself in; though he's lanky enough, he has to climb using his elbows and knees instead of his hands and feet. Before long, however, Hark hauls him up, and all three are sitting on top of the ledge, which is revealed to be yet another platform, though the challenge is different than what they've seen before. There're no handholds or weird walls or other things that would fit with the other challenges. Instead, there are two large pots and an obvious pressure plate. One pot sits on either side of the plate, with the pots labeled three and five, and the plate between labeled with a four. Additionally, in the wall, is a little fountain.

I'm actually a bit proud of this puzzle, even if I did steal it from *Die Hard*. Using the two jugs, put four gallons of water on the plate. Mechanically, it's a modified flood trap. If they don't put the correct weight on the plate, water will push them all off the platform and into the drink once more.

The three look around, wondering if they've missed anything. Hark speaks up first.

"Where's the four jar?"

Mlynda frowns. "Well, it's not here. I don't think there were any pots at the previous obstacles, either." She looks back the way they came, but the position makes it difficult to see much.

Vnarl thinks as well and shakes his head. "I don't remember one either. Maybe it's hidden in the water?" Hark looks in the fountain and shakes his head as well.

"Not in here, unless you meant the water down there?" he asks, pointing over the edge.

"If we go looking, we'll need to do it all at once," points out Mlynda, and none of them are especially eager to throw away their victory so soon. They spend a few minutes looking around, and even pick up the pots, but don't make the connection of what to do with them just yet. With no other ideas, they collectively sigh and dive into the water, and I let my mind wander to other things.

Honey has been getting a bit frustrated with the library. She's got it cataloged and organized, but she is starving for more books to put in it. She's been asking to be able to send expeditions to get more, but I've been telling her no. I get the feeling something isn't translating through the empathic bond, though, because she keeps requesting.

I poke Teemo to go and speak to her, and it's fun to watch him talk with Honey. The other scions make their various sounds which he seems to hear as words, but bees don't really communicate with sounds. They either use pheromones or they dance. I'm pretty sure she uses some pheromones too, but she mostly dances to talk to Teemo, which I find to be just too adorable.

When he gets to the library, she's working in the hive, laying some new eggs for new workers, but he's able to get her attention easily enough. She comes out and dances for him. He says she and Queen call me the Emperor, and Teemo is my Emissary, and no matter how many times we try to get them to drop the formality, they refuse to.

"The Boss wants to know why you keep asking about expeditions despite him telling you no."

She dances, and he translates after a few seconds. "She says she doesn't want to go stealing books, but to get knowledge."

Okay, but how does she propose to do that? He relates my question, and she dances her answer back.

". . . She wants to write her *own* books from her own knowledge, gathered from expeditions."

Oh? Now that sounds like a good plan. Tell her to start coordinating with Poe and Leo for her bees to join their expeditions. I might send an aranea along with them, too; they're not the most dexterous, but they have facsimiles of fingers at least, and can make bags to bring back samples. I'll probably try to get them to offer trades of silk stuff for blank books, too. I have my notebooks, but I don't think I can just make blank books for her to use in the library. Does she have anything specific she wants to study?

He chuckles at her response. "She's very interested in plants, but she says she wants to gather pollen from all the flowers of knowledge."

Hmm. I wonder if I should try to teach her what I remember about math? Algebra is pretty simple, all things considered, but there's also a lot of stuff that I don't know what the function actually is. Trigonometry is all about sin, cos, and tan, but I don't think I've ever had to actually try to do those functions without a calculator. Even the few more common valuables for them are either in or result in fractions of pi! In fact . . . how do you even do a square root? I can work backward and guess, but that feels awkward.

Well, she's a clever bee. Maybe she can derive that stuff?

Honey

The Emperor is wise and possesses an endless garden of knowledge! The Emissary speaks of things of such wonder, and Honey only wishes she could ask her Emperor her questions directly. Even if she has to respawn a thousand times, the pain would be worth it for the knowledge!

Though the Emperor also trusts her to find knowledge herself. He is willing to share some, but there is so much for her to learn on her own! That's why she kept requesting to have her workers join the expeditions. There are so many plants and creatures to discover and learn about! The Emperor has been wanting his scions to expand their aspects, after all, and she thinks this is her best option.

She sends workers to communicate with the Marshal and the Warden. They each have their duties to attend, but perhaps later that night she can ask about joining them, as well as about having an aranea along, too.

She still feels a sense of horror when she thinks of them. No, not because they are arachnids, nor that they can be unpleasant to look at. No, her sense of horror comes from their senses of *spelling* and *grammar!* At least she's been able to get through the thick chitin of their heads the fundamentals of writing. They still prefer three-word, do-the-thing style of signage, but they now do so properly, and so don't insult the Emperor.

She doesn't dwell on that thought for long, however. No, she still has eggs to lay and plans to make. She has a few ledgers and such she can write in. Perhaps she can make a proper presentation to the Marshal and Warden? The Emperor managed to gift her with a flash of a bearer of knowledge projecting an illusion to help illustrate their points, writing and pictures created on a large curtain for all to see, rather than the smaller print of an individual book.

Could her aspect allow her to do that? Perhaps. She idly flexes her magic as she works and plans, following in her Emperor's footsteps and delegating what can be delegated as she works toward her goals.

Chapter 69

Looks like Honey's working hard to prepare to talk with Leo and Poe. She's doing something with her magic, but I can't really tell what. Whatever it is, I don't think it'll be ready by the meeting, but I'm glad to see her practicing. I'm not sure that the graphs and such she's writing down will do much to convince the two to bring her workers on expeditions, but it probably won't hurt her chances, either.

Especially since I can see the two have kept a few expedition groups in reserve. They seem to have already decided to at least do a few test expeditions with her. I hope they let her do her presentation despite that. She's looking like such a happy little nerd bee, heh.

I decide to watch the terrible trio while I wait for the evening, but they're not doing much today. I think they're all grumpy about the puzzle. They still haven't found the pot labeled four because it doesn't exist. I think they're starting to realize that, too.

Fine, if they're going to be boring, I'll check in on Aranya and the ratkin. She's been hanging out with them even after the whole ceremony that officially made them dwellers. I think she's just glad to have company. There's not a whole lot of chance to socialize in the deep tunnels, after all.

She hasn't joined any of the hunting expeditions, but that's mostly because she's not a very good hunter. That, and her only weapon is still the sword I gave her. She practices with it every day, but it's still something more designed for self-defense rather than hunting. I've tried to have Teemo tell them they can hunt and eat the stuff in me, but they don't want to be a drain on me like that.

It's not exactly a drain, but I can appreciate their desire to be able to support themselves. While delvers killing and gathering will give me mana, and invaders give me nothing, my dwellers doing stuff is basically a zero-sum. I get back some mana, but only enough to cover the cost. I guess it's *technically* a drain on me to wait for things to respawn, but that's no big deal. But my dwellers don't want to impose even that much, and I'm not going to force them. Besides, I'm proud of them for being able to find their own path and have the strength to walk it.

But back to Aranya, she'll usually talk philosophy with Larx, or whatever Crystal Shield guys the ratkin allow to visit. Interestingly, the former Head Acolyte has been coming down to talk a lot. It looks like his demotion and punishment has taught him some humility. He's still pretty gung ho about the Shield, but now he's willing to actually debate and listen instead of smite and exorcize. I wonder if I should suggest they do a couple public debates? My dwellers interacting with the delvers earns me boatloads of mana.

There are several different merchants who come by over the course of the day and trade for stuff. They mostly want hides and meat and such from the things the ratkin hunt, and the ratkin mostly like to trade for cloth, though one of the merchants is looking for crops which might grow underground.

With the feel of winter on the way, thoughts turn toward making sure everyone has food. Nobody is exactly *worried* about making it through the winter, but everyone would like to have more food. Besides, with underground stuff, crops can grow basically year-round. Temperature doesn't change much, so there's no real single growing season.

Hopefully, they can get a bunch of spores before the routes basically lock down for the winter. Listening in on their conversations, it seems we're not usually snowed in for *all* winter, but there's generally a couple weeks with too much snow to make it worthwhile, and it's not a consistent few weeks. Besides, in the depths of winter, there's not a whole lot of new things to trade. That might change with my ratkin, but they're not established well enough to really be able to do much this year.

By the time the last merchant leaves, it's about sunset, and so most of the activity dies down. There are more night delvers than I used to have, but that's still not saying much. It's mostly a group or two of lower-leveled people doing stuff in the manor, which gives Honey her chance to talk with Poe and Leo. I poke the two to let them know she's ready, and I poke Teemo to go translate for me.

Honey seems surprised to see Teemo along with my two expedition leaders, but he quickly explains.

"The Boss mostly just wants to listen in on the presentation, Honey. He likes your idea and wants to be able to offer any assistance or ideas. And he can tell you've been working hard on the presentation, so he wants to hear what you have to say."

I don't need to speak bee to know that's her happy dance. Teemo takes a seat a little farther away than Poe and Leo, mostly because he's going to be quietly translating for me the entire time. Honey passes out a few small packets of information before she starts.

"Esteemed Marshal, Warden, and Emissary; thank you all for your time and presence. I've asked the Emperor to allow my workers to join your expeditions. Our library should be overflowing with combs full of knowledge, but our stocks are practically bare! So, I would gather knowledge like pollen: by going out and obtaining it directly.

"I've made several graphs to show how I expect our stores of knowledge to increase, but I also want to get into a few details. While I don't think we'll be able to get much information in fields like history or mathematics, there is a wealth of information to be gathered on biology! There are numerous plants, animals, insects, arachnids, and more to discover and study!"

"How do you propose to do that, Librarian?" asks Poe. He looks interested, but he's ever the pragmatist, so wants details.

"If you'll refer to the packet, I can help explain," starts Honey, who gives the two a chance to take a look before she continues. "For the surface expeditions, plant and insect samples should be simplest for the ravens to gather. They may be able to gather specimens of smaller birds and animals like rodents too, but I want to start a bit more simply.

"For underground, Emperor Thedeim has offered the service of several aranea to accompany the expeditions. I've calculated a wolf should be able to carry one with little difficulty. Can you confirm that, Warden?"

Leo thinks for a few moments before nodding. "There are some spots they'll have to get off and walk on their own, but my wolves should be able to carry them to wherever we're going to get samples from. You're not going to use the ratkin?"

Honey wiggles her rear in the negative. "While they are very helpful to our Emperor, he doesn't want to impose on them for this. If the first expeditions go as well as I hope they will, there also simply won't be enough ratkin to keep up, either. The aranea can weave some kind of packs for the wolves to be able to bring back samples, too. I've included a diagram of what they may look like, and the design can be improved with field testing."

Teemo speaks up at that. "Heh, sounds like the Boss is going to need to expand the tunnels around here, then. If you're going to be getting that much stuff, you're gonna need a lot more room to examine everything. He's also going to need to have the aranea offer trade quests for blank books."

Honey does a little embarrassed shuffle. "On the back of the packet, I have projections for those, yes. I don't wish to impose on the Emperor like that, but I couldn't think of any other way to get and keep the knowledge. That is, if the Warden and Marshal are willing to allow this?"

Poe fluffs himself up and nods. "I think it is a great opportunity to extend our Lord Thedeim's knowledge, and it may be just the thing to whip my ravens into proper shape. I've been having trouble getting them to pay attention to the details. With your workers wanting samples, they may finally start to understand that shiny things are not the only valuable things."

Leo speaks up directly after. "I also think it would be a good thing to do. The ratkin have some knowledge of the deeper tunnels, but there's a lot of room to keep track of, and a lot of stuff in there besides. And with that Violet down there, too, I want to know as much as possible. The Alpha says a Warden is supposed to protect his territory and his charges, and I need to know what I need to protect them *from*."

Honey looks like she might explode from how hard she's doing her happy dance, but Teemo can still translate for her. "Wonderful! If the Emperor could get the aranea to weave the packs tonight, we can start the first expeditions in the morning, then?"

Nobody has any objections, so I spend a bit of mana to get the aranea to do the weaving. The first pass is basically just a pair of open saddlebags, though they're designed more to lie across the wolf's withers than the side. I can't wait to see what interesting stuff Honey discovers.

Chapter 70

Having all this mana just sitting in my proverbial pockets is making me a bit antsy. I wonder if that's a dungeon thing, or a me thing. Having a big bank account doesn't make me want to spend it, but in games, I tend to spend my resources as I get them so I can get more resources.

Whichever the case, those expansion options are calling to me. I've been upgrading the alchemy and enchanting labs so Queen and Thing can do their things, but I still have a good chunk saved up, and I really want to get some more room to do stuff.

I also think I've come full circle on how I'm going to expand. Past the cemetery could be interesting, but it'd make me more than a bit lopsided to do that. Up keeps whispering like a temptress, but I keep thinking of what happened the first time I expanded downward. I don't want to cause a hurricane or tear a hole in the sky or something to actually facilitate my upward expansion. Maybe I can ask the ODA about that. Telar seems to be working on an information packet, but I think she's going to wait for Tarl to get back before she tries to tempt me with it.

The ratkins' hunting tunnel was a really tempting direction to go, until I gave it a bit of thought. They are deliberately hunting outside of me. If I expand down their hunting tunnel, they'll be back to hunting inside. Not to mention that Violet would probably freak out at having a powerful neighbor rubbing elbows with it. So I think I'm back to the original plan: expand down the tunnel Aranya came in from.

I take a few seconds to simply look at the area I'd be getting, though *look* isn't really the right word. I can just sense the volume that will become mine. Oddly, the volumes for the different expansions are not all the same, nor are the costs. The smallest expansion would be taking part of the town, but that's also the most expensive, while expanding up gives a ton of volume and costs less than everything else.

I wonder why? Probably another question to ask the ODA.

Alright, enough waffling. Time to either do my business or get off the pot.

I spend the mana to expand down Aranya's tunnel.

Yvonne

Yvonne, Ragnar, and Aelara walk through the wilderness on their patrol. The birdkin ranger feels she's shirked her duties in this regard long enough, and her friends are happy to help her with it.

Well, for certain values of happy. While the dwarf manages to look vaguely interested at the wooded surroundings, Aelara the elf is looking a bit haggard.

"Why are we doing this, again?" asks the city elf rhetorically once more. Yvonne smiles at her friend and spreads her arms to take in the nature around them.

"Ranger duties," she replies with a smirk, which earns a snort of laughter from Ragnar before Yvonne continues. "I suppose we're deep enough out here now that I can actually show you. It's not some secret ranger rite or anything like that. I'm actually surprised you haven't figured it out, Aelara. I thought you studied magic."

Aelara sighs and mentally puts on her big-girl pants. "I have, but more in actually using it. I can feel the mana around us, but if I paid attention to it all the time, I'd never be able to focus on anything else."

"Well, focus on it now," encourages the birdkin. Aelara obliges, and she can even feel Ragnar giving it a shot. With her elven friend, it's like she's opened her eyes and is now looking around. With her dwarven friend, though, it's more like a blind man reaching out and poking what's around him. It's not too surprising to Yvonne that his mana sensing is terrible. Like most physical classes, his magic is a lot more internal, so he's a lot less sensitive to magic around him.

Aelara starts to look intrigued as she takes in how the magic is behaving around them. "I can tell something is different than in the city, but I don't know how to put it into words."

Yvonne nods at that. "It is different, yes. In cities and towns—and even some forests—the ambient mana is turbulent. Ranger teachings say complex life makes mana move, and like life itself, it's more than a little chaotic. But in quiet places like this, the mana is still and stagnant. It's like the difference between a frothing river and a scum-covered pond. And like a scum-covered pond, unpleasant things can develop in stagnant mana."

"Monsters?" asks Aelara with interest. None of her studies really talked much about monsters. Now, she supposes she should have been looking for ranger texts instead of diving deeper into wizardly mana theory.

Yvonne nods. "Yes, monsters. Some seem to breed like ordinary life, but others seem to simply form from the stagnant mana. They attack because the waves we cause are a threat to them. They want to keep the mana stagnant, while we seem to only churn it more and more."

"Ach, reminds me o' wha' the' cragstriders like t' talk about. They say th' dungeons try t' smooth th' mana out, making a middle ground b'tween rapids and ponds, as ye'd say?" starts Ragnar, and Yvonne nods before he continues. "Tha's why they attack dungeons. We make a mess o' th' mana, and dungeons smooth it out and get th' mana movin' over a huge area. Th' beasties try t' destroy it so they c'n get back t' whatever it is they do."

Yvonne nods again. "Yes, or they may come after the settlements instead, ignoring the dungeons. After all, the dungeons need the energy of delvers to exert their control over the local mana. If the monsters destroy the 'food' of the dungeon, it'll starve, and the mana will go still once more."

"Are the monsters really that smart?" asks Aelara with concern. Yvonne shakes her head.

"It's not so much intelligence which guides them to attack people. To them, there are two threats: the big dungeons and the smaller people. If they can't attack the dungeon, they'll attack the other threat. It's like when two large predators' territories start to encroach. Neither really wants to try to fight the other directly, so they'll instead compete for food. Either there's enough for the both of them, or one is eventually driven off."

Aelara gives her a flat look. "I don't think I like the idea of being dungeon food."

Yvonne just shrugs. "It's not my best metaphor, but it's not that far off. Wandering monsters are a threat to people and dungeons alike."

"Is that why you're out here, then? To protect Thedeim?" asks Aelara, and Yvonne smiles and shakes her head.

"Technically, I suppose, but I've had this duty for longer than I've been a resident. Besides, I like being out in nature like this, even if I sometimes have to cull undesirable things," she says, pointing down at a large print left in the loose soil, an obvious sign for her friends of what she's been tracking for a while now, before giving her friends a playful smile.

"Though that's where you two come in. It's a lot easier to deal with wandering monsters with a couple friends at my side."

"Aye, and the experience isnae 'alf bad, either."

Chapter 71

Man, have I really not expanded since I ate Neverrest? I had forgotten how much goes into actually making the new space livable. I haven't forgotten about the new spawner I get, but I'll focus on that in a moment.

For now, I'm just taking a few minutes to get a feel for what I've got now. It's one thing to be able to list off the volume of moveable space, gallons of water, and raw area I gained with the expansion, but it's another to actually understand what that all means and how it all relates to each other.

While the area immediately under the manor has mostly tunnels and small caverns, the new expansion has more . . . *cavernous* caverns. I'm pretty sure the rock is different, too. The tunnels were some kind of brown stone, probably something sedimentary? The new caverns seem to me more like granite or something, probably more igneous. I'm hardly a geologist, though. All I know is the rock down here seems to be much stronger than above, which allows for those large caverns.

I hardly need to tell Teemo to head down there and work his magic, though I do tell him to pay special attention to how he makes his shortcuts. He's been making no progress at all with trying to expand his control into temperature, which makes me wonder if his shortcuts are *really* non-Euclidean and somehow manage to have larger inside dimensions without actually increasing volume. Or he might just have trouble visualizing it, I dunno.

So I'm having him concentrate a bit more on how his magic flows and actually works when he's making his shortcuts. I figure, worst case, he'll understand his Spatial magic better. You know, get a bit more depth before trying to widen it into temperature and other stuff.

I *do* have to tell Coda to head down there and survey, though. I think he expected his assignment would be mostly in the general tunnels, but if he's going to be my Architect, I'm gonna need him to get a good look at each expansion.

I wonder if I can get him to go on expeditions to survey stuff before I expand. Maybe I'll even get a discount? Getting my scions to do stuff has gotten me discounts on everything else, so why not?

I think the first thing I'm probably gonna have him do, once he's finished surveying, is to dig a more direct route from the largest cavern up to the tunnel system. I think I'm going to keep working and making the crypt complex be my strongest area, so now the caverns will get to be my tier between the tunnels and the crypts. Besides, most delvers tend to stay away from the undead. Thankfully, the Crystal Shield guys love the area. I bet that gnome Head Priest is telling everyone he can to come here to train, too.

But, if I'm going to leave the crypts as a place for priests, paladins, and whatever other divine classes are a thing, I'll be using the caverns to help train the more ordinary delvers. So I'll need a good path there for them to reach. The only problem is that I don't know if my little ratling crew is going to be up for it.

Pretty sure explosives are the preferred way to get through tough rock, and I don't really have any boom. With the lab being expanded, I think Queen is looking into making some, but I'm not exactly holding my breath on it. Not that I don't think she can do it, just that I think I'll have a better way to get through that stuff: my new spawner and scion.

While most of my stuff has been pretty mundane, my new spawner is probably the most "fantasy" of the stuff I've gotten so far. Yes, I have undead and slimes, but they're both still fairly normal, at least in my head. My new spawner is an elemental spawner. An earth elemental spawner.

Right now, it's just spawning stalactsprites, which are little vaguely conical stone things. They make me think more like snails than sprites, though. They have a single foot like a snail, and they like to climb and rest on ceilings, then drop on baddies. They seem to be really good at dealing with the gremlins, too. The little resource thieves just can't pick them out from the normal outcroppings on the ceilings. I'm gonna want to get them to propagate in the tunnels and my various mining nodes, to help keep them secure.

My new scion, however, is different from them. He's a vaguely humanoid pile of rocks and sand. He has shoulders and arms and a head, and even fingers when he wants them. Aside from that, though, he's a kinda lumpy column all the way to the ground.

I have a vague idea of what I want him to do, mostly because it's a terrible pun and I can't resist. It'll be a while before I can even start working on that, however, so I'll just name him Slash and leave it at that for now. I tell him to take a look around, meet the other scions, and just get a feel for how things will be working around here.

And, with the extra room, I can try to get those other two spawners I've had my eye on ever since Leo joined: gremlins and moles. Moles are my top priority for the moment, though, and are the reason I'm not going to pressure Queen for explosives too hard. If I can get a mole spawner, I can either upgrade it enough for it to make some kind of mole thing that can dig through rock, or I can have Queen transmute their claws to steel, and they can dig that way.

Or both. I remember how quickly that scythemaw was tearing at my walls before Tiny took care of it. If I could get something similar but with *steel* diggers, Coda would be able to carve out stuff with ease! But, before I go counting my moles before they hatch, I need to actually catch one.

I tell Leo I want him to capture a mole and convert it, then I start looking into what other upgrades I can make to the jail. I'll probably be able to decouple it from the punishment gauntlet soon, but not quite yet.

The upgrade options seem to lean more into inquisition territory rather than rehabilitation, though. I'll probably have to finagle something . . .

Leo

The Alpha has a new mission for him, and Leo is excited for it. The trio with that *halfling* are probably going to be freeing themselves within the next week or so, which will leave his jail rather empty. But with the new expansion comes a new order: convert a mole! He's not certain how well that will work, but the Alpha's strange thought process isn't too outlandish.

Thankfully, the Alpha doesn't seem to expect it will go as smoothly as it did for him. Leo didn't have much other option, so had no problem changing his loyalty to the new dungeon.

So now he needs to find a mole . . . which is the first hurdle. He's a wolf, not a ferret. He can't exactly go diving down a mole hole to grab one of the things. He might be able to with the help of the Voice, but he has his own new duties to attend to.

The other problem with catching a mole is that it's shockingly difficult to grab one without killing it. He still doesn't have thumbs. *Okay . . . think outside the box.* Maybe an aranea can help him?

He goes and tracks down the one who will likely be going out on expeditions. She's weaving the sample bags as he approaches.

"Aranea. I need your help to weave a trap for some moles."

"No," comes the simple reply. Leo growls.

"Why do you refuse?"

"Not my job. Job is weave. Job is make. Make to wear. Not to grab," she explains, and it's pretty clear to Leo he's not going to get anywhere trying the aranea. Sure, they're smart for denizens, but they're still pretty simple. If the Alpha ordered them, they'd probably listen, but Leo doesn't want to go running to him at the first sign of trouble with his task.

So, if the denizens are too simple to help, he should try a scion. Fluffles could probably handle catching a mole without too much difficulty. The only problem is he's almost as hard to track down as the Voice.

Leo patrols the tunnels as he thinks, trying to figure out who he can ask for help. He notices Jello oozing by, and he stops in his tracks.

Could the Purifier help him capture a mole? Could she even help to convert the mole? His instinct is to ignore her . . . but trying this is just the kind of strange thing Alpha Thedeim would do. He thinks it over a bit more and comes to a decision. If it won't interfere with her duties in the tunnels, there shouldn't be any harm in trying.

He approaches her, and she notices him. She burbles in friendly welcome, and he nods in return. "Purifier Jello. Could you assist me on the surface? Alpha Thedeim has tasked me with capturing and turning a mole, but I'm having difficulties catching one," he explains.

"Jello can help friend Leo! Tunnels are full of friends, so Jello can leave the defense to them for a while. Where do you need Jello?" He motions for her to follow, and the two quickly slip through a shortcut to the surface. Many of the delvers there look with confusion at Jello, but nobody does more than give the pair strange looks.

Leo shows her a few of the more active mole tunnels. Queen and her ants do their best to collapse them as they find them, but some are good to leave open for the snakes to be able to hunt. "Here is one of the main mole tunnels. If you cover this entrance, I can cover a different one, and hopefully, with the two of us, we'll be able to capture one."

Jello burbles in affirmative and moves to literally cover the entrance while Leo goes to a different one. It doesn't take him long to notice something strange with Jello. She's burbling again, but not saying anything. Perhaps she cannot handle the sun very well? She's been in the tunnels for perhaps her entire life.

"Is everything alright, Jello?" he asks, concerned he may have made a mistake in asking her to help.

"Yep! Jello is fine! She's just exploring these tiny tunnels some," she replies without further explanation.

Leo tilts his head at her in curiosity. "Exploring? How?"

In answer, she oozes herself off the entrance and soon reveals a long thin tendril that she had sent down the hole. "Like this! Jello likes to be a cube most of the time, but she doesn't always fit like that. So sometimes she does other shapes." She leans toward him and whispers, "She's even tried to be a sphere like the Voice, but a sphere is a lot harder than it looks!"

". . . Teemo is a rat, not a sphere," is all he can think to reply, to which Jello just burbles in laughter.

"Not *that* Voice! The other Voice!" she says, like that explains anything. After a few moments, she tries to help her fellow scion. "You know, the Voice that tells us what to do? Voice Thedeim?"

That makes . . . not quite *sense*, but at least Leo understands what she's trying to say. And with that understanding comes the understanding that he made the correct choice in asking for her help in this, too. "So you can extend yourself down these tunnels without difficulty? Can you grab a mole for me like that?"

"Jello would love to!" she replies, taking her spot above the hole once more.

Leo watches and wonders if this is how his Alpha tends to get such strange ideas for how to do things. He didn't expect to be spending his afternoon watching the Slime Scion hunt for a mole, but that's what he's doing. None of the steps along the way were too outlandish, but the final result is just the kind of weirdness he'd expect from Alpha Thedeim. He supposes he's doing his job right, then.

Chapter 72

I don't know what I was expecting when I asked Leo to capture and try to turn a mole, but I'm pretty sure I wasn't expecting him to get Jello's help. The two barked and burbled at each other before she followed him, and now she has a mole in a little pocket of air inside her. The mole looks pretty upset about it, too. I have no idea how Leo will turn it, but I'm sure he'll figure it out. Even if it takes a few practice moles to learn.

Jello has started wandering a bit farther, too, now that she's had a taste of the surface. She seems to really like watching the delvers gather resources, or maybe she just likes catching the invaders that want to nibble on my nodes. Either way, I don't tell her to get back down to the tunnels. Instead, I go ahead and tell Rocky he should patrol.

In fact . . . he really *should* patrol. I'm not sure it applies to someone whom I don't think breathes, but cardio is a big part of boxing. He seems happy at the idea and jogs down through the catacombs, occasionally throwing a punch or juking his head. I wish I could get him a real mouthguard, but I have no idea where to even start with plastics. I might be able to manage something with some leather, but that's going to taste terrible . . . though Rocky probably wouldn't care.

Slash is still learning how things work around here, but I think he's fitting in well so far. He's met all the other scions now, and I think they've all given him what advice they have to give. From what Teemo says, it mostly boils down to: Yes, I'm weird. Yes, delvers are cool. You'll probably get a weird job and/or title soon, don't worry about it.

He's also found the ratlings doing their mining, and he seems to have decided his best job for now is to help them. I'm not going to complain. Rock parts like weak Styrofoam for him, which makes the expansion on the library a lot easier.

I don't have access to a research lab room, but I'm not letting that stop me. I seriously doubt it'll stop Honey, heh. Maybe she'll even be able to turn it into one? Her workers on expeditions have been bringing her all sorts of interesting things, and even Queen has been taking an interest. While Honey seems to want knowledge for its own sake, Queen is hungry for new things to try alchemy on.

She's been working on making a lot more go-juice, as well as Liquid Steel, but storing it is a bit of a problem. The alchemy lab doesn't really have many options for industrial storage of products, which is annoying. I might need to figure out how to make glass to get her storage. I know it needs silica sand, but I don't know how to actually identify that. The stone in the caverns might be silicate, but I honestly have no idea.

I'm leaning toward the shallower stone being silicate, but even if I have the right rocks to grind, I don't know if I have the right *heat*. I might be over thinking it, though. The ratlings have been able to make steel in the forge, and I'm pretty sure that's supposed to be a pretty big pain in the butt to make without modern processes. Maybe glass will be easier than I thought? Either way, I ask Slash to grind some of the stone as fine as he can, and the ratlings to take it to the forge and see what they can do to get it to melt.

If it works, I expect it'll be dirty and cloudy, but that's fine. I'll probably try to line a barrel or something with rough glass before trying to get anything clear. I think I read something about it needing sodium carbonate, but that's probably as useful to the full process as knowing stainless steel has a bit of chromium in it.

The trio, who I've stopped thinking of as terrible now, have started to puzzle out the water jars. Mostly, they've realized they can put water into them from the little fountain, and putting the wrong weight will wash them out to do the whole thing over again. They seem to understand they need four gallons, but they haven't realized they need to math it properly instead of trying to guess and pour the right amount into jar five.

Still, I doubt they'll be too much longer in solving it, and then, they'll be on to the final puzzle I've made for them. It's kind of like an escape room that's been cut into thirds, like three escape hallways. There are sliding blocks, scales, and all sorts of complex things they'll have to figure out, with the solutions only obvious with proper communication between the three. I think they'll understand what they need to do fairly quickly, but the execution will probably take them a bit.

I turn my attention elsewhere once they seem about ready to wash out again, and instead focus on Freddie and Rhonda, who have just returned from the rat-kins' hunting tunnel, and presumably Violet. I poke Teemo to go and chat with them and see if there are any new updates with the little baby dungeon.

The kids are taking a little breather with the ratkin and Aranya, and my little kobold is possibly even more interested in Violet than I am. She's been asking all sorts of technical questions that the kids just don't know the answers to, but she relents once Teemo makes himself known.

"Hey, kids. Aranya still trying to chew your ears off about stuff you don't know?" My kobold blushes a bit at that, but the kids laugh it off with smiles.

"She just knows so much more about dungeons than we do!" exclaims Rhonda with a tone of wonder, and Freddie nods.

"Yeah, she needs to talk more with Mr. Tarl once he gets back. I think they'd both learn a lot. With us, though . . . it's like showing advanced axe forms to someone who's only just picked one up for the first time."

"I'm sorry," apologizes Aranya. "It's just that I've never been close to a Nascent Sanctuary before! The legends mention them, but usually focus on the First and his children once they're established. There're so many questions!"

"And speaking of questions, anything new with Violet?" asks my Voice, and the kids nod. Rhonda pulls out her little notebook while Freddie gives the basics.

"The borders seem to have stabilized, so I think it's fully established now. It still just has the mushrooms and centipedes. No scions yet, either. I saw a couple stronger centipedes and a different mushroom, but Rhonda has the actual details on them." Freddie looks to his friend, who now has her book open to the correct page.

"The nascent dungeon had least centipedes, but now has some lessers mixed in. Miss Telar told us a few signs to look out for to figure out if they got specialized, but I don't think they have yet. The mushrooms have also upgraded a bit. They are still mostly aggressive cordyceps to deal with insects and such, but today, we saw a spotted sweet demise. They're a poisonous mushroom that I think it's using to help deal with the mice down there. The rodents love to eat the caps, which doesn't go well for the mice." Rhonda realizes she's talking to a *rat* about pest control, and looks a bit abashed. Teemo, however, just laughs.

"I eat mice all the time, so I'm not going to feel awkward about Violet killing them." Rhonda relaxes a bit before he continues. "Still, if Violet is a bit more situated, it might be time to say hello."

The kids look confused, so Teemo explains. "See, the Boss has been wanting to talk to the little dungeon ever since we found it, but he doesn't want to freak it out. But with it now more established, we might be able to make contact. I'm a Voice, after all. I should be able to talk to it." He looks over at Aranya. "The Boss would also like to ask if you want to come, too. Just because it should be able to understand me doesn't mean I'll be able to say anything it wants to hear. You know a lot about dungeons, so you could help with what I should actually say."

"Do you think it'll listen?" asks Rhonda, looking a bit nervous. "What if it's more like Neverrest than like you?"

"That's why the Boss wants to talk to it. If it's nasty like Neverrest, he can just subsume it. If it's friendly, like it seems to be with you two, he might be able to give it some pointers. Everyone is always going on about how the Boss does things differently. Well, he wants to see if doing things differently will work out for dungeons besides himself."

Chapter 73

Teemo and Aranya get ready to head to Violet, and I tell him they can loot a couple potions, just in case. Aranya also needs to go get the sword, so it'll be a little bit before they head out. In the meanwhile, I look in on what Jello's up to.

She's been hanging out with Leo ever since they got that mole together, and she'd had to get a couple more since then. The moles act kinda rabid, or at least what movies say is rabies, minus the foaming. They lunge at the bars whenever they notice my scions, and they'll lunge at the walls when they sense the trio resting in their own cell. And just like a bird diving into a window, it doesn't end well for the little fuzzy missiles.

Leo growls as he disposes of the latest mole and thinks aloud, yapping and grumbling. A lot of my scions do that when frustrated or confused, and I try to parse their body language and what I get through the bond to understand what they're saying. It's not great, but I still try to give them what advice I can through the bond, or have Teemo come say something. He's a bit busy, though, so Leo just vents to the air.

Jello soon comes with a fresh mole, and Leo stops in the middle of directing her toward the cell, looking closer at her. I do the same, wondering what seems to have captured his attention. Jello doesn't seem to know either, and she contorts herself in ways a cube shouldn't to try to see what we're looking at.

Something about music drifts through the bond with her, but I don't hear anything. I probably shouldn't be surprised, though. She's not very good at explaining herself; probably comes with technically not having a brain, heh. Still, she's doing *something*. I just don't know what.

I take a moment and focus on her status, which I rarely do anymore. It's partially because I don't want to go sticking my nose in other people's business, but also because it takes a bit of effort to do, and details can kinda . . . fuzz out if I'm not paying attention. I wonder if I'm not actually supposed to be able to peek? Or maybe it's something about my Fate affinity? Either way, I should focus on her status.

She's level twelve now, which puts her just above the average for my scions. Come to think of it, she's about the middle kid right now, as far as scion age goes . . . I think.

Slime, gelatinous cube—yes, thank you for the obvious.

Jello the Purifier for name and title.

Huh.

Does Purifier not just mean she's good at dealing with undead?

I guess it's time to try an experiment. I do my best to impress the idea upon Leo, and he seems to nod in understanding.

Leo

"I don't get it . . . I knew they'd be more difficult than I was, but this is getting ridiculous! I've made no progress with them at all!" he growls and paces as he waits for Jello to return with a fresh mole. He can feel the Alpha sympathizing with his frustration, but he has no solutions to offer just yet. A few upgrade options for the jail can be glimpsed through the bond, but the Alpha's distaste for them is plain, and Leo agrees with the hesitation to use them. A rival can be cowed into submission and obedience, but a scion should be an equal, a peer.

He paces and thinks, and before long, Jello returns with another mole. Leo sighs and nods at the cell. "Just put it in . . . Wait . . ." He pauses and looks closer at Jello. He can feel the Alpha do the same, wondering what he spotted. Even Jello seems confused and is trying to look at herself, which mostly has her bending her cube in weird ways.

"What is it? Did Jello accidentally get a mouse again?" she asks, hoping she didn't mess up, but Leo shakes his head.

"No, it's a mole. It's just . . . a lot *calmer* than when they're in the cell. Did you knock it out or something?"

Jello wobbles a negative. "No, Jello just grabbed it. Oh, she *is* quietly singing to it, though. Otherwise, they try to escape, or they screech about noise."

"Noise?" repeats Leo, tilting his head once more. "The moles in the cell never make any sense, just bellowing in mad rage."

Jello wiggles in affirmation. "Jello can't hear the noise, but the moles all shout about it when she grabs them, and they start working themselves into a fit as she carries them. So she started singing to them, which calms them some. She doesn't think they really *like* her song, but it seems better than whatever noise they're hearing."

That's interesting and strange all at once. Leo can hear no music, and it feels like the Alpha can't hear anything, either. The Alpha can sense *something*, though, and seems to be focusing on the Purifier to try to figure it out. Jello is a worthy scion, diligent in her duties, but she can be difficult to get information from, so Leo mentally goes over what she's said and done. She's doing something to calm the moles . . . but what? Maybe she's gained some strange ability?

She burbles as the Alpha looks closer at her. It's not often Thedeim's attention is so intense, but at least Jello doesn't shrink under his scrutiny. Numbers and concepts flash past the bond, and Leo doesn't even attempt to understand them. Even if it didn't give him a headache, the Voice has said that is what happens when the Alpha is looking at someone's status. He's also said that status is private, so Leo does his best to give Jello that privacy.

After a minute, the importance of her title is impressed on the bond, and Leo thinks about that. "It seems the Alpha feels your title as Purifier may help in converting the moles, Jello. Keep that one for now, and we'll see if we can work from there. We've been nipping and barking to try to get them into line, but your playful barks may be the better option."

"Okay! Jello will do her best!"

Teemo

Teemo fetches a few useful potions for Aranya while she prepares for her sojourn to Violet. The Rat Scion isn't too concerned about her getting hurt, but it's hardly a *bad* idea to bring a few things for an emergency.

He has to ferry the potions one at a time, but with the shortcuts, it doesn't take him long at all. He gets to see the little kobold prepare like watching a slide-show. With the first potion, he sees her putting on the studded leather armor the ratlings have made. It's not the best, but they're getting better with time. With the second potion, she's putting on the sword, and with the third, she's putting the sword on again, after having put on her white robe. Three should be more than enough, so he speaks up.

"Ready to head out?" he asks, and though she looks nervous, she nods. He's not too convinced. "You sure? I think the last time you looked this skittish was when you helped move the core."

She sighs and slumps a bit, nodding. "Okay . . . yeah, I *am* really nervous, but that's not going to change, so we should probably get going."

"What're you nervous about?" he asks as he hops onto her shoulder, letting her lead the way as they chat.

"It's just . . . Sanctuary Thedeim asks so little of me. So when he *does* request something, I want to do a good job!"

The rat laughs at that. "So that's what the Boss means when he says something is like seeing his life from the outside." Aranya gives him a confused look, so he continues. "That's just how he works. Tiny and I have been here from the start, and we could probably count the actual orders for the both of us on his legs."

Aranya just looks more frustrated at that revelation, rather than relieved. "But you're his scions! And I'm not just his first resident—I'm his High Priestess now, too! Shouldn't he be guiding us all more than that?"

Teemo calms a little and shrugs. "Should he? The Boss isn't above giving advice on stuff, but he doesn't like forcing anything. And I think it's been working wonders so far. Even Leo and Slash are adjusting quickly. Slash is a bit lost at the moment, kinda like Coda was for a while, but I know the Boss has a plan for him. And he doesn't make Slash do nothing until the plan is ready. He lets him help as he can."

"So how can *I* help?" asks Aranya, slumping a bit.

Teemo considers that for a few moments, then shrugs. "I dunno." Aranya looks like she wants to throw him against a wall, so he chuckles and continues. "I don't know what a High Priestess does. Do High Priestess stuff, I guess?"

"But *how*?!" she insists, and Teemo can only shrug once more.

"Talk to delvers? I don't know, and I don't think the Boss knows anything else to try, either. You talk to the Crystal Shield guys a lot, right?"

She nods. "Yeah, they're interested in this kind of stuff, and some of them want to make sure they're not allowing a dark cult or something to take root under their noses. But they're not going to convert. They're kinda all spoken for already."

"Then try the other delvers. Maybe even get the ratkin to help. Larx would probably be happy to spread the word a bit; he's definitely an adherent already."

"But . . ." She shifts uncomfortably, and Teemo smiles.

"You still feel awkward around the delvers, hmm? Well, you won't get better by hiding from them, and you won't be able to do your High Priestess stuff if you hide from them, either."

She deflates and nods at that, and Teemo gives an encouraging squeak. "You'll get the hang of it eventually. Just keep it as casual as possible. It's been working for me."

Chapter 74

While Teemo and Aranya walk and chat, I use the time to go over what I want to do with the new expansion. One of the big things is to get the Aranea Enclave going. I've been sitting on that for a while now, and now, I actually have the room for them to grow. I'm also going to need to upgrade some of my other spawners to help fill in the caverns a bit.

My snakes have an upgrade or two before they max out, and they'd probably do pretty well down there. I spend the mana to upgrade the spawner, and it spits out a couple spitting cobras, which is pretty cool. I'm a bit low on denizens with ranged attacks. I don't think they'll be good for in and around the manor; maybe one or two in the tunnels? They look pretty tough. They should be fine in the caverns, though.

I'm not going to upgrade my birds for down there. It'd be kinda mean to put them that far down, away from the sky. I could upgrade my bats, instead, but. I'm gonna put it off for the moment. I've been ignoring my slime spawner for way too long. I haven't even specialized them yet.

Looking at the options, there are a couple which are interesting. The choices look like either slimes, jells, or oozes. The slimes look like they'll be the walking jello-mold variety of slimes: big, squished spheres which may or may not have faces. I'm leaning away from that one, mostly because, while they look cute in a cartoony way in a lot of games and such, I feel like they'll sit squarely in the uncanny valley in reality. They're the physical specialization. I could use some more bruisers, but I think I'm going to be taking my earth elementals down the bruiser route.

Jells appear to be the magic specialization, and I think I can give them any aspect I want. I wish my experiments with breaking the magic system could have progressed further by now so I'd have a better idea of what could really break things. Still, more magic could be nice. On the other hand, I have my tundra wolves and the go-juice, so I do have *some* magic to throw around.

Physically, the jells are vaguely humanoid, looking like someone took a soft clay doll, removed all detail, and slammed the thing down so the legs squished into a puddle. They get a maybe.

The one that's drawing my eye, though, is the oozes. They're the resource specialization, but I have no idea how they'll work. My other resource denizens are mostly focused on plants, though the ravens and packrats get general loot stuff. What would an ooze do? Would they be like gold slimes or something, rare spawns who drop really cool stuff? A big experience reward would be cool, but I don't know if that kind of thing even exists here. This one's tempting just for the mystery. What to go with—Oh, looks like Teemo and Aranya are there now. Let's meet the neighbor.

Violet

Danger comes. Strong . . . far too strong! What is it?! The new centipede and mushrooms will not be enough, but they muster all the same. If they are to perish, it will not be without a fight!

The doom looms close, and the young dungeon can finally sense with more detail what it looks like. One is a larger invader, the soft ones of teeth and claw. Unlike the lesser vermin, this one radiates power and purpose. It alone could very likely destroy the young dungeon!

The other is large and unique. It is neither hard like the centipedes, nor is it soft like the invaders. It *wears* softness, but underneath, it's like a moving pile of stones. It, too, radiates power . . . the same power of the larger invader.

These are not simple invaders, nor are they delvers like the big mushroom and bigger not-mushroom. These are conquerors!

The denizens gather to make the outsiders pay in blood if they wish to take their dungeon!

The conquerors deliberate just outside for a few minutes . . . and then they are inside. They don't simply step across the border. They move strangely, and suddenly, they exist deep in the dungeon, well past the desperate denizens.

The one of stones says something that the dungeon doesn't understand, and a wave of orange spreads from it. It washes over the denizens, and their movements are slowed, their panic calmed. It washes over the small core, and the dungeon itself is much less terrified as well. Before it can work itself back up into a tizzy, the invader speaks.

"Easy there. We're not here to hurt you."

Not hurt? Lies!

The invader shakes its head. "It's the truth. We haven't harmed you nor your denizens. And if you don't believe that, just check our designation."

The dungeon cautiously does so, knowing it will simply be told there are two conquerors inside. It looks at the designation with confusion, and the invader smiles.

"See? We're envoys. We're here to talk." The dungeon doesn't know how to respond, and so the invader soon continues. "I'm Teemo, and this is Aranya. We represent Thedeim, a dungeon not too far away. He's known you're here for a while now, and even helped get Rhonda and Freddie to come take a look and help you."

The big mushroom and bigger not-mushroom?

The invader . . . *Teemo* laughs and nods. "Yes, them. They can help you grow stronger, and soon, other delvers will come to interact, too. Thedeim would like to help you grow, give you some pointers, and help you avoid pitfalls. Will you accept his help?"

Accept Mentor? Yes/No

Protection?

Teemo nods. "Yes. He already has been sending expeditions around to ensure nothing too nasty stumbles into you."

Accepted. Protect. Help?

The dungeon can feel a portion of its mana income be reserved for its mentor, and it worries if it's made the correct choice.

"Don't worry, Violet. The Boss will do everything he can to help you. He's got two things for you to do, too. First, secure your core. The mushrooms aren't fooling anyone. Even worse, if something big comes and actively *wants* to eat them, your core might get gobbled up along with them!"

Alarm!

"So you should get it somewhere secret. I even see a good spot for it. You've got a lot of cracks in your ceiling. Delvers never look up, so you should hide up there." He looks to the one of red stones. "Can you give me a toss up there? That little space between those two stalactites? Thanks."

The large one moves, and Teemo sails toward the small crevice, somehow disappearing inside. The dungeon can feel *something* happening, like an expansion but on a smaller scale . . . and without costing mana. After a few minutes, Teemo jumps out and is caught by the one of stone.

"There, that should give you plenty of room for a Secret Sanctum for now. Your centipedes should be able to get you up there, and a few mushrooms should be all you need to keep flies and stuff out."

The dungeon looks at what Teemo did, and is confused, impressed, and grateful. The space is perfect to secure itself. It can feel some strange kind of magic, but it appears it will not fade unless it is deliberately broken. As it examines the new space, Teemo speaks up again.

"The other thing the Boss suggests you do is get a resource node. Normally, that might draw a stronger invader, and it could be trouble with you so young. But with the Boss here, his expeditions should be able to keep anything too nasty away. Delvers love nodes. They've been picking your mushrooms probably thinking *those* are a node, too."

Why?

"Well . . . delvers like to make stuff. It doesn't matter if it's a big, powerful sword or a simple mushroom stew, delvers will take what they can get their hands on and do something with it."

Mentor Thedeim does stuff with me? Change me? He is delver?

Teemo seems taken aback at that for a moment, but thinks it through and nods. "A bit, yeah. He doesn't want to change you into anything different. He wants to make you a better you."

Better me?

It's a strange concept, but an appealing one.

Chapter 75

I was a bit surprised to get a notice to be a mentor, but I accepted it without difficulty. What I had Teemo propose really was a mentorship, more or less, and Violet accepted it. So now I have a protégée, which is interesting. I can take a look in on Violet's territory, and it seems like any denizens and even dwellers are seen as friendly, so they can wander in and do stuff and generate mana. A couple ratkin have already gone and picked a mushroom or two, probably looking to expand their options with their mushroom beds? Oh, and while I can leave little suggestions around or offer quests (like the two that I've already given), I can't make any decisions.

If I had to guess, I'd say that comes with the next option I have. I haven't floated the idea to even Teemo just yet, but he probably knows it's an option . . . and Aranya probably knows it's a thing, too. I could take Violet as a vassal.

Yeah, not really interested in that right now. I have enough on my plate running just *my* stuff without having to try to run a *second* dungeon. I could probably delegate a lot of stuff, but I dunno. Maybe if Violet asks, I might.

But speaking of my own stuff, I think I managed to miss the trio figuring out the water jar puzzle. I guess they finally stopped trying to cheese it and actually used their brains. Or they just started pouring one jar into the other and realized they'd get there eventually if they kept doing that.

Either way, they're on to the final challenge, and they're doing about as well as I expected: steady but slow progress. I get a lot of satisfaction listening to them chattering away as they try to figure out the big complex puzzle in their own corridors, and I get a lot of mana from it, too.

"This lever do anything for you two? I can't see anything changing here," calls Hark. His current section has a bunch of different levers, as well as a slot for something.

Mlynda hums as she moves a peg in the wall along a track. She can see it'll eventually be able to come out, once she gets to the end of the track, but there

are a lot of hidden blockers between where she has it and where she wants it to
be. "I can't tell anything different over here."

"I might have something," speaks up Vnarl, his own puzzle involving pres-
surized pipes and needing to get the pressure just right to get it to spray into a
specific hole. "These two valves are acting different, I think."

I might actually miss them when they're gone. Leo won't, but I don't blame
him. I get a flash of loathing from him whenever he sees the halfling in the group,
but he's a good Warden and hasn't been sabotaging their efforts, which I'm glad
for.

He's also been busy with Jello trying to convert a mole.

They've managed to calm a couple down enough so they stop braining themselves trying to escape, but something in what Jello does seems to pull all the
fight out of them or something. As far as I can tell, they all just want to be let go
once they're out of Jello. Leo's getting a bit frustrated, but I do my best to encourage him. There're plenty of moles to try.

I also have him try with a couple gremlins, just to see if maybe moles are just
weird. The gremlins dash themselves against the walls if they don't get purified
by Jello first, and also just want to be let go after.

Maybe I need to try a different approach? Getting them calmed down feels
like the proper first step, so now I need to figure out something to make them
want to work for me. I need some incentive, but I have no idea what to offer
moles or gremlins. I could try to bribe the gremlins with ore or gems or something, but that doesn't feel quite right. I don't think I need to pay any of my other
denizens? Maybe a little mana. I dunno.

I think I might have something to tempt the moles with, though. If they like
digging, I can offer them the metal transmutation on their claws, which should
let them dig even through stone. I bounce the idea off the empathic bond with
Leo, and he seems to approve, which is great.

Especially since Queen should be able to make bigger batches of stuff now.
The lab is nicely expanded, so all she needs is something to be able to store the
stuff. The ratlings have managed to make glass in the forge, too. It's ugly and
lumpy, but still seems to be glass. At the very least, dipping it in some of the
metal transmutation doesn't change it, so it's good enough for me.

I spend a bit of mana to get a couple aranea to come help, and they get the test
barrel up on some webbing. They should be able to rotate it easily as the ratlings
pour the molten glass inside.

They have to work in batches, but they have everything set up so that the
previous section hasn't *fully* set before the next section gets poured. If they do it
right, the entire inside should get a single coating of glass. I hope.

They start to work, and the forge fills with smoke. It's a delicate balance to
keep the wood of the barrel from burning out of control without cooling it so

quickly that the glass just shatters. I tell them to keep pouring water on the outside and let the inside char. I don't want water inside because that will *definitely* shatter the glass. I probably should have asked Rocky to come and try to help, come to think of it, but it's a bit too late now.

It's smokey, dirty, hot, dangerous work, but it seems to be successful! I let my denizens take a break, and ask Queen to inspect the barrel to make sure it's still sealed. Once she gives it the okay, she can get down to some serious alchemy.

Coda has finished with the surveying, so now it's time to actually do some stuff with the caverns! First thing: *Slash, please go help Coda and the ratlings with the access tunnel.* That's probably going to take a bit, which is fine. There's still the normal tunnel to the caverns; I just want to give a more direct route to the largest cavern in there.

This cavern over on the side, though, should be a great spot for my new enclave! I'm a little nervous about making more intelligent people, but it worked well with the ratlings, so I think pitfalls can be avoided and hurdles overcome without too much issue.

After taking a moment to approximate a breath, I designate the enclave.

Interestingly, only about half of the aranea get the progress bars. When I did it for the ratlings, all of them got it. Though, come to think of it, I have a lot more aranea than I did ratlings at the time. The ones with bars are now labeled *Spiderkin*. I guess they're not suddenly going to become half elf, half spider, then.

Much like with the ratlings, the ones with bars start gathering things. It looks like spiderkin are going to be a bit more martial than the ratkin, however, because they grab a lot of simple spears and a few picks, though they also grab a few things from the couple of underground herbalism nodes. Do mushrooms count as herbs?

As they prepare to go to the enclave, I also notice the ones who go are the ones who seemed to have the least to do. The ones with signs and the ones that have been organizing the warehouses and such all seem to be staying. The exception seems to be the one who weaved the sample baskets for the wolves.

I'm actually surprised none of them managed to convince a wolf to go with them, actually.

Either way, with an enclave getting settled in there, I poke Teemo to let Aranya know. She did a great job with the ratkin, so her help would be greatly appreciated with the spiderkin, too.

I think the last thing I'll spend my mana on for the moment is to specialize my slimes. The oozes with their claim for resource specialization have a grip on my curiosity and won't let go. The spawner immediately spits out a copper ooze. It's mostly clear, but it has some green flecks throughout, which are probably oxidized copper? I think the name is a good hint for what it'll do, too. Sure enough, the thing oozes its way to the nearest copper vein and does . . . something. I'm not sure if it's purifying it or adding more copper or what, but the node ticks upward a tier.

Instead of moving on, the ooze just kinda absorbs into the node, leaving it looking a little wet, but otherwise fine. Maybe it'll help deal with gremlins and stuff, too. Between oozes and the stalactsprites, maybe I can get the gremlins to join me just so they don't have to face those terrors to be near my resources. I doubt that'll be all it takes, but a dungeon can hope.

Chapter 76

The caverns are coming along nicely. It'll probably be a week or more before they're truly *ready* for delvers, but they're not barren anymore. The access tunnel is going well, and Slash is being a great help, too! I can't help but hum "Sixteen Tons" to myself as they work, and they seem to be working to the beat. I'm pretty sure he's trying to sing along or something; it's difficult to tell. His rumblings are changing in pitch, so I think he's at least trying.

It makes me wonder what I can do to make progress on my plan to basically make him a bard. I need to figure out how to make an electric guitar for him, and how to combine that with an axe. The puns run deep with him, even if nobody here will understand them. I also need to get him a top hat, but the axe is the more important thing.

I'm pretty sure I can at least get the basics for an electric guitar, though I might need to give Slash some go-juice to give him electrical affinity. Heh, that'll be a good surprise for anyone who fights him. Who expects an earth elemental to sling lightning? I look into the stores of go-juice, and it seems Slash will need a way bigger dose than the more ordinary denizens do, but that's fine.

I'll probably need to ask Teemo to talk to the ratkin about actually forging the axe for him. I don't think my ratlings can manage the kind of quality I want for it. Grim's scythe is fine to be a bit rough. Slash's axe needs some style to it . . . and needs some specific detail work done to make the guitar part work properly.

For one, I need to actually make the guitar parts. The basics are simple: strings with adjustable tension to change the pitch. The first thing is that guitar strings are not simple wires. They're really long springs, basically. I *think* my ratlings can manage that. It's fine work, but once they draw out wire thin enough, they just need to wrap it around a stiff, separate piece of wire, so I don't think I'll need to bother my dwellers with it.

I wonder if silk would vibrate right? Eh, I'll put it on the list to test. I don't think it'll do the job, but it should be simple enough to check. Which makes me glad Honey's library expansion/lab is up and running. It's still not officially a research lab, but there doesn't seem to be anything actually stopping us from using it as one.

Strings planned, now I need the pickups. A normal guitar uses the hollow body as an amplifier, basically, to make the small vibrations of the strings actually loud enough to hear at any distance. An electric guitar uses pickups to change the vibrations into an electrical signal. I might be able to get Thing to enchant something, but I also want to try something there.

I'm pretty sure actual electric guitars use magnets to get the electrical signal, but I want to try using quartz instead. I'm pretty sure it's piezoelectric, which means pressure will get it to squirt out a bit of electricity. It's not a *lot* of electricity, but it's the principle that sonar works on, and I think quartz watches actually use it for power? Maybe?

Either way, sound waves are pressure waves, so it should make electricity. My hope is to use some magic to grab the electricity, amplify it, and transmute it back into sound. So yeah . . . probably going to take a lot of work to actually make viable. Maybe I can get the aranea to trade something for an instrument, just so Slash has something to practice on until his actual axe is ready.

Still, I do my best to explain the concept to Thing and Honey. The little bee seems to adore any new information, while the hand is looking happy to have a direction to take his studies in. He's hit a wall in trying to come up with some counter to Lifedrinking, aside from just overwhelming it with healing magic. As far as I can tell, that's the only accepted way to deal with it. Considering the level one needs to reach to be able to drop that kind of magic, I don't think it's a very viable counter.

He's tried attacking weak points in the spell, but it looks like it tends to go off like a bomb, rather than just collapsing into rubble.

I'm sure he'll think of something eventually. Maybe playing with electricity and sound will inspire him. At the very least, he should be able to confirm if Slash will even need the electrical affinity to use the axe. I'm not going to force either on the guy, but if he really has been singing along while digging, he'll probably be more than happy to help introduce the world to some rock music.

Tarl

The seasons are certainly turning. Down in Fourdock, it's a bit less extreme, but further inland and higher up, it feels like winter is already preparing to bully autumn out of its place. There's already been some snowfall, which has not helped his trek at all. At least he doesn't need to inspect the Southwood this time, so that's a good week trimmed off the trip already.

He's a bit surprised the White Stag didn't meet him at the border. It seemed like Southwood wanted the information more than usual, but it's not making it any easier for him to deliver it.

He mentally shrugs and leaves that train of thought. He's almost at the clearing, so the Stag should be making his entrance soon anyway.

As if on cue, the soft sound of chimes drifts on the wind, and soon, the White Stag steps forth from the trees. "Inspector Tarl. My Lord bids you welcome and hopes you have brought news of the new dungeon of Fourdock."

Tarl takes a few moments to straighten himself and let his breathing calm a bit from the rough journey. "Indeed. As a representative of the Dungeoneer's Guild, I have come to complete the quest: to exchange information for information."

The Stag regally nods, sending more chiming music from the lights adorning his antlers. "Then proceed, inspector."

"The dungeon is named Thedeim, and has been officially recognized as a cooperative dungeon. Each of his spawners has a scion, and he shows little sign of straining under their costs. He has a Voice now: his Rat Scion and Scout. He has a Ratkin Enclave, who are peaceful and cooperative, still feeling out their place in the larger world. He has a Conduit, gained from subsuming Neverrest."

"So Neverrest is truly gone?"

"Indeed. What's more, he has remade the cemetery to allow its intended use. Heh, he's even assigned a scion to care for it: the Skeleton Scion, Grim. Despite having inherited several undead spawners and having created scions for each, his outlook appears unchanged."

Tarl starts to continue, but the Stag tilts his head, clearly listening to Southwood itself. The elf waits patiently, knowing how displeased the Voice can get if his lord is interrupted while communicating with him.

"This Thedeim truly subsumed Neverrest while so young? The same Neverrest that has consumed other young dungeons?" asks the Stag once more, and Tarl nods.

"Yes. He planned with the local adventurers' guild to help. He feinted with his denizens in the tunnels below Fourdock while sending three of his scions along with what adventurers were available on the surface. One of which is now his second resident."

The Stag listens to its lord again before speaking. "My Lord would entreat with this Thedeim. Something is stirring in the Green Sea. If this Thedeim can defeat the likes of Neverrest, perhaps he can defeat whatever is out there. My Lord has been forced to upgrade his spawners to deal with the influx of invaders from the north, and is uncertain how much longer he can manage. His mana gains are up, but so are his expenditures.

"Bring his Voice, so we may speak."

Tarl stares for a few seconds before his brain kicks back into gear. "I will try, but winter is not far off. I don't think he'll be able to send anything until the spring at the earliest, if he's even willing to help at all."

The Stag looks unconcerned. "My Lord should be able to hold out that long, at the least. The orcish nomads slow their wandering in the winter months, and so tend to delve more often. But that is later. For now, tell me more of what you can of this Thedeim. If my Lord is to ally with him, I would hear his measure."

Tarl chuckles and nods. "I can do that. He's told me not to reveal too much of his current strengths, but even if I were to tell you everything I currently know about him, he'll have many new tricks to spring soon, besides the ones he's kept secret."

Chapter 77

The aranea/spiderkin are developing a lot differently than the ratlings/ratkin. I don't know why that surprises me. Basically, the only thing they have in common is that they come from my spawners. I guess the biggest difference is the dimorphism . . . and trimorphism? Have I mentioned I'm not a biologist?

The ratkin ladies gained boobs as the bar filled. Not enough to go bouncing around me, but enough to feed their children like the mammals they are. The spiderkin are . . . Well, I'm pretty sure if I *was* a biologist, I'd be yelling about how that's not how any of this works.

Where do I even start with how they're changing . . .

Well, I'll start with the male spiderkin, since they're not changing much at all. Well, okay, that's not fair. But compared to the women, their changes are pretty minor. Their faces are changing, gaining a bunch of smaller chitin plates that can move a lot more, making them way more expressive. It makes me think of maybe a detailed helmet or mask with some animatronics. They're getting over the hump of being ugly to being cool. I wouldn't be surprised if some version of *Power Rangers* had helmets like their faces. Their mouths are also kinda sideways; it's weird to explain. I think that might be more like their lips than their actual mouth parts, though. There's a jagged vertical line around a rough square for their mouth. I've seen them yawn, and past the "lips" is a nightmare of mandibles and pedipalps and whatever the words are.

Still not a biologist.

The males aren't growing larger, however. I'm pretty sure most male spiders are smaller than the females back home, so I guess it makes sense. I just thought they'd grow to similar size when they're smart. The other big difference between them is that the males are still staying pretty low slung. While the two pairs of legs at the front are gaining definite hands for both sexes, the male hands are still being used to help walk. They kinda knuckle-walk on the ground, and then use the hands to actually grip when climbing stuff. The women only sometimes use their hands to help climb, and they've been moving more toward a spider-centaur body shape.

So I'm pretty sure they're growing a lot of extra bits. Pretty sure spiders only really have two sections: the butt, which has their organs or equivalents, and the section that has all the legs attached. I think the head is just kinda tacked on to that part? I could go look, but that's not really my point. My point is they've gained a torso bit that stands more or less straight up, and that two sets of arms have migrated there. They also have actual heads. They seem to still have eight eyes, but only the two in the normal spots are big. They even have an iris lid, like a camera. It's really cool. The other eyes are smaller and ring the head, making them easy to forget about if you're not looking.

They also appear to have grown . . . *something* on their chests. It could be boobs with a chitin plate covering them, spinnerets, venom sacks, or even just muscle. I honestly haven't been brave enough to try to take a closer look. The nightmare of seeing inside the mouth of one still haunts me.

The part that I really think would make a biologist have a fit, however, is that they're growing an internal skeleton . . . or maybe just in certain places? Or certain species?

This is what I meant about the trimorphism earlier. While the males are smaller and a lot different from the females, I'm also seeing three races, I guess would be the proper term.

There're the relatively small ones that seem built like jumping spiders. There are a lot of different colors and patterns, though the classic wolfspider grays and stripes seem to be the majority. They're busy little spiderkin, and seem the most inclined toward going out to hunt. There's always at least one party of them out in the tunnels and caverns past my borders, looking for food. I'm not exactly surprised by that, at least. I've never heard of a spider growing mushrooms to eat or anything like that, so my spiderkin being carnivores is no big shock. I do wonder if they'll be able to eat other stuff, too, or if they'll be staying with meat.

The normal-size ones are definitely more based on black widows. They have shiny black carapaces, rounder backsides, slender limbs, and have the red hour-glass marking. I expect they have potent venom, too, but they haven't really bitten anything. Instead, they seem more content to stay inside the area for their enclave and build. Widow web is supposed to be stupidly strong, so I suppose it makes sense.

Interestingly, the males help out a lot with building, too. They seem to be the ones to use the picks they brought with them, and with stone and webbing, the enclave is coming along nicely. I think they're even building a little animal pen, so maybe they'll be able to ranch later? Oh, I should have Aranya try to introduce them to fishing. There's gotta be *something* aquatic around here worth eating, and should be a lot easier to domesticate than something like a scythemaw, or whatever else wanders around on land down here.

The larger ones seem to be based on tarantulas. They're built stockier, and their carapace looks like it's growing around muscle. It makes me think of Roman ab armor, as seen in movies. But the presence of abs is why I think some of them are growing internal skeletons. Normal spiders don't really have muscle. Instead, they have hydraulics, basically. Muscles need internal bones to be able to leverage for movement. I wonder if they're doing a hybrid kind of system? Muscles for fast movements, hydraulics for strength? However they actually work, the tarantulas are taking the place of guards, with a couple helping move around heavy stuff.

Interestingly, Tiny has taken a couple trips down to the enclave, too, along with Aranya and Teemo. The big guy has apparently been dispensing the "Wisdom of the Weaver," which even has Aranya listening.

Great, just when I thought the whole cult business might quiet down. He is also being something of an oracle, apparently, saying he can read the pattern of the weave. I would usually ignore that kind of talk . . . but I *do* have Fate affinity. I probably should have expected at least one scion would lean into that aspect instead of whatever else they have.

I should actually try to grill the big lug about how that works, come to think of it.

I poke Teemo about the fishing potential, and he squeaks at Aranya from her shoulder.

"Hey, Aranya, the Boss suggests trying to teach them how to fish, maybe with weighted nets? He says a rod and reel might be a bit much for them to try right now."

The kobold brightens at that. "Ah, fishing! That should be a lot simpler than trying to teach them how to domesticate whatever is walking or flying in the deeper tunnels. Thank you, Lord Thedeim!" she says with a slightly bowed head. Teemo takes the chance to hop off and onto Tiny.

"I'm gonna stay here with the big guy. The Boss wants to talk with him." Aranya nods at that and heads off to gather as many spiderkin as she can to teach how to fish. Tiny shuffles his legs slightly when he hears Teemo say I want to talk.

So. Reading the weave?

I can't hear anything from Tiny as he explains what he can from my question to Teemo, which makes me wonder how my favorite rat actually hears everything. I can't chew on that puzzle for very long, however, as Teemo starts talking.

"He says he can see the tapestry you're weaving, and if he concentrates, he can see the greater tapestry around us being woven as well?" says Teemo, clearly weirded out by the description. That's pretty cool, though. *Can he tell if the winter will be a harsh one?*

Teemo asks and is answered, and he shakes his head. "He says he can't read that far ahead . . . or that far away? He says there's a lot of distance between the cause of a harsh winter and the effect of feeling one."

Hmm. I probably shouldn't expect him to be a more accurate weatherman than people with radars and satellite images and stuff. Maybe if he could get a read on more of how the weather is on the entire planet, he'd be able to take a guess.

I go to ask Teemo another question, seeing him rubbing his head. *Oh . . . sorry about that.*

"It's okay, Boss. You weren't too focused on those things, so it was more disorienting than painful. I've been getting better at ignoring deeper implications for things, but how am I supposed to ignore the idea of an eye so high up it can hide in the stars?" He shakes his head and chuckles. "We're both getting better at it, though. What else did you want to ask him?"

Oh. Uh . . . I was going to ask him how he reads the stuff, what's it like. He must be using Fate magic to do it, but I know almost nothing about it, and only have the vaguest ideas of what it even could *be.*

Teemo relays the information, and soon replies, "He says it's like he can see a web as it's formed right now, and also see the ways it might be finished, all at once?"

Ah, brace yourself then, Teemo. That sounds like quantum superposition. Ask him if looking changes things.

Even with the warning, it looks like Teemo loses his balance for a moment, but thankfully, only a moment. He looks a bit confused at my question but relays it anyway.

"He says no?"

Maybe not quantum, then? Or magic can measure without changing the results because magic, heh. Either way, that's very interesting. *Does he spot any potential snarls in my web?*

Teemo shakes his head. "Tiny says he doesn't see anything, and he likely wouldn't say anything even if he does, barring something catastrophic. He says you integrate problems much too smoothly for him to try to keep them out."

I chuckle at that. *Well, tell him thanks, I suppose.* I'm a regular Bob Ross over here, making happy little accidents, heh. Still, that does make me want to keep myself prepared for something potentially dangerous. He seems to need to be able to observe the different causes to see how the web will change, so some big surprise could make a mess of things and blindside him, and so us.

Tell him thanks for me, and to keep up the good work. The hedge maze is the wild success it is because of him. And he's the only one who seems to be delving into Fate magic, so I'm sure I'll need to pick his brain about it eventually, too.

I get the feeling I won't be able to ignore that magic forever.

Chapter 78

"Over twelve . . ." says Vnarl, peg in hand at what looks to be the final puzzle for the gauntlet. Each previous room gave part of the solution, and now they just need to decipher the clues and put the pegs in the correct hole. The only problem is that the final chambers are all covered in holes. Still, I think they've managed it.

"Up five," calls Mlynda, confident in her answer. I'm still surprised at how much they've all grown just from the gauntlet. Then again, growth is the whole point of the place, so that's a great success.

"Back seven?" finishes Hark, and all three place their pegs. They've tried this several times before; if it's a failure, they get washed back out to the start. They all flinch at the click once the pegs are inserted, but instead of a wall of water, the doors open.

The three cautiously head through. Hark is the first to speak. "Did we do it? Are we free?"

"That depends. Did you learn your lesson?" All three jump at the sound of Teemo's voice, but at least none of them try to attack.

"What do you mean?" demands Vnarl before he remembers how well provoking my scions went last time. Mlynda elbows him, and he looks abashed at his response, so at least they're still trying.

Teemo just grins at their antics. "Yeah, I think you have. Next time, don't go assuming things about a new dungeon. Not all of them are as nice as Thedeim."

All three look wary at the revelation of my name. "Wait . . . it has a *name?*" asks Mlynda incredulously, and Teemo laughs.

"Of course he has a name! You three could have learned it earlier if you had just asked!"

The three exchange looks that say they all just dodged a bullet. It seems like dungeons with names are not ones to trifle with, and probably have harsher punishments for those who draw their ire.

After a few moments of appreciating life, Hark speaks up. "So we're free to go?"

"Yep. Thedeim isn't banning you from the place, either, though he does suggest you take the time to learn the rules before you try delving again. Oh, and probably go get some gear. He's not giving it back."

The three slump slightly at that but don't argue. Vnarl straightens up slightly before addressing Teemo again. "Then . . . we'll take our leave. Please give Dungeon Thedeim our gratitude for his mercy."

The other two murmur similarly before the group heads off toward the exit from the tunnels and the front gate beyond. *I think that went pretty well. What do you think, Teemo?*

"Yeah, I think you've actually managed to beat some sense into them," replies my Voice, nodding. "Need anything else?"

Not right now, no. You can get back to making shortcuts or doing whatever.

It seems like he's leaning more toward whatever, as he hops into a shortcut that leads toward Violet. She's done the two quests I gave her and seems to be pondering which way to expand. For the moment, my only advice for her is to not expand in a direction which doesn't have an obvious path. She's deep enough that she probably wouldn't make the kind of quake I did, but going deeper just yet feels dangerous, and going up will only make further upward expansions more likely to produce a dangerous earthquake.

For now, she seems to be happy just upgrading her mushrooms and centipedes, and her little animal node. Yeah, animal node. She has a little . . . cave bunny node or something? The things are adorable and fluffy and, apparently, pretty dang tasty. The ratkin like to hunt one or two on their way back from the deeper tunnels, which seems to suit Violet just fine.

She's even specialized her mushrooms into some resource spec. It's called Nutritious Hyphae, which seems to make the mushroom patches produce little fungus balls, and the cave bunnies love them. With a stable source of food, the bunny population would be spiraling out of control if the ratkin weren't keeping their numbers manageable.

Spawner and node upgrades aside, she's saving the bulk of her mana to see if Coda's surveying will give her a discount on expansion. To be fair, I'm looking forward to seeing if that idea pans out, too. He's currently out on expedition right now, surveying what will probably be Violet's next expansion. The caves kinda west-down have a lot of water in them, looking a lot like small lakes and large ponds, along with shores.

He's been staying away from the water, happy to survey via sonar from well above the surface. He hasn't seen anything leave the water yet, but he's not taking chances, especially since some of those shapes and sizes hint at scythemaws. I might actually let Honey send a few expeditions to try to learn about the life in there, but I'll probably need something to give the bees either Water or Wind affinity to get an actual look under the water.

If that *is* where scythemaws come from, why was one chasing Aranya? If that's *not* where they come from, where do they *actually* come from? I've seen a couple signs that I think are from scythemaws, but nothing looks especially fresh. I dunno.

I rub Honey's bond with the idea to study them, and she looks to be all for it. The smaller gathering expeditions have been going great, so I think she's been looking for some bigger research to tackle. Learning more about what seems to be the apex predator in the Deeps can only be a good thing.

I also rub Queen with the idea for something to grant either Air or Water affinity, and she also seems happy for a bit of direction. She's been dutifully experimenting with the expanded setup, as well as producing more of the three alchemy things we have available: Bottled Lightning, Liquid Steel, and Healing Essence. We had basically stopped production of the latter, once the healing ants got up to a good population, but I want to get a bit more and see if I can make a healing *slime*. I feel like the ants are good for more minor stuff, but a healing slime would be like a portable sci-fi healing pod.

I don't even need Queen to run the numbers to know it's going to take a ton of the stuff to make even a single healing slime, but I'm not worried. Slow and steady wins the race. Besides, she has her ants working on constantly expanding the lab now, thanks to the ratlings taking most of the digging duties elsewhere.

Speaking of elsewhere, the Spiderkin Enclave is shaping up nicely. The bars are about halfway full now, and it seems like everyone is mostly the shape they're going to be. Aranya has been working with their apparent leader, Folarn, who used to be the aranea who made the sample baskets for the wolves. She's the largest of the tarantula spiderkin, and has actually made a large axe for herself, rather than the simple spears the others prefer.

She's pretty no-nonsense, and has shot down a couple of Aranya's suggestions for how to do things. But the ones she *does* take into consideration get her full attention until they're complete. Take fishing, for example. The watery caverns outside my borders are more swampy than the ones outside Violet, which actually makes net fishing a nightmare. After just a couple attempts, Folarn put the kibosh to the idea.

I had Teemo explain to them the idea of a basket fish trap, though, and that seemed to get their attention, especially after Aranya explained the basics of aquaculture. I'm pretty sure there's a book on that up in the library, too. Folarn didn't seem to like the idea much, but she allowed a couple traps to be made as a pilot.

The traps worked like a charm, and they caught a bunch of lobsters. Well, probably not technically lobsters, but they're way too big for me to call a crawdad.

They have more of a mottled gray shell instead of the mottled brown that most lobsters have, and they turn a bright blue when cooked.

And the spiderkin love them. As bottom-feeders, they should be pretty easy to care for, too. Aranya is currently helping them dig out some ponds to keep them in, while some of the other spiderkin are gathering various plants and other stuff from the swamps. Teemo's warned them about potential scythemaws, but none of them look too worried about it. They're not exactly *ignoring* the warning, but they're confident and cautious enough not to let something like that scare them off. Not when there're tasty cave lobsters to domesticate.

Chapter 79

Most of my current projects are proceeding nicely. The access tunnel from the caverns up to near the tunnels' entrance should be done in a day or two. Sure, I could have dug in a straight line, but that'd hardly be useful as a way up and down. It kinda spirals and loops and wanders, and I'll probably have Coda and his crew dig out a few rest areas, maybe with some aranea trading/quest posts.

The easy gauntlet and the hard gauntlet aren't the major draw that the hedge maze is, but the maze is also designed for nonadventurer types. The more physically active people have been enjoying them a lot. The easy one has been beaten a couple times now, but nobody has managed to get past the water jar puzzle on the hard one yet. I think they can smell the chest at the end, though. It's probably going to be an amazing bounty once someone actually gets there.

The Spiderkin Enclave is also progressing nicely. They've been weaving tight baskets to bring in water to their ponds, and they are working on figuring out how to get it just the right level of stagnant for the cave lobsters to thrive. They're also experimenting with some of the plants they've found. There's some kind of tuber that I'm going to call a swamp spud, and the spiderkin seem to actually like it once its cooked. I figure their bars will probably be just about full once they get the ponds running smoothly. No idea how long that will take, though.

One project that's *not* going smoothly is trying to convert a mole or gremlin. Leo is starting to get pretty stressed about failing, too. I poke the bond to get him to relax and suggest he focus on the wolves and expeditions for now. The tundra wolves haven't had a whole lot of guidance and could use him to help get them into shape. While I want them mostly in the caverns, I also want a couple in the catacombs to be strong encounters, and to mix things up a little for the Crystal Shield guys. If they only have experience with undead, even with my ones which are resistant to a lot of holy magics, they'll be unprepared for going out into the world at large. I think.

It's not like I actually *know* what threats are out there in the world. I can guess, but that's really all I *can* do. I could ask, but asking what threats are outside even back on Earth would produce a list that drags the floor.

I'm also going to ask Jello to try to do things a little differently. I think she's using Fate magic to calm the invaders, but even Teemo can't get much detail out of her. So I'm going to try to get her to do a bit more Fate stuff. Instead of just grabbing the first mole or gremlin she sees, I want her to wait and grab one that feels right to her. I'm not sure if it'll work, but the idea had her burbling in what Teemo said was a thoughtful manner, so I guess we'll see.

My three research scions, Honey, Queen, and Thing, have all started working together more closely. Honey is all for working with the two to learn more, but Thing and Queen hadn't done a whole lot together; I guess enchanting and alchemy don't have that much overlap.

But that changed when Thing's work with the quartz started yielding results. He's still a long way from making pickups, but he *has* been able to produce a measurable current from quartz and been able to make a separate piece vibrate from the signal. I don't think that's how it works back home, but then again, there is magic involved. Anyway, once Queen heard about that, she had to come see for herself.

So now, all three are comparing notes on basically everything and seeing if they can produce anything else interesting. I think Queen is experimenting with using quartz in the go-juice process to try to make a Kinetic affinity potion, or maybe a Sonic one? Either way, she seems more inspired than usual. Not only does she have some interesting new ideas to play with, but with Violet and the underswamps, there are a bunch of new reagents for her to try.

Coda is still doing his thing with the digging crew and Slash's help, and my Bat Scion has been experimenting with a few concepts I was able to squeeze through the bond: harmonic resonance and interference. They're just fancy words to describe how sonic waves (and basically any wave, pretty sure) can affect each other. They can add together and make quite a bit of force, or they can cancel out. They can even be aimed to only be stronger at certain points, which has been the major application so far.

He's been trying to use it to cause weak points in the rock so the ratlings can hit it and produce a stone block with a single swing. He's still got a long way to go, but they're reliably hitting out large chunks of the wall with each swing now, instead of just little pebbles or sand. Slash is also helping out, and I'm wondering if he'll somehow manage to become a bard or some other Sonic class just from helping out. He doesn't have the affinity yet, but I can already see his earth magic moving more in a wave rather than just grabbing a chunk of earth and moving it.

Teemo, on the other hand, isn't having any luck at all with expanding his magic. He's making so little progress that I think we're going to have to do some experiments to see just how things work. It feels like I'm missing something on a fundamental level when trying to explain pressure, volume, and temperature to him. Hopefully, a few experiments will clarify things.

On the other end of the spectrum is Rocky. He's kinda becoming a beast. He's gotten that Ice affinity now, officially, and I'm pretty sure he's been going easy on Rhonda and Freddie for a while now, too. I'm going to try to have Teemo explain some new concepts to him and see if I can't get him to have Kinetic affinity, and maybe Lightning . . . maybe Sonic.

I don't know if it'd be easier for him to take the concept of Kinetic and apply the vibrations of heat to get to Sonic, or get him to make the energy bob and weave into the waves of the electromagnetic spectrum. Or maybe I should have him focus on the heat part of fire to more or less distill the idea of electromagnetic waves out of thermal radiation. I dunno. I'm gonna have Teemo talk to him soon.

One scion that has hit a bit of a wall in basically all magic has been Fluffles, though. He's basically stopped casting things. I'm pretty sure he's obsessing about efficiency and not wasting my mana, but if he's my Conduit, I want him to be a magical powerhouse. And he's going to need practice for that.

So I poke Teemo, Rocky, and Fluffles to meet up in the caverns for some practice and maybe a few experiments. Teemo gets there first, of course, and perches on a blunted stalagmite to wait for the other two. Rocky elects to not take a shortcut, yet he still gets there before Fluffles, who seems to want to slink in and avoid notice as much as possible.

Yeah, that's not happening. *Teemo, would you ask Fluffles why he's acting so skittish?*

"Hey, Fluffles. You okay?"

My wingnoodle hisses, and Teemo doesn't even bother to translate before he adds, "That doesn't answer the question. Come on, Fluffles. You're making the Boss worry."

Fluffles's head shoots up at that before he deflates and starts to explain.

"He says he's sorry for wasting your mana?"

Tell him to waste more.

Fluffles starts to object to that, but I have Teemo just talk through him. "The Boss needs you to practice, Fluffles. You're his Conduit. If I'm his mouth to speak, you're his hands to smack someone who needs it. You need to practice. If you're worried about wasting mana, he says to get used to efficiency. That's partially why he has Rocky here, too."

My Zombie Scion stops idly chewing his mouthguard and focuses on the two before him as Teemo nods. "Yeah, you too, Rocky. Thedeim says you've surprised him with your progress with getting the Ice affinity, and he wants you two to practice together and spar to learn."

My Voice looks at Fluffles as I start to explain what I want him to do. "For starters, Fluffles, smash that rock there." Fluffles looks a bit uncertain about that but does as asked, producing a loud crack and a spark of heat from the kinetic impact he puts on the rock. Rocky seems to notice the spark of fire, and I can feel his rotten brain trundling along, trying to figure out how that happened.

"Thedeim says the sound and the heat are inefficiencies. The kinetic energy gets wasted into sound and heat. So he has three things he wants you to do, Fluffles. First, learn to reduce those. Translate the kinetic force directly into movement, without wasting any on heat or excess sound. Second, expand your affinity. You've seen how Kinetic can create Fire and Sonic affinities, so learn to harness them directly. And third, spar with Rocky and teach him about kinetics. You've both seen how kinetics and fire can be related. The Boss says he can give some technical details later, if you guys end up needing it."

The rat looks to Rocky and continues. "You, Rocky, should listen to Fluffles and learn about Kinetic, and hopefully Sonic as well. And once Fluffles picks up Fire, teach him how to translate that into Ice, too."

The two nod and start to talk and demonstrate to each other. Fluffles is looking relieved, too. I guess the thought of wasting my mana was a big weight on his proverbial shoulders. But now, he not only has my blessing to use a lot more mana than he was, but he also gets to teach and spar with someone who can give him a run for his money.

And if this works out, I'll probably bring in Slash to practice with them, too. If he really can translate Sonic from his Earth affinity, he might be able to teach them how to work backward from Sonic into Earth. It's not like I have any other ideas for how to get from the various scientific aspects into the more arcane ones.

Chapter 80

Mana Gained!

Whoa, it's been a while since I got that popup. Last time was . . . the last time I got a new invader! I have a new invader! I have a new invader? I thought I basically already *had* all the invaders I was going to get.

Mana Gained!

Again? Okay, what's going on?

I start looking around in the caverns, as it's my newest expansion, wondering what it could be. It's been open for like a week now, so it's probably something sneaky. Hopefully not *too* sneaky.

I don't see anything deeper in the caves, so I try to backtrack the notification.

I've never really had to do this before; it's weird, like trying to remember something that's on the tip of your tongue. So I do what works for me when that happens: I try to go over what I was thinking or what I was doing, looking for something that will make the thought finally click.

I zoom out and try to only focus on areas with activity. It was something active; that ping happens when my denizens kill some new invader. So, who's looking busy?

Well . . . everyone, more or less. Who's doing something different, then?

Rats? No. Snakes? No. Stalactsprites? No, and I should probably upgrade their spawner again, come to think of it. Spiders? Hmm . . . maybe. Something feels weird with them. I zoom in on the webs nearest the caverns, and after a couple minutes, I finally track it down. My spiders have caught a mosquito!

Just when I thought wasps were the worst, mosquitoes had to show up and remind me whose throne it is. Ugh, I hate mosquitoes! Thankfully, they're pretty small, so I start nudging my smaller spiders to head into the caverns and keep the little vampire bugs at bay.

Speaking of spiders, I check in on my Spiderkin Enclave, and notice they've nabbed a few mosquitoes too. But these ones are about the size of Teemo! Thankfully, the denizens-for-now are handling the dire mosquitoes well. I listen in for a few minutes, and the general consensus seems to be: not bad, needs a bit of pepper, kinda gamey. Cave lobsters are tastier.

I think they're going to hunt and eat them as a backup to the lobsters, as they're still getting them all settled in and trying to work properly. I'm probably going to ask Yvonne to give them a hand with that once she gets back. I think she's more of an expert on life above the ground, but she'll probably know at least something about domestication.

I reluctantly take a closer look at the dire mosquito, and yep, that's a *big* mosquito. Oddly enough, I don't think it was one of the mana pings. I get mana from the technically-still-aranea killing them, but I guess the notifications just count them as big mosquitoes . . . or it counts the smaller ones as tiny dire ones.

Before I can try to track down the other ping, I can feel my protégée having a bit of a panic attack. When I look over at her area, I can see why.

One of my wolves has dispatched a . . . I don't know what. It makes me think of an amalgamation of a ferret and a badger, with just a dash of fox in there for flavor. Whatever it was, I'm pretty sure it's the new invader, seeing as there are several dead cave bunnies around Violet's little area.

I take a few minutes to focus back on the notification, and I'm pretty sure these things are the largest mana-per-kill invader I've encountered so far. It looks like I got the lion's share of the mana for that, but it's still a good windfall for Violet, even with my cut taken out.

I don't bother Teemo with trying to talk to her right now. She's a bit shook up, but she is not in any danger. She *is* a bit sad about the bunnies going without producing her any mana, though. I give her a quest to upgrade her centipedes a bit more, at least to where she can choose a specialization. I also try to impress on her that expanding would be a bad idea, even with the discount from Coda. She'll be getting another invader when she expands, so she'd better be ready to handle *this* one before she goes and adds another.

Part of why I don't bother Teemo is because I have him setting up for a couple experiments to try to figure out how his shortcuts work. I actually drag in Leo, Grim, and Poe to help. I have an inkling of what might be going on, but I need bigger people to be able to test it.

The three aren't upset about being asked to join the experiment, but they all seem a bit confused at what I want them to do.

"Yes, guys. That's what he wants you all to do. Just go through this shortcut together, and I'll come get you each after, one by one," repeats Teemo, also clueless as to what I'm trying to discover here. I've tried to explain it a bit, but his attention wanders pretty quickly. I'm not sure if the concept is one that he wants to let slide off his brain without thinking about it, or if it's boring for him. It could even be both, honestly.

The three scions all nod their understanding for their parts, at least, and take the shortcut down to the training room. I wonder if that room will eventually become an official training room if I keep having Fluffles and Rocky work in there. I still want to make Rocky's boss chamber look like a boxing *ring*, but I'd still need a place for a boxing *gym* for him to practice. And if he's getting to practice, I should accommodate the others, too.

Anyhow, back to the experiment. I tell Teemo to take a separate shortcut and tell Leo to come back using the one he took to get to the training room. My Warden still looks confused about what I want, but he doesn't argue. Once he's back in the war room, I get Teemo to ask him a couple questions.

"The Boss wants to know how much room you had when traveling as a group." A couple growls and yips later, Teemo translates for me.

"He says it felt like the wall was just slightly farther away than he could reach. Same with the ceiling."

And when returning by himself?

Leo tilts his head when Teemo relays my question, clearly thinking for a few moments before answering.

"He says it was the same. Like the walls and ceiling were just out of reach?" relays Teemo, now looking really confused. I'm trying not to groan at that revelation, instead asking him to bring Grim back.

He gets the same questions and gives the same answers, which further confuses Teemo and Leo but confirms my suspicions all the more. I have my Voice go get Poe and tell him to fly through the shortcut instead of just walk, and then he gets the same questions and gives the same answers. That leaves me with four confused scions and one annoying result.

I think distance in the shortcuts is subjective, rather than objective. That means, instead of something being a definitive X feet away, it is simply *over there*. That's why I couldn't get Teemo to notice the change in pressure and temperature when he makes his shortcuts. He's technically not messing with the volume at all!

Trying to consider the math makes even my non-existent head hurt, so I don't think too hard about it.

"Is teaching me new magic a dud then, Boss?" asks Teemo, a bit disappointed.

Heck no. It just means we need a different approach. I'll find a hat and figure out how to eat it if a bag of holding isn't Spatial magic, and they definitely *do* have a defined interior volume. I think the shortcuts are more like balloons but with a constant volume instead of a mostly-constant pressure. It makes me glad we didn't get one to pop while anyone was inside. I don't know if them popping is even a thing, but I'm in no rush to try to test the limits and find out.

Anyhow, Teemo. You're going to be spending a bit of time with Thing. Ask him to get a good schedule going so you two can work on making a bag of holding. We still have that one from Tarl to compare with. I want you to feel that thing out and how it works, and how it's different from your shortcuts. I don't need them to become more defined like the bags of holding, but I do want you to be able to make a defined space into a larger defined space. Once you do that, I'll be able to teach you some serious stuff.

Chapter 81

Yvonne is back, and so she and Teemo are relaxing a bit. He demands belly rubs, and she's more than happy to give them. I want to ask her about what her ranger stuff actually entails, but that can wait for now. She's been on the road for a while, so I want to give her at least a bit of time to just relax with Teemo and not need to do anything.

I'll also probably ask her to look around in the caverns and in the area by Violet that I'm going to call the aquifer. The expedition wolves are getting unsettling feelings coming from both the aquifer and the underswamp. Right now, my worst-case scenario is an army of undead from a piece of Neverrest that somehow managed to escape.

It's also probably the least likely scenario, but better to be prepared. My most likely scenario—and honestly, still pretty bad—is some unknown dungeon with scythemaws as denizens. Then the next couple on the list are other variations of "lots of scythemaws want to eat us all." I'm considering asking Thing to try to make magical traps that I can trigger directly, but not yet. He's got a lot on his plate right now.

The work on the axe has stalled a bit. He's made some serious progress, though. It wasn't difficult to make the quartz pickups, and not difficult to get it to make a separate bit of quartz vibrate with it. The problem is getting it to actually sound right.

We first tried putting it in several different boxes, to see if the vibrations would work. It made sound, sure, but it sounded like a box with a big bee in it, not like an electric guitar. We then tried a couple slats of wood, trying to make it sound like a xylophone, but . . . well, it sounds like a xylophone. It also wouldn't work to perform a wide range of sounds with. It'd take an entire array of crystals and . . . keys? Do xylophones have keys? Either way, I'm not going to make Slash haul around something like that.

My next idea was to try a pipe and make it be more like an organ, but after the xylophone experiment, I shelved it. Besides, now that I think about it, it might come out sounding more like a kazoo than a pipe organ. And, you know, pipe organs aren't exactly the most portable instruments either.

I do have an idea for an amp that could sound how I want it to, but that's going to take a lot of effort. Right now, I have Thing experimenting with copper coils and steel plates, to help him get a better understanding of how electricity works. He's going to be making a magical Tesla coil, and once he has that running as efficiently as I need it, we'll work on making it sing. If all goes to plan, it can be integrated into the tophat.

Slash is going to make a lot of invaders and hostile delvers wish they wore their brown pants, once he's ready.

The ratkin have been working on making the axe itself, too, but they're having some difficulty with the processes. They don't have any problems smelting the ore. They also don't have any problems working on the alloy . . . kinda. Actually, *making* alloys is a breeze for them. Smelting was one of the first things I had my ratlings do back when I first got them, before they even became ratkin, so it's basically in their blood.

The real trouble is in making the correct alloy. They've been mixing numerous different steels, adding in various other metals to get it right to where I want it. Honey has been helping test the parameters.

I need a steel that hardens properly so it'll keep an edge, but not so hard that it'll shatter from repeated impacts. I'd like to make it stainless, too, but I'm uncertain how well stainless works for weapons. Considering the process involves an acid bath and . . . maybe electrolysis, it might be a bit too complex for a weapon. It might mess up the hardening or mess up the edge, or just stop being stainless once it's resharpened.

Maybe some magic can make the weapon stainless, too, but Thing still has more than enough projects to keep him busy right now.

Another trouble the ratkin are having is that they simply don't have a lot of experience making large weapons like an axe. They've made ones for chopping wood, spears, and arrowheads, but an axe is a totally different beast.

For starters, a classic double-headed battle-axe is *big*. Like . . . big enough that there are a lot of people who argue that something like that would have never been used in actual combat. Weight is less of an issue here, at least. Pretty sure Slash can swing something heavier than a battle-axe all day long without tiring out. The problem with it being big is actually forging something that large.

I think it's going to have to be done in three pieces: two separate heads, and the piece in the middle. The middle will need to have the space for the pickups as well, and the three will have to be forge-welded together. I might be able to get some of Queen's fire ants to weld them together . . . but we're nowhere near ready for that.

And speaking of people getting ready, Larx is on his way to greet his soon-to-be fellow Dwellers. They still have about a quarter bar to go, but I get the feeling he has a lot he wants to talk with Folarn about.

He makes his way to the caverns easily enough. My denizens don't stop him, and he's still in my territory, so there's not a whole lot of other potential trouble to come get him. When he approaches the enclave, the tarantula guards don't bother him, and so he enters and looks around with an approving eye.

Aranya soon notices him and brightens up. "Larx! I didn't expect you'd come visit!"

Folarn simply eyes the elderly ratkin as he approaches, using his staff/scepter/whatever as a walking stick. I can see her tense slightly, though none of her arms move for the axe on her back. I guess she's not going to let the grandpa schtick get her guard down.

Larx, for his part, utterly ignores her tension and smiles at her like she's his daughter. "Folarn, right? Aranya has told me so much about you! She was instrumental in helping my fellow ratkin ascend to dweller status, you know." He smiles and glances around. "Looks like your people are growing strong quickly."

Folarn slowly nods, still cautious of the ratkin that smells so strongly of magic. Seeing as it's *my* magic, however, she's not hostile. "Yes. I take her advice when I feel it will work for us, and refuse when it won't."

Aranya chuckles at that and nods. "I think it's about fifty-fifty. I've tried to push a couple times, but the decision really is on her and her people. Lord Thedeim doesn't like to force a specific choice on someone, after all."

Larx and Folarn both nod at that, and the tarantula lady speaks up. "The Weaver adapts to the situation at hand instead of forcing the situation he might prefer."

"Indeed!" agrees Larx with a wide smile. "I might have to come down here more often just to discuss theology, Ms. Folarn. As it is, though, I came more to ask you about what you have on your back."

She gives him an odd look but takes the axe from her back to hold in her hands. "Why?"

"Because Lord Thedeim wishes to make something similar for one of his scions, and he has asked my enclave to try our hands at it. He wishes one made of metal, rather than stone, as well as some other differences." He shakes his head as he avoids getting off topic. "My point is, you've made one already, so you know at least the basics. Together, our people could forge the artifact Lord Thedeim wishes."

Folarn seems to weigh her axe along with the decision. She looks around the enclave for a few seconds before focusing back on Larx and nodding. "We will do this. We will build forges down here together. You will teach us to use them, we will make weapons and armor, and this axe the Weaver desires. Your people are the intricate swirls of fine threads in the weave. My people are the thicker strands of support and strength. Without both, the tapestry would be lesser. Together, the Weaver makes us more."

The other two smile at that, and soon, Folarn and Larx are talking shop about forging and weaponsmithing. I expect they'll talk about their ceremony for becoming true dwellers, too, so I let them have their fun. I let my mind wander with the implications of what Folarn said about the spiderkin.

I was actually getting a little worried for them. They've been growing more militant, and I was afraid they'd go full skull throne on me. Thankfully, they seem to appreciate the finer things in life, even if they seem to feel they can't produce them on their own. I'm going to need to have Aranya remind them about their weaving. I don't mind them wanting to take up a position as strong support, but I don't want them to think they can't have a softer side, too.

Just like with the steel I need, if the spiderkin are too hard, they'll shatter.

Chapter 82

Teemo lounges on Yvonne's lap as she reads by the light of my core. It's kinda adorable, watching the two interact. I'm tempted to let them relax some more, but I really do need to ask her what she was doing with her ranger duties. They sound important, but I don't actually know what they are.

Alrighty, Teemo, break's over. You two can relax some more later, but I really want to ask Yvonne about what her ranger duties actually are.

Teemo sighs but doesn't fight. He knows I've been letting them have some time, despite my burning curiosity. He rolls over to his feet and speaks up.

"Hey, Yvonne. The Boss wants to ask a few questions."

She quirks an eyebrow at that, wondering what I could want to ask about, and marks her place in the book. "What's he need?"

Well, I also want to ask her to help with the spiderkin domesticating the cave lobsters, but the real *thing I want to know is what she was doing. I thought rangers were basically violent hippies, but hippies aren't real big on duties.*

"What do rangers actually do? The Boss seems to think they're just people into nature who use bows."

Yvonne giggles at my apparent naivete in regard to rangers. "It does look like that from the outside, doesn't it? People always talk about encountering rangers in the wilderness, just giving vague warnings or hunting some random thing. But we actually have a big duty."

Teemo sits up and pays attention as she gathers her thoughts. "I suppose rangers aren't so different from dungeons, come to think of it."

Uh . . . what?

Teemo also looks confused. "What do you mean?"

"I mean we both do similar jobs."

You're a source of loot and XP?

"You're a source of loot and experience?"

She laughs at that, thinking it's a joke, but her smile fades when Teemo continues to give her a genuine expression of curiosity. "You really don't know what a dungeon does?" She pauses as she lets that sink in before smirking over at my core. "I suppose that explains some things, heh."

"So what do dungeons do?" repeats my Voice, and Yvonne takes a few moments to answer.

"Okay, um . . . you *can* feel mana, right?"

Yeah. It's like I'm in a bubbling hot tub with the mana around here. It's warm and active. My own mana feels more like a pool at the perfect temperature, circulating enough to keep algae from forming and with just the right chemicals to keep the water nice and clear. Below ground, though, it feels more like a cold pond, with all kinds of stuff growing that I probably don't want to get on my feet.

Teemo relays my metaphors, and Yvonne nods at them. "That sounds like you're feeling the mana around here, yes. Normal life agitates, and I suppose, warms the mana just by living. But, just as everything goes to the bathroom, it's unhealthy to let it build up. It becomes difficult to actually use the mana when it's hot and agitated, and I've even heard some rangers say it's a cause *of* slums, rather than just caused *by* them."

She shrugs and continues. "And similarly, the cold, stagnant mana is also difficult to use. Even worse, monsters live in the stagnant mana, and need it to survive. They can't stand warm and moving mana, which is why they attack people and dungeons alike.

"Because dungeons are the equalizers of mana. They cool and calm the mana of life, and warm and move the mana of monsters." She smiles at Teemo and my core. "So, while dungeons like you treat the disease of stagnant mana, rangers are more concerned with treating the symptoms by hunting monsters and helping out natural life that wanders into the stagnant places."

Huh . . . I do all that? I thought I was just a playground, but now, I'm a sewage treatment plant.

"Eugh, didn't need that idea in my head, Boss."

What? You'd rather all that just get dumped out into rivers and oceans?

"Please, stop."

"What's wrong?" asks Yvonne, and I laugh as Teemo answers.

"The Boss . . . apparently has ideas to turn gross sewage into something *not* utterly vile and disgusting," answers my Voice with a shiver, and Yvonne laughs as well. I would have never expected a *rat*, of all things, to be concerned with cleanliness.

The Trio

Mlynda and Hark sit in the tavern, nursing their ales. Vnarl is trying to get a message and reply to their guild about what's happened, and he's taking a while. The message service in Fourdock isn't the *best*, but this kind of delay feels more like he's getting news he doesn't want, rather than not getting any message at all.

"What do you think is the holdup?" asks Hark. Mlynda can only sigh.

"I don't know. Hopefully, they're just making him fill out some paperwork for a new regulation or something."

Hark nods at that. "There was talk of a deal with a crafter's guild before we came here, yeah? Maybe he's having to negotiate something with them to get us new gear."

Mlynda absently nods to that. She doesn't think that's what the delay is for, but she can hope. They all have a bit of savings, so it shouldn't be *too* difficult to get new stuff. If it *is* a deal with a crafter's guild back in the capital, though, they'll have to wait for it to get shipped here. With winter not too far off, they could be stuck without gear until spring!

Her thoughts are interrupted by Vnarl stomping through the doors of the tavern. He quickly spots the two and stomps over to them before collapsing into a seat with a scowl.

"Are we going to have to buy our gear from a guild back at the capital?" asks Hark. Vnarl growls and shakes his head.

"If only. No, the guild declared us dead! It was easy enough to clear up with the kingdom, but the guild is refusing to let us back in! They said the best they could do is to start us fresh, including our pay!" He only just manages not to shout, but the entire tavern hears. It's not exactly crowded, but there are a few sympathetic glances at the table.

"They can't do that!" objects Mlynda, and Vnarl deflates a bit.

"That's what I said. They said they can and have."

"Where does that leave us?" asks Hark, and the three all exchange glances. Before being captured by Thedeim, they would have burned their savings on new gear and would have become freelance delvers. After having a lack of information bite them in their collective butt, however, they all want the security that comes with a guild, and the steep discount on Dungeoneer Guild prices.

Before any of them can voice an idea, a fourth chair is pulled up to their table. Three sets of eyes land upon a skinny orc, but none of the eyes are relieved at the sight. They've been adventuring long enough to recognize a rogue when they see one. It's something about the smile, not quite a smirk, and the way they seem to even *sit* light on their feet. The signs aren't too difficult to spot if one knows what they're looking for.

"If I could make a suggestion?" he speaks, meeting their eyes one after the other. Vnarl immediately shakes his head and lowers his voice.

"We're not doing work for the thieves' guild."

The orc laughs loudly at that. "Hah! Ah, it's been a while since someone thought I was working for them, heh." He takes a few more seconds to calm himself while the trio looks confused.

"I couldn't help but hear you're between guilds at the moment," he says, and the three look a bit embarrassed about how loud they were. "Nothing to be ashamed about. How many others spend that long inside a dungeon and emerge unscathed? I imagine that's why your old guild declared you dead."

It's a small consolation for the three, so the orc continues. "I'm Karn the Slight, leader of the Slim Chance guild, the local adventurers' guild." He smiles as they all perk up, Hark letting his mouth run first.

"We can join your guild?"

"Well, that depends. On what terms did you leave the dungeon?" he asks, his whole demeanor tightening slightly. The trio exchange looks again, all seeing the truth in what he's not saying—if they're on poor terms with the dungeon, they're going to be on poor terms with him, and possibly the entire town as well.

"Amicably," answers Vnarl. "The dungeon put us through a gauntlet, and we couldn't leave without escaping it first. We eventually worked our way through it, and that rat Voice told us we're free to return, but suggested we get some new gear first."

Karn relaxes and nods at that. "Sounds like water under the bridge, then. Now, I can offer you three a party slot, though you will be starting at the bottom." The three deflate at that, but he just smiles and continues. "Don't be like that! We're a small guild, so the bottom isn't so far down, heh. I even have a quest that I think you three would be uniquely qualified for."

They look suspicious, and Mlynda speaks up first. "What quest? We're unequipped."

The orc answers by pulling out a small plank of wood and setting it on the table for them to read. "I'm sure it's changed at least some since you've escaped, but I want to be the first guild to be able to hang this up as a trophy for completing it."

The three look down, and slowly, they all realize what the orc is getting at. Guilds love having trophies to show how good they are in various dungeons. Vnarl speaks up before any of them can get blinded by the stars in their eyes. "We get to keep the loot?"

"Guild dues aside, of course," replies Karn, holding out his hand. All three shake with him over the crudely painted sign.

Beat the Gauntlet

Chapter 83

I watch as Yvonne's head emerges from the cave lobster pond, quickly followed by the rest of her. She stands nearby as she considers what I've asked her to look into.

"What do you think?" asks Teemo. Yvonne hums in reply.

"I think I'm better at things that live above ground. Still, it's an interesting challenge. I think it'll work, though they'll probably have an easier time of it if they just section off a small part of the underswamp. I'm going to go take a look there, next. From what I can tell, they're getting what they need. I don't know if full domestication will be an option, however. That usually entails the creature seeing you as not a threat at all, and I don't know if these things are smart enough for that. I'm pretty sure they'll be able to breed and feed, at least, so that's close enough."

"It's not too stagnant?" asks my Voice, and Yvonne shakes her head.

"You really want stagnant water with these ones, actually. They live to eat stuff like algae and moss that will grow in stagnant waters. The spiderkin will just need to introduce fresh lobsters every so often to keep inbreeding down."

"Cool. Shall we go check out the swamps?"

Yvonne grins at him. "I don't know . . . swamps can be pretty gross. You sure you want to come?"

He gives her a flat look. "I'm never going to hear the end of that, am I?"

She laughs and kneels down to let him hop onto her shoulder. "Of course not!"

He grumbles but climbs aboard, and they head out toward the underswamps. Yvonne speaks with wonder as they walk. "I never expected the underground to have so many biomes! I should have asked Ragnar to come, see if he knows more about this than I do."

Teemo snorts at the idea. "I don't mind him coming along, but I think he'd be more at home in a mine than wandering the great indoors."

Yvonne laughs at that and nods, though she takes a few minutes to inspect something on the wall instead of answering right away.

"What'd you find?"

"I'm not sure. It's covered in moss, but it looks like a territorial marking." She reaches out a hand and brushes away the plant, tracing two long gashes in the wall that meet at the ends. "I've never seen a clawmark like this before." Teemo peers at the markings; he has the same worried inkling that I do.

"I think I have. Test your sword in the gashes," suggests my Voice, and so she does. Yvonne pulls the large, curved blade from her belt and tries several ways to make it fit the mark on the wall. After a few different positions, she seems to have one that she likes.

"I think you're right, Teemo. They're sword slashes." My best rat sighs and shakes his head.

"It wasn't always a sword, remember? You never saw the scythemaw it came from. It's . . . a mandible? Big, nasty, teethy things that stick out of the face sideways."

"What's a scythemaw?" asks Yvonne as she looks more closely at her sword. It's pretty easy to tell she's trying to gauge how big one would be, based on the weapon in her hand. I don't think she likes the picture it's painting.

"A big, scaly lizard thing with two of those sticking out of its face. One actually chased Aranya to the Boss. That's how she got here. He had to bring in Tiny to handle it. I think she called it a tunnel horror."

Yvonne's eyes widen as she looks at Teemo, then back to the sword in her hands. "This is an *actual* tunnel horror's fang?! I thought it was just modeled after one!" She looks like she's ready to have a panic attack before she closes her eyes and takes a deep breath.

When she opens her eyes again, she's all business. "This wasn't the only territory marking I saw, just the one that looked freshest. There's not a whole lot known about how they actually live. Most people who try to research don't come back to report their findings. The ones who do were usually too busy running to take any notes."

My Voice attempts to lighten the mood a little. "Don't tell that to Honey. She'll take it as a challenge." Yvonne's demeanor softens a little, but she's still in business mode at the moment.

"We need to investigate. There are way too many markings for a lone horror."

Yeah . . . now that I'm looking, I'm seeing a lot of those slashes in my walls all throughout this layer of the caves. The tunnels under the manor are looking fresh, but deeper, there are gashes in the walls all over the place. I ping Coda, Slash, Rocky, and Fluffles to come take a look, then let Teemo know.

"Looks like the Boss wants to help, Yvonne. He's got a bunch of scions coming down to see what to look for, and then check the rest of the walls and such for more signs. Don't forget Honey, Boss."

Ah, right. She should be able to help organize the markings. Are you two still going to the swamps? We haven't found scythemaws anywhere yet, but with all these markings, they've got to be close, and the underswamps are the closest place they could be hiding.

Teemo glances at Yvonne while she walks, a hand on the wall as she feels out more gashes. "Yeah, looks like it, Boss. We'll be careful."

You'd better. We might need to make some kind of rowboat or something to travel in there, too. A fanboat is the peak of swamp travel, but we should probably crawl before we try to sprint.

"Ooh, that's a neat boat design, Boss."

"Hmm?" asks Yvonne, the odd statement pulling her from her focus for a moment. Teemo takes a few moments himself before he replies.

"The Boss has an idea for a boat to travel swamps. It's a flat, shallow boat with . . . kind of a windmill on the back. But instead of capturing the wind with the blades, they *make* wind and push the boat along."

Yvonne considers that as she returns to looking at the wall, and the slow transition from light mushroom forest to mushroom swamp. "It's an interesting idea. I don't know if it'll be practical for cave swamps, though."

"It'd still be neat to make." Teemo chuckles at himself after a few moments. "It'd also be a long ways off to make it. Thing has his hand full enough already."

Yvonne doesn't answer before shimmering wings can be seen, and Fluffles makes his entrance. He nods at the two as he lands while Teemo speaks up. "Yvonne has found a lot of scythemaw markings on the walls here. We're going to be heading to the swamps, but you stay here for the others and show them what we're looking for, then all go search the other deep layers. The Boss says he's seeing a lot of these markings, but it'll be a lot simpler if we get a lot of scions on this, instead of just me trying to dictate what Thedeim's seeing."

Fluffles nods at that, flicking his tongue as he examines the wall. After a few moments, he hisses at Teemo, who frowns. "Yeah, Fluffles says he tastes scythemaw. It's been a while, but that last one made a pretty significant first impression."

Oh, joy. Well, better to have bad news with time to prepare than it just showing up unexpectedly. Teemo nods at that, and soon, he and Yvonne continue on their way.

At the swamps, they can't make too much progress, unfortunately. It's almost all water and kinda mangrove mushrooms. They look cool, but they aren't exactly the best things to try to traverse dangerous waters by.

Yvonne still manages to pick out a few shallow paths, but it's slow going. Meanwhile, my scions scour the deeper passages for more signs. We've spotted a couple before, but never paid them much mind, thinking they were old and the scythemaws were more lone hunters. From the number of gashes everyone is finding now we're looking, though . . . I'm getting a bit anxious.

It takes Yvonne about half an hour before she gives up on trying to traverse the swamp on foot, and she and Teemo start working their way back. "I'll talk to a shipwright and see if they have anything for a swamp."

"A canoe would probably be best. Nice and narrow for easy maneuvering, and easier to ditch than a kayak," says my Voice. Yvonne gives him a confused look.

"A what and a what?"

"Oh, uh . . . different boats. Thedeim says they're usually made from single logs . . . which would be pretty heavy, come to think of it."

Yvonne shrugs. "Boats aren't exactly light. I'll ask the shipwright, though. I'd really hate to get stuck because the boat's too fat."

They chat for a few more minutes until they get back to the Spiderkin Enclave, which gives Coda the time to give me more bad news, which I relay to Teemo to pass on to Yvonne.

"Uh . . . so. There are markings all the way to, through, and past Violet's area. There's a big aquifer not far from her territory that also has a lot of scythemaw markings."

Yvonne slowly blinks as connections get made, and she glances at the lobster ponds. "That could be bad. This much marking says it's clearly their territory, but the markings are also old. There are also two different areas with water for them to potentially hide in.

"I think there are two options." She holds up a single finger. "Option one, they live in one of the bodies of water and migrate periodically across the land, possibly to mate. The other option"—she points her finger at the lobster pond—"is that there are *two* scythemaw populations, and they migrate to mate so they don't inbreed too badly. They might even mate on land, who knows? One thing's very clear, though: they come through here a lot, for whatever reason. I don't know how long between active periods . . . but my gut says it won't be too much longer. If the markings were new, they'd have just gone through. With the age, though . . . I think we're getting very close to a scythemaw migration being due."

Chapter 84

Hey, Telar," greets Teemo, deliberately waiting for her to start taking a sip of her tea before he speaks up. She jerks to a more attentive position and looks around, but she doesn't bless him with the spittake he so desperately wanted.

"Voice Teemo!" she replies as she stands and gives a small bow, which makes her miss him rolling his eyes at her formality. "What can the Dungeoneer's Guild do for you? I'm still working on that information packet you asked about. I just need Inspector Tarl to check it over," she says, still uncomfortable talking with me.

I don't get the feeling she's scared of me, at least. It feels more like she's scared of her boss, or scared to mess up the account of some bigwig client. I can spot the extra books on her desk which appear to be about etiquette with dungeons. While I'm playing Sherlock with her and her desk, though, Teemo sticks to the business of why I asked him to talk to her.

"Do you know anything about scythemaws? Or tunnel horrors?" he adds, liking my name for them a lot more than the colloquial term.

Telar's eyes widen a bit. "*Tunnel horrors*? I'm sorry, I don't, but they don't sound pleasant. Has something happened?"

"Eh . . . more like something is *going* to happen. The Boss has been exploring outside his new expansion and around Violet, and he has been seeing a lot of signs of scythemaw activity but no scythemaws. As far as we can tell, the various caves between the aquifer and underswamps are their breeding grounds. The markings and such are pretty old, too, so we're expecting them to want to use those grounds fairly soon."

Instead of answering, Telar starts digging through scrolls and books, mumbling to herself. She opens up one of the books about talking to dungeons and seems to be referring to it as she scribbles something illegible, then she's off to look at a map one of the ratkin sold her, looks like.

It's quickly apparent that, though she's taking the question seriously, she's also taking her duty to her guild seriously. Notes are written, scratched out, rewritten, references pulled out, put away, pulled out again . . .

"Now I understand why you try to stay away from bureaucracy, Boss . . ." mutters Teemo, turning to leave. *Yeah, I don't think we're getting any answers from her today. Maybe go check and see if Yvonne is having any luck with her guild?*

Teemo's not about to turn down a chance to go hang out with Yvonne . . . and come to think of it, I haven't visited the adventurers' guild yet. The birds on expedition don't count.

It doesn't take Teemo long to get to the guild and slip inside. Right now, it looks a lot like a tavern, and is fairly busy. Looks like a lot of parties are either winding down after some quest or winding up to go do one.

Oh, hey, I even see the trio over there. I resist asking Teemo to go see what they're up to, as we're here on business, not exploring. He heads up the nearby stairs to what appear to be rooms for sleeping, so he climbs further up. He's stopped by a boot landing right in front of him, quickly followed by a second one and a voice connected to the person in them.

At first, I think he's a tall goblin, but the features don't add up. Goblins almost have little fangs that don't pass their lips, but orcs have definite tusks. He smiles at Teemo.

"Ah, you must be Teemo! At least I hope you are. I don't usually let rats stay long, heh."

"Uh . . . yeah, I'm Teemo. Is Yvonne up the stairs?"

He nods but doesn't step aside just yet. Instead, he kneels and offers a finger to my Voice. "I'm Karn the Slight, leader of this guildhouse. It's nice to finally meet the Voice of Thedeim."

Teemo slowly reaches out and shakes the finger after I prod him to. "Uh . . . thanks?"

Karn stands. "Did you spot that group downstairs? The ones that recently escaped you?"

Teemo nods. "Yeah, they made it through the gauntlet and earned their freedom. I thought they were from a different guild, though?"

Karn sighs. "They were, but they were declared dead when they didn't come back. So I took them in. There's no bad blood between you, is there?"

Teemo shakes his head. "Nah, they're fine. They were obnoxious at first, but Thedeim was able to beat some humility and cooperation into them."

Karn laughs and steps aside. "That's what they said too, hah! I just wanted to take the chance to verify that with you. Library's on the third floor." With that, the orc heads down the stairs.

Wait . . . wasn't he at the bar when Teemo came in?

". . . I'm pretty sure he was, yeah, Boss."

Then I think you might not be the only one around with shortcuts. Teemo doesn't dwell on that, instead heading up the stairs, only to find Yvonne glaring at the full shelving.

"Something wrong?" asks Teemo. Yvonne turns her glare on him for a moment before she softens and slumps slightly.

"Yes. Karn does his best to buy everything about monsters, delving, geography, and more. He wants to make sure his delvers are armed with knowledge as well as weapons and spells. The only problem is he hasn't had a guild librarian since he started." She waves a frustrated hand at the books. "They might be in even worse disarray than Neverrest's books!"

Oof, don't say that where Honey can hear. She's liable to pull out her own secret-raid-boss mode and take over the place. Teemo laughs, and after relaying my joke, Yvonne joins in.

"But seriously, Teemo. It's a disaster! I'm pretty sure I can find what I need, but it'll take time."

"You have your nights pretty free, Yvonne. Maybe you could start organizing the place?"

"Oof . . . that'll take a long time to do."

I think she could get Honey to help. I can probably keep her from obsessing over the library here if I keep reminding her about our library, not to mention her research lab. The ratlings should be able to make a card catalog, too, so people can actually quickly access what they need.

"The Boss thinks you can get Honey to help at night, when her other duties won't demand her attention. It'll still take time, but not nearly as much."

Yvonne smiles at the idea. "That'd be nice. Once it's organized, I might even act as the librarian here at night; reshelving books, putting new ones in their proper place, and making notes about the gaps in the knowledge kept here."

"Cool. I'll help you find the thing on scythemaws today, and we'll see about making this an actual library tomorrow." With that, the two get to work, and I turn my attention to trying to prepare for the scythemaw problem.

Probably the most pressing thing is making sure my spiderkin are going to be alright. Aranya is working with them to ensure they have most of their residences built more toward the ceiling than the ground. I think Folarn was inclined to fight any scythemaws that tried to start trouble, but after Aranya told them about how much of a fight just one gave Tiny, they seem to accept that discretion can be the better part of valor at times.

I'm glad, because I'm still not sure what to actually do about the impending scythemaw invasion. On the one hand, sure, they're big and dangerous. They even count as delvers, so I'd get boatloads of mana from killing them.

But I don't really *want* to kill them. Killing one that's chasing someone, sure, self-defense right there. Killing a bunch of them who are just looking to make babies, not so much. Besides, I don't know what they might be keeping at bay. Big predators tend to be a good way to keep other things away. The scythemaws are scary, but they seem to mostly keep to themselves.

I don't want to go and destroy the ecology in the caves just because I'm scared of an overgrown alligator/insect thing. People may have killed wolves for the threat they pose, but people also domesticated the things for the same reason.

Which is another opportunity, too. I'm pretty sure actual alligators like to lay their eggs on the shore then wait for the babies to come back to them. We might be able to steal a clutch or two to try to raise. That's a lot of mights and maybes, though. For all I know, they give live birth by the babies eating their way out of their mom! Hopefully not, because ew, but I'm pretty sure at least one insect does that, and the scythemaws have those big bug mandibles. I dunno, still not a biologist.

No, I'm an engineer! So how do I build a solution for this? I don't think it's going to be as simple as a salmon slide which lets them get around dams so they can spawn, not that *that* is a simple thing in the first place!

Even if I do dig out a bypass for them, I think they actually need dry land to do their thing. There will probably be fighting for mates, fighting for good spots to make a nest—fighting for everything, really. Somehow, I doubt their courtship involves just peacefully making the best wall marking to attract a mate.

Still, might as well get that project at least started. I'm hopeful Yvonne will be able to say we have plenty of time to make the bypass, but I seriously doubt we'll be that lucky. And I do mean *we*. For me and everyone in my dungeon, it'll be simple enough to just get out of the way and clean up the mess after, like dealing with gigantic army ants.

But Violet is going to be in some serious trouble. She's been working on getting her centipedes to dig out a proper core room for her in the ceiling instead of the little space Teemo made for her. She seems to find the place weird to be in, which I don't blame her for. Everyone else just goes through them in a couple minutes at most, but she was planted in one for a while. She's technically out of the inflated space now, but it will take her more work to get a proper Sanctum made.

But all her spawners and nodes are on the floor. And she seems to be just off the main path of the migration/breeding ground. Thankfully, she's not panicking, which is great. She seems to be taking it as the proof of the wisdom in getting her core up off the ground and hidden. She seems confident I'll be able to keep her safe.

So that makes one of us.

Chapter 85

I have an idea for how to help Violet. It's not exactly the kind of thing I think my scions would expect of me, which is actually kinda hilarious. They're all expecting something big and complex, or some strange concept that makes no sense to them. My idea is probably going to disappoint them for how simple it is . . . and maybe for how long it took me to come up with it.

It's a door. Just build a big stone door at the entrance to her main cave. It won't even lock. I can't lock my door, after all, so I'm not going to provoke the system by trying a work-around. It hasn't popped anything up at me in a while, so I don't know if it's giving me the silent treatment or if I'm just behaving better now.

But yeah, I want to build a door for Violet. Just a simple thing that opens outward. To a scythemaw, it should look like a weird wall. It'll probably get a couple gashes in it, but that should be all they do. Her cave isn't really connected anywhere else; it's not a thoroughfare, just a little cave on the side.

Of course, *building* a door for her is another matter. In theory, it's pretty simple: big hinges, two stone slabs—*bam*, easy. In practice, however, I need to make hinges strong enough to support a huge slab of rock and still be able to move with the friction of all that weight. And I kinda need it to open outward, not inward. If it opens inward, a scythemaw could just push it open, which would be bad.

I'll probably end up using something like a vault hinge for the two doors. At least, I think vault doors work like that.

No, not a big gear that has to be rolled out of the way. Lowercase-*v* vault, like a bank. Basically, one entire side will be a hinge. Lots of points to hold weight, lots of stability. The downside is needing everything to line up perfectly to open smoothly, but I don't think I have much other option.

I wonder if metal or stone would work better for the hinge. This will require some testing . . .

Tarl

The elven dungeon inspector smiles as Fourdock comes into view from atop the final hill in his way. The travel to and from the Southwood is long, but it was worth it. The Southwood needs some help with the new invaders it's somehow attracted, and Thedeim seems just the type to be willing to lend a hand.

He smiles as he imagines the crazy things Thedeim might do to aid the Southwood. He especially enjoys the absurdity of the idea of using bats to carry hands to drop on whatever foes need to be dealt with, literally lending the Southwood hundreds or thousands of hands instead of just one.

The image, along with home in sight, helps put a spring in his step, and soon, he's opening the door to the Dungeoneer's Guild. At her desk sits Telar, looking a bit sleep-deprived but not too worse for wear.

"Thedeim keeping you up at night, Telar?" he asks with a smile as he moves to relax in a chair. She sighs before answering.

"Only tangentially. He's been busy since you left, but he's easy enough to work with, for the most part. What's been keeping me up is trying to learn and follow the regulations for actually interacting with a dungeon!" She glares at the pile of regulatory books stacked on one side of her desk, like everything is their fault. To be fair, it mostly is.

Tarl just laughs at that. "That's why inspectors have to apprentice before they can work on their own. It takes experience to understand which regulations can be bent, which ones to follow, and which ones to ignore completely."

Telar looks scandalized just by the thought of ignoring a regulation, so Tarl continues before she can work herself up into a huff. "What's he been wanting to talk to you about?"

"He wants information about . . . *everything!* He wants to know about other dungeons, the surrounding area, the kingdom, *beyond* the kingdom . . ."

"Well, at least there are only two dungeons to tell him about."

This time, it's Telar who has the mischievous smirk. "True, but that's only because *he's* the expert on the third one that's shown up."

Tarl freezes for a moment, then leans forward in his chair. "A new dungeon? Do I need to go and inspect it?"

"Eventually, but it's not too pressing. Thedeim's Voice told me he found a new dungeon in the Deeps, and it only recently graduated from being nascent. Dungeon Thedeim has been guiding it, and Rhonda and Freddie have been acting as provisional inspectors. I've been teaching them what I can of the basics, and everything seems to be going well with it so far."

"Give me details! What spawners does it have? How big is it? Does it have any scions yet? *What's Thedeim been teaching it?!*" he presses, emphasizing the last question.

"It has centipede and fungal denizens so far. Yes, fungal *denizens*, not nodes. It does have an animal node, though." She pauses to rifle through some papers before finding the report. "Cave rabbits, to be specific. They've attracted deep stoats, but Thedeim has been helping the dungeon deal with them. Ah, yes. He's also made her his protégée."

Tarl rolls his eyes at that. "Because we need more dungeons like Thedeim."

Telar smirks and nods.

"I think we do, yes."

After a few moments' thought, Tarl agrees. ". . . Yeah, we do. He's hard on the paperwork, but that's really it."

"You're telling me," says Telar, nodding at the stack of scrolls on a different part of her desk. "I've been compiling as much information as I can, but I'm uncertain what knowledge I should actually offer."

Tarl gets up and looks at her desk. "Do you have any reports on Thedeim? I can relax and look them over now, then go inspect him and the new dungeon tomorrow."

Telar stands and hands him a couple scrolls before heading toward the back rooms. "Would you like some tea? A few gatherers have given me a nice blend that goes well with the Bee Scion's honey. It's somehow both relaxing and focusing. I feel like I've been running on nothing else for the last week."

"Sure, I'll try some." He accepts the scrolls and gets to reading. "Hmm . . . good, none of his denizens nor dwellers were involved with the new dungeon for a while . . . Mentor and protégée relationship established . . . Looking like a toybox in training, which could be interesting. There's a lot of good stuff to be had that far down, but most dungeons that deep are belligerent at best.

"Wolf Scion is a Warden, interesting. I haven't seen that title before. Usually, it'd be a Jailor or maybe Inquisitor in charge of a prison. Jello has been seen on the surface? Odd, but she's peaceful enough, and has earned enough of a reputation among the Crystal Shield followers that people leave her alone . . .

"Expeditions have been changing? Strange . . . but that lines up with wanting more information. Bee Scion is involved in them; seems to be gathering samples of all sorts of things? I'll need to look into that tomorrow, then. Ah, thank you," he says with a smile as Telar hands him a hot cup of tea. He takes a sip and is greeted with a gentle sweetness alongside a bright and acidic undertone.

"Ah, that *is* nice," he agrees, and Telar nods.

"Anything of particular note?" she asks. He shakes his head.

"Nothing so far, but I'm not too deep into it yet."

She leaves him to his reading as she organizes her desk.

He takes another sip before returning to the scrolls. "Let me see, where was I . . . Ah. Scion activity. Uptick in Lightning-affinity denizens, Ant Scion has likely expanded the lab." He pulls out his note stone and speaks into it. "Note:

Attempt to barter information to get a look at the secret lab as well as Thedeim's core. Oh, and the Bee Scion's work with expeditions." With that, he sets the stone on his lap as he resumes perusing.

"Raven Scion's new titles recorded. Do not engage in combat." He laughs at how understated the official record is on what Poe can do. "Oh, a new scion? An Earth Elemental Scion named Slash? Not Bash?" He looks over to Telar, who just shakes her head at his suggestion of a typo.

"Thedeim probably has something weird planned for him already, then." He squints as he looks at the next entry, then reads it aloud, "Rocky. Zombie Scion. Boxer. Affinities: Fate, Fire, *Ice?*"

Telar just nods at that, but Tarl frowns. "He has Ice affinity now?"

She gives him a confused look. "Hasn't he always?"

"No. When I tested him, he only had Fire. Well, and Fate. Have other Ice-affinity denizens been spotted?" He flips through the scrolls while Telar thinks before she shakes her head. "I don't believe so. There have been some with metal transmutations, but nothing else with Ice."

Tarl frowns at the scrolls for a few more seconds. "He's done something that I'm pretty sure is impossible." Telar smirks at that, but it fades when the inspector doesn't seem to share in the humor. "Ice and Fire are opposing affinities. A scion with both is rare, but not unheard of. A scion *gaining* an opposing affinity, however, *is*. If it was alchemical, we'd see other denizens with it, too. With this, though . . ."

He picks up his note stone once more. "Note: Ask and barter with Thedeim for the knowledge of what he's done with Rocky to grant him an opposing affinity."

Chapter 86

The birds are making a racket, so that can only mean one thing: Elf Guy is back! I should get the aranea to make him a hat or maybe a shirt that says Elf Guy on it to give to him. It looks like he's the one bearing gifts today, though. He's got a backpack on, and I can tell there're books and stuff in there just from the shapes.

Heh, I should get Poe to teach the ravens how to say Elf Guy, too. But that can come later. The birds settle down and get back to their various jobs as he steps onto the porch, and he looks at the notice board before clearing his throat.

"Dunge—"

"What's up, Tarl?" interrupts Teemo with a cheeky grin. With the growing concerns of a scythemaw apocalypse in my basement, I think everyone is looking for a bit of an excuse to have some fun and keep from just worrying in circles.

The inspector gives Teemo an exaggerated glare for a few seconds before cracking and smiling at the rat. "Hello, Teemo. Telar tells me you've been busy while I was away."

"Heh, yeah. The Boss gets bored easy, so he's always up to *something*. You probably want to start with Violet?"

Tarl gives him a confused look. "Violet? Did you get another resident too?"

Teemo chuckles and shakes his head. "Nah, that's what the Boss calls the new dungeon downstairs."

"Ah. While that dungeon *is* one of my concerns, it's not my biggest. What have you been doing with Rocky?"

It's Teemo's turn to look confused. "What do you mean?"

"I mean that, not only is he a zombie with Fire affinity, but he's also picked up Ice affinity somehow. That *should* be impossible," he states, staring at Teemo like a teacher whose student has given a suspiciously-correct answer.

I had suspected my experiments with magic would shake things up, and now

Tarl's confirmed it. *Sorry, buddy, but that's need-to-know information. Come back when you're a resident, and maybe I'll share the secret.*

"Sorry, Tarl. Boss says that's a secret."

"Hmph. At least he understands the potency of that kind of thing. It's not just some new affinity potion, like the lightning elixir, then?"

"Heh, nope. I'm pretty sure I *can* say that Rocky isn't the only one working on expanding their affinities. So don't be too concerned if more pop up. Heh, or if Rocky gains more."

Tarl just sighs and shakes his head. "A lich with arcane power wouldn't be a surprise . . . but you just *had* to figure out some way to make a *zombie* do it instead." He grumbles for a few more moments before stepping back into his inspector shoes. "Then my other concern is exchanging information. Telar says you've been wanting to know more about what's going on around Fourdock and beyond. Additionally, the Southwood has requested you send an envoy at your earliest convenience. It has somehow attracted more and stronger invaders lately. After hearing how you were able to handle Neverrest, the White Stag of the Southwood has asked to normalize relations and see if you are willing to lend aid."

"A dungeon wants to ally with us? Where is it? Somewhere to the south?"

Tarl shakes his head. "It's to the north. It's called the Southwood because it's in the southernmost area of the Green Sea Forest."

Hmm . . . I'm all for making friends, but I don't know how much I can offer in aid. I'd probably be able to send some tundra wolves, but I think anything else will have to wait until spring.

"Boss says he can send some tundra wolves pretty quickly, but anything else will have to wait until after everything thaws."

Tarl nods. "That should be fine. He's not expecting *anything* until spring anyway, and is confident he can hold out at least that long. The other piece of information I'm hoping for . . ." He shifts his pack to draw attention to it. "I have a lot of information, but I need something in return, Thedeim. Can I barter this pack full of knowledge for access to your core and other secret rooms?"

Hmm. I really would like to have that pile of info on his back, but can I show him my core? I trust *him*, but I'm a lot less trusting of a big guild that specifically peddles knowledge.

"Why?" asks my Voice.

"Because the guild gets nervous without being able to check a dungeon core. And there are theories that core shape and color influence how a dungeon works. I can vow to not give away the location of the core or other secret rooms, and only give a basic description of the core itself," he offers.

I consider that for several seconds before giving Teemo my answer.

"Come back tonight. The Boss will let you in to see his core and the other secret rooms, too."

Tarl smiles at that and shucks his pack, setting it on the porch. "I know it takes a lot of trust to let me see it, so I will trust you and pay you now. With that settled, I'd like to inspect Violet . . . and then probably you, too."

"That works. Follow me," says Teemo as he opens a shortcut for Tarl to use, and they quickly arrive at Violet's cave. Immediately, Tarl looks confused.

"What are you doing?"

"Building a door. I'll explain why later," answers Teemo. He lets Tarl do his job, just watching as he pulls out his recording rock.

"New dungeon is deep underground and is the protégée of the established dungeon Thedeim. Some influence can be seen, but nothing that seems domineering." With that, he steps inside and looks around. "Confirm centipede and fungal denizens. Fungal denizens are odd, but not unheard of, especially for deeper dungeons."

The centipedes watch him for a few minutes before deciding to ignore him as he wanders the cave that Violet inhabits. "Centipedes appear non-threatening despite size. Cave rabbit node spotted; larger centipedes likely a reaction to the stoats it has drawn. No sign of core." He looks around and even up, but he doesn't spot anything, even with his experienced senses.

"Mentor likely told protégée to hide the core. Will ask for description of it later." He plucks a mushroom and nods as he puts it in his pocket. "Experience gained for taking a mushroom. Could be an even better place for new adventurers than Thedeim's manor. Dungeon appears to be a burgeoning toybox, likely intending to rely on mentor for protection. Considering mentor, though . . . any scions should be avoided. Speaking of . . ." He looks around some more, but can't find a scion, either.

"No scions apparent. May be in Secret Sanctum, or possibly doesn't have any yet." He glances out the entrance, where Teemo sits waiting for him. "Unlikely, but possible. Dungeon seems safe to delve, if sparse at the moment of inspection. Will follow up soon." With that, he pockets the stone and returns to Teemo.

"Does it have any scions yet?"

Right . . . I knew I had been forgetting something in my advice for her. I give her a quest to make a scion as Teemo chuckles.

"Not yet, but the Boss just suggested she get one. He's been a bit distracted with the new expansion and the Spiderkin Enclave. And the other problem he wanted to ask you about."

"Another problem? I thought Fate-affinity dungeons were supposed to have *good* luck," answers Tarl with a smile. Teemo chuckles in return.

"Well, we keep surviving. I'd say that's pretty lucky."

"I hope it's nothing like Neverrest." He pauses at the idea. ". . . It's not another murderous dungeon, is it?"

"No. That'd be a fairly simple solution. Here, let me show you." With that,

Teemo scurries up the nearest wall and into a particularly-deep gash. "This is the problem."

". . . Moss?"

Teemo shakes his head and motions at both ends of the deep gouge in the wall. "This slice in the wall. There are a lot of them. Do you know what made them?"

Tarl examines the room, noticing the cuts in the walls and their age. "No . . . What made them?"

"Scythemaws. Tunnel horrors. Big, mean, lizard things with mandibles. Yvonne thinks they're mostly aquatic because there are two big areas of water down here: the aquifer over there, and the underswamps over by the Spiderkin Enclave. There are markings all through the caverns and tunnels between the two. We're pretty sure they come out every so often, and it's been a while, so we're about due for them to come out."

Tarl looks concerned at that, then uncertain. "But isn't that a simple solution? Just fight them? It won't be easy, but it's not complicated."

"They're not monsters. Thedeim says that if he destroys the apex predator in the area, the ecosystem could collapse . . . or something even nastier might move in."

The elf thinks that over before slowly nodding. "If you can't just kill them . . . that *does* complicate things. Does he have a plan?"

"Part of one. The door for Violet is part of it. He's mostly hoping to stay out of the way and let them do whatever they do quickly. The spiderkin might be in trouble, though."

"Right, you said they're near the other body of water. I'll inspect the new expansion and see if I can introduce myself." The two take a quick shortcut to the caverns, and Tarl pulls out his stone to take notes as he looks around.

"Average encounter level higher in caverns than even in the crypts. Dungeon continues to follow an idea of progression. New spawner is earth . . . elementals, not earth spirits. Stalactsprites abound, as do more valuable mining nodes. Mining guild will probably want to post to the adventurers' guild for escorts." He lowers the stone and looks to Teemo. "New scion?"

"Slash, an earth elemental. The Boss says he's on his way to becoming a bard. He's making a few special things for him, too."

"Scion confirmed to be an earth elemental dubbed Slash, planned to be a bard. Special equipment also planned. Advise against attempting to fight scion for said equipment, whatever it ends up being."

Before too long, they get to the enclave, where things are busy. The spiderkin have their bar most of the way full; I'm not sure what's keeping it from finishing. Their forges are basic but functional, built high up the wall to be out of the reach of scythemaws. The ponds seem to be doing fine. Maybe they need to actually get the things to have babies before they'll count as having domesticated them? And then they'll probably have a little ceremony to finish it off, like the ratkin did.

The bustle comes from what looks like a fresh hunt gone right. Tarl can see a dead scythemaw in the enclave, even past the tarantula guards who silently bar his way. At least they're being chill about not letting him in. They've just done the classic crossing of their spears rather than pointing the sharp bits at him.

Still . . . how'd they get a scythemaw?

"How'd you guys get a scythemaw?" asks Teemo. The guards share a glance before one speaks.

"Hunters ambushed it at the shore. Folarn wishes no interruptions while they prepare the meat, hide, bones, and fangs." They look at Tarl with mild suspicion while Teemo sighs and hops off his shoulder.

"I'm gonna try to get some better info out of them, but I don't think they want to share with you, Tarl. Come back tonight, yeah? You should get to see the core and other rooms then, at least if we're not up to our ears in scythemaws."

Chapter 87

Thankfully, it doesn't seem like the scythemaws are gearing up for anything just yet. My spiderfolk wanted to confirm if the scythemaws were even a thing, so they started baiting the shoreline. It would have been quite a fight if they weren't prepared, but they were. According to their retelling, the thing was pretty much dead before it even knew it was under attack. And now that they have a corpse to poke and prod at, they seem to be coming to the same conclusion I have: one isn't too bad, but several could be *real* bad.

I kinda wish they hadn't killed one, but all's well that ends well, I suppose. Despite having killed one without too much effort, it was still the best-case scenario, and Folarn is smart enough to understand that, at least. They're still going to keep an eye on the swamps, but I don't think they are expecting to keep scythemaw on the menu.

I think they were considering trying to use the mandibles for the axe, but the shape is all wrong. Maybe they'll just use them as a trophy or ask for them to be transmuted to metal for swords. Whatever their plans for them, they're working on butchering the big beastie and processing the meat. I think smoking it is their best option for now. Salting it might be the classic, but I don't think we have enough salt.

I'm sure the town has plenty, but even my ratkin have only just normalized trade relations. My spiders still need to officially become dwellers before they can expect to trade in the kind of bulk they'd need to salt the whole scythemaw.

Anyway, I've been getting everything ready for Tarl to come visit the Sanctum and see my core. Aranya and Yvonne say it's pretty cool, but they're kinda biased, heh. I think it's pretty cool, too, and I'm clearly not biased in the slightest. Mostly, we've just been organizing the secret rooms a bit and tidying the place up some.

It's not exactly a *mess*, but it is lived in and worked in. The alchemy lab is basically running nonstop, Thing is doing a lot of work in the secret enchanting lab, and the war room has expanded quite a bit since I last actually needed it. It used to just be a map on the wall, but now, it's its own entire room, with a model of the town and various other maps on the shelves. Poe and Leo have been doing good work.

I still haven't gotten proper beds for Yvonne and Aranya, but they both enjoy the modified hammocks, so there hasn't been much of a need. I'd like to stuff a slime into a mattress for them, but we'd need something slimeproof . . . and two slimes who were willing to do that. I bet some would volunteer, but even with how mentally slow the slimes are, I think they'd get pretty bored pretty quickly as mattress stuffing.

Tarl arrives at the gate exactly on time, and I send Teemo to greet him.

"Heya, Tarl. Ready to see behind the scenes?"

"Almost, Teemo. First . . ." Tarl clears his throat and stands straight. "I, Tarl, the Unseen Blade, swear on my honor as a Dungeon Inspector to record only that knowledge which Thedeim deems fit. In no way will I pass on what he wishes to keep secret."

Impose Geas? Y/N?

Oh wow, he's serious about not betraying my trust with this. For a moment, I consider selecting No. I *do* trust him, especially after this, but it somehow reminds me of how Telar was acting around me. I might consider him and her to both be my friends, but they do work for someone who doesn't know me from a hole in the ground. Better to dot my t's and cross my i's when it comes to the ODA.

Geas Imposed

Tarl relaxes a little at that and smiles at Teemo. "Now I'm ready. Most of the official stuff is just busy work, but sometimes, a regulation is passed that's actually a good idea, heh. So, how're we going to do this?"

"The Boss wants me to shortcut you to the entrance; you can walk in from there." With that, my Voice jumps to Tarl's shoulder, and the two are quickly off to the spider lair.

The spiders all look at the elf warily as he enters reality proper, but don't stop him as he looks around. "Ah, it *is* in here somewhere. It's a good spot to hide the entrance. Even a strong party wouldn't want to go wandering around in a spider lair when they only know of one entrance. It's a good way to get trapped."

He slowly walks around, looking for the entrance on his own. By now, there are a lot of different rocks covered in webs and eggs, so the fake rock is hidden well among doppelgängers. Even with his elf-eyes and other senses, he can't pick out the actual spot.

"Where's the entrance? I can feel the core is closer in this room, but I can't feel the path to it."

"That's because the Boss went through a lot of effort to make it hard to find, heh. To your left, four boulders over."

He follows the instructions, and even staring at the fake rock, he can't seem to figure out how to get past it. "Is there a switch?"

Teemo laughs. "Nope! Just pick it up!"

Tarl gives Teemo a suspicious look but moves to do as told. As soon as he touches the edge of the "rock," he realizes something is up. It only takes him a few more moments to lift the silk and see the passage beyond. He replaces it and looks closer, eventually giving a low whistle of respect.

"Fully-mundane camouflage? Well . . . not *fully*, but no illusions or anything. The only magic is to make the mana flow around the rock and entrance like they were mundane stone. Very subtle." He nods in approval before ducking through the cloth, making sure it's properly in place before he takes in the small hallway.

I've had to expand the secret base quite a bit since I first made it. It used to open practically right into the Sanctum, but now, it's a decently-long hallway. It's pretty plain, too. Maybe I should see if the ants or ratlings want to try carving something in the walls?

The first arched doorway leads to the alchemy lab, on the left. Tarl peeks then steps inside once he sees there's room to. Ants cover practically every surface that's not covered in alchemy. It's quite the scene of organized chaos. He doesn't go and look at the different stuff going on, though. He's probably not an Alchemist. He, instead, walks over to the barrels and cautiously peers into them.

"What are these?" he asks, looking confused at the contents.

"The yellow is go-juice, or Bottled Lightning. That's how we give Lightning affinity to the denizens. The Boss is considering trying to give it to Slash, too."

"A Lightning Bard?" asks the elf, eyebrow raised, before chuckling. "Not the strangest thing he's done. And the other two?"

"The metallic stuff is Liquid Steel. It transmutes stuff to metal. We're not quite sure if it grants a Metal affinity or just transmutes. A couple ants tried to drink it . . . and it didn't go so well for them, so we're only dipping things into it for now. And the red barrel isn't blood; it's Healing Essence. That's how the Boss made the healing ants, and he's working on healing *slimes*, too."

"Is it granting Life affinity, then?"

"We don't think so, but we haven't had enough of it to do much testing until recently. Queen's been inspired by something with quartz, so that's been her main focus for new stuff."

"How much does Thedeim want others to know about his alchemy progress?"

"As little as possible. Old Staiven has a sample of the go-juice, so you can probably record whatever you know about that one, but the others should be kept a bit closer to the vest. Especially the transmutation elixir. Queen was inspired by something the Boss told her about how reality works to make that one."

Tarl's eyes widen at that, but he just nods instead of asking questions. "I'll leave the metal one out of the report fully. The Bottled Lightning and Healing Essence are not too far out of what dungeons with access to alchemy have produced."

He pulls out a notebook instead of his rock, and a charcoal stick, jotting down a few quick notes before returning to the hall and going through the first door on the right: the secret enchanting lab.

Honestly, the crystal array in the public lab is still better, but the one in here is cheaper and easier to replace when something explodes. Which has happened several times. Tarl runs a hand over some of the scorch marks as Thing watches . . . or does whatever he does to sense things.

"What made these marks?"

"Failed experiments in countering Lifedrinking. Thing blew three arrays before accepting he can't just pick them apart like other enchants. At least he knows what to look for now."

Thing slumps slightly at the retelling of his failures. Tarl just chuckles. "Well, he learned from his mistakes. I've had enchanters flat-out tell me some enchantment is impossible even after tripping over the same magical trap a dozen times."

His mirth falters a bit when he sees his bag of holding next to a chalkboard with the runes sketched out. "Is that my bag of holding?"

"It was, but it's ours now, heh," replies Teemo with a smile. Tarl soon smiles at the situation as well.

"What are you doing with it?"

"We're trying to figure out the Spatial magics that make it work. And Thing is trying to teach it to me. The Boss says something about how a bag of holding works will let me expand my affinities."

"Like Rocky?"

"Yep. Probably don't let that tidbit out either."

Tarl nods and absently takes a few more notes, mostly about the secret lab being used for research into countering Lifedrinking. "Well, take good care of that bag. It cost me a lot. I liked that bag . . ."

Teemo laughs as they exit and take the stairs at the end of the hall that lead to the secret war room.

"That's a detailed model," notes the inspector simply, and Teemo nods.

"Yeah, Poe's been working his tail feathers off to get the details for this right. There're also a bunch of maps for farther out and down in the drawers."

Tarl opens a couple drawers and glances inside. "Nothing too out of the ordinary in here, seems like."

"Leo's working on getting more detail for the other maps, too. The Boss wants to know what's living out there, instead of just the topography."

"Makes sense. I've seen some dungeons have huge complexes for their war rooms, with little enchanted figurines for particular people of interest to walk around and keep up-to-date in real time."

"That's kinda creepy."

"I'm actually surprised you don't have something like that for Freddie and Rhonda. And me."

Teemo laughs again. "The Boss doesn't need to keep that close an eye on everyone! Besides, it's not like he can react quickly enough for that to make much difference."

Across from the war room are the . . . apartments, I suppose? There's a dining area, cooking area, the secret library is in there too, as well as the sleeping quarters behind one last set of doors. Tarl looks over the books for a few moments before nodding.

"Neverrest's books, and a few notebooks I can't read?"

"Heh, that's the Boss's writing. He says he can read it, and Honey and Queen can make it out, but I can only tell what it says because I'm his Voice. Boss has *terrible* handwriting."

Tarl slowly nods at that, then looks at the last set of doors. "That's the Sanctum?"

Teemo nods. "And Aranya and Yvonne's rooms. The Boss offered them both separate rooms, but they both like sleeping close to his core."

Tarl hums at that as he heads for the doors. "That's pretty normal. Residents have a closer bond to their dungeon than anything except the scions." As he opens the doors, he can see the truth of his statement. Yvonne and Aranya both stand just inside the Sanctum, wearing their spider-silk clothing and their scythe-maw swords at their hips.

"Inspector," greets Yvonne with a slight nod of her head, which he returns.

"You will not harm our Sanctuary?" asks Aranya fully serious, and the elf nods once more.

"He's taken a geas to only record what Thedeim will let him. It's alright," reassures my Voice. The two share a look before stepping aside to let him in.

Yvonne breaks from the pomp and circumstance first.

"You're our first visitor to the core, Tarl. We had to come up with some kind of ceremony or honor guard."

"Maybe I should get a staff or something like Larx has . . ." ponders Aranya as she thinks about their duties to guard my core.

"Nah, the sword and silk looks good. Maybe a necklace or a little tiara or something to show off your High Priestesslyness?" suggests Teemo. Yvonne sniggers at that, and Aranya smiles, though it becomes contemplative as she chews on the idea.

Tarl, for his part, is looking at the thick silk curtain keeping my core from sight. "Do I just walk past it, or . . ."

I cut off Teemo before he can joke about how looking directly at my core would melt his face. He sulks a little before speaking. "You can just pull it aside. It parts in the middle. We put the curtain in to make it easier to sleep near."

My residents let him open the curtain to my core, revealing my . . . kinda boringness, in my opinion. Maybe I'm just used to looking at it. My core sits in . . . kind of a giant egg cup. I'm over a yard across now, my sphere slowly swirling with various shades of orange. There are layers to the swirls, as well as little sparkles. I think I look like an overfilled spherical lava lamp that ate a glitterbomb.

Tarl just stares for about a minute before shaking himself and speaking up. "Core is an orange sphere with swirling depths. Close to four feet in diameter, approximately. Emits soft light to match the movements inside. Rests in receptacle." He looks to Teemo to see if he has any objections to him writing that down. I don't mind if he records that, so he does.

"So, what's the core theory thing say about the Boss?"

"Hmm?"

"You said there're theories about how core shape and stuff determine things about the dungeon. What's Thedeim's core say about him?"

The elf shrugs. "I don't put much stock in the theory. I've seen a lot of cores, and at best, it gives vague guidelines about how a dungeon is and will progress. It's a lot easier and more reliable to get to know the dungeon, rather than trying to look at the core and guess."

"Aw, that's boring," says Teemo, and my residents agree. Tarl just chuckles.

"That's most dungeoneer work, really. Anyway, I should get out of your hair and get to bed. Late-night inspections aren't the worst of my duties, but I still have to get up at a decent time and report back to Telar."

Teemo nods. "I'll get you back to the gates in a jiffy," he declares, pointing the way from Tarl's shoulder. The elf gives my core one last look before going, his expression unreadable.

Chapter 88

Aranya and Yvonne exchange looks when Teemo leads Tarl out, and it's not difficult to tell what they're thinking. Something spooked him, and spooked him good. I just can't imagine what. He was unhappy about the affinity broadening, but I think this is something well beyond that.

Teemo quickly returns once Tarl is gone, and he doesn't waste any time.

"What do you think has him worried?" he asks my residents, but they can only shrug.

"Whatever it was, it was plain as soon as he laid eyes on the core," points out Yvonne, and Aranya nods before giving her two cents.

"Nothing about the core seems out of line with the legends, but I haven't seen any other cores to be able to compare. The inspector has probably seen more than even most in his field. He's pretty knowledgeable, it seems."

Yeah, which makes me concerned. Do I have core cancer or something? I think he'd tell us if that was the case. I just hope that whatever scared him is something he can keep secret. If he entered a geas with me over information, he's probably entered one with his guild, too.

Tarl

The elf lets his feet slowly guide him home as his mind races. Even so late at night, Fourdock is safe enough that he doesn't have to worry about potential muggers trying to stop him . . . and generally low enough level he wouldn't need to worry about muggers who actually might try.

It's part of why he likes it here. It's quiet, for the most part. Sure, there was Neverrest and Hullbreak, but the cemetery was mostly contained. Even with the painful memories from Hullbreak, it's content to keep to itself and ignore the world around it.

After what he saw in Thedeim's core, though . . . he worries for the peace and quiet of not only the town, but the kingdom as well. Maybe even the world. He shakes himself to keep his imagination from running away from him, trying to process what he saw in the core.

He had heard that Fate-affinity dungeons could produce visions, but he never expected Thedeim to give him one. If only he could fathom what he saw.

It started simple enough. The layered swirling orange depths almost seemed to part and showed him . . . he's not sure.

Perhaps even stranger is that it didn't seem to be deliberately done. Teemo didn't give him any cryptic or sarcastic clues to what he saw. There were no knowing looks from the residents from having their own visions. He's just glad they didn't try to press why he needed to go. It wasn't his most subtle of exits, but he needed to get some fresh air and try to make sense of it all.

It hurts to try to remember the details, so Tarl tries to focus more on the big picture. Teemo has talked about being hurt from trying to understand some of the things Thedeim does and thinks, and the elf isn't in a hurry to test how resistant he is to mental damage. So what *can* he understand about what he saw?

Danger, for starters. The talk of expanding the affinities available to his scions may only be scratching the surface of the danger that Thedeim poses. And yet, despite the intense feeling of *danger*, he gets very little feeling of *threat* from the dungeon. After all his experience inspecting, he trusts his gut when it splits hairs like that. It was almost the opposite as with Neverrest, come to think of it. The cemetery dungeon always gave off an aura of threat, but very little actual danger to back the threat up, scions aside.

His thoughts continue to race as he enters his small home, and his body practically moves on its own as he gets out of his work clothes and into his breeches to sleep. He closes his eyes, trying to get some rest, even as his mind continues to race.

Neverrest wanted destruction, but never truly had the power to back it up. So does Thedeim have that kind of power? It doesn't take him long to admit that yes . . . he does. Just the *number* of scions the dungeon has gives him incredible power, and *none* of them are slouches when it comes to strength! And that's just the known capabilities. He'll be shocked if the other scions don't have secret levels of power they can tap into like Poe did.

Even Teemo probably has a few tricks to let him punch well above his level, and that's not even counting the insanity of expanding affinities!

He grumbles and tosses in bed, hoping maybe he'll find a comfortable enough position to take his mind off Thedeim, but he's not too hopeful. He tries a different tactic to get *some* sleep tonight, focusing more on the mundanity of most of the secret areas in the dungeon.

The alchemy lab, while busy, isn't anything for him to get too worked up over. Even with the cryptic remark about the metal transmutation elixir, he's not too worried about it. Petrification is a rare thing, but not outside reason. Curing being metallic should be similar to curing petrification, and that's even assuming Thedeim would ever use the strange liquid like that.

It seems a bit difficult to manufacture, so even if he *did* want to fill pitfalls with the liquid, it'd be a long time before he has enough to do that, and he doubts Thedeim would want a trap like that.

The enchanting lab is also something to help ease his mind. Maybe Thedeim will stay focused on a counter to Lifedrinking. It'll probably keep him out of trouble for a bit, and if he actually succeeds, that'll be a positive for the world as a whole.

He relaxes slightly at the thought, finally letting some of the tension out of his muscles. He can feel his mind finally starting to drift, and he nudges it to Thedeim's core itself. If anything will help him sleep, it'll be thinking about the inanity of core composition theory.

He chuckles in bed as he thinks about the arguments just on spheres. He couldn't have been a shape that adherents to the theory agree about, could he? Facets of a core are generally taken to be how complex the thought of a dungeon is, how many ways it tries to approach a problem.

Spheres and eggs and other round shapes are always argued, as some think it means there's only one facet, while others argue they're theoretically infinite facets. Someone once tried to show him the math behind it, but the equation took up an entire wall of chalkboards, and Tarl had better things to do with his time.

He finally drifts off to sleep as the theories of colors and movement of those colors drift through his mind, his sleep deep and dreamless. In the morning, he feels much better, and the details of his vision are comfortably muddled. If that's the kind of thing people with Fate affinity have to deal with regularly, they can keep it.

He goes over his notes as he enjoys the morning air and rising sun, mentally mapping out what he can and can't put in the report. He's glad nothing clashes with his promises to the guild or to Thedeim. Sure, there's dangerous stuff in the dungeon, but that's dungeons. As far as he's concerned, there's no actual threat, so no obligation to play word games to get the guild extra information.

His preparations for work are interrupted, however, once he gets close to the guild. Sitting on the sign is a seagull, squawking its little bird brain out. As he looks, curious, he notices it has a scrap of parchment in its beak. It eventually notices him noticing it and gives a louder squawk before dropping the paper and flying off.

His instincts tell him there's something odd, and so he spends a few minutes searching for the dropped paper. He gives it a shocked look after reading it, rereading it a few times to make sure he's not misunderstanding. He even takes the time to examine it to make sure it's not just some joke . . . but everything seems to check out.

He briefly considers destroying the note, but soon sighs and stuffs it into his pocket, heading inside. He doesn't like Hullbreak Harbor, but he can't bring himself to hate it, either. And even if he did, he doesn't bear the dwellers any ill will. If their dungeon really *is* starting to starve, something will need to be done.

Chapter 89

I've been trying to get Tiny to help narrow down the window for the scythe-maws to do their thing, but the big guy can't get much of a read on them. He agrees that it'll be soon, but he also says it seems like it won't just start instantly. So the best he can do is say it's not imminent, but still should happen soon.

Ugh, it's like waiting for a patch for a game that forums insist will ruin the whole thing.

If I had an actual time, I could accommodate the stupid things. You know, dim the lights, put on some good music, maybe light some candles . . . set the mood.

But no, they're going to do it on their own time and just improvise. If I thought anyone would get the joke, I'd make a bunch of fake cars so they could do their business in the back seat.

Alright, enough grumping like that. The door is progressing as smoothly as can be expected. It's difficult to line everything up so each part of the hinge actually helps support the weight and let the door open, but it's not impossible. Queen's ants have been lifesavers for the fine adjustments that have been needed.

Speaking of Queen, I finally understand what she was so interested in the quartz for: she wants to grow crystals. I'm not exactly sure why, but the idea has Thing inspired, too. Maybe if they can get specific shapes, certain spells will work better? I also wonder how they'll react when they learn that quite a lot of gems are the same gem with different impurities. I just don't remember which ones are in that family.

Still, I think they're planning to grow the quartz pickups for the guitar to their specifications, and then we'll be that much closer to bringing some rock music to this world. Slash is definitely going to blow some minds.

Speaking of minds being blown, Rocky is kinda blowing mine. He's figured out the Kinetic affinity. He was sparring with Fluffles when something just clicked. He tossed a cool swirling vortex of ice and fire at Fluffles, who put up as strong a barrier as he could manage. It was quite a drain on my mana, too. Luckily, the attack wasn't held together too well and hit the barrier with all the force of a wet noodle. Still, Rocky has another affinity under his belt.

Fluffles is having a harder time with gaining affinities, but at least his Kinetic mastery is being refined pretty quickly. He's a lot more efficient, and I almost wonder if he'll manage Wind affinity out of the blue instead. I don't think he's quite figured out that air is still made of matter, but I also don't know if grabbing air and throwing it around with kinetics will count as Wind affinity. If anything, that might count as Sonic instead.

I'm probably getting ahead of myself, though. Rocky's hardly a master of kinetics yet, and even Fluffles has a ways to go before I think he'll have the fine control to get an extra affinity. Stop worrying about the tools you don't have; get ready to do the job with the ones you do.

I start drawing up an access passage for the scythemaws, if only to feel like I'm doing something. Maybe I'll get lucky and not only get it finished, but the things will actually use it.

Old Staiven

The aged ratkin can't remember the last time he had something so interesting to experiment with! Nor can he remember the last time he had something so *frustrating* to experiment with, either!

He's distilled, desiccated, crystalized, and everything else he can think of to get at the secret of the Bottled Lightning, but it continues to insist it's made with only ochredill and spell spore! (With trace amounts of ant drool, soil, and other impurities.)But no matter what he tries, once he separates the reagents, they refuse to recombine into the yellow fluid!

Oh, but what he can get that fluid to do! He didn't have much left after the initial experiments to make something useful, but even a minor infusion of the liquid into a wand made from a tree struck by lightning made it the kind of lightning-spell conduit that even a master mage would pay dearly for!

Maybe he'll try to trade it to Thedeim for some more of the Bottled Lightning . . . or something else. He'll round his ears and declare himself a giant mousekin if the dungeon doesn't have other unique alchemical creations. He had joked with himself about becoming a dweller or even a resident to get access to just the Bottled Lightning, but now, he finds himself sometimes pondering the logistics.

Of course, they never work out. At the end of the day, he has his lab just the way he wants it, and moving it would be too much of an ordeal . . . not to mention there would be various dungeon things poking through everything at all hours, wanting to pick his brains as much as he wants to pick theirs.

He smiles at that thought and stands from his notes. He's out of Bottled Lightning now, but there's a master alchemist not far who knows how to make it. Maybe he can make a new friend.

"Rhonda!" he shouts, and soon hears her muffled reply drift down to the lab from the store floor. "I'm going to the dungeon! I want you to practice with that lightning wand I made the other day! If you're going to earn a proper mage class, you're going to need to get a feel for mana more than Meta and Ice!"

She shouts an affirmative as he gathers a few things. If he's going to go and try to make friends with the dungeon, he should do some delving. He's hardly a battlemage, but he's learned enough tricks over the years to get close enough.

Hullbreak Harbor

The First Mate swims slow circles around the shipwreck-turned-jail. The whole situation makes her uneasy. She's not surprised the Captain put the dweller in there. The great white had hoped he'd somehow not notice when the merman swam off, like the First Mate pretended not to, but they had no such luck.

She was pushing it by not immediately going to chase him down when he wandered away from the fishing expedition, but chasing after the one would have left all the others without her protection. That didn't stop the Captain from wanting to keelhaul the merman for wandering off, even if he actually was chasing a large fish.

Whatever he was up to, the First mate is pretty sure he accomplished it. She can't imagine what it could be, though. As far as she could tell, he swam off, outside of even her senses, and swam back not long after. She actually expected him to have abandoned the Captain. She wouldn't blame him.

Things have only gotten worse since that fateful day, so long ago. She can remember the sound of the anchor chain snapping on that merchant vessel, then the horrible crunching of it being swept into and onto the trading hall atop the reef.

And then . . . a frenzy. The next thing she remembers clearly about that day is there being so much blood in the water . . . and an inspector's badge stuck between her teeth. She returned it to the journeyman inspector at the time, now full and experienced Inspector Tarl.

He still comes back every couple months, in that little dinghy. He still heaves the anchor over the side, still respects the border, still asks if delvers can return. She longs to be able to tell him they can . . . but the Captain refuses. He was always suspicious of the delvers, but the mana they brought eased his concerns for a time.

But when his precious dwellers were killed, even in an accident, every paranoid whisper in the Captain's head started screaming. She tells herself he's just mad with grief . . . but mad is still *mad*, no matter the cause. But what can she do?

She's a scion, and the Captain's Voice to boot. Even if she knew how to stage a mutiny, she couldn't do that to the Captain. He just wants to keep his dwellers safe. But he's killing them, and he's too scared to see that.

She peers through the hole in the hull where she can plainly see the adult merman in the brig inside, idly floating behind the bars and looking off into the distance.

Hmm . . . off toward where the delvers used to come from. Just what did he do? If he somehow got their help . . . She doesn't think it'll make much difference. The delvers haven't been able to do anything in the years since the disaster to help the Captain. Nothing could have happened to change that.

About the Author

Khenal is the author of the Dungeon Life series. Born and raised in a small town in Northern California, he studied mechanical engineering but graduated from college in the middle of the Great Recession. Unable to find an engineering job, Khenal turned to content creation, streaming videos on Twitch and posting stories to Reddit and Royal Road.

Milton Keynes UK
Ingram Content Group UK Ltd.
UKHW031211111124
451035UK00007B/806

9 781039 453944